BEAUTIFUL WRECK

BEAUTIFUL WRECK

Larissa Brown

COOPERATIVE TRADE

an imprint of Cooperative Press

REVIEWER PRAISE FOR BEAUTIFUL WRECK

Paranormal Romance Guild calls Beautiful Wreck pure poetry.
"A saga worthy of the firesides of the Vikings … lavishly woven into a story about loving family, dangerous plots, and lost love."

A 2014 Best Book, All About Romance

"It's the kind of book that shifts everything you knew, or thought you knew, about writing and love. The world just looks different when you're done."
—Heather Monroe Kinne, Fiberista Files podcast

"With a plot as exciting as it is bold, and with characters as real and important as family, Larissa Brown's *Beautiful Wreck* weaves an intensely gripping tale about the strength of women and the love they carry. This is the story we've been waiting for."
—Rachael Herron, bestselling author of *How to Knit a Love Song* and *Splinters of Light*

"The setting in Iceland is a breath of fresh, glacial air. The era of the tenth century is depicted with vivid, stunning clarity. The prose is elegant and the characterization of the hero, almost unbelievably realistic. His desperate loneliness, his longing for love and acceptance, his courage; all are written deftly and touchingly."
—Jill, Romantic Historical Reviews

So lyrical and so personal that it literally stole my breath.
—Melanie, All About Romance

"As I read, I kept seeing the story as a painting—definitely an Old Master—a vast landscape of a bygone time, vibrant with life and detail."
—N. J. Layouni, bestselling author of *Tales of a Traveler*

"If I could give six stars, I would. I adored this book. I began reading it at seven in the evening and read all through the next morning until I was done. The experience was like falling into another world, one where words transported, challenged, and oh so pleased me.

"Read it."

—Dabney, All About Romance

WHAT READERS ARE SAYING

"A tale of ancient Iceland told with such touching, haunting truth that you will swear you have seen it yourself."—Julie

"A feast for the soul and the imagination." —Meg

"Crisp, stunning, vivid writing. This is the happiest a book has made me in a long time. Happy to bursting, and sad and fluttery because it's over." —Claire

"Just finished and am overwhelmed with ALL THE FEELINGS. Spectacular.... Read it right now." —Julie

"I didn't want to put the book down. I found myself reading most nights until I literally could not hold my eyes open any more!" —Angela

"Sleep is overrated." —Holly

"*Beautiful Wreck* is engrossing, thrilling, frustrating, and heartbreaking. I devoured it in about three days (and spent a good portion of them in a legitimate mope because I was vicariously tormented by dark, sexy, tortured Vikings)." —Alex

"GET THIS BOOK, PEOPLE." —Jennifer

"Clear your schedule because you will start reading and not stop until you reach the last word." —Penny

"I really didn't want to say goodbye." —Anna

BEAUTIFUL WRECK
ISBN-13: 978-1-937513-31-3
Third Paperback Edition

Published by Cooperative Press Trade,
an imprint of Cooperative Press
www.cooperativetrade.com

Every effort has been made to ensure that all the information in this book is accurate at the time of publication. Cooperative Press neither endorses nor guarantees the content of external links referenced in this book. All business names, trademarks and product names used within the text are the property of their respective owners.

This novel is a work of fiction. With the exception of those persons appearing as personalities under their own names, albeit in fictitious circumstances, all other characters are imaginary and any resemblances to actual persons, either living or dead, is entirely coincidental.

For information about licensing, custom editions, special sales, or academic/corporate purchases, contact Cooperative Press: info@cooperativepress.com or 13000 Athens Ave C288, Lakewood, OH 44107 USA

Join the Cooperative Press Trade email list at http://eepurl.com/DS-m1

CONTENTS

A NOTE ON LANGUAGE

The old language in this novel is a storybook composite—it's meant to be fictional, not entirely real or correct. It is based on Old Icelandic words, modern Icelandic, Old Norse, and a few composite words I made up by blending those languages and speculating about how people thought of the world and put it into words. I have used real Icelandic letters in many places. English speakers, for that little voice in your head:

Ei   long *A* sound, so Heirik's name sounds like *Hay'-rik* and nei is *nay*

J or j   a *y* sound, for example Jul is the winter Yule festival

Á or á   *ow*, so Hár's name sounds like *Hower*, and já sounds like *yow*

Þ or þ   soft *th* as in *thing*

ð   hard *th* as in *brother*

Í   long *ee*; so the farm, Hvítmörk, sounds like *Veet-mork*

"FARM NOTE"

Iceland, circa 900

Everyone settled.
Goodnight to sheep and cows and horsies. To grassy field, rough
walls.
To stars and hearth and strong house. To woods and whales and sea.
Goodnight to the circle of young girls, their long braids lit by fire.

INTO THE STEAM

The future
Inside "the tank"

THE CARDBOARD SMELL OF SIMULATED BEER WAFTED THROUGH
the crowd.

True, vivid smells were something I yearned for, but tonight I
was grateful the programming team couldn't get them right. Realistic sweat and stale beer, and the iron tinge of blood, would have
made the Ultimate Fighting simulation hard to bear.

A meadow would have been lovely. I'd come into the tank
every day if I could feel lush, slippery grass between my toes, the
gentle nudge of a breeze at my frothy hems. But the programmers
couldn't accomplish the immense reach and power of outdoor
scenes. Not yet.

Besides, who wouldn't want to visit a vintage, turn of the century cage match between two men who hit and kicked each other
and struggled on the floor in the slippery, knee-length pants of the
aughts and teens? Jeff couldn't imagine anyone not adoring this
sim. The whole programming team loved it so much, they named
the extraction signal after this kind of wrestling. To leave the tank,
a user just had to tap out.

Outside this lab sprawled our real place, the city of Iceland. But
in here, we immersed ourselves in fighting arenas, castles, grass
longhouses. I designed Old Norse voices, gestures and idioms for
the high tech company that was creating it all.

Jeff's fight sim wasn't entirely lost on me. I enjoyed one part
of it—the voices. The wash of them in this simulation was complex and nuanced. The setting was Atlantic City in the old United
States, designed with a strong primary accent. Weekend visitors
from the north. I absorbed the aggressive voices, the language
punctuated with jabs and dramatic eyebrows.

The sounds of talking in any language drew me—the motions and rhythm of speech, the spikes and quiet spaces of arguments, the steady murmur of flirting. I craved the sounds of lovers, hiding and seeking, the voices and movements of the desperately angry. As a linguistic artist it was almost impossible to just listen without analyzing, but when I could I had a vision of humans as animals. Great flocks and herds, sometimes majestic, sometimes frightening or gross. This arena sounded like a field packed solid with geese.

What I thought geese might sound like. I'd seen them in the electronic arcs. I knew geese and hawks and ravens, dogs and foxes, from years of personal study. A thousand afternoons spent with my nose pressed to an archive screen, trying to feel the silky threads of a horse's mane.

I heard there were fanatic realist farms, out beyond the glacier. But those were dreams. I checked the one time I flew in an airplane.

"They were still called shorts." Morgan leaned over to shout in my ear. "They were practically down to their ankles in the early 2000s." She was talking about the wrestler's pants. The shiny reds and greens and yellows were so bold and pure, stunning in their dumb glory.

The audience's clothing was a more complex expression of hopes and needs and sexual invitation. Tattoos on the curves of women's lower backs were displayed like tail feathers, paired with hair that was every color and shape of plumage. Cowgirl boots and tight jeans were prevalent. A sheen of iridescent powder covered it all, as though the women had stood together under a gentle rain of it, faces upturned. A blessing for long life and a brawny boyfriend.

New Jersey circa 2010 didn't seem like something Morgan, a blacksmith who designed Viking weapons and buckles and locks, would care much about. But she pointed out that the men were dressed surprisingly like Vikings, with heavy boots, long hair and neat beards. Their markings encircled their upper arms like the precious metal rings worn by chieftains. Jewelry showed at their throats, an echo of the torcs and silver Thor's hammers of tenth century Norsemen. The decorations of farmers and raiders from the Rus' States to North America.

"Isn't it awesome, Jen?" Jeff blared in my ear. "I worked on the voices with Shank."

Come to think of it, Jeff himself was silver-necklaced and fair in a big, Norse kind of way. He wore the clothes of the second tech revolution, headphones at his throat rather than the fangs of stylized dragons, but he was Viking in his family's real blood. Tonight he was close, touching me casually, as if it were the fault of the tiny seats in the arena. We had the best ones, of course. We were the only real humans. A perfect view into the eight-sided cage.

I floated the symbols and stats. Mateus Vida was imposing even in teeny yellow shorts. They glowed against his dark skin. Information wafted beside him, telling me he stood six feet tall. Beside his bald head, white letters read, *Weight: 83 kg (184 pounds). Reach: 188 cm (74 inches).* I read a litany of Black Belts: *Brazilian Jiu Jitsu, Judo, Taekwondo.* He specialized in Muay Thai.

"That's kickboxing," Jeff told me, and he gestured at the cage, poking at the stats with the same finger that held his plastic cup of beer. Some of it seeped into my authentic jeans.

They all had Viking style bynames, just like Aud the Deep Minded, Eirik Bloodaxe. Here stood Vida the Locust. His opponent was Yusef "Superior" Cruz, a self-important choice of name, I thought. At six feet tall, 186 pounds, and with a couple of similar Black Belts, he seemed to my untrained eye to be a fair match for Vida.

I found moments that weren't ugly. Time seemed to stretch out and I could appreciate a snapshot of two men tumbling in midair, one lifted high like a dancer. The sour face of a referee looking at me from between a wrestler's legs. But those moments of clarity were scarce. Mostly, it was a kind of grueling hugging on the floor, with grunting and some vicious punches. Bodies would sometimes slam into the cage, right in front of us, and adrenalin left my hands and feet tingling. Sprays of blood and spit just missed us. I pretended it was true. I let the stats drop and watched.

The fight was brief. Just three minutes of circling, jabbing, inviting with bared teeth. There were a few terrible punches, hard and gross. I couldn't imagine being hit even once and getting up again, let alone so many times. Cruz circled, waiting, wanting to hit, to take down. And then Vida kicked him.

It wasn't just a kick to the shins or belly or even the chest. From a standing position, he kicked him in the face. Time slowed down, literally now, for the replay. The kick was elegant. Vida's leg was poetry, long and accurate, the ball of his foot smashing up from under Cruz's chin. The man's face rippled like rubber.

Then time rushed forward again and he hit the mat, knocked cold. Everyone flew to their feet with the madness of shock, outrage, and glee. Tall, cheering bodies obscured me on every side. I could still just see the cage. Vida was spinning in a tight circle, ecstatic, fists clenched in triumph. He looked like a giant figure skater corkscrewing down, down into the mat. Down onto one knee.

A metallic screech split my head—a brutal ripping sensation in my brain. My hands flew to my ears, but the wrenching was deep inside and I couldn't reach it. Something unfathomably delicate was tearing. I shut my eyes.

And opened them to see the ocean.

The green waves were almost black, laced with white foam in the moonlight. I knelt, my hands sinking into cold, moist sand. Every grain felt sharp and clear. The last ripples of a wave reached close to me, like fingers searching blindly for my knees. A glow cast the beach in bluish white. I turned to it, and it dazzled. Mammoth letters lit the sky, each at least three stories high. They were brilliant against a black expanse of space. STEEPLECHASE. In smaller letters, THE FUN FACTORY fought to outglow dozens of swags of white bulbs, tiers of them climbing the facade of a fairy tale castle.

My head ached and drifted onto my shoulder, making the scene cant. A hundred people seemed to slide off the tilting boardwalk. They were lit with colors of the dead, faces blue under a million incandescent bulbs and shadowed by the brims of broad hats. A hundred ankle-length skirts caught and riffled in unison by a sharp wind off the water. It blew my hair forward and blocked out my view. A strong smell, like salt and fish, burned behind my eyes.

I felt a rushing, fast building roar of applause and chanting. "Vida! Vida!" The audience crushed me. I swayed into Jeff, and he dropped heavily to his seat, the glow of cheering on his cheeks and in his eyes. He seemed unaffected by the ripping sensation, the exterior view. I hadn't seen him at the beach. I'd felt sand and wind and water. An outdoor scenario? Without Jeff or Morgan. I'd been alone there.

Vida spoke to a reporter in Portuguese, the words flowing, scrolling through the air in English a moment ahead of the human translator who was programmed to be there, just like he had been on that historic night. Vida was thanking people, his family, his trainer. "How does it feel to be middleweight champion of the world?" He grinned. Smiled for the flashing cameras.

He was given a massive silver belt, so big it covered his considerable abs, and he held it across himself to show it off, but he didn't fasten it. Instead, he approached Cruz and placed the belt at his opponent's feet. The champion bent low over it and touched his head to the mat. He looked like a knight, pledging allegiance to the man he'd just knocked flat with a kick to the face. It was one of the things I understood intellectually, but never did get in my heart. That you could beat each other so savagely, and then bow down to one another, honorable brothers. I knew many words for it in Old Norse, for honor. I knew it existed. I saw it. But it wasn't mine.

"WHAT HAPPENED IN THERE?" I TRIED TO ASK BETWEEN KISSES, from under the weight of Jeff's sweet-smelling body and searching mouth. He had me pinned against the wall outside my building, my insides starting to melt in his heat. I struggled to remember my question. "With the beach?"

"What?" He was distracted, shoving kisses at my mouth.

"When everyone was cheering at the end." I got one arm free and pushed at his chest. "For a second I was outside by the ocean."

"Huh." He paused briefly, his troubleshooting mind engaged, but then his body took over again and he swept the hair off my neck and bent to kiss it. "You must have been in a botched test for a second." He nuzzled into me. "I'll look at it tomorrow." We forgot it in a clumsy press of bodies against the wall, a deeper kiss.

It wasn't that I didn't want him. Sometimes I did. Sometimes I fell into a daze of skin and tongues and our long blond hair mingling, and there were moments of stark beauty. I would look down at him, at us, and I would see how fair and pretty we were, and I would feel nothing. Or no, I would feel something, and it was flat as scents in the tank.

Outside my door tonight, he pushed his hips into me. We never did meet. It was as though some emotional mismatch was echoed in the body, a truer judge than the mind. Jeff gave up and pulled away, disappointed, but not really upset. He didn't wonder why I wanted to be alone, didn't worry about whether I loved him or even wanted him. I'd see him at the lab. He'd pour me coffee and we would smile, he would wink.

He'd never know what I did instead, on nights when I went home alone.

I zipped up my snowsuit and pulled on big, spiked boots. I left by the back door of my building, the one for the odd people like me who went beyond the gate. I stepped into the night and started walking up the waves of a motionless sea.

My building backed up into the glacier—the only one left, stabilized and gutted by the same company that owned the tank. Past the back gate, the white expanse I walked on stretched forever, an ocean frozen in the midst of rolling and crashing. Marbled darkest green and white, ancient and unmoving. I read that there were once thirteen glaciers, some of them unfathomable at fifteen times this size or more, far beyond anywhere I could see.

When I climbed high enough, I turned back to see the Atlantic Ocean twenty miles away. Towers of glass and metal filled every space between me and that water. A million lights glowed steadily in windows, never stirring with any breeze or breath. Twenty million people lived there, not caring that their flames could never flicker. Buildings piled on each other like boulders. A cairn, a grave mound for the walking dead.

I whispered to them all, an ancient lullaby.

Everyone settled.

I said the words from the Farm Notes, a Viking Age diary I had translated.

Goodnight to smali *and* kyr *and* hross. *To sheep and cows and horsies.*

To grassy field, rough walls.

To stars and hearth and strong house. To woods and whales and sea.

I whispered sleepy words of young girls, their braids lit by fire. The ends of my own long braids glowed pale in the night. Warm, synthetic flur scratched my forehead and cheeks, but my nose and lips felt nothing. I stiffly kissed my gloved palm and raised my hand to let it free, in case it might reach someone.

I went inside to read.

Wall screens glowed with a verdant pasture full of flowers and horses—the few colors in my neutral apartment. My bare toes gripped the grooves in the kitchen tiles, my boots and suit discarded on the living room floor. While I waited for the coffee machine to choke and whir to life, I told my contacts I wanted to see the diary.

Jeff said it was impossible to feel the moment when the opaque tint closed like an iris from every side, covering the eyes for reading. I always thought I did, though. I could almost hear a snick, like a lock turning.

The letters jumped to life. The scan of the ancient book showed them as they'd been written, the common alphabet, not sacred runes. Letters so tiny, traveling down the pages of birch bark that had been worked into a rough paper. Along the edges and top, upside down, words small enough to fit dozens of observations on each precious sheet. The ink had spread until the words were almost unreadable, as if they'd been worked with a bristly brush.

I'd done my own translation, and I could recall every word choice, every line and turn of phrase. I would read it all again anyway.

I'd found the diary in a disused museum—a Viking ruin that sat three levels under the city. There were open stacks of electronic files, compiled when someone used to care and then never deleted. They contained the dating of stones, comprehensive lists of artifacts, notated images of spindles and combs and scoops to clean out ears. One wooden doll. Its cracked form was cradled in an electronic grave.

Among the jumble of information, someone had collected snips and quotes from later sagas, from the stories attributed to the family who once lived there. They told of a formidable chieftain with eyes of precious metal and a face like death itself, a man who could form new gods from his own hands. His wife was a shape shifter. It was fanciful and electric and very Viking.

But even in such a dramatic household, someone must have spun the thread. Someone fed the children, stoked the fire, strung up the fish.

I dug around in the database and found her. The farm wife. Among a bunch of ancient scientific papers about the devastation of Iceland's forests, behind long lists of extinct animals, lumbering auks and leaping salmon, there sat her diary.

Her words laid captured in a wooden, iron-hinged box. The scan said it was no bigger than my two palms. The front of the box swung open like two doors, an entrance to a fairytale world. Guarded by an iron dragon's-head clasp.

The image of the box hovered next to the rough pages, all cracked and stained. The first few contained simply dates and trades, numbers of cows and days. After the last entry, words appeared that caught the breath like a flash of light—a lullaby! It was the first entry among the wife's quotidian moments.

Her words went on for a dozen more pages, filling up all but the last few centimeters of space. There, on the last wisp of birch-bark, sat a love poem. The kind of poem that was not believed to be written down until a hundred years later. The dangerous kind, that could get a Viking man killed.

> *… of yellow birch leaves spattering light*
> *across lattices of bright white bones*
> *where kisses*
> *come without question or consequence;*
> *where my hand would rest on your belly*
> *and move only with your breath.*

These words were crafted by a hand unused to writing, the letters shaky and uneven. They traveled to the edge of the page and stopped, as if the poem might continue somewhere else.

The pages must have been delicate to scan, and in places they were lost altogether. Just twelve remained, in various states of crumbling decay. Three for animals and weeks and silver, and then the diary, filling up everything else.

The woman who wrote it was concerned with cod and fleeces and butter, not spirits. I pictured a niece of the scary chieftain maybe. A young woman who wrote surreptitiously in the dark, binding her words in a leather book, lovingly made by a normal husband. A farmer with grass and animals and axes on his mind, not a quest for fearsome power over settlers and spirits.

I cherished the well-kept secret of this book, which would have been some of the earliest colloquial writing. Her language was strange and wonderful—a poetic and unexpected mix of Norse and Icelandic and something unknown, in between worlds. The words of a completely foreign territory—a rugged wilderness on the cusp of becoming a governed country. A language slowly turning from what was left behind in Norway to a new set of sounds, a new voice in the air.

Mostly, I loved her everyday moments. In a time of vivid imagination and people who were larger than life, this diary was intimate, life sized.

I read it as easily as drinking water. Word choice, order, rhythm, came freely like waves. A flash of raven hair against cool linen, the smell of birch tar and herbal bite of a root called snowbloom, a winter-sparked landscape seen from the threshold of the farm wife's house at bluest dawn.

Other translators might have called them "dark hair against a shirt," or "a snowy morning," but I saw them fully detailed as though the memories and words were alive on my tongue and in my hands. Eyelashes on cheeks, the beloved shape of an ear. *Crushed juniper on my hands and throat, for heat,* she recorded. *For scent.*

Sometimes I threw the words up on a wall screen, huge. *Skating the stream. The sky was big today, all ice and violet.* I could tunnel deeper and deeper into the strokes of ink. Each year, each night, each word gone by. I looked harder and harder, as though I could climb inside.

I tried not to read it too much, on lonely nights. It was pitiful to huddle in my blankets surrounded by her trees and buzzing flies, her grass and horsies and enormous sky. Her family and husband.

There was someone real for me somewhere. Someone I could really know, could really love, and some part of me admitted I would never find him here in my room, my eyes shuttered, heart in the past.

The boundaries became indistinct. The coffee, the pillows and covers, the way I thought real fur might smell, the green wet grass and pungent scent of stripped bark. The presence of people seemed real. The farmer himself, her husband, so clear I could touch him. He'd been her bones and blood and home—her house itself—in a way that I hadn't ever known. The words intoxicated me. *Full dusk, orange light on fourteen good fleeces. Rinsing his hands, he is sweet to my eye.*

My empty mug cooled between my palms, the apartment's heat winding down for the night. I slid into the couch cushions, eyes heavy under their contact glaze, and I let my cup drop softly to the floor, burrowing deep in blankets, sleep coming. Inside my closed eyes, the words still hovered. *Hot from haying. Exhausted and hungry, backs thrown into feeding us for the winter. Mine sleeps, reckless as a child.*

My irises opened on my room with a jolt, the farm diary thrown open, daylight screeching in. I shaded my eyes and turned away from the window, and blinked hard.

I thought I'd left my walls on a farm scene, but now they showed an eerie, dark green blue. I sat inside a liquid ocean, and a crystal ice-colored sun reached from above the surface. My ceiling glowed with an icy, sun-sparkling blue.

A dark hump moved, just a shadow, a place of even deeper blue against the thick water. A familiar beast I'd seen and heard in arc videos.

"Gone in the dark to the whale road," I whispered, then thought the rest of those words I'd memorized. *I dream them at the camp, all spears and fire. Four nights now, alone in our bed. My hand closes on this white fur, his on black sand.* The whale's haunting voice, just like it sounded in the arcs, swelled to fill my room.

I woke again to the apartment blaring at me, shouting the time. I was late.

I dressed in a stumbling daze, dribbling drops in my eyes and muttering for the alarm to stop. I pulled on clothes—linen shift, overdress, apron, beads and tools. I wrapped my signature bead-and-needle-case necklace twice around my neck. My braided leather belt kept slipping through my fingers, tangling in itself. I was going to hold up today's tests of the tank. We were warned about lateness, given an image of the minutes running freely like blood when the tank was online and no one was in it.

I shouted "the usual" at my apartment. It would lock after me, get warmer near 19:00, lights at 25 percent. I grabbed my little knife from the hall table and slipped it into the leatherette sheath at my waist. At the last second, I grabbed a beaded necklace I'd been making for Morgan. I was out in ten minutes flat.

Coffee splashed onto my dress, a fine spray misting my cheeks and eyes. I stood still and dumb in the door of the cafe, staring down at the stain spreading across rare, handspun flax.

"Gods, I'm sorry."

A big Viking took me by the arm. I looked down at his huge wrist where he gripped me. It was covered in a tattered leatherette bracer with iron buckles. Both hand and gauntlet were scarred, bit by dozens of weapons. My heart raced. Was it real, from a cow? Was he a fanatic realist?

Chain mail clinked as he drew me aside to the edge of the doorway. I looked up to his eyes, and they were amiable and sky blue. I watched them light up as he noticed my hair and clothes—the long braids, simple fillet across my forehead. The glass beads and pewter needle case that hung at my chest.

He switched to Old Norse. "May I help you, Maid?" He sounded practiced with the language, almost perfect. His voice was deep, and for a second I imagined he was a little dreamy. But I had to go.

"Neinn," I answered in the old tongue, almost a sigh. "It is nothing. I'm near my place of work."

An impatient Ninja pushed past us, iced latte sloshing.

The Viking and I looked at each other for a moment more, and then his eyes softened and lost focus. He was reading something. My height, maybe, or a weather alert. The smile faded absently from within his bushy beard.

"Fare well, Viking," I told him and ducked away.

He didn't say anything. I left him lost in his own eyes, not a fanatic realist after all. He'd looked so alive in an unusual way. But he seemed too sweet to sacrifice real animals, to wholeheartedly plunder or hurt a maid such as me. Besides, he was holding a tiny espresso.

Clear and sunny, my contacts told me it was 65.2 F, 18.4 c. Cool for an August morning, but the rays were warm enough to make the coffee on my chest start to dry and smell bitter. Fine then. I'd have something real to smell in the tank all day.

A clutch of men came toward me, laughing, wearing the cornflower jackets of Confederate soldiers, one with a faux musket casually resting on his shoulder. Words came up before my eyes, appearing to float alongside the soldiers.

The Civs have roots in 1960s centennial reenactments of the American Civil War, when living history was a hobby practiced by few.

Now in the 22nd century, everyone lived—to some degree—in a world that had happened before. We studied and debated and reanimated the words and fashions of a hundred yesterdays and adopted them as though we'd run out of original things to be. In the aughts and teens, being part of an anachronistic culture had been unusual. Now it was the norm. Everyone had a place and time they loved, and they lived in it every moment they could.

I threaded my way through a crowd that had stuffed itself into a park for a picnic. The ones who were standing cast a canopy of parasols over my head. This little spot of green surrounded one of the few intact structures in the city, a charming, arched stone bridge maintained by those who wanted to pretend at riverside picnics. But water no longer flowed underneath it. Crows—the only birds we knew—lined its arching walls, waiting for bread and meat.

Strewn with baskets and blankets, only a few square feet of grass poked through, muddied and weak. I sank to my knees, and combed my fingers through the blades, helping them to stand up straight. I petted the grass, like people used to do with dogs.

A sharp heel came down on my hand and a woman stumbled and fell over my back.

"What the fuck?" she barked at me. She sported the little white puff sleeves of Jane Austen's summertime Bath. A man in a long-tailed jacket stood her upright and straightened her tiny umbrella. They huffed off.

As I stood, words swam in my eyes. *This stone bridge was built in 1928.* I shook my head. Somehow I was stuck in tourist mode. An impatient flick of my eyelids turned off the contacts.

I wiped dirt from my nose.

In a world where fragile, intangible threads connected us, we should have been able to find each other in the physical mess of the past. Painful, joyful, disgusting, romantic. People spent their days and nights, to varying degrees of fanaticism, in authenticized settings. They were in lust for their worlds. They shared them with a fervor.

But the truth always comforted them—that they were playing. They wanted ale feasts and spears and Valkyries, not the messy beauty of a real farm, the stink of animals and work of many hands. They wanted to sacrifice a barrel of mead, not a horse, and they wanted someone to clean up after.

Into this reality, the company I worked for was going to drop "the tank." An immersive environment that felt absolutely real.

People would be insane for it. The chance to dive into a fully realized world, interacting with people who didn't know they weren't really Vikings—or Ninjas, lairds, courtesans and knights—would be a revelation. All they had to do was pay dearly and endure the sensation of entering the tank. Their feasts and fights would all disappear conveniently behind them when they were through. They could be home for dinner.

The company had a team of us designing and testing it. Our expertise reflected the presumed mass desires of the world, especially those people who would pay dearly when the tank went public. Costume and linguistic artists, period smiths, fiber artists, leather workers. We specialized in the gallant armor and chivalrous utterings of Medieval knights, the long plaids of men who romantically roamed the Scottish highlands, the drapery and curlicued speech of Roman aristocrats, the rags and weapons of gladiators. Elegant Gatsby suits and the gloom of the eighties punk scene in London.

I'd created the accents and dialect for the Viking heartstone scenario, a scene inside an authentic tenth century longhouse. I loved the sounds, the words and voices, but I didn't want to immerse today. I would miss this air, this day, when I went into the scene, a house lit only by flames and a tiny square of sky. I wandered slower as I approached the company.

A nondescript door said nothing, and the building itself seemed only two stories high. Most of the company's vast corridors, its glinting clean offices and labs and spas were carved inside the stabilized glacier. They'd delved further into the ice than anyone knew—stories and stories below. When I entered, I would step through another set of glass doors, those three times my height, and into a sparkling blue cathedral.

I felt especially reluctant.

I said goodbye to the chaotic buildingscape around me. Goodbye to the puffy clouds endlessly reflected in planes and angles of glass. The buildings showed an airplane, its many selves moving in a hundred directions at once. It droned, and I felt a consuming laziness. For years, I hadn't known they were singular machines. Not until I took the subterranean train out to the airport myself and flew to Norway to study.

I'd looked down eagerly to find the fanatic realists, to find their houses in the open interior of Iceland, where they could feast and rage and breathe life into the kinds of festivals and battles real Vikings knew. Out beyond the glaciers, where the realists lived, my airplane would appear to fly by alone. I imagined it made a sound like a bee.

But I didn't see any farms, only the city stretching from the coast all the way up to where it met the glacier. I'd seen my own building, the very last one before the natural boundary, a frozen ocean lapping its walls.

I dreaded the first moments in the tank. Jeff said the sensation of water was one of the first complex virtual triumphs made by long-ago pioneers in programming. Even now, the sensation of moving water was the best tool they had to jolt the senses and blank the mind. After what he called the "impression of a brief shower," the mind was ready to enter anywhere, anytime. And so, I had to drown in order to emerge in Viking times.

The company's plain-looking door slid a soft, shushing welcome.

Morgan's auburn hair burned against a sea of gray. Her studio contained every expression of metal, from the whitish gleam of silver on her workbench to the iron smudge of smoke that ballooned in the air just before it got sucked into the filtration system. The only color as vivid as her hair was the flame of the real wood fire that jumped and burned in the corner. A massive hood loomed over it to take and process the smoke, but remnants of the smell lingered and mixed with the metallic bite of tools, filings, pewter, copper. All together, the scent of Morgan herself.

The little necklace I made for her was nothing at all, just a few pretty beads I'd found. I wasn't very good with my hands, and I bumbled with the little metal clasp, but I thought she might like it.

She didn't see me standing here yet. She made soft popping sounds with her lips, along with music in her earset. She was tapping a few hundred tiny dents in a mighty arm ring.

The clarified air came back into the room cold, like I thought a woodland stream might feel. I held my fingers up to the vent and the air moved them like riffles of water. I imagined my hand submerged, shiny and distorted. *Make me a stream, Jeff.*

I sent him my request, gently, as if he really could hear it. I could fall for a man who gave me a stream and a horse.

Jeff couldn't, I knew. No far-ranging outdoor scenes in the tank. Not yet.

Morgan stopped her percussive humming, and I turned to find her watching me with her head cocked. I drew my hand out of the stream of clear air and said hello. She blinked off her music and said, "Look at you, Lady."

I picked up the skirts of my new, gorgeous dress and curtsied. "I spilled coffee on the other one."

"You did not." She was horrified, and then bust out laughing. "Gods, I wish I could've seen Vera's face." Morgan puffed up her cheeks like the costume historian.

"It wasn't my fault," I told her. "It was a man. At the cafe."

"The Linux Club?" Morgan asked about the coffee shop. It's what we called Jeff's period hang-out. Jeff was mid technical revolution, turn of the 21st century. He and his friends played at doing programming and design using only the old tools. They also spent a lot of time with the baristas.

"Já. He was a raven feeder," I sighed. "Done up in mail." The man had been a warrior, yes, or at least a raider. "His ax knocked into me."

There was a kind of gauziness to my mood, leftover from looking into the big Viking's eyes in that moment before they'd glazed over. "Mmmm. There was dirt too, from the park," I told her.

I lifted my arm and studied the lovely curve of my belled sleeves. The hand-dyed, cherry colored wool somehow glowed with an amber undertone. It was the only available replacement. Thanks to the big Viking and my sniffing in the park, I was no longer a farm maid but a Norse princess. I'd be the richest girl in tenth century Iceland. Not really authentic for the "heartstone" scenario I was testing, but it would have to do for today. And it made me feel pretty.

"I'm late and not ready," I continued. "And everyone's going to kill me, but I wanted to talk to you."

"Já, I want you to wear a couple new things." She came over and knelt in front of me, taking off my knife and replacing the sheath with a new one. I raised my hands up out of the way. The bones in my fingers looked stark in the artificial light. I flexed them, still dreaming of a cool brook. A bit of ecru linen showed at each wrist, peeking out from under the red wool.

"No, I wanted to talk to you," I told her. "I have something to give you." I drew the necklace out of my purse.

Morgan stopped messing with my belt and looked briefly at the beads.

"I see," she said, "The attachments are wrong here and here." She pointed at the metal parts, then set it aside. "I can work on it for you later."

Oh.

I closed my eyes tight against a sudden sting.

She told me to sit so she could do my hair. She had a newly-etched hair comb. While she brushed and twisted and yanked on my scalp, I kept my eyes closed against any tears that might come. I opened them once, to blink into a reading state. The irises closed, and I muttered "Steeplechase, Atlantic City."

Words came wafting by. *New Jersey, United States, turn of 20th century. Steeplechase was one of several wooden piers that reached out over the Atlantic Ocean and housed entertainment venues and amusement rides. Opened August 1899. Destroyed three times …*

I flicked my eyes to make the history go by faster, to get to the early 2000s. But the dates ended. *In 1932, a fire started by a 26,000-light advertising sign—*

"You can't do it, you know." Morgan's cold finger on my spine startled me, and the words dropped away. "Right here."

She touched the nape of my neck.

"Já, I know," I said. "The raven."

I desperately wanted a tattoo—a stylized bird made of swirls and lines in darkest blue-black. I'd wanted it for a while and had asked Morgan to design it, but the arcs said nothing about ink in settlement Iceland. That kind of extensive ink wasn't known in any Viking land, let alone on a woman. I imagined it would give me a fierceness and indifference that I craved. The bird's beak would be open as if cawing up my spine, ready to bite into my hair, the only color a round amber eye. But it came down to a choice. Authenticity, or the raven?

"Skyndi, Kona!" Jeff was there suddenly, standing at the door with a chipped coffee mug, showing off his amateur Old Norse. He knew how to say exactly three things. Besides Hurry, Woman, there was How do I undo this? and That was not my fault.

I took the coffee from him, holding it far away from the red dress, and sipped carefully at it. "So late this morning," he said, "and you didn't even let me in last night."

He winked, like I knew he would, and the room lit up. Jeff was brilliant, his strawberry blond ponytail falling in messy strands over two layers of worn t-shirts. The headphones around his neck met at his throat like a Viking torc. I literally shook my head, astounded at myself for spending the night with the diary.

It just wouldn't have been right. *Mine sleeps*. I recalled the farm wife's words. I knew Jeff was not mine and wouldn't ever be.

"Let's go, seriously," he said. "I need you on your knees, now."

He was teasing me. The sensation of rushing water as I entered the tank—his "quick impression of a shower"—was so powerful it had physically knocked me over more than once. I'd made a habit of kneeling at the heartstone to immerse.

I waved at Morgan as Jeff dragged me out of the studio.

"I won't be around tonight," she said, gesturing toward the necklace I'd made for her. "It's turn-of-the-century night."

The turn of the century tugged at my thoughts. Oh. Right. Atlantic City.

I'd meant to tell them both about those whipping skirts in the boardwalk light, and the wash of hats, brims atop every single person. It seemed wrong, the costumes far older than the Ultimate Fighting era. But Jeff had me by the hand, and we were gone down an ice cold corridor, swallowed by a cloud of steam from the vents.

BEACHED

I WOKE FACE DOWN ON A BEACH OF BLACK SAND.
My cheek pressed into moist, stinging grains, and the elements of the scene came to me slanted, the details building one by one. Pebbles and rocks of all sizes stretched as far as I could see, shimmering in a thousand shades of ebony and slate.

Big boulders loomed over me, shaggy with seaweed in shades of rust and gray. Farther, two rock formations, taller than a building, knelt like gigantic trolls before a frothing sea. Sparks of white light bit at my eyes, and then a message glowed with the ambient temperature. *54.3 F. 12.4 c.* My contacts. I'd forgotten to take them out before immersing. *No coordinates found*, they said, power sliding down toward nothing.

Moisture from the beach must have seeped into my linen shift for a long time. It was bound tightly around my legs and stuck to me everywhere, miserable. A nasty wind came, and it whined and whipped at my hair and wool cloak.

Dark closed like a flower over my eyes. I woke again, and it was the same.

I counted pebbles, starting over and over as I failed. They were more bluish than black. Almost purple, some of them. A watery light played on them from high in the sky, but I couldn't seem to roll over and look up to find the sun. A very faint sensation of its heat reached the back of my neck, tantalizing but nowhere near strong enough to make a dent in the prevailing cold.

This wasn't right. This wasn't the heartstone. I didn't know where I was.

I tried to raise my head, but fell back to the sand. I couldn't feel my arms, but I wiggled my fingers. I flexed one foot to find it was the same, frozen solid inside my heavy, clogged boot. I tried to recall the symptoms of hypothermia from a long-ago documentary. Labored movement, confusion, that was all I could recall. I dragged my arm up to where I could see my fingers. They were bluish and wrinkly like a crow's claws. I considered their color against that of the sand. Fingers like skim milk against the darker blue of flint.

A wave lapped my leg and jolted me awake. I scrambled, useless, limbs completely numb. My hands and feet moved like dumb blocks. All around me, boulders crouched patiently, furry with damp seaweed. Ragged, wet. Oh. It meant water would come here. This whole place would be submerged, and I would freeze in a minute. I'd drown.

I struggled forward, away from the seeking waves. I tried to roll on my back and sit up, but crawling was the most I could do. I got one knee forward and then the other, dragging myself through volcanic sludge. It felt like a hundred pounds of dress and cloak dragging with me. The splendid red dress. It was saturated with muck.

I drew myself far enough onto land to be sure I wouldn't slide back in, and blessedly closed my eyes. Under the shushing of tide, there was a mournful, inhuman voice. The whale's song sounded pretty, and I smiled into sleep.

Two faces hovered over mine.

Two men, but not techs from the lab, nor scholars who had the pale skin and organized hair of those who worked in clean seclusion. These faces were bronze from the sun and red from biting wind and cold. Both men had ash blond hair that hung over me in waves, with braids that fell from their temples.

They were from the simulation. They were Vikings. I was still in the tank.

"Chief," one of them called in thunderous Old Norse. "She is awake." His breath told of recently-eaten fish, a vivid and complex smell, disgusting but fresh, not the rank smell of old bad breath. Jeff had made a breakthrough in the design quality. I wondered at the glitch that was giving the man an odd accent, though. He'd spoken just a few words, but I knew inside and out what he was supposed to sound like. I'd designed it, and this wasn't it. I had never heard the lyrical language spat so roughly before.

He helped me to sit and held me up. My head swam and contacts struggled, sputtering. *LX89.9scssXXZ998877zp*. An attempt at temperatures, heights, a last gasp. The data faded, and there were four men. Four horses. One of the riders swung his leg over and dismounted with an elegant ease. I thought about the detail, and who among the geniuses at the lab had bothered to program such grace. The two men who hovered about me had called him Herra. Their chief, then. Their leader, the protector and commander of their clan. Or perhaps the word was slightly altered, used to mean simply boss, or—I smiled drowsily—perhaps like one might call a little boy "Hey, Chief."

Regardless, I hadn't expected there to be one in today's session.

My two rescuers quickly gave way to him. In the damp sand, he knelt before me on one knee. He was no little boy. His forehead, the long straight line of his nose and high cheekbones reflected gold in the setting sun. Strong features were framed by hair of the deepest black, shot through with the blue of a crow. Drawn back on top, it fell in tangles and waves over his shoulders. His beard was trimmed close to the skin. Raven hair and eyebrows contrasted with shocking eyes like sunlit straw. They evaluated me. But behind the scientific and wolfish gaze there was a hint of something softer.

In the next instant, hair and eyes were eclipsed by the scar. I drew a sharp breath. It was a birthmark. A massive one that darkened most of the left side of his face in shades of mud and blood and berries. Its edge was indistinct and fractal, like a coastline lapped with an angry tide. I followed the mark with my eyes as it continued down his throat and disappeared into his linen shirt. He seemed so real, I actually felt sorry for insulting him with my stare.

He stood abruptly then, and with an economy of motion turned and mounted his horse.

"Bring her home." He said this without looking back, sure of being obeyed. His voice was quietly commanding, not warm, but I idly thought I would follow it anywhere. Something about it tugged at me. Again, the accent, the almost-not-right words. I knew the pronunciation conventions that historical linguists had agreed on, the options in cases where experts didn't agree, and I knew for a fact what I had chosen for this sim. I'd heard all of six words since I woke up in the mud, but I could tell this was different, almost like a riff on the language that I knew in my sleep.

I was lifted onto a horse and without thought I leaned back into the strong body sitting behind me. I had no idea who it was programmed to be, but it was warm.

The animal turned in a tight circle, orienting behind the chief's dark horse, and the animal's warm, moving body beneath me was shocking. Dizzy and sick, I clutched at anything, a mane, surprisingly tough in my hands. I focused on the chief, directly in front of me. His hair was lush and black and tied with leather, and it stirred with the restless movements of his mount. He was balanced and at ease on the horse, his body moving in sync with the animal's restless stamps. And I wondered who she was, the woman who'd programmed him. He was made with fascination and love. Did she intend to come into the tank and meet him herself? I rifled through my memory of the programming team and vaguely came up with a couple of faces, two women and one possible man, who might have the skill and passion. Then I let their faces swim by and out of my mind. So tired, so cold. I needed to lie down.

The chief turned to look back at me. He smiled with one side of his mouth, so briefly I wasn't sure I'd seen it.

"Name?" he asked me.

I dreamily blacked out.

I woke on a moving horse, and I tensed and scrabbled at the dusty mane. A huge arm closed tighter around me. I'd always wanted to ride a horse, I thought wryly. The animal's body was alien, the way it adjusted and shifted constantly. So wrong, feeling bones moving, alive under my thighs. The man's beard brushed my temple, and the sky slid into a purple glow, replacing the sunset that had burned on the horizon at the beach.

The beach. Yes, I remembered going into the tank for the test, and then there was ocean and black sand.

In summer, there would be a night, but a short one. Maybe 20:00 when the sky turned like this. Except that I had never seen any sky like this—an epic wilderness of color and clouds, roiling, descending overhead.

The tank created a tightly local environment. It wasn't good enough yet to do anything like this, to carry me through a complex and far ranging landscape.

Acid crawled up my throat. I couldn't remember anything I'd been trained to do if a sim went wrong. I'd memorized and recited so many good ideas. My head was so sogged with water, though. Contacts sputtered to life and told me the ambient temp again. They shouldn't be working in here. They didn't work inside the tank.

I was in here too long. I had to get out, tap out. I hadn't even thought of trying to tap out!

I reached with my right arm to tap on my left, right over my wrist. My fingers fluttered under the sleeve of my dress, entering the short sequence. Nothing.

Cold uncurled in my gut, despite the heat of the nameless Viking who was holding me up. I tapped out again, expecting the unpleasant tingling that came with extraction. No response. Again. Nothing. The wind was scouring my bones, and either with the cold or the fear, I cried. No matter. Beyond the sounds of weather and hoofbeats, no one heard me.

I whispered English words into the wind. *"What is this?"*

A tank malfunction? If so, it was the most spectacular mistake in history. I could smell the horse's hair and the leather of the bridle. Feel the rough surface of mane and the shifting of the big man behind me. I turned to watch a forest pass by, the twisted trunks of thousands of delicate trees, their coppery bark flaring with a last bit of light before they would be consumed by night. A single last tendril of brilliant orange was suddenly snuffed out by deep rust, the purple filling over all of it and lifting for a moment into pure electric blue.

It would be an accidental quantum leap in technology and pure artistry. For this was art, magnificent in its fervent detail.

It was the electric blue moment between day and night, and we picked up our pace. The chief was so beautiful, silhouetted against a darkening sky. He carried a torch now. The soft flame lit up the blue in his hair as it rose and fell with the gait of his horse.

In the dark, we arrived somewhere. Frightened, numb from the horse, I couldn't walk or speak. The big man carried me. I heard muttered phrases, men's clipped words, women's voices like a flock of practical birds. "Found," I heard in the odd Old Norse, "almost drowned" and "make room." I felt a wooden bench against my back, a wool blanket dragged up and over my clammy clothes and body. I was asked my name.

"Jen," I struggled to say. I was so, so tired, and my voice sounded small and hoarse.

A woman was holding my hand. Her face was tough but curious. With her smooth palm she petted me. "Ginn," she said.

She was surrounded by the glow from a fire, and I looked beyond her to see more than a dozen faces, people crowding on benches that flanked a long room—so long I couldn't see the end. It was the heartstone setting, but so much bigger than we'd designed it.

The characters were different, too. Swirls of smoke singed my eyes and when I choked, tears blurred their faces, but I could still see detail. Fear and curiosity alighted on each face in a different way as they considered me. And each pair of eyes was illuminated with a rich inner history that brought them to this moment. This was no Jiu Jitsu sim, and they weren't playing house.

It felt real. Like I was really here, in Viking Iceland. But that wasn't possible.

None of this was. The vivid stink of fish and horse and smoke, the long stretch of fairytale forest under an epic sky that changed with the hours, a far-reaching landscape that deepened into night. None of this could happen in the tank. And so I wasn't in it, was I? Even as my mind refused to consider it, some small part of my heart knew it was true.

Iceland, circa 920

I CHOKED INTO CONSCIOUSNESS, MY LUNGS ON FIRE. A WAVE OF smell washed over and into me, the stink of fire and wood and bodies. The berth was dark, and the bench beneath me bit into my hips. I could just about stretch my toes to the opposite wall. Concealed behind a pair of thin curtains, I was alone. But I remembered a bony body tossing next to mine, someone yanking on the wool cloaks, the low sound of female voices. "Shhhh, go to sleep."

Now, a stack of folded blankets and sheepskins sat tidily against the wooden back wall, everyone gone but me. I pulled myself up to sit and lean into the corner. Strong smells made my eyes well up. I turned my head and pressed my cheek to the wood. These must be the scents of sap and bark, mixed with the familiar tang of metal from Morgan's studio. Such small sips of air made my head throb.

I sluggishly tapped out and nothing happened.

My sleeve was different. A soft, fluffy underdress that wasn't mine.

Jeff said smell was the most basic of the senses in terms of primal response, behavior, memory. Basic scents were achievable in the tank, but subtle and complex smells were beyond current programming capabilities. This dress smelled like soap and bright, glacial water. The scent of this wall flushed my body so strongly and specifically, opening up dark and sensual in my gut. The smell of dirt brought back moments from this morning. Memories of anemic park grass between my fingers. The glimpse of sun through angry swirls of skirts already felt like a million years ago.

This smell wasn't emitted by the cold workings of a molecular generator. It was wood. I was in this world.

I looked around, but didn't find a place to vomit.

Time still passed, which was impossible. The wrongness persisted—the vivid smells of birch and wool and sweat, the unknown characters and voices. The sound of words I didn't design.

Some dwindling piece of my heart still believed I could tap out, despite the fact that this world could never exist in the tank. And so I tried again, and then I shook and cried. I cried silently, my forehead pressing tight into my palms, mouth open. I cried for home, for Morgan and Jeff, for safety. For facts inside my eyes, my contacts showing me how I could choose words, define them.

I cleared my eyes of tears and then blinked them on, but they didn't respond. Nothing glowed or twitched, not one letter or fact. My dread became shapeless. The definition of the word itself and no more.

Then the chief's voice was there. Outside the curtain.

He sat on the bench right outside and talked about a tool—a word for *earth cutter*. Another man spoke about how many, how sharp. The chief talked about how many walls, how far. Men's thoughts and calculations. I sensed the heaviness of his body, so close I could feel the bench move when his hips shifted. I could have touched him, if I'd stretched out my arm.

Old Norse words were often round and thick, spoken with the cadence of a lullaby. Voices layered upon one another around the heartstone, phrases rising like questions. Then barks of joy pierced the softness. Clipped tones of irritation. No other language had its range, its ragged roughness and yet its capacity for melody and intimate murmurs.

I thought I'd immersed myself in this language. But I'd been playing at it. My god, I was hearing the real thing. I closed my eyes and drank in the chief's voice. Hoarse like gravel sometimes, very grave, but something about it was good.

Feeling the solid weight of his body on that bench, I wanted things. I wanted to see the gestures that went with the words, to see peoples' faces when they spoke. I wanted to go to the bathroom, wash my hair, eat. And I wanted to look at the chief again. I remembered every line and detail of his face from the sea. The high forehead, black waves of hair and dark angled brows, knife-like cheekbones, wolfish eyes. I raised my hand to lightly brush the curtain that divided us. I wondered what he was named.

The men left the house, and even through the curtain I could feel the sigh of readjustment in the way the women talked.

I sat up and stretched as best I could in the cramped space, and I seized with pain, a thousand needles and aches and pinches. I leaned into the wooden wall and groaned. My fingers tapped on my arm out of habit, but I wasn't surprised nothing happened, nothing at all.

I lay my head against the wood and felt its scratchy surface snag my hair. I had no more ideas. I was just here.

"She needs to get out." A woman was speaking. She said "the bath," and something like "it will ease her." The voice was soft but slightly hoarse, like the scratchy mane I'd clutched last night. A tiny lisp, no more than a push behind esses, so small that no one but me might notice. A formation of the mouth.

Someone drew the curtain aside and let in the light of a nearby torch and a strangling wave of smoke. Sun reached through a hole in the roof, enough so I could see her clearly. She placed her hand, slim and bony, palm down against the bench near my feet, and she looked at me with pale eyes. Quiet, but not hesitant.

She was younger than me, maybe by several years. It was hard to tell, because of the light, and because of her hair, both childish and severe. It was pulled tight in two French braids that gripped her head like talons. They made her angular features stand out, accentuated in the lamp light. Nose straight and prominent, high cheekbones, chin like a point. But her lips were full and rounded, a soft mouth for such a sharp face.

After a moment, she moved her hand farther into the alcove, as if gentling an animal in a cage. It was easy to let her come all the way in. She folded herself like a wading bird, all arms and legs. It was simple to let her sit with her knees drawn up just a few feet away.

"I am Betta," she told me. The rich, smoky voice I'd heard outside the curtains now came from those lips, a sensual surprise. She smiled, and her teeth were just a little too big for her mouth. Somehow it softened everything, gawky and charming.

I smiled too, and breathed in a rush of smoke. The air burned going down. I croaked hello. Mutual intelligibility, I thought. If people who speak different versions of a language can equally understand each other.

She focused on my mouth, eyes intent and curious, and I wondered if she'd never seen anyone with a gap in their teeth. Her hand twitched in her lap, as though she wanted to reach out and test me. As if where language failed, her fingers could find out what I was. She wasn't afraid of openly observing.

"You're scared," she said. Everything was stated matter of factly.

She couldn't know how deep my fear went, spiraling down inside me like a funnel of dark birds. Varieties of fear. I was insane, definitely. And stranded, abducted by realists? Stuck forever in some twilight of the tank? Or not. Afraid to admit it, my gut knew what was true. I was twelve hundred years from where I began.

The shaking started again, and I drew five pounds of wool and fur up around me.

"You have no need to be," she told me. "The farm is green now. It's summer, já?" She looked at my blankets, then reached for one and very slowly drew it away. "You need to come outside and breathe."

Breathing! The idea of fresh air came to me as if from a long ago story. I'd forgotten about it. There would be clear air outside the house. Air and sun and light. Suddenly, I couldn't wait. I needed it. Tears sprang up, and I nodded, already gulping for it, singeing my lungs.

Betta slid to the edge of the alcove and opened the curtains all the way. "Let's see if you can walk." Her strong fingers closed on mine, and she helped me out of bed and into the house.

I stepped into a Viking dollhouse, lit by two dozen lamp fires that twinkled and flared along the walls.

Benches stretched far away to my right, scattered with gray and white furs and sheepskins, their ends disappearing into the dark, limitless longhouse. In the firelight, the benches and walls were colored in butter and copper. Outside the reach of the small flames, they shifted into shades of rust, plum and darkest brown shadows.

Objects glinted in angled rays of sun that shot through a vent in the roof. Tools, axes that had been laid carefully aside, women's knives and needles flashing. Two women sat like spirits in the drifting smoke and revolting stink of body odor and fish. I swallowed hard.

It was the hjartastein. *Heartstone.* A word that, in the Viking way, made a tiny poem out of the most ordinary thing. It was the main fire, the center of the living home. An elongated oval of rocks contained it. Sunlight coming through a hole in the roof carved a swirling column of ashes and smoke that rose slowly toward the sky.

I blinked the sequence to save an image, and a little tear of loss and frustration stung my eye. My contacts were gone, wouldn't work anymore.

I searched the room, desperate to take everything in, every detail, for when I got sucked back into the future. I had no idea when it would be. I had to seize this, and I had to do it alone, with just my eyes and mind. I reeled, trying to see and listen and memorize, and when I stepped down out of the alcove I stumbled and my knees hit the ground.

From the swept-dirt floor I looked up in wonder. Across the way two stories of sleeping spaces were set into the wall, divided by big posts, entire trees holding up the house and dividing tiny sleeping quarters like animals' dens. Most were enclosed with thin linen curtains, a rusty orange color that glowed almost pink where it was lit.

A few alcoves on the lower level were open to the room. In one of them, a man slept heavily with his mouth open against the wood bench, his belly crushed against a metal cup and several knives that hung from his belt. One arm bent, his hand rested on his ax blade like it was a lover's cheek. Other than him, no men were present. Just the two women at the heartstone. They stared.

I reached blindly for Betta, and she squeezed my hand with her capable fingers, her cool and reassuring palm. She helped me up, and when we both rose to our full heights, she stood an inch or two above. A very tall woman in her place and time, probably five and a half feet.

She helped me walk the length of the room and through an archway into another. The second room was smaller and paneled with a blond wood that made it shine. I'd read about this! The room for women's work. At the center, around a smaller fire, were a small clutch of women, vaguely threatening. Two sat spinning on glowing blond benches. The third paced with a baby at her breast, whispering to it and kissing its white head. Its soft hair waved with her breath. Betta didn't introduce me, and I was grateful. They nodded, a couple smiled, and we moved on.

A door stood at the end of the room, all golden wood with iron hinges and a little gable with crossed dragon heads above it. A child's dream door. Something breathtaking and special should be on the other side, like a world made of candy. And it was.

The mudroom at the back of the house was a great profusion, lit with the same little wall lamps stuck into the dirt walls here and there. They illuminated a rich and abundant life. Dozens of wool cloaks hung from pegs, leather boots lined up below, a tall stack of big bowls, so many baskets, tools, brooms. Bows and arrows hung on the wall, next to a pair of long, curved blades and a string of blunt ax heads, everywhere lay knives and axes and other bits of metal made for cutting. One corner was filled of wooden handles of every length from hatchet-sized to taller than Jeff. Another corner was stacked with crude snowshoes and long, flat slats that were the skið I had read about—*snow skates*—like thin wooden skis. Low benches lined the back wall, one piled high with folded blankets and sheepskins. Under the bench, a small wooden sword and tiny shield lolled, forgotten. The home's true heart was not the fire pit, but here.

The room was chaotically alive and yet neat as a tack. A house run strictly but bursting with love, kept in order by a good wife. Maybe it was the one with the babe. Had she worn keys at her waist? A pang of emotion erupted in me, an anger so sharp that I staggered onto the bench. Who did she think she was, the woman who kept this house so beautiful? I was confused. Shocked at myself. Frustrated and mad at being lost and weak. This was a gorgeous home, bigger, more extravagant and comfortable than any longhouse I'd imagined, and I was lucky, so very lucky.

My head was a dead weight in my hands.

A little girl with long, brown braids knelt in front of me. "Come Lady, are you alright?"

I lifted my raw eyes to her, and she told me she was Ranka, exactly six. Betta knelt beside Ranka, looking speculatively between my feet and a little pair of leather ankle boots. I noticed my own by the door, two salt-watered lumps. She pursed her lips, matching my foot to a sole. Ranka gave advice in a sing-song voice about girls with growing feet.

Besides the way we came through, there were two other doors. One went outside, I assumed. Another had a complex iron latch. And there was also a passageway—a simple opening in the floor with steps going down into the earth, extending into a dark, unknowable interior.

I stood and wobbled, reached out my hand for the latched door, and Betta and Ranka nearly knocked each other over scrambling to pull me away. "Nei!" Ranka's eyes were wide. "We do not go there." I let them steer me away and down the dark stairs into the earth.

THE TUNNEL WASN'T FRIGHTENING. JUST HIGH AND WIDE ENOUGH that Betta and I could walk comfortably, it looked like something built by friendly elves. Betta let Ranka hold a small torch, and I winced when she waved it too close to my face. We hardly needed it. In less than half a minute we could see a square of light where the tunnel ended. It was a charming little door with a paneless window cut out of the top half. We seemed to be inside a hill, and right ahead of me I could see the clean air.

I stepped out, and the sun off a million blades of grass slashed at my eyes. I cried out, covering them with my hands. I opened my fingers slowly, and when I was able to look, the world was stunning. We stood in a small bowl in the land, and emerald hills climbed everywhere, up from us in every direction. The grass grew down off them and right onto the roof of the tunnel door. The grass yielded to soft moss all over the stones at our feet. A circular, sea green pool sat calmly, waiting, glittering. And we were in the green. It wasn't something seen against a screen or a white tile or metal tabletop. It was around us.

Betta took me farther past the pool, to a place where I could go to the bathroom. The future word stood out in my mind as ridiculous, given the circumstances—this bath that stood without walls, under the sky, a "room" that was no more than a private space in the bushes near a stream. In privacy, I took my dry contacts out of my eyes, rolled them up and stashed them in the cylinder of my needle case.

Then I floundered, figuring out what to do with my bundle of skirts. Grass scratched and tickled. So different from my apartment, I could barely comprehend what I was doing. Where I had come.

When we got back to the pool Betta started ordering me around, and her exaggerated gentleness dissolved into easy cama-raderie. "Afkloeði, Kona," she demanded. *Off with your clothes, Woman.* I burst out laughing at how much she sounded like Jeff. I would have to teach him that one.

My laugh stuck in my throat. Jeff. I wondered when I'd see him again. Would I be whisked out of this scene, back to the lab, at any moment—the wrenching metal in my brain as unexpected and fast as last time?

Betta's toothy smile drew me back. She was easy and sweet, and when she smiled she was beautiful. Not pretty at all. She held the promise of later grace, of becoming gorgeous with age, growing into her wide eyes and learning to loosen her hair.

She helped me with my dress and got my shift off over my head. Belt, needles, necklace all heaped on the rocks. Holding onto her arm, I stepped into the pool, expecting it to be pleasantly warm. But it was almost hot, just on the edge of comfort. It was luscious, and I sank gratefully down into it and it cradled me.

We had a spa at the lab, a floating, melted space inside the heart of the glacier, but none like this. I'd never seen a pool that sat like a tiny bowl under a peach and moss-colored sky. I tilted my head back and an immense weight of openness—a sky unbroken by steel and glass—pressed down on me like a heavy blanket. So big. I breathed slowly, calming myself. I brushed my thigh, and the water was like silk on my skin. I gripped the silty bottom with my toes and played with the resistance against my hand as I swiped the surface. Mesmerized.

"Have you not had a bath before, Lady?"

Ranka sat cross-legged on the stones at the edge of the pool, her head so far to one side she was dipping a braid in the water. Her brows were scrunched into a tight V, a very adult look of concern on her face.

What did she think of me? As new and amazing as this pool was to me, I realized that's what I was to her. Ranka's world must have been small. Unbelievably small. I was the one glittering new thing that would come along probably in her entire childhood. She wanted to be part of me, of the occurrence of "Ginn."

Worry crept over me and a chill shot through my bath. She was a child, open and intrigued, but what would the adults think? Where did they suppose I'd come from? I pictured myself lying on the black sand, my dress like a splash of blood against the dark. I had no explanation, and that seemed dangerous.

I floated over to the edge and asked if Ranka would do my hair.

"I will see what I can do," she told me in a scolding voice, and Betta and I glanced at each other and stifled our laughter.

While I soaked, Betta swished her feet in the pool, and Ranka bathed my forehead with a linen cloth dipped in some sweet smelling water she'd mixed with flowers. White sprigs like bits of Queen Anne's lace bobbed and swirled in her soapstone bowl. Snjorbloms she called them. *Snow blooms.* The farm wife had used that word in her diary, and now I knew it was angelica, before the Christians and botanists brought such notions to this place.

Ranka wiped my temples and the back of my neck, moving my hair around in soggy ropes. She talked in her little voice about how she would one day have jewelry like mine, and about feeding horses and learning to cut and sew a shirt for her father. It was a very big shirt. Soon she would need her own new dress, she was so tall.

She combed my hair with a beautiful comb, bigger than my hand. It had a curving back and delicate teeth, each one carved from bone. It gently scraped my scalp, waking up a million tingles and itches. I'd been sleeping on a hard bench, my hair damp and matted with sand. Every stroke of the comb made me feel a bit more human. Ranka industriously and carefully worked at the tangles, obviously proud that she was helping to wake me up and get me "ready." She dipped the comb in the water and ran it down my hair, and I leaned forward so she could comb all the way down my back. Bunched with worry, I wondered. "Ready" for what?

She asked if she could wear my necklace someday, and I said yes, as long as she would tell me what this place was.

She paused. I'd said something strange.

"Já well, you're at Hvítmörk!"

This was meant to thoroughly answer the question. And her tone strongly suggested I should be thrilled. Yes, I should know what Hvítmörk was. *White Woods.* It must be the name of the farm that lay before me, where these people worked and lived, where the chief went this morning when he left the house. The place I would eventually go, when this bath was through. It was a farm full of people who would expect me to behave in all the normal ways they did, and to know every common thing they did, let alone know where I'd come from and what had befallen me. How could I tell them? It was unthinkable. I didn't understand it myself.

Ranka went on about her little girl topics. She talked about everyone on the farm, and I could hardly comprehend or remember any of it. She had an urgent need to tell me everything she'd ever absorbed or thought. I could feel her unstoppable will to grow, and to be, and it made me ashamed of hiding back in that bed for even a minute. My heart filled with her excitement, and I breathed the fresh air and smelled grass and dirt, more vivid and animal than any city park. Bliss and pure wonder coursed in my veins.

Then she was talking about me.

"I heard that you came from the sea," she said. My worry came back, a sudden hard ball in my stomach. She went on, oblivious to me. "My Da found you."

An unaccountable feeling stabbed at my heart. My voice came out smaller than I intended. "I thank him, then."

"Já … " She trailed off, and the silence was stark after so much chatter.

She wanted to ask me something. I could hear it in the echo of her *yes*, the inflection that lingered in my ears, and I could feel her swaying back and forth on her knees while she arranged the wet hair around my shoulders. Finally she burst out, "So are you sent by the goddesses or not?"

Betta and I laughed out loud, then looked at each other and smiled. I thought of the programming team, of Jeff, and he was no goddess. "I don't think so."

Ranka's father had found me at the ocean. She was his child, then. She was a bright and wonderful girl. So why did it make my heart hurt to know that she was his?

"So the chief is your Da." I said it lightly, but the words burned in my throat. It was the smoke, still thick in my lungs.

Ranka gasped and dropped the comb with a glunk into the bath. The intensely bubbly girl who'd hardly stopped moving for a second in all the time I'd known her, became still.

"Oh nei, Lady, nei," she whispered.

Betta was alert, watching me without moving. I'd said something wrong. I felt like I'd been walking in a grassy meadow and stepped in a cavernous hole.

Then Betta returned to herself. "Ranka's Da is Arn."

"And my Ma is Kit," Ranka joined back in, picking up speed. "I have a little brother. We sleep in the next bed after you. The chief has his own room." And she was off on a number of tangents at once, until my head was full of sheep shearing and spinning and horsies and kids who are nice and not nice. Betta lived down the hill at the thralls' house. And Hildur—she was in charge. There were four girls who needed to be betrothed soon, in order from least pretty to prettiest: Betta, Thora, Grettis and Svana.

Ranka stopped short, realizing what she'd done, but Betta was turned away and I couldn't see her smile fade. I only saw her sit up taller. Least pretty.

"It's okay, Ranka," I said, breaking into the silence. "I think it's time for me to get dressed."

Betta gave me a pair of gauzy wool pants for underneath my skirts, and I pulled them on quickly. We were far enough down from the house to be mostly hidden, but I could still see a swatch of the grass wall. A trick of the landscape that made this little spot visible from the yard. The bite of air felt unfamiliar on my breasts and thighs.

The pants were so finely woven, like clouds around my calves. I drew on the shift and underdress they'd given me. My extravagant red wool was still clogged with mud, so a borrowed, oatmeal-colored dress went on top. I thought of the Viking in the coffee shop. If it weren't for him, I'd have washed up as a peasant girl, not a Norse princess in a lavishly dyed dress. Perhaps the chief would have sent me to Betta's house, down the hill.

He could still send me there.

I looked back at the door to the tunnel. Grass grew off the hill down onto its little gable. Dragonheads crossed, frozen in the act of biting the crisp air. I took a few extra deep breaths before heading inside again. Before heading to meet this man who held my fate.

"Do you remember yourself?"

Betta's question was asked so softly I almost didn't hear. I turned to her, but she didn't look at me. She watched the horizon and waited.

I thought about me—Jen—about my friends, my empty attraction with Jeff, my clean apartment. Thought about my job building fantasies for other people who had similar friends and lovers and homes. I thought about reading the farm notes alone in the dark.

"No," I said, actually wishing it were true. That I didn't remember me.

And then I knew my answer, that this is what I would tell everyone. Betta, Ranka, the chief, the staring women. My worries about explaining myself were over. I just wouldn't remember anything.

FINALLY BETTA AND RANKA HAD DONE ALL THEY COULD. THEY'D bathed and dressed me. Fed me a big, delicious cloud of goat cheese that I ate in great gulps with a spoon. Let me floss with thread and brush my teeth with a carved stick. I swished with the angelica water left in the bowl, trying not to think about how the comb had dipped into it so many times. Ranka arranged my braids one more time, drawing them down from my temples, smoothing the rest of my hair that hung long over my shoulders. I was ready. I would have to meet the chief.

While they worked on me, I thought about the way he talked, outside my bed curtain. He sounded cold. The way Betta and Ranka acted, I imagined he must terrorize this family. They were afraid he would be mean to me. But it was more than that. There was an icy dread underneath everything having to do with him, and I couldn't name it even enough to ask. What was it that they feared?

By the time I was fully prepared, I didn't know if I should expect to be welcomed to Hvítmörk or backhanded across the face and told to live in the stables.

Ranka pushed me in the right direction and ran away.

The chief was working with iron over a hot fire. He was sharpening a nasty looking blade, pounding it with a hammer against a rock. Again and again, flattening, honing. His hair—all of it this time—was tied out of the way with a strip of leather, and his temples showed slick with sweat.

He worked in linen pants and a thigh-length shirt. No, it was two shirts, layered like Jeff's old t-shirts. They covered him completely from his throat down to a pair of leather gauntlets on his wrists. Not the romanticized version of a horn-helmeted warrior, the chief was big and lean and powerfully built from hard work in the sun. I was lulled by the changing curves of his shoulder blades as he worked. The elegant flow of muscle and bone under linen, so far beyond the reach of any programmer's skill.

I shaded my eyes to watch, and the hem of my dress fluttered and caught in the grass. A quiet moment alone with him. It felt natural.

He stood up, dragging one hand across his forehead and the black strands that stuck there, looking as though he'd half forgotten about me. He had, I think, and he was bewildered and freshly annoyed at the idea of me. I had been soothed by the sun and breeze and his rhythmic work, but now that lurking dread came again.

I was lost. Stranded in a place where no elegantly curved Viking ship could take me home. At the mercy of a man who held his own family—every woman and child in the house—in fear and awe. What would he do with me? Scenarios flashed through my mind. Wind and rain whipping at me, cast out alone in the wilds of Iceland, or working on the farm, a slave. Bringing him his food, slipping the boots from his feet at night. What else might he want? Whether he threw me away or kept me, I would have little choice.

Then those gold eyes fixed on me.

"Heirik Rakknason," he said of himself, without extending a hand.

Two boys fluttered around him, picking up his task where he'd left off. Heirik stepped away from the fire, and clearly I was supposed to follow. He crossed his arms over his chest and settled in to stand and talk.

"I take care of this family, this land."

I looked past him and down into a stunning valley, where smoke from small fires climbed the air currents. Cows grazed randomly, like in a children's book.

"Hello Heirik," I said, amazed at how small my voice sounded, The hard A up front, the softly rolled R. "I'm Ginn."

I tried out my name. Like my skirts, soft and mysteriously new.

I was afraid I'd be unable to look away from his birthmark. But I looked at him head-on, and in an instant it was as if the mark dissolved and I saw only him. His face was as sharp and breathtaking as I remembered from the coast.

He kept his arms folded tight, but he repeated "Ginn," and a fleeting lightness lifted his voice. My name seemed to turn his eyes to honey, and a smile played at one corner of his mouth. It lit there for only an instant and was gone.

The forge stood uphill from the house, and he looked into the distance, down into the valley, in a direction I thought was the sea. A chill breeze came up and lifted the loose strands of hair from his face. He was head of a huge household and farm. Probably two dozen people lived in the big house alone. He was young, not much older than me, but still in this time and place he would have a family, a wife and kids already. He no doubt counted farmers, fishermen, hunters and traders among the extended family whose land and huts sprawled in this valley and on the slopes of surrounding hills. He was bound to protect and lead them. What I amounted to was a small irritation. He needed to decide what to do with me, so he could move on to the next challenges of the day.

He smelled like fire and leather.

He took a deep breath, as though he knew this would go nowhere but he just had to ask. Looking out over the grassy vista he said, to the air as much as me, "What happened to you, Ginn?" The bracers at his wrists were tied with leather strips, and with his right hand he began loosening the laces of the left. It was as though he cast the question out like a stone in a pond, and then focused his eyes elsewhere while he waited for the ripples.

"I don't know."

It was the truth. I didn't know anything about how I'd come.

He nodded. He looked at me again, looked into my eyes for a moment that was too brief. His half smile returned. "Have you seen the woods?" He raised his chin.

I turned around to follow his gaze and gasped. I had been staring at him, watching him work, looking down into the grassy slopes of his farm, and all the while behind me was Hvítmörk. A glorious, heart-stopping forest stretching for miles, farther than I could see. From up here, the woods stirred, alive with a thousand whispers and breezes. Mysterious and lush, a place for elves and land spirits to live, for children and lovers to hide. The canopy gleamed, dark and glossy from above, but the slanting light of afternoon reached the interior and lit the woods with a haunting white glow. *Oh.* I was looking at a million trees, every one of them a silver birch.

"Oh, Heirik," I whispered. "Your woods are beautiful."

I turned back to him wanting to see his smile again, but found him considering his ax blade. "Go to Hildur," he told me, the lightness gone. "She will have you work." He walked away.

SPINNING

IT WAS TO BE THE LAST TIME I'D USE HIS NAME. HILDUR MADE that clear soon enough.

We sat atop a grassy wall that was pleasantly heated by the sun. It was a rock and turf circle that enclosed the stables, no more than fifty feet from the back door of the house.

There were five of us women and Ranka, like birds in a line. We'd helped each other get up to the top, which was just about my chest height. A pretty girl named Svana clasped her hands for me to step on. Her fingers were so slender and white, I was sorry to plant my damp leather boot on them. She just smiled and then climbed up on the next girl's hands in turn. When she met me up top she was a little breathless, and she laughed and brushed my cheek, sweeping off something, some twig or dirt that clung to my face.

"Have you never climbed a wall, Woman?"

Even Hildur, at twice my age and around four foot ten, climbed up in a heartbeat. The whole time, she maintained an air of strict superiority.

Keeper of the keys. I learned Hildur was mistress of all that happened inside the house and everything women touched and made. Every ounce of spun fiber, every slab of fish and drop of ale were hers to demand or deny. I knew intellectually that this was how it was done, that a woman ran the house and a man the farm, but they were usually married. I guessed Hildur was about fifty. I thought she was much too old for the chief.

She had not grown tired, though, with decades of work, nor plump or doughy. Not overly kind like a fairytale grandma, either. She was short, slim, and sinewy. Her eyes were quick and dark under a severe arrangement of graying blond braids, and her expression flashed rapidly and frequently from exasperated to resigned to mirthful. It seemed she could be funny as well as fierce. And as far as I could tell, she ran a perfectly functioning, huge and prosperous house. She and Heirik made an oddly matched set of tough strategists with changing eyes. Together with him, Hildur ruled this place.

She was smart. I was sure she could see me calculating, wondering.

"You will call him Herra," she told me. *Chief.* "No one uses his name." She nodded to herself, checking that off her list of the many things I needed to learn.

In a sideways manner, Hildur had welcomed me. She'd watched me put on the new socks and boots I was given. I wrapped and tied the leather with little hitch knots, and Hildur, without breaking her sewing stride, glanced at me and raised an eyebrow. I wondered if this was not an alright way to tie my shoes. Finally she said, "We have enough." Meaning, I could keep them.

She'd also made it quite clear that I would work immediately. Today, I would re-learn how to spin, considering that I must have known and lost the memory. Tall, angular Betta handed up a basket with several spindles in it, and billows of cloudy, whitish fiber, before she pushed herself up, too.

The stables were set into a single round building with cave-like openings on all sides where the animals huddled and slept. Since it was summer, Svana explained, the stinkiest animals—the sheep and cows—were in the highlands grazing. There were a couple of goats here, a mess of chickens, two house dogs. A few of the horses stayed down all year working. The smell of animal hair and dung was stunning, like a physical blow, and I had trouble imagining how much worse it would be when the entire population came down from the hills and gathered in close.

My eyes watered from the stink. I blinked and cleared them and lifted my face to see the farm.

Only when the chief showed me the forest had I gotten any sense of the enormity and wonder of this place. Coming out here, and sitting up on this wall, a green and purple and white immensity opened up and crushed me.

I was small. A breathless speck under this sky, boundless without buildings to divide it. My breath came fast and shallow and I dug my fingers into the sod on either side of me. I told myself it was just the outside world the way it used to be, before glass towers and labs. I'd dreamed of it. I forced my lungs to work slower, to breathe deeper. I let my mind adjust. And finally my fear fell away, dissolving into the grassy, velvet beauty.

The house and stables sat on the only flat plane in sight. Hills climbed and fell in a dozen directions, like green waves slapping and sloshing in a pail. Chaotic, and so vivid I could taste grass in my throat. Down to the bath, up to the forge, and beyond, maybe, to the highlands. Land seemed to spill right from our laps and all the way to the distant sea. The merest sparkle of ocean lit the horizon, or perhaps I dreamed I could really see it. A river of impossibly sky-blue water ran past not far below the house and wound through the landscape toward the sea. Where I'd come through. My one link to home.

Far down the slope, almost too far around the curve of the forest's edge to see, a single big fire sent out gray billows. I squinted and could make out a long building, another house. A neighbor, so close? Nei, it was the thralls' house. Where Betta lived.

I blinked in sequence to save the image and shook my head. Would I be here long enough to learn? My contacts would have been able to take an image, and would have told me just where I sat on the map of the city. Now they sat dry and curled like dead bugs inside my needle case.

I turned to Hildur, resigned to try spinning.

I dreaded it. Morgan had replicas of two dozen of the spindle whorls discovered in excavations across Europe. Hers were stone, ceramic, and even one dazzling beauty carved of amber. They were conical, flat, convex, all manner of shapes and weights, and I'd tried at least one of every type, without success. These seemed to be made of bone, though to carve these solid pieces, it must have been the bone of something massive. I looked around nervously, my eyes settling on the edge of the trees. Only little animals lived here, I reminded myself. Birds mostly. Foxes.

Hildur handed me a spindle that was already started. She placed the shaft against my leg and drew it from knee to thigh, knee to thigh, three times over, then lifted it away and it was spinning. She showed me how the thread was forming, how to feed the fiber, like spun sugar in my hands, a tiny bit at a time. I took over the spindle and tried to let in the right amount of wool, but a familiar sense of being chased came over me.

In the arcs, the demonstrators said spinning was relaxing, but I felt threatened by it. It was menacing, the way the twist climbed inexorably toward my hand. I knew I would never feed just the right amount at the right time. I would get bound up, the twist getting out of control, the thread turning on itself and bundling. It was exactly what happened every time I sat in front of a screen and tried to mimic the motions. My stomach clenched in a familiar knot that perversely made me homesick. It made me miss Morgan's hands turning over her rare spindles to show me their beauty, pointing with her deep blue polished fingernails. The closest I'd had to a friend.

Hildur's nails were pale. Her hands were thin and avian.

She ordered me to keep starting over and trying again, and she remained patient for a very long time. Her assertion—no, command—was that any woman with two hands would learn. "Slow and sure." Yes, I thought, definitely slow.

Three more tangles later, she looked at me skeptically. "You make me wonder if you're lazy, Child. Remember," she said with a wink, "no battles are won in bed."

The girls giggled.

"Mother!" Svana gasped.

I gasped, too. Hildur was Svana's mother? Svana, whose neck was long and lovely like her namesake bird's, whose hair was soft like buttercream frosting. Ranka had noted her as prettiest on her marriageable list. Tough, middle aged Hildur had made this vision of loveliness. I tried to imagine the housekeeper younger, picture her flitting, lovely, through the trees, presumably with a gorgeous man. An image lost to time. She must have been pregnant when she was over thirty. Svana must be around fifteen.

"Keep your hands moving," Hildur chided her pretty daughter.

"And you can stop wondering, Girl," she said with a jut of her chin toward me, as if she might dispatch with all my questions in one swift stroke. "There is no real wife of this house, and there will not be until the chief's brother returns."

She said this brusquely, and with absolute finality, and no one—not even her sweet, pouty daughter—spoke up. In fact, Svana dropped her eyes and blushed. There were undercurrents here, underneath the surface of this idyllic pool, and Hildur's statement had hardly stopped my wondering.

VARIETIES OF PAIN—STABBING, DULL, CONSTANT—OCCUPIED MY shoulders, my spine, my lower back. I'd spent what seemed like endless days, eight or more hours each, trying to make thread. My fingers were silky soft, my skin a red and tenuous barrier. My neck throbbed, and still I spun for three hunched-over days.

The time passed in a strange, uneven way. Was it a hint that I might suddenly return? The way a moment watching thread twirl could last a hundred years? The way sleeping seemed to last a second?

Every time I woke, it was another teasing moment when I expected the soft nudge of my apartment's voice, the clean light through glass windows, the smell of coffee. Then that still moment of potential would pass, yet again, into the heat and stink of the longhouse.

To pass the time and keep our blood flowing, we broke off in pairs and small groups and walked and gossiped. And I learned about Betta. Like Hildur, Betta's father, Bjarn was a kind of hired help. A thrall, but more like an upheld servant. If not for her Da's healing gift, Betta would live somewhere else, not as lovely and rich as Hvítmörk. He'd made a good life for his little girl. And as a third generation thrall, Betta was free.

Besides this tale, and lessons about the family tree, there was not much else to talk about.

Everyone longed to go places. Roundup would come in a few weeks, where they would see other families from the surrounding farms, and from all over this clan's own land. The women talked about minor intrigues, stolen horses, lazy shepherds. About boys, some that were attractive, some dumb. They talked of Eiðr who was ugly but smart and strong. His big brother Ageirr, a pinch-faced man whose house was renowned for its grimness. It hadn't always been so sad, and when the women said so their voices were chilly and fascinated. Hands fluttered nervously in clouds of fiber.

Their words turned broad and free when they spoke of Egil, a bear of a man, descended from one of the greatest settlers. His house was magnificent, his farm as vast as Hvítmörk. Haukur was his son. The chief fostered the boy here, and Haukur wouldn't see his Da again until the Jul festival. Egil's animals grazed farther away.

The women planned for a trip to the coast. Most of them went twice or maybe three times a year to gather eggs and herbs and juniper berries and to help process the birds and fish the men would kill, the "leaping salmon" of the arcs, the "great and clumsy auks." They would ride every one of their horses, pulling children and supplies on sledges, stopping to walk down rocky slopes between here and the ocean.

Betta dreamed bigger, of someday riding to the gathering of all the men in Iceland. The chief and Har went every year to a new kind of meeting, of everyone from everywhere. It had been growing until men from all over Hvítmörk now joined in the trek.

They went without children and with only a few of the women, but Betta had heard stories from Har. He told them around the hearth at night. Stories of riding so long they had to stop and sleep three times under the sparse stars of early summer.

In Betta's mind those stars shone on a landscape of gold and icy beauty. She pictured herself riding through it on a soft brown horse. There would be booths and tents to live in at the gathering. Merchants, other families and different chiefs, betrothals, liaisons and feuds. Betta was absorbed as she told me, and she set her spindle down without knowing she'd stopped making thread. There would be parties! More people than she had seen in her life. There would be jewelry and blades to look at and want. She spread her hands out in the air, palms down as if to contain the profusion of her dream. The river would run bigger and bluer there, she said. The knives would glint in a different sun.

I'd seen the place she spoke of, where the althing was held each spring until centuries after Betta herself would be gone. It was a deep rut in the ground, surrounded by glass towers that blocked the sun. A track of ground where people walked single file, their eyes furtive as they consulted their contacts. *The althing was formalized here circa 930 AD.* I recalled the dry lesson. *Chieftains and their men assembled each summer until the end of the Old Commonwealth in the 13th century.* Betta made me want to go now with her, to see the real thing. To see a bigger world through her eyes.

But she would never go. At best, she wasn't important. She would stay at Hvítmörk when the real men and women were gone.

A WEEK LATER, I REMAINED.

One night, the air turned crisp with a bite of something cold, the prickling of rain to come, and everyone left the house after the evening meal to walk and breathe. They smiled, chatting, calling to each other. Ranka's Da lovingly grabbed her mother, Kit, and dragged her away from talking with the girls. Three-year-old Lotta stopped to adjust her little boot and tried to race after the bigger girls wailing, "Nei! Nei!" I drifted a little bit after them, drawn by their wake, then stopped and stood. I didn't know which way to go, or who to bother. Awkward and frozen, I looked toward the ocean.

No more than ten days ago, I'd washed up there. Carried into a place of profuse, willful life, so vivid I ought to feel submerged in it. But I floated, so alone, even here in a place I'd fervently dreamed of.

The loneliness was most often a subtle little thing casually chewing at my edges. Now, in the languid stretch of evening, it hit me like a blow. The force of it drove me to the ground. I sat right there, a hundred feet from the house, my skirts in a cherry red billow around me.

I drew my knees up, and they felt bony when I rested my chin on them. I was thinner already. The food here choked me, and a slight hunger was my constant companion. Sour whey curdled in my throat and gut, porridge lodged like dull cement. I drew a braid the texture of straw over my shoulder. My hair was wrecked from just two washings with lye soap. I wrapped my arms tight and allowed myself to sob, just once. Gods, how had this happened? Why wasn't I sucked back into the twenty-second century, as randomly I'd been forced here?

I wasn't going to be. I could tell.

I rocked myself and drew a few hitching breaths.

I cleared a small space in the dirt, and with my finger I drew Iceland. I'd done this before, a few times since I came, trying to piece together where I was. Whether I sat, right now, where my gleaming apartment would stand, or whether I'd gotten lost far across the island as well as through time. I remembered Betta's words, about how the men had to sleep outside three nights to reach the althing. I drew lines emanating from Thingvellir. How far could that be, if it took four days? My finger was too big, the lines too fat. I brushed the map away. I had no idea.

I could see people far off down the hill, heading toward the edge of the silver forest a mile away. They were tiny, and the forest was a living mass of twisting, swaying green. I closed my eyes and thought of salad tossing in a giant bowl. I would hold it in my lap and eat it with my hands—all of it—like an animal.

Something wet and cold touched my temple, and I yelped and whipped my head up. The dog beside me yelped too, and sprang up facing me. My heart raced, and I looked around wildly for help. I'd never been this close to a dog. He stretched his paws out toward me and pushed his tail up high, wagging it, ready to wrestle.

"Nei," I laughed. His tongue hung out and his ears were two triangles standing in the air. He looked at me a moment longer, as if I might change my mind about wrestling. "I am not a puppy," I told him, offering him some grass to eat. He looked at it, and then at me as though I were dim. He seemed to adjust his expectations, and turned himself around to sit beside me, facing the sea. He smelled like sun and bare feet, and waves of stink came rapidly as he panted, but I liked his presence. My loneliness wasn't the dire, choking stone it had been a moment ago.

I picked little yellow flowers from around my feet and tucked them into the braid that went across the top of my forehead, making myself a crown. The dog yawned thoroughly, forming an amazing curl with his tongue, and then lay down with his paws pointing straight forward. I touched his back, and it seemed his whole body vibrated with his breath. Soon I was petting him, telling him nonsense words and how he was a good dog.

The chief and his uncle Har came from the house and stood down the hill to talk, about what I couldn't hear.

The chief was not easy with people. Most often demanding, matter of fact and seldom warm. But something subtle hid in his voice, so dark brown and lush, the way his tongue curled around the old words. I might wake each morning thinking I would be home, that this was just a bad dream, and when I found I was still here I would panic. Then I'd hear him say something. It didn't matter what. It was like waking from a childhood nap, someone big and safe nearby.

From where I sat he and Har were silhouetted against the late summer sky, and I was stunned once again by Har's size. He was the man who'd held me all the way here from the coast, his arms bigger around than I could grasp. His body had shielded me like a blanket. He'd kept me alive.

I'd been watching him with interest all week, and he was the only person who was not at all scared of the chief. He had led the family before Heirik was old enough, and he raised the boy like a son when Heirik's parents died. If possible, he was even more of a revered and mythic creature than the chief himself.

Most often grim, when his face and voice broke into joy it was overwhelming. His laughter rolled like thunder. The little children—almost all of them his own grandkids—were in turns awed by his imposing silence and charmed by his messy eyebrows and funny faces.

The two men turned my way, and I could see the chief's flaxen eyes. The family's unspoken dread seemed reflected there. But why?

He seemed hard and ungraceful today, and I felt like it was because of me. I wondered what he was deciding about me, what he might do.

The flowers were childish, and I untangled them from my hair.

Only ten days I'd been here, certainly no more than two weeks. I needed to give myself a lot more time than that, months or maybe even years, I thought. I needed to give everyone here a lot more time.

Betta came tripping down the hill to land beside me, breathless. "Ginn, you are still here."

"Já," I said, surprised at how often she seemed to read my thoughts. "I'm still here. Look!" I patted the dog, depositing crumpled yellow flowers on his back. "I think he likes me."

Betta shielded her eyes from the low sun, looking away toward the men and the farm. "Já," she said absently. "Já, I know he does."

Since I had no memory, Hildur took a good deal of the spinning time to lecture me.

Now, she talked about winter. She explained that while everything that happened inside the threshold of the house was her domain, in winter the line was blurred. Men brought work—from bits of char cloth to entire animals—inside. It was a messy, wet and cold time, and I could see that she was uneasy with the thought of it coming. As she talked about last year's waist-high snow, I pictured the threshold of the house, the actual line in the dirt, as a neat little handhold in a swirling wilderness. A charm against the uncontrollable frontier.

In reality, she told me, a woman could shear a sheep if she had to. A man could mend a shirt or cook a meal. I would rake windrows in the fields just two months from now. "We keep each other alive, já?" Of course. I found I could very easily imagine Kit's husband Arn, or even the chief himself cooking. I was sure there were limits, though. There had to be. For one, I could not picture a single one of the males of this family learning to use a drop spindle. I envied them with a great sigh.

Watching the wool endlessly become thread, I absorbed Hildur's conclusion. One overriding law. Always, inside or outside any house on the farm, the chief was as the gods. I was to do whatever he told me to do. He didn't often step into Hildur's way, but when he did, she let him. His orders were above question.

All the women had become quiet. Even while their spindles twirled, each was looking into the distance, or inside themselves, seeing their chieftain. There was that unease that came with any talk of him, an apprehension so vague I couldn't name it even enough to ask. I pictured the contemplative young man, his resolute mouth, honey eyes. What was it that they feared?

I closed my own eyes and saw a dark cloud and white lightning, an afterimage of the line of thread I was making. I must have looked scared. "He isn't always terrible, Child," said Kit. "Nei."

"He's not, nei," Dalla agreed, her sisters nodding. Svana assured me he would never hurt anyone, that he wouldn't even touch any woman. That it was okay, I'd be safe.

They were all completely unconvincing.

At least Betta didn't try to dissemble. She sat silent and intent. Hildur made tisking sounds, her face severe.

Thoughts and impressions jumbled together. He seemed off-putting, já, cold and a little frightening. But something in his voice made me respond with a still and open heart. "He doesn't seem terrible at all to me," I said finally.

Every voice faded, and they all gaped at me. Ranka listened with big eyes, and it reminded me of how she reacted when I suggested the chief was her father. She had dropped the comb into the bath and gone still.

"Ranka," I asked. "Why are you afraid of him?"

The little girl stared like she was trapped, and I was sorry I'd asked.

"You see what he is, já?," Hildur answered in something close to a low hiss. She was transformed by the subject, no longer kind.

I shook my head slowly, still ignorant.

"Child, clear your eyes," she continued. "The gods spilled blood on him. A terrible omen."

I was lost. Blood was spilled on him?

It came to me slowly and dreadfully. "His mark." I breathed the words.

"Já, his mark." Hildur's fingers grazed a glass bead, a charm that hung from her belt, as if warding off the danger of even speaking about him. She was truly scared, brimming with it.

"We don't speak of it," she explained with irritation, as though I was a willful child who had pestered her for answers. She continued anyway. "The chief was clutched from death by his father's hands so that he could learn from him and take his place."

"Ulf," I said, reviewing my lessons. "His father."

Ulf was there when Signé brought forth their firstborn, Hildur told me. The baby who was now the chief. The moment he came into the world, a blast of wind passed through the house, flattening the heartflame. The servant woman who had helped Signé tried to wipe the blood off the baby, but it would not come. When Signé realized the blood was part of him, she clutched the baby tight to her breast, frightened for his life.

I imagined her, a new mother, her baby just minutes old and in danger. I saw her tears, her wild eyes and determination. Her kisses on his warm head.

Ulf drew his seax, Hildur said, and ordered everyone away, the doors shut and bolted. And then with the gentlest love for Signé and for his new son, he set his knife down and placed the baby on his lap. He sprinkled him with water and named him for his own grandfather.

Something tugged at my awareness, something odd about his father, Ulf, naming him, but the feeling was gone in a second.

With a name, Heirik had been accepted and could not be exposed and left to die, no matter the family's superstitions. Still, Signé wouldn't let anyone touch him. She took baby Heirik in her arms again, and did not let him go for seven weeks. She charmed and glared the family into submission. She bound them in fear, not with a curse, but with a blessing. She blessed anyone who would follow and serve Heirik.

Signé's blessings were powerful and not to be spurned.

"And so we follow and serve him," Hildur finished. "And he is his mother's son. Untouchable."

Untouchable. They kept using that word.

In their flutter of assurances, Svana had mentioned I shouldn't worry, that he would never touch a woman. Could she possibly mean it literally? The times I'd seen him interact with people, he hadn't reached out. He hadn't touched me when he knelt and looked in my eyes at the beach. He folded his arms and turned away when we talked at the forge. Ranka's little voice came to mind. *The chief has his own room.* My god, what did they think might happen if he touched them?

"And the eyes of a wolf," Hildur was still talking. "And that hair. A blue swan."

It was a poetic phrase for raven. I thought it was kind of pretty, until she finished the thought. "The bird of corpses."

In the uncomfortable lull that followed, I bent my head to my work and really tried to spin. My thoughts kept following paths that branched and narrowed and became mired. It was a birthmark, huge and ugly, yes, but in my world practically inconsequential. It wouldn't be fraught with fearful meaning. It would probably just be removed.

This was not my world. Looking out over the vast land, I tried to imagine the depth of belief that could allow such cruelty. For a little boy to grow up without the comfort and joy of touching other people. I kept coming back to his eyes. The troubled thing I'd seen in them when he stood with his uncle, silhouetted against the sky. Maybe he'd seen my loneliness. And now he knew what it looked like from the outside.

"But you thrive," I said. "The farm thrives under him."

Hildur's eyes were like sparks on steel, but I held her gaze.

"Intelligence," she said, punctuating the word with a smack of the spindle to keep it moving. "Leadership, fierceness, strength. And a face and body disfigured by an ugly curse."

She contemplated this, her fingers expertly pinching fiber, her lips pursed to match. "It is a complex thing, what the gods have given him."

I supposed so. No matter how much I might believe or disbelieve about the Norse gods, some force of nature had made the chief into what he was.

"And you," she raised her chin at me. "Now the disir have given him you to figure out."

There were glances, as though the ancestral spirits who'd invited me were now sitting like ghosts among us on the wall. I dropped the spindle and reeled it up carefully. When I got it back, I placed it in my lap. My hands shook and I couldn't spin. What could I say in answer to that? I was another complication in his difficult life. And he was a feature of what was to become my lonely existence, too, forever stranded far from home, in a place where no one knew me. Tears stung the corners of my eyes, and I let my gaze blur until the hills and valley were a sad, green wash. A big cloud came and turned it all dark blue.

"Hildur?"

Ranka was speaking. I kept looking blearily into the distance.

"Já, Child."

"What does a blue swan look like?"

"Oh ..." Hildur hesitated for just a second. "It's a terrible beast, little one. A bird as big as a horse. With great black wings that sweep the ground, wider than a man's outstretched arms. Bloody eyes and claws, and a carrion reek."

It was a horrible joke to play on the child, but I imagined Hildur winking to let Ranka know it was just a story to scare and thrill her. Then Hildur finished, in a hiss. "Its beak is gory with the flesh of men. Its shriek rips souls from their dying bodies."

And I realized it wasn't a campfire story. She was serious.

She must have never seen a raven. She knew of them because of religion and superstition, passed down through the family and clan. But they didn't fly around the farm, apparently. And Hildur had gone nowhere else in her life, just the coast, the hills, this wall. Had she spent her days in a place so small, such a tiny crevice in the universe, that she'd never seen a black bird? In her mind, they'd grown to be tremendous and gruesome beasts. They ate the dead. When a warrior saw them, he knew his end had come.

And she thought the chief was aligned with them, because of his long black hair, its intense iridescence. All these girls thought so. They thought he was perhaps one of the ravens himself, come in human form to lead them, willing victims, to what? I opened my mouth to say something. I wanted to tell all of them that I'd seen ravens in documentaries. That they weren't gigantic beasts, just birds. Big ones, yes, inky black, but just birds. In the city we had crows. I'd seen a few of them eat a lost, old pancake in the park. I'd certainly never seen one eat a dying soul.

I felt crow-like and dark myself. It came over me like fast-moving storm clouds, anger as rotten as the flesh in Hildur's vision. It came up in my throat. With a great effort, I didn't say a word, just turned back to spinning with a vengeance. My best thread all day.

I could feel Betta looking at me. I saw her in the periphery of my vision. She had the largest, roundest eyes I'd ever seen, clear green and almost expressionless, her whole body transformed into the act of observing. I noticed, then, that all the other women and Ranka were looking downhill.

The chief was coming from far down the slope. They were stunned, each one mentally comparing the atrocious vision Hildur had just described with the flesh and blood monster who approached. The monster sworn to protect them, who kept them alive and safe. Who was right now working to raise food for them to eat, coming home from chopping wood to keep them warm. He was closer now, and I could see the mark on his face clearly. A bloodied man, who held their lives in his revolting hands.

He was lovely. He walked with an unhurried, steady gait, an ax hanging casually from one hand. His hair glinted in the sun, and it was exactly like a crow's feathers, mysterious and deep.

IT WAS THAT TIME OF NIGHT WHEN EVERYONE ROAMED THE FARM, walking in the clear sun of ten o'clock. Women and girls took off in groups to wander around the pretty birches and watch the rushing water. Up behind the house, Magnus and Haukur trained the little boys with wooden axes and shields.

I hadn't found anyone in particular to be with, to follow, and I didn't want to spend the time with the dogs, so I walked alone. I watched my boots smash the grass as I tramped up a series of hills that took me farther and farther from the house. The air was alive with moisture, and I raised my face to the sky and the dozens of peaks and slopes that surrounded me.

White mist rose from every hilltop, evaporating off of lavender and black rocks and dissolving into the sky, only to be followed by more and more steam, always coming off of the landscape. It shifted and billowed and covered the very tops of everything. And I was below, looking at the underside of earthly clouds.

I came over another small hill and stopped short, a sound of surprise escaping. A lovely glen opened up before me. Birds glided casually over the narrow little valley, a stream rambling below them. Grass grew right over its banks, almost covering it, but I could hear its constant gushing. Louder and wilder than the stream I'd wished that Jeff could give me. I had to touch it.

I skidded and tripped down to the water.

The grass, when I got very close, was cushy. The stream was less a waterway and more a drenching of the land. What looked like a bank was a cushion of saturated moss, and everything that appeared solid was sluggishly floating. My boots started to sink. My heels were sucked down by greedy mud. I panicked for a second, lifted my skirts and drew away.

I followed the thread of the stream at a safe distance, up where the ground was solid. I picked my way through grass and yellow flowers that grew taller and taller. Birds traced oblongs in the sky, lower now, close enough for me to see their long, curved beaks. I was so close to real birds! Ones that could fly with air under their wings, not pixels on a screen. One perched on a lump in the grass and complained, its call rhythmic and harsh like a honk.

The bump in the land looked unnatural, not like the other lumpy rocks that sat about the glen and streamside. The shape was familiar.

Birds opened their needle beaks and scattered as I took the last few steps to reach it.

Oh. I exhaled with surprise.

It was a longhouse. Just like the one the family lived in, but knee height. The tall summer grass and wildflowers almost obscured it, but a diminutive gable peeked out, and I cleared the way to a door no more than eight inches tall. Over my shoulder, a bird blared its rhythmic cry once more. My skin prickled with the thrill of it—of being in a world of actual brooks and animals. Being near creatures who circled in the air above a grass-roofed dollhouse. I knelt all the way down and got onto my elbows to open the door.

A hole in the roof let in just enough light to see.

The house's interior was spare and eloquent. The floor was packed dirt, and an oval of little rocks formed a heartstone—the bones and pulse of a house, nothing more. A bird passing low overhead made the light flicker as though the hearth was lit with flames.

I walked my fingers over the threshold but didn't reach in any farther. There was a pleasant stillness that I didn't want to disturb. I imagined the little girls playing here and wondered if the house had belonged to generations of children. Whether Betta had used it, whether Uncle Har had kept it in shape, trimming the weeds each summer and shoring up the little walls.

A rush of blood hit me when I sat up and rocked back on my heels. I'd had my head down longer than I realized. I looked to the sky, and my view swam with birds. A dozen or more defining elegant curves against the colors of evening. The mist had closed down tighter, now a translucent but oppressive gray. My feet tingled when I stood and I stamped them gently, wincing at the sharp pins and needles.

A bird swooped by just ten feet away and lit on a mossy rock. It scolded me, its long beak open. Another whizzed past my head, even closer, and then a hint of anxiety came, a gentle nudge of something not right. Wild birds weren't like house dogs. They didn't come over to be petted.

I turned to head back to the house, and the glen had changed to a big valley stretching endlessly up and away in every direction, disappearing into the growing mist. My heart pounded. Which way was home? I walked fast, taking big squelching steps. Birds were massing on every side. They flew in close to my face, so close I could see their round and unemotional eyes. Up close, their beaks were as long as my hand, curved and thin like the biggest sewing needle.

With the stream and little playhouse as a guide, I made a desperate stab at the right direction, and I ran. They followed me, crying out, and I was rushing now, my head light and full of adrenalin. I imagined them stabbing at me, tearing at my skin and hair. I stumbled up and out of the glen and kept racing, tripping over rocks, dress catching on flowers, nose running. The birds fell back, but I still struggled ahead.

I thought I saw the house, our big one, but in the green of full summer it was almost invisible until I was upon it. Sagging against it. Home.

Betta stepped out from the front door, saw me and came toward me, and she looked like salvation. I could tell her how I was so afraid and she would listen and say it was nonsense. I could imagine her comforting arm around me, her cool and sure hand on my forehead. But she froze in her tracks. Curious for one moment, her fingers clutched at the neckline of her dress, then she ducked her head and went back into the house.

"Ginn."

The chief was behind me.

He said to my back, "What happened?"

"Birds," I started, and it sounded so dumb. "I was walking in a pretty place." I pointed vaguely away from us, up the hills. "There was a tiny house just like this one, and then birds attacked me, all around my head—"

"—You are here now." His voice was safe, like a lullaby. He moved closer behind me. "Touch the wall."

I put my palm on it and it was strong. I gripped a handful of grass. My cheek felt hot against the relief of the turf. "My body hurts from spinning," I admitted. Then the words started to come fast and free, every one of them condemning me as ungrateful and lazy. "I'm sick from wool and dry fish and smoke and my lungs burn and I'm hungry all the time. And the farm is so beautiful. I'm just so alone."

It felt good to say it out loud, that I was lonely. "And I'm afraid of birds."

My words hung pathetically in a brief silence.

"Turn to me," he said with a sort of demanding kindness. Different from the way I'd heard him command Magnus to settle the horses or direct Hildur to prepare for an earlier morning meal for the men. There was no question that I would obey him, but the instruction wasn't cold.

My face felt wet and raw when I faced him.

I expected his to be implacable, but it wasn't at all. His emotions were visible and chaotic, surprise foremost. His eyes, wild gold, quickly searched mine then looked elsewhere, the house, the ground. His fingers found the grass between us. "I apologize," he told me.

"For what?"

He looked back up, and his dark brows briefly drew together. He looked for something in my features, but whatever it was, he didn't find it. "I only wanted to see your face." He was flushed and ashamed, and I didn't know why.

"Follow," he said abruptly. He turned and walked along the house, around toward the back, his palm trailing on the wall. Grass sprang up where his hand passed, and I followed, gliding my fingers over the same disturbed places. I was careful not to touch him.

He must have seemed like a giant to Svana or Hildur who stood shy of five feet. I myself had five inches on the women here, and my eyes were even with the leather tie in the chief's hair, the nape of his neck and the collars of his two linen shirts. I thought of Jeff, whose broad, easy smile was a foot above me. Even in his arms, he'd always seemed so far away.

"My mother showed me this," the chief said, moving along the back of the house. We turned a corner to follow the contours of the pantry. "When I was alone ..." He trailed off. Since we started talking, he'd been losing whole phrases, sentences, quietly losing control. I hadn't heard him this way before.

He was still facing away when he finished, a bit more neatly. "Know this house is here for you." Another tender command.

I tried thinking of his home as mine for a second, and it felt immediately natural. My house.

"One hundred fifty six of my paces around the back," he told me. We stopped at the corner and he faced me. "Now that I'm grown." The corner of his mouth turned up in a disarming way, a smile there and gone in a heartbeat.

He smelled like fresh sweat and something else, like cinnamon.

"All grown up," I repeated softly, like talking to a child.

He smiled again. "How old do you think I am?" I could see he wanted to amuse me, occupy me and take away my sadness. It was charming.

I didn't know what to say. He was grown up, yes, very much a man. But I had a feeling it had little to do with age. He couldn't be more than thirty. I guessed. "Twenty seven?"

He laughed, a sound I hadn't imagined.

"You would have me with the ravens so soon?" He told me seriously, "I am twenty-two years this fall."

My god, he was a boy. Younger than me.

A breeze rose, and the scent of iron came too. He held his ax, so easily I wondered if he remembered it was there. The birthmark reached to the back of his hand, mostly hidden by his scarred leather bracers.

He saw me looking. He was so open right now, I could hurt him if I stared. I had to do anything but focus on his mark. Desperate, I said "Your ax is lovely." Duh, I thought.

He lifted it, slipped it into his right hand as though it weighed nothing, and said "Já, it is," and I was relieved to find that it was entirely ordinary to him, not at all awkward to receive such a compliment about a tool. "Ulf's ax," he explained. "My father's." And then I realized what I was looking at.

It was not the ax he normally carried. It was gorgeous.

"Slítasongr," he said, the long ee up front, the r dissolving into nothing but a brief shape in the mouth.

His voice was fluid and changeable, turning sweet and then to hard stone and back. A voice to study.

It meant rending song. It was the ax's name. This was not just an everyday tool, but a beloved, named weapon. Delicately balanced and sharply honed not to cut turf or trees, but bones of animals, of people. My mind shied away from what it was capable of. I could see by how he held it that it *would* sing in his hands.

He looked up from it and seemed to shake something off, retrain his features.

"Go in." He gestured toward the house with his chin and I nodded.

I was dismissed. Before I ducked into the door, I saw him heading toward the stables. "Vakr!" he called to his horse sharply. I stepped inside.

"The iron pot brings out pink," Betta told me as she and Thora tipped a cauldron of hot water and birch leaves. The scented water poured over a screen I was holding and then, strained of leaves, it flowed into another pot.

Steam rolled like great flowers bursting open all around us. I stirred the leaves with a long wooden spoon, and a gorgeous sent rose up, like cooked apples and black tea.

"The leaves by themselves make yellow," Thora said.

They were showing me how to dye thread. We worked around a small fire, close to the river. Little Lotta, about three years old, watched with a finger in her slack mouth. Darling and blond, her name was Ginnlaug—"just like you, Ginn!" She was entranced by our work, watching what bigger girls do.

"The pink brings more trade," Betta said, then smiled and added, "and it's pretty."

Her big teeth made her seem just ten years old, until her face fully resolved from the steam and became that of a young woman. She held her braids back and leaned over to breathe deeply of the birch water.

"I'm seventeen today," she said out of nowhere. With her own long spoon, she joined me in stirring and spreading the soggy greens.

I grinned and smacked playfully at her spoon with mine. "You didn't tell me it was your ..." I trailed off and couldn't find a word for *birthday* in the old language. "... your day," I ended dumbly.

"You'll have flowers for a crown tonight," Thora said. "Ranka will want to make it."

"*I* want to make it!" Lotta broke in.

"You can let your hair down." I tugged on the end of Betta's braid.

"Nei!" Betta reccoiled. She pulled away from me and flipped her braids over her shoulders, outside my reach. Suddenly, I'd been too familiar.

She never took her hair down outside of the sleeping alcove, she told me. She'd started braiding it as a little girl, when her Ma died and she and Bjarn moved to this big house. Now, nine years later she had a habit of keeping it bound in the same way every day, and no one but the girls she slept with down the hill had ever seen it.

I thought of little Betta, alone without her mommy in a big, strange place, thrust into the company of giant men and stuck up girls. "You were just eight?"

"Já. The oldest of the children down the hill, though. I took care of them." Betta smiled, and for no reason added, "The chief was thirteen." She cast a glance toward the stables.

Heirik stood with a couple of boys—Magnus and Haukur—and a bunch of horses. His head was bent in concentration, listening without looking at gangly Magnus, Har's son, just about fourteen himself. The chief was clearly teaching him something, waiting for the lesson to be absorbed and proof sent back. And not getting the response he needed. The chief's natural grace was gone, and right now his body was cramped. He was impatient. After just a couple weeks, I knew the subtle physical expression of his moods.

"Your brother will take over the job of chief, then?" I asked Thora.

"Já, the baulufotr." *Cow foot*. A hundred times dumb, with not enough words for her to express it. He would probably inherit the position, she told me, and keep it if he could. Her idiot brother, with the chief's holdings, tenants, burdens. From our perch, we could see that his work featured prominent elbows and a lack of physical ease that was stark next to the chief.

"Soon after I came here," said Betta, "when the chief was old enough to marry, it was decided he never would."

As though drawn by the illicit subject, Svana and Grettis walked up, spinning. They joined in telling me the whole story.

The chief could not marry. It would endanger all of Hvítmörk if he were to father a child. He could bring heartbreak and ruin. Heirik was not just dangerous himself. He could be a harbinger of something, or someone, far worse.

Thora summed it up in the crudest possible way. "He's vowed to keep his bloody atgeirr to himself." *Thrusting spear*. It would have been an apt and witty metaphor if it weren't so cruel. She looked toward the stables as if the chief might have heard her and cursed her in some new, extra way.

A sudden voice came from behind us. "He is the breaker of rings," Hildur declared. A phrase for *chieftain*. She'd been observing us, listening, while we didn't hear her approach. Her cheeks flamed crimson. "I will not have this kind of talk."

My heart fluttered. Bits of leaves and twigs clung to my spoon.

For a moment all was suspended, then Hildur spoke to Betta. "You, Girl, will stay with our guest and sleep at the house now." Then she walked away to go oversee someone else.

In the tense aftermath, Betta pressed on the leaves and curbed a small smile. I smiled a little, too. Everyone else watched Hildur's back, their mouths open.

Was this one of those times when the chief gave orders and she let him? Hildur seemed bunched and angry over this new arrangement. I couldn't imagine the housekeeper feeling all that charitable toward me. But somehow, I'd been given Betta.

My new friend deftly turned the conversation back to something that would draw attention. "It is possible that a child might be normal," she said, utterly reasonably. She looked at me evenly while she spoke. "A woman might be unaffected by his touch." Unharmed, I thought, but not unaffected.

"Well, it is a closed door," said Thora. And as chief, it was his door to close.

Magnus would someday become a big man like the rest in his family, like his father Hár and cousin Heirik. And like both of them, he would one day protect and guide a clan of farmers and fishermen and traders more extensive than Betta or I could imagine. At the moment, he seemed completely incapable.

"The chief teaches Magnus everything," Thora said, "as though this is a good plan." She touched a charm that hung at her belt, just like Hildur's. A ward against Heirik's ugliness and a blessing for his long life in one complex and brief swipe of the fingers.

That night, I made room in my little sleeping alcove for Betta. I curled up beside her and felt an unfamiliar pressure, painless, happy, in my heart.

Each day without fail the women mentioned the chief's brother. Younger than Heirik, and so wonderful.

He was called Brosa, but he was a character to me, his face unknown, with no real name on my lips. He was beaming and broad, I was told. Strong and kind and generous. Brosa was capable. Sweet. Each woman added words to the litany of his greatness. Expansive. Funny. Bright like the heart of a flame. Tall as the chief and just as fierce.

"And handsome to make the girls go mad," Kit added wryly. She gave Svana an amused glance.

Svana didn't mind being exposed as lovesick. She exhaled, "Like the sun." She let her spindle sink and slow.

The whole family had a love affair with him, an infatuation just as great as their fear of the chief. He'd taken the boat away on a trading voyage. His return would announce celebration, and he would bring abundant, luxurious goods to the farm. A hero.

I imagined a vaguely rugged man at sea, his curved wooden ship slicing the waves, his perfect face to the wind.

The way they offhandedly called it a *boat* confirmed what I already knew. This house was prominent, rich, and the chief more powerful than I could understand. And no woman for him, no one to carry on the family line. Hildur's comment—that there would be no real wife of this house until Brosa came home—began to make sense.

I asked why this wonderful brother hadn't married already.

"Já, Child, there was a wife for Brosa," Hildur told me with that pinched tone she used for half-forbidden, half-delicious subjects. I could hear the fiber slip through the hooks of our spindles. Sometimes I knew nothing about what things meant here. It was an open and honest and bright place, and I kept stumbling into pits of darkness that this lush grass was meant to hide.

"Esa died." Kit finally said, matter of factly. "Birthing their son."

"Oh." A stunned answer. What else could I say to those two statements? To the grinding pain and dashed hope those words conjured?

Betta completed the miserable thought. "The babe died, too."

Brosa had married the sister of Ageirr, a young farmer with adjoining land. Ageirr's father once had a great holding, but he grew old and demented, until finally he sat useless and blank eyed as his farm suffered a quick decline. The marriage of Brosa and Esa was meant to save Ageirr's remaining family. To dig them out of the mess their father's illness left behind.

Their union merged Ageirr's farm into Hvítmörk. A stroke of generosity and strategy, the marriage added to Heirik's collection of followers. It was not far, Betta told me, raising her chin toward the horizon, and I wondered what vast distance she considered to be nearby.

Ageirr missed his sister Esa with an unseemly passion. Hildur told me that at night he sometimes walked in goat's form and came to our house. He'd lean his head and horns against the grassy wall all night, right outside the pantry where Esa and Brosa had made their bed.

Brosa was sixteen then, the girl fifteen, "so beautiful like a breeze." They were married only a year when she died. When Brosa returned from trading this fall, he'd be nineteen.

There were great gaps in the story, whole pieces submerged in sorrow. I was getting only the child's version.

I glanced again at Magnus. If Heirik would have no son, couldn't Brosa still have one?

As if she read my mind, Betta added. "Brosa wants no other wife."

"That will change." Hildur said with finality, and she cast a glance at her daughter. Svana blushed becomingly. "It's too much of a waste."

"And a man like that," tisked Kit.

"Já," Thora agreed, "light to the chief's darkness. Da calls them the wolf pups." Because of their father's name, Ulf, *wolf*.

Heirik's eyes came to mind, and they were quite wolfish. But similarity to any of a half dozen prophetic and fearsome animals could be found. A wolf's eyes, a crow's hair, the mane and elegance of a god's steed. His black beard, his birthmark were of no consequence. Heirik was not dark. He was entirely lit by sun. What candle could Brosa hold to such a stunning older brother?

"IF YOU SQUEEZE HER SO HARD, YOU'LL BE AT THE SEA IN NO TIME."
Magnus, amused, watched me cling to the back of an old mare named Geirdis. The horse wanted to go somewhere, and she pulled her head side to side to loosen the reins. Magnus held them in his hand, up near her chin, and in the sonorous, loving voice these men reserved for horses, he called her Gerdi. I gripped her mane and tried not to clench her sides with my feet.

"Grab her with your legs only if you want to fly," he told me.

"Já," I told him. "As if I might ever want that."

Under all my clothes, I was already sweating. Together with my apron, loose pants and ankle boots, I was a generous bundle of linen and leather. I melted from the effort and embarrassment of hoisting myself up onto the saddle—a primitive arrangement of two wooden boards that hung at Gerdi's sides, hollowed slightly so my thighs fit into them. Iron stirrups swung like two curved raindrops. My toes reached to just barely grip them. The two boards were held together and slung over her back with leather straps, so there was no actual seat underneath me, just moving bone and muscle.

Gerdi's hair felt like silk and straw at once, complex and alive. I pictured her mane flying white and free as she ran off with me clinging to her back, racing away past the edge of the earth, me tumbling behind in a bloom of skirts and elbows. Or maybe she would dash headlong into the white woods. Far enough to maim, if not kill me.

Magnus raised one eyebrow just like his Da. He snickered almost soundlessly, his chest shaking with it.

"For slow riding," he said, "sit straight. Tap her with your heels."

I did, and she started walking. I gasped and clenched my teeth instead of my thighs, and we moved, one sleepy, slow footstep, then another. I was riding a horse!

Lotta could have walked faster. I watched Gerdi's head bob slowly up and down, and though she was clunky and smudged a nondescript and dirty white, she looked fair and delicate to me. After a minute or two, I lifted my eyes to see what was going by.

"Let your body move with her steps," Magnus shouted from across an expanse of grass that had grown between us. I'd ridden farther than I thought.

A memory came to me, of pushing my way through a crowd at the very edge of the city. I ducked past people with parasols and bayonets, went too far and got lost, alone inside the multitude. And then I broke through to the ocean. The spasm of fear was brief, and then I was overcome with the water's immensity and motion—like a moving glacier. Buildings and streets ran right off the edge and into the water, but I could see out over it, and it felt good. Good to look that far. Good to ride Geirdis.

I looked over at the boy who leaned against the stable wall, his arms crossed over an honest-to-God Viking Age tunic, iron knives and fire striker hanging from his belt, blond hair cropped at his chin. This was farther than I ever expected to go, truly.

I smiled at him, and just then Gerdi dropped her head to chew at the grass and my smile turned to a gasp. Magnus laughed like his father Har, a bark of amusement. Then he settled on smiling a little sideways just like his cousin, the chief. It was darling on his young face.

"You are riding her now." He walked toward me. "But not telling her where you want to go." He began talking about using the reins gently to draw her to look in the direction I chose. To go right, I pulled in a little of the rein on the right and let a little go on the left.

I closed my eyes and listened to Magnus's voice shift and lurch, sometimes break, then unexpectedly dip into deep water. Just fourteen. The hint of a smooth voice like the chief's underneath. I thought about how melting and fluid Heirik's was, and how it too would continue to change as he got older. It would acquire the sandpaper of age like Har's.

All three men sounded unlike anyone I knew in the future. Their very thoughts were formed of a different ether. Their minds and tongues and bodies used words that were built entirely differently. A mix of Norse and emerging Icelandic. It seemed, suddenly, like a system of sounds custom made for this family, this moment in time.

"Thank you," I told Magnus. "This is …" I searched for a word for *fun* and didn't find one. "Sæll," I said. Something like *happy-making.*

That was it. There was a summer stillness. The only things to hear were Gerdi's sniffles and Magnus's instruction. I liked the animal scent of the horse's hair and the frank green of the midday grass. I felt something very simple and unhurried. Plain happiness.

FALLS

IT WAS POSSIBLE THAT GEIRDIS WAS THE OLDEST HORSE IN ICE-land. Reserved for children, or amnesiacs like me, she was steady and slow and placidly disinterested in anything but grass and blossoms to chew. Indifferent to the world beyond her pink, flaring nostrils and square teeth.

But she would be like a winged dream to me, if I could just ride her without fear.

I planned to practice a little every day. The morning after Magnus taught me, I got up early and tiptoed to the mudroom. My head no longer ached every morning without coffee, but I was still fuzzy from sleep and I knocked a great weight of cloaks off their hooks and into a heap. I picked each one up, shook it and folded it again and again and again into a rectangle, a perfect envelope. I folded a half dozen cloaks and laid them on top of one another. It was a blessed relief to do something well. I pressed down on the top of the pile, and it was springy. Something palpably good I'd done, a neat stack on a bench.

I glanced around for something more to straighten before I faced the horse, and beside me stood the door to the chief's room. I'd forgotten he slept so close. I wondered if he heard me out here crashing around and folding. Wondered if I'd woken him from his bed.

If indeed a mythic creature like he would climb into a normal bed each night and sleep, instead of crossing a dark wing over his eyes or curling his wolf's tail around his body. I thought of Hildur with a stab of anger.

I did wonder about his bed, though—whether he had a real one that was more comfortable than the benches where we slept. Did he have pillows? I salivated, thinking of mine from before. Covers fresh from the dryer, their forms like great marshmallows, clean and bright. He wouldn't have those, nei, but maybe something like them. I pictured Heirik lying on his bed, fallen down tired from the endless chopping and moving of wood. Too exhausted to even take off his boots. Maybe just his gauntlets untied, his belt and clutter of knives loose on the floor. His hair was splayed black and wild across a creamy white sheepskin. His features would be loose in slumber, not contained by the demands of being the chief. Just a boy sleeping.

The wood of his door was warm to the touch, the latch cool and complex under my fingertips. A kind of keyless lock that only he could open.

I shook the drowsiness from my head and pulled away from his door. I found a dark green cloak to secure over my shoulders, and I stepped out into the misty pleasure of morning.

The stables smelled ripe and ugly, and my breath frosted the air. The light was still there in the sky, always in summer, but for a few hours it dimmed on either side of midnight. The lower temperature and dip into gray marked the passing of each day into night into morning.

I called quietly for the horse and waited a long moment. Just looking, breathing in the farm.

Lavender crept into the sky, as if pushing its nose under the big, gray quilt of nighttime. A breeze moved across my face, and with it I felt the stirring of every kind of animal as it woke. I felt the goats' and cows' and foxes' hearts beat. I imagined a chicken opening one eye, the yawns of house dogs. I knew the baby would be struggling in his half-sleep to find Dalla's breast, Lotta turning over next to them and thinking, *I am awake.* In an hour it would be warmer and the flies would stir, too, and start to buzz.

Gerdi's nose came cool and inquisitive, tickling my cheek, and I laughed out loud before shushing myself. I didn't want to wake anyone, to call attention to us. I needed to ride Gerdi by myself, needed to do something bigger than expertly folding a pile of blankets.

I got the simple saddle onto her and then the more complex reins. It felt good to do something with quiet determination, just me and Gerdi breathing and waiting for me to get everything right.

It was so easy to climb up on her. One boot on the teardrop stirrup, the other leg over her back, my skirt like a giant red wing opening, and it was done. When her bones shifted, I did too, naturally as floating in the bath. And then she took off. With an uncharacteristic surge of direction, Gerdi whisked me away down the rocky lawn that sloped away from the stables. I held on tight, quietly grinding the word "Ho!" through my teeth until finally she slowed.

By then, we were gone.

As soon as we were away from the yard, she began to amble. I untangled my clenched hands from her mane, and tried to give in to her sleepy and sensual gait. My breath slowed, and I became peacefully thrilled that I'd gotten on her and rode away, alone. I was happy now to let her pick her own slow way over the uneven ground.

This volcanic rock had been battered and bashed by time until it came to sit here in a variety of sizes from giant boulders towering over my head to dark black pebbles and sand. Every surface, everywhere, was grown over with pale moss and frilly white lichens that opened like bouquets of oak leaves. Wildflowers in every shade of yellow were sprinkled throughout it all. Gerdi nosed at them and chewed, and it was as familiar as breathing to just let my body yield and balance when she dipped her head low to eat.

We followed a dusty path that was worn through the moss. It disappeared into a stand of twisty birch trees, their branches so gnarled and low they stuck in my hair. Then in a second, we were through the trees and out the other side. In paradise.

It was a place of unapologetic prettiness. A ravine that opened before us, just under our feet.

Steep, rough masses of rock plunged down from where we stood, down into a storybook world a long way below. Gerdi and I looked out across a chasm to where twin waterfalls cascaded down a black rock face. They joined and finished falling together into a clear, round pool at least twenty times the size of our bath. It was rimmed with a kind of beach made of blue slate that had been sheared off in a thousand overlapping layers.

The water left the pool to travel a complex course, feeling its way around plants and boulders and islands no bigger than the heartstone. A striking blue, like sky and navy and silver flashing and flowing together. The waterway turned to skirt the corners of the crags we stood on. The rock walls of the ravine were carved out with child-sized caves, cut by time to inspire bedtime stories and legends.

The whole scene was surrounded by little birches like the stand we'd just passed through. A giant ring of trees enclosed the entire grotto, and we were inside it. Gerdi had taken me to a secret garden. A place for lovers. For people like Ranka's parents, who could tumble breathlessly together on the shale beach or hide in a million intimate places where no one—not even their intrepid little daughter—would find them. The sound of rushing water hiding even their sighs.

I would sit right here every second I could. For the rest of my life.

"Are you leaving?"

The chief startled me, his voice harsh, his question so at odds with my peace.

Behind me on the ridge, he and his dark horse emerged from the little forest, as silent as the mist until he asked his jarring question. With his long straight nose and high cheekbones, he looked stark and angry. Or in pain. He stopped a safe distance from me and regarded me.

"I saw you going …" He waited a moment, I could see him consider his words and decide to stop there. Then he started again. "You remember how." He nodded to indicate Gerdi.

That seemed right, yes. My body seemed to know something that my head had forgotten, about moving in harmony with a horse.

"I just tried," I said, "to see if I could do something by myself." Then it occurred to me. *Oh.*

"I wasn't leaving you," I blurted. "Leaving with your horse."

His face closed. I thought maybe he didn't believe me. But he smiled, then, and was transformed. "You would get far with her," he said. "But it would take the rest of your life."

I smiled, too, and laughed. "This is far enough," I said. I looked down into the grotto. "I would stay here forever if I could. It's so beautiful."

He drew up beside me.

"Good," he said. "Flotta straumi." He relaxed with the words, his voice deep and respectful. *Splendid stream.* We watched it go by.

Then he straightened himself again, like I'd seen him do before—a gesture of deliberately waking from a dream. "In winter, we skate it."

"Skate it!" I was thrilled. This wonderland would be made even finer with a dusting of snow. Images of cold laughter came to mind, of frosty breath and fur coats and freedom.

"Já, have you not skated?"

"No, never." I said it for sure, knowing I hadn't, and he watched me with calm interest.

"You will, then," he told me, and he seemed to accept how sure I was. That even with my complete amnesia, I had no doubt I'd never strapped skates onto my shoes. His horse stepped in place, shaking his hooves out, and the chief looked into the grotto. A moment more, standing in a quiet covered over by the sound of endless, speeding water. Oh, I wanted to skate in this enchanted place! This swift rushing could be stilled after all. Frozen. And we could fly over its surface.

Would I still be here? Or would I be grasped by the tank, taken through time?

I took a deep breath, readying myself to leave the ravine, to return to the house and work. "Next time, I'll find a way down there."

The chief turned to me with his brows drawn. "What do you mean?" He asked me as if I was dense. "Come down." He gave the slightest pull on Vakr's reins, almost imperceptible, and the horse walked right off the edge of the earth.

"Follow," the chief called, but he didn't have to, because Gerdi had understood and was already walking exactly where Vakr did. She took a step off the cliff, and my heart fell free.

Of course, it wasn't a direct plunge, but it was so steep, it hollowed my stomach and dried my throat. We descended the uneven rock face, the horses stepping down without a care. It was one of the hardest things I'd ever done, to hold onto Gerdi and let her find her way down those jagged rocks. I held my breath, until I knew I would pass out and fall off her back. Gerdi knew what to do. That I had never done anything like this was irrelevant—and electrifying.

We reached the bottom, my head alight and dizzy. I got off the horse clumsily and turned around, my skirt a bundle of confusion. The chief was composed, not struggling with anything.

He sat on the rocks, already using a stick to trace something in the sludge at the water's edge. The fearsome Viking, reduced to a curious boy poking at a stream with a piece of birch wood.

I sat down several feet away from him, drawing my skirts away from the water. I touched my fingertips to it. It was frigid and clear, its blue borrowed from the sky, its rushing sound so much louder than I expected. It moved fast, flowing off in the direction of home. This water would become the wider river that ran below the house. The chief didn't speak much, and I didn't either.

I looked at him closer and longer now. His legs weren't bound, and his fine wool pants hung loose around his ankles, only his short boots underneath. He wore no bracers either, and his wrists showed under long loose sleeves. His black hair was free. So undone. I imagined him waking early as I rummaged and clanked around outside his room, imagined him walking outside to find me stealing his horse. The chief had left in a hurry to come after me.

I untied my boots and set them aside, rolled my woolen pants up and stepped into the water. The cold felt knife-like, and all sensation began to slip from my toes. The water reached above my ankles, rushing hard against me and tugging more than I thought it would. It felt wonderful, and I waded out farther into the current, my skirts lifted in my two fists to stay dry.

I looked back at the chief and he seemed open and relaxed in his silence. He'd brought me down here, and in return I would coax him into the stream. "Follow," I said with a thrust of my chin, playfully echoing his earlier command.

He didn't play.

When we had walked along the house, my eyes on the back of his neck, he seemed life sized. But as he rose to stand now, I was overwhelmed. The intensity I'd heard about was directed at me, his gold eyes on me, and I was emptied. The blood rushed out of my hands, fingers tingling, everything gone. I backed away and stumbled on the rocks of the stream bed, the freezing water closing like fingers around my ankles.

He stopped, and turned his head away, rested his palm on the rock wall beside him. And I waited for him to do any of a dozen things, to banish me from his home, to draw a knife from his belt and bury it neatly in my heart, to simply leave me here in the water, rebuffed.

Instead he placed one foot up on a rock and untied and removed his boot. Then the other. He set them aside and walked into the water.

He stepped onto a little island, no more than three feet across, and crouched on the moss. He drew black stones up from the bottom of the stream and piled them. A fort, or tiny cairn. While he built, I let my heart settle. I swirled my foot around, feeling the freezing drift and pull, and watched my hiked-up skirt hover just above the surface.

His voice came, overly easy and light. Sorry he'd scared me? "You love the water," he said.

I always knew I would. I stopped just a breath away from saying so—just short of admitting that I remembered a time and place where I lived without streams or horses or chieftains.

Here in this lovely place, I felt like I could tell him. I wanted him to know about how I remembered my apartment, the lab, the sounds and unearthly light of screens. Flat pictures of farms. I wanted him to know me. I felt almost like I could say everything, and that he would accept my truth.

"Já," I said instead. "It feels calm to me. So good and easy."

This moment felt easy, too, and I was no longer scared of him. No longer scared of birds or steep rocks or anything. Giddy with the rush of relief, I swept my foot in a bigger arc, and I kicked, splashing water on his island.

He pretended not to react, but I could see him hide a smile.

"I am that way with the woods," he said, and without looking up he sliced his hand into the water and expertly splashed me back. He soaked my pants and the hems of my skirts and my laugh echoed through the rocks and all around us. He told me, "I have the men cut from the far side."

The far side. *Oh.* Of the white woods, yes. The gorgeous, glowing woods that were being devoured every day to become boats and beds. To become the fires that gagged and sustained me. But the chief was an early settler, and there was still so much forest left, trees twisting and leaves tossing farther than I could see. It made me happy that there was a place like that for him, where he felt easy.

He still worked on his fort. Approached me indirectly with his few words. "You go places alone."

I laughed. "Maybe I shouldn't. I might get eaten by birds."

The chief laughed, too. "It was the elf hollow," he told me, sitting up on his heels.

The elf hollow? I recalled the glen that held the tiny house as if in a great palm. *Oh.* Yes, it made sense. I'd read about this! The little home I'd seen was not a dollhouse for playing, it was there for the hidden folk.

"You keep the small house ready for them?"

He pressed his lips together, literally holding words back. In a moment he answered. "If not, they will come and tramp on Hildur in her sleep." He tried to say it without disdain, but a hint of stress on her name came through, and I had to hold back a smile.

"They bring dread dreams," he finished.

"Did the birds protect the hollow," I asked, trying for one moment to believe what he might. "Because they thought I'd see the elves?"

"Já, well," He took a deep breath. "I suspect you would have seen many nests, too."

Nests, I thought, and a second later I got what he meant. *Oh.* The birds were protecting their eggs! A nesting ground turned legend.

I smiled broadly at that, feeling closer to Heirik knowing that he questioned such things. Besides both of us being isolated, we were odd in this way too. Words tumbled out without my thinking. "It's less lonely," I said. "To go out by myself."

My eyes stung suddenly, and I turned to regard the waterfalls. "I know it doesn't make sense."

Level and sure, he answered. "It does."

I waded back to the shore and he did too. We sat apart from one another, but both of us kept our feet in the stream. I couldn't feel mine any more, but I didn't want to break the stillness and pull them out. I knew if I did then we'd leave here. We both watched the water, moving and yet unchangeable. I tried to follow a single bit of it with my eyes, and for a moment the falls seemed suspended.

If I came to this place in the 22nd century, it would look wrong. It might have carved a different path by then. This was now, this small moment sitting with our toes in the water.

I lost track of my little piece of the current and it was consumed. My voice trailed off to a whisper that went with it. "It's what I came for." Over the stream's hard rushing, the words disappeared.

The chief broke into my reverie, but gently. "My grandfather knew poetry," he said. "He put the house here."

The house came to mind, a living thing, its walls grown so thick with grass that it melted into the hills. The chief looked up and back in its direction. We couldn't see it from here, but the word hús itself seemed to pull at him. His mother's house. The place he remade every year, shoring it up, making it solid and safe. The place he entered every night, into a world where everyone turned away.

I thought Heirik himself knew poetry. He spoke so sparely and bluntly. Statements so evocative with three or four words.

"Haying is soon," he said. "We'll have enough wood stored." He looked at his own unmarked palm as if the echo of his ax lay there, then turned his hand over to rest on his knee. He raised his eyes, so pale in the morning light.

"We'll go," he told me, and he drew his boots on.

I didn't want to, but I knew it was time. We weren't truly suspended here. The day would begin and I would cook and sew, and he would tell men what to do. He'd cut wood and sharpen axes blunted by constant chopping. And roundup and haying would come soon, time passing as it should. I liked that idea.

Gerdi fell in exactly behind Vakr, nose to tail, and once again I found myself watching Heirik's back. His glossy hair stirred with a breeze, and I felt like I'd observed him this way not only once or twice, but always, for twelve hundred years. The farm was beginning to feel that natural to me.

We didn't talk anymore, and at first it was easy. By the time we reached the house, he was different. Working. Roughly calling to the foster boy to bring another horse up. I was completely forgotten, and the ease of building a fort and splashing were displaced by the demands of the day.

Hildur stood framed in the mudroom door. "There you are, Child!" She sounded relieved, as though she'd been worried about me. She watched Heirik ride off, and once he was gone, her voice turned unkind. "You have work to do." I nodded and slid off Gerdi's back.

Bye, I thought after the chief.

Hildur waited, the palm of her hand pressed against her waist, her charm.

Hvítmörk was a low, dense forest.

The trees were maybe twice my height. Just tall enough to get forever lost.

I was alone here, as I was many nights after a late evening meal. The women didn't wonder or worry about me. Betta did sometimes, but not always. Some nights she was gone, walking with someone else, and I would go alone to the ravine and listen to the rapid water. Or come here, to the edge of the woods.

I ducked in under the trees, a few feet in, just to see how it felt inside. It was cool and creepy and smelled alive, like wet dirt. Gerdi would know where we were. She'd find our way back. Holding her reins, I drew her into the enchanted woods.

At first, everything looked white—the bark of the trees, the tops of the angelica flowers, even the horse by my side. The light itself was blasted out and white. But as my eyes adjusted, I saw a subtle chaos of color. Underneath the peeling white bark were copper and fire and pale apricot. The snowbloom stalks were electric lime, set against a forest floor of black dirt, creeping with low evergreens and their navy blue berries.

The trees did not stand majestic and straight. They were elaborately twisted, each with three or four trunks growing from a single root. Some spindly, some strong and intertwined with others. Each tree seemed a complex mess, but when seen together they all slanted in unison for the same light. An eerie reaching, as though the forest had a million skeletal hands all desiring the same thing.

I ducked under branches and picked my way through the underbrush, looking for something myself, I didn't know what. It was too dense for Gerdi now, and I let her go, knowing she would be content with so many blossoms at our feet. She would stand eating until I returned.

The woods got thicker and closer, and when I stopped and peered through the branches, the tangle of trunks went on forever. They pressed in from all directions. This time I wasn't afraid to be alone, though, out here in real nature with no companion but a horse. Twelve hundred years in the future, I would be born. I'd come so far. There was something negligible about the dangers of wandering in the woods.

I ducked low, branches snagging in my hair and creeping juniper grabbing at my hems. The trees peeled white, revealing a coppery red so dense it was hard to look at. Brushing leaves out of my eyes, I stumbled into a little stream bed.

The dirt and stones that lined it were almost completely dry, but a waterway still trickled, so tiny I could step across it with ease and not get my boots wet. I knelt and washed my hands, then dipped water into my palms and drank. It tasted cold and honey-kissed, and I knelt and dipped my head low to smell its dirty, vivid scent. I stood too quickly, snared my dress on a branch, and fell into the open palm of a tree.

Five gnarled trunks grew from its base, and I had fallen in a cherry red heap right in its center. I leaned back and saw the sky, peaceful through the leaves. I ran my finger along the glossy side of a leaf and it was tough like old leather, like the chief's bracers would be, worn slick and strong. I lay my head against a scratchy trunk and drew my body in, curling up inside the tree like a fort. Colors changed and my eyes grew heavy. The sun was sinking and dimness coming on, and the branches were turning from snow and blood and peach to the simple darks and lights of night.

I felt the cage-tree holding me, and yet I wasn't there at all. I was in my apartment, shocked at the cold, unyielding tile under my toes. The farm on the wall screen lay ridiculously flat, and I laughed at myself, the self who used to know anything. I muttered at the apartment to turn up the heat, and then I had a thought—I asked the apartment to let me go. And with a rush, I was outside, looking back at my building against the night sky. I saw myself. My body was still there. In the windows all around me were people, above my head, right under my feet, laughing, watching screens, feeding each other. A couple making love.

I stood out against a flat pasture, a single hand against the glass.

On the real farm, then, I saw a girl playing bride. An imperfect crown of twigs and flowers sat on top of her tight braids. She laughed and threw her bouquet of grass up in the air and it fell all over a dog who sat panting in the sun. She looked up and almost seemed to see me. She smiled, and her teeth were enormous.

I tried to look around behind little Betta. The chief was there somewhere, in that yard, his thirteen-year-old self. I wanted to see him.

But all I could see was his face the way it looked now, in his twenties. *Now that I'm grown,* he'd said. That smile, it was devious and charming and too brief. His eyes were dark amber. "Stay," he said, as if I might ever go. He reached for my face, and I lay my cheek in his hand and thought Gods, he's touching me. I turned to kiss his fingers, and his palm was warm and dry against my lips, mine to touch, to own, all mine. I woke. My sweaty cheek stuck to my own hand, my whole body curled in the palm of a tree. Newly born and glowing.

I must have been attracted to Heirik all along, but I sat in the cup of that tree and felt the weight of realization. Oh, yes. I saw it now. How I'd assumed my interest in his voice was academic. How I felt defensive of him, but it was no more than I would feel for any outcast. The way my heart was peaceful and open around him, the way I looked for him coming from the fields at night, listened for him first thing in the morning. Those meant nothing.

Except that I'd fallen for him.

He'd given me a stream, after all. He'd given me his woods and animals. He talked to me, like he did with no one else. He told me to put my hand on his house and call it my own, and I wanted to. I wanted to hold him in the heart of that house and have it be ours. I would be the one, the only one, to touch him.

I floated home, a blissful idiot on Gerdi's back. The world was navy blue, with white lichens glowing like starbursts in the dark. The horse stopped to sniff and chew things, or sometimes just stood and looked around, as if moving had no appeal. I didn't care. I was reliving every moment I'd been with Heirik, every word he'd said since the day we met. They were few, and it was easy to recall them all. *Turn to me,* he'd said. *I only wanted to see your face.*

His eyes frightened me the first time I saw him, at the coast, and again at the ravine. Now I wanted to look into them for long hours, to spend days learning the shades they went through with the changing of the light, sun-bleached wheat in morning to amber at night. I wanted to touch his dark brows, explore his mouth and bearded chin, my fingers small against his jaw. I wanted to see his fleeting smile, and maybe ask him if he'd let it linger a moment more.

Gerdi ate a flower and I thought languidly about his hair, how bits of it stuck to his forehead. I wanted to brush them away.

The old mare eventually steered us around to home. My heart picked up when we passed the bath, almost to the top of the hill and the stables. I dreaded the moment I would see him, and yet I desired it. I needed to look at him. Maybe I would be able to tell whether he felt some unutterably tender thing for me, too. Gods, could I hope he might be moved by the sight of my straw-like hair sticking to my sweaty forehead?

And then I saw the house waiting. His mother had shown him how to pace the walls. *When I'm alone …* Since Heirik was young, he'd known he would never have a companion. It was probable he wouldn't even recognize desire in my eyes.

I brought Gerdi into the stable yard, removed her reins and saddle, and I felt an unusual stillness. An absence.

It was very late, and the dark was already lifting again. The light of two in the morning was beginning to rise, and with it the steam that emanated from everything. It rolled off the bath and hillsides and house, and the world was mysterious. I felt hidden inside a cloud. When Betta whispered behind me, her voice was like the voice of the mist itself.

"Hello, Ginn," she said, and I turned to find her changed.

Her hair was a wind-stricken mess around her head and shoulders, the uneven waves of loosened braids everywhere. Long, it trailed down over her breasts, down her back. It was amazing she had such ample beauty always tied up on her head. She looked alive, sensual, her lips and cheeks stained pink. Her eyes sparked with surprise and delight. It was as though the wind were a lover who'd left her tousled and flushed.

"What happened?" I whispered.

"Nothing," she said, and dipped her head, a way she had of hiding in plain sight. She was so changeable, one minute a direct and fearless woman, the next a blushing girl. "I was just out riding," she said.

Riding, yes. I dropped into a waking dream of Heirik and I, riding into the depths of the ravine. I walked beside Betta into the house to go to sleep, both of us up too late, and I thought only of the chief. Of seeing him soon.

Scents of cold dirt and musty wool wafted out of the mudroom door, smelling like comfort. Peoples' cloaks and boots were half gone and Lotta's doll sat on the bench, propped against the wall, waiting. The latch on the chief's door was closed tight, as always, giving away nothing. His work ax was gone. Not *Slitasongr*, the beautiful tool—or weapon—he carried like a companion, but the other one, that he took to the woods.

It was a sharp awakening, realizing that I knew not only his ax, but his lesser ax too. Oh gods, I had it bad.

Carried along by my crush, I floated into the main room and looked through the smoke for him. I sat on the bench outside my bed and listened for his voice, like I had every day, every moment since coming here. Where was he? The wall was hard against my back, and I slumped into it, sleepy and soft. It was at least two in the morning, and my eyes grew heavy with waiting and I crawled in to bed.

Betta's soft nighttime ponytail lay across the sheepskin in our alcove. As I crawled in next to her, I thought about her wind-driven freedom. Betta had told me herself—she hadn't let her hair down in public once in the nine years she'd lived at Hvítmörk. And only now, staring at her sleeping back, did I realize that "out riding" was no explanation at all.

He did this sometimes, Betta told me—left for days and didn't tell anyone but his uncle. And no one knew where he went, not even Hár. Gone on Vakr into the white woods, to another farm? Or to the sea, maybe? The days seemed to stand still, endless. There were moments I felt like I was waiting the way these women waited for Brosa, for a trader long gone on the water, without the comfort of knowing when he would return.

I buried myself in work, barely looking up to the horizon. I applied myself to dyeing and combing fleece until it was fluffy and wispy enough for the other women to spin. I helped with cooking around the mealstone—the small fire that burned in the room used for weaving and feasts. Massive blond wood tables hung suspended over our heads. The giant loom shushed and clacked, and Ranka showed me how she made flat bread. Hildur had, uncharacteristically, given up on teaching me to make good thread. Instead of relief, I only felt worry that I had no useful place here.

The man who told me I did have a place was gone himself.

Reasons circled like crows in my mind. Gone to trade, to talk with men, visit the highlands? To see another woman maybe, outside the reach of this family's fear. The thought rent my heart, and I turned my head away as if it were a physical blow.

I learned to make socks with a big needle and thick yarn, and I slipped loops over my thumb again and again and again. Binding, it was called. I tried to empty my mind while I did it, sliding into a repetitive stupor. The hum of women's working voices and the buzz of flies rising around me. A sock, two socks, falling from my fingers. I would not count the days, I swore. It didn't matter. I would let my new and tenuous feelings go, let them dissolve into the equally ethereal world of dyepot and bath steam.

Ranka and I braided each other's hair. We crowned the dogs with flowers.

Two washing days passed, and both times I forgot the chief in the bold chatter and splashes of eight women in the little pool. I watched my fingers divide the water, watched it close so completely behind them. Naked, bumping into the slippery bodies of other women, I thanked the gods I didn't have that tattoo I'd wanted so much. No indelible raven biting at the nape of my neck.

I imagined Heirik looking there with his yellow eyes and desiring me.

Sweet fantasies came then. To be the first woman to touch him, even just his hand, his wrist, with tender intention. I imagined the look on his face when I reached for him, when our fingers first met. Imagined being his, right in front of the whole family. Sitting by an outside fire in the twilight, Heirik behind me, keeping the cold away. I would lean back against his chest and he would surround me, gently holding, mind wandering. I would have someone who was mine. Someone gorgeous, graceful, intelligent, shy. The sparest poetry on his lips. Gods, what would it feel like to kiss? I couldn't even imagine it.

On the second washing day, the women cut the mens' hair. It was sweet.

Thralls brought wood up from the far side of the forest. Chopping endlessly, eating away at the enchanting birches. I did count the days, after all.

On the eleventh he came back.

In the stillness of midday, he rode up on Vakr. Only Magnus greeted him, everyone else tensing with his arrival. My pulse quickened, and my heart broke when no one rose, no one ran to him, happy he was home. And I was standing then, leaving my binding in a pile on the ground and walking toward him, where he stood still on his horse.

Suddenly, there were a gaggle of excited voices coming up behind me. A wave of kids and women and dogs swept past on both sides, rushing so fast my hair blew forward in the breeze. Their voices rose in happily panicked tones, with questions, exclamations. Ranka's stood out—"Is she for me?" Lotta said, "Ansi!" *Pretty.*

I didn't care. I was a still point, wondering about nothing but Heirik. He was here now, with me, after so many days of wanting him to come. On Vakr, his shoulders far above me against the sky, he was more splendid than I remembered. More gorgeous by far. He saw me and there was his flash of smile, fuller and brighter than ever. He was happy to see me. I felt my own eyes soften with happiness and lust. I let him see. Anything he wanted, my hope, my desire. I pleaded with him silently, *Like me like this. Feel this way, too.* It was that lovely moment when it was still possible that he might. That he did.

His face closed.

Like a great door coming down, with a last glimpse of emotion before it shut. There was a second where he was confused, irritated. A moment of regret, maybe. Then his smile was replaced by the unemotional face of the chief. I felt the loss in my chest, constricted and sour. I wouldn't cry.

"Our guest names her," he said, and turned his horse to walk away.

I turned to find the family huddled around a darling horse.

She was the color of bittersweet chocolate, with a pure white splash across her back. Her mane was white, too, and hanging free except for a single hank that was twined in a loose braid. Unbound, the strands were coming apart, probably from the wind that must have combed through her hair as she ran. I imagined the formidable chieftain whispering to her and plaiting her hair, just that one bit. A casual, maybe even subconscious gesture as he spoke, telling her stories of her new home.

She leaned heavily into my shoulder and I smiled, thinking of them together that way, the chief and his new horse.

"She likes Ginn, not you," another of the girls told Ranka.

"Nei," Ranka said. "She wants me to ride her every day."

Without warning, the horse let out a tremendous, honking cry that went straight into my ear. I shrieked and jumped back. Then we all laughed, everyone crowding around me.

I glanced at Heirik at the stables, his own messy braid falling down his back. Our guest names her, Heirik had said. As though it was normal, not special, to bring home such a beauty and let me choose her name. Normal to whisper sweet love stories to a horse, but close himself off to a woman. Or perhaps not. Perhaps he gave me this gift to try to tell me something that words couldn't. I dared to hope that, with no evidence.

He stood at a safe distance, far from me, but I sent a silent thanks to him. I thanked him for bringing the horse, for so many reasons—her loveliness, her obvious spirit. How he used her to make it clear that I was welcome here. With great relief, I handed the horse the mantle of being the newest thing on the farm.

I chose Drifa for her name. *Snowdrift.*

She didn't belong to me, really. Only the men had their own specific horses, Hár and Heirik and Brosa, whose horse Fjoðr went unridden until the boy returned from his voyage. Drifa belonged to everyone, and Ranka rode her with abandon all day the next day. The rest of us hardly got near her.

After evening meal, the adults sat on the stable walls with our cups and watched the children race. Somewhat used to the sour barley ale, I took bigger sips than I had a couple weeks ago, and it made my mind wander in a tipsy fuzz. I leaned back happily on the grass wall and watched the older boys take the fastest horses down the hill. Here in the yard, Ranka rode Drifa, racing one of Hár's little granddaughters on Gerdi. It was a ridiculous match. The new horse outstripped the old white mare in seconds every time. During the final race, little Drifa stopped running and turned around to wait for Gerdi to catch up, and it was adorable.

The smaller of Hár's grandchildren batted at a hapless chicken with sticks. They were sweet blond bundles, while Dalla herself was pale and thin, as if she were hollowed out by nurturing such a crowd. Just now her husband was brushing a wisp of hair off her forehead, telling her something soft, and she was listening with big, tired eyes.

It was very late. Time for sleep, but not at all dark. The challenge of summer bedtime. The kids were called in to clean their teeth, and Grandda would tell a story.

Given a helm and shield, Hár could have sprung, imposing and grim, from the pages of any children's encyclopedia. A classic Viking. His ash blond hair was turning pewter and fell shaggy around his shoulders, framing ice blue eyes. A scruffy, silvering beard and mustache covered half his face, and an assortment of scars littered the rest. His speech was boisterous and strewn with curses, but also laced with humor and affection for the other men. Massive, tall for the time, he filled up every space he moved through, physically terrifying.

But then, looking past the terror, everything about him was familiar—the way he held himself when he sat to sharpen a knife, the way he looked into the distance like his nephew. His face, the high cheekbones, angular jaw, flashing eyes. All his features were cruder, like a first draft of what would become Heirik.

He made sure all the children were settled in various laps and pools of blankets, and then he began.

"You remember that Frigg is the greatest goddess, and she has many handmaidens."

"Já!" the children all piped up, Ranka the loudest, sitting up on her knees in agreement. Lotta shifted in my lap, and I leaned back into the wall to try to settle us both.

Watching Hár, I was fascinated. "Grandda" was, I guessed, about 40 years old. He'd taken care of the family before Heirik was old enough, and I was told he had over a dozen living children from two wives and at least one lover. Whenever I heard about them, I lost track of the family, the daughters and sons and grandchildren all sliding into a blond heap in my mind. I wished for the clean zipping of a pen across a screen, so I could make a drawing, a family map. Magnus was Hár's son, I knew that, yes, and I knew several of Hár's daughters. Even more lived out there in other places, on other farms.

"Frigg sits at the head of the hearth—one just like ours," he told us. "And twelve maids' faces shine by the fire."

He spoke of them all. Of Sjofn, who directs peoples' hearts to love. Lofn, who clears the way for impossible unions, and Var who hears the oaths that men and women make in the privacy of their beds and hearts and bowers in the woods. He spoke of Snotra, the one who knows the ways to live by, some of which bear great importance to men. Hár gave an example, "Don't wake your man up early for spring cleaning when he's been drinking the night before." This drew muffled agreement from the men, who raised cups as quietly as they could, so as not to wake the drifting children.

"And you may remember Saga," Hár said. "The fairest of face. Frigg likes her the least, because every night Frigg's old husband Odin goes to visit Saga in her shining castle under the waves, and they drink together. She gives him the water of time in a golden cup." He coughed and waved his own cup for more ale. "They sit by the banks of a cold river and she shows him the past and the future."

"Now, Frigg is above all sorts of jealousy," he continued. "And she doesn't mind if Saga pours drink for her husband every so often." He pulled his bushy brows into a serious V. "But night after night is too much for an old man to be spending with a maid."

His scratchy voice cast a hush over the room. I started to listen just to its sound, its cadence and waves of deep and shallow tones. I tried to imagine the "old man" with a young maid in his arms. He was comfortable with his own things: axes, knives, horses, walls. So far beyond the need and reach of a woman. It seemed he might brush emotion away like a fly. Had he ever yearned for someone? I tried to conjure up an image of him with one woman, let alone the three he'd had.

Had they loved him? Had one of them wanted him so desperately she watched his mouth, watched the way he walked? His eyes?

With long and vigorous will, the children stayed awake. Even though the light through the hole in the roof and the small windows had finally begun to dim, they were still restless. Bouncing with the remnants of summer excitement, even after several handmaidens' names and faces and stories had passed by. And so Hár asked them if they knew what an apple was.

"Já, they are like a hard berry," Ranka said in a sure voice, and Hár laughed.

"A little, já. They are fruits, and they are bigger around than a berry and come only from your great grandparents' home. Now put your head down, and I'll tell you something about them."

She lay her head on her mother's lap and stared at him, waiting to absorb every bit of a tale she must have heard dozens of times before.

"Well now, Idunn is the maid who has something the gods need very much, já? She tends the garden where special apples grow that keep the gods young. All the greatest of them, Odin and Thor and everyone, come to her garden and kneel down before her and ask if they can eat her apples."

He smiled at someone, in the darkening room, and it was a smile like a wink. Perhaps for the men, who laughed and softly smacked their cups together.

Hár told a long story of Idunn being duped by Loki and taken into "a certain forest," gesturing with his head to mean Hvítmörk. Loki said Idunn would find some apples there that she liked just as well as her own. But a villain came in the form of a great bird and locked her up in his pantry for weeks and months.

"Now the gods began to grow gray without Idunn around." At this, he pulled his own beard and there were giggles in the darkening night. "And so they held a Thing to talk about it …" *An assembly.*

Lotta felt dreamy in my arms, a sturdy girl, a warm chunk of life snuggling into me. Her breathing slowed, became more regular, and it made me sleepy too. The wall felt welcoming and cool behind my back, and I gave into it and gazed off into the long room. The darkness had finally taken the house.

Heirik was there, and it stole my breath when I noticed him. He didn't always stay for these family moments, for the stories and long hours of talking or walking after evening meal. He was a delicious surprise, at the other end of the room, sitting outside my own sleeping alcove. One knee bent, he rested his foot right on the bench where I would stop later and remove my shoes for the night.

Something in his hands glinted, a small knife. He was carving something. Intent on it, he kept his head down but he nodded absently, perhaps in agreement with something in the story, a subconscious gesture. His hair was sparked with the light of the hearth.

I no longer knew what Hár was saying.

Heirik raised his head just then and caught me looking, and I couldn't turn away. I couldn't deny for a second that I'd been watching him. I was fifteen years old in my heart, sinking deeper into an uncontrollable, delicious crush. Would he understand what my face must be revealing? He watched me back, and for a moment neither of us drew apart.

"Nei!" There was a delighted outburst from the older kids, and Lotta and I were roused.

"She does not fit through the window!" Ranka said with authority, and Kit pushed her daughter's head back down into her lap. Lotta blinked and tried to answer "nei" through drowsy pink lips.

"No more questions, Da," Dalla warned, and Hár laughed.

"You're right, Idunn did not fit," he continued. "And so what did Loki do? He turned her into a nut, and flew off with her in his beak, as fast as he could bring her home."

I murmured soft words back to Lotta—"Be still, Little Hazelnut"—until she burrowed again into my dress and cloak.

When I looked back up, Heirik was carving again. Like drinking the sweetest honey ale, I took him in, the easy way he sat against the wall, how close he was to my bed. I watched him with half-closed eyes, a secret gaze in the dim light. He'd forgotten about me, absorbed in what he was making. One of his hands went to his hair, to tuck a piece behind his ear.

I pressed my hand to Lotta's sleepy, blond head. I would be still, too. This was a good place. She was entirely asleep, as deep in her dreams as I was in mine.

WALLS

I approached the stables and called for Drifa, and she leaned her chin on the turf wall and sniffed in my direction. So curious. Gentle and small but full of lust for running. Her hair was fuzzy, like a baby's, her mane a lot like mine, pale and long and so straight it was almost stiff.

She came around the wall and nosed at my chest. Her dark tail brushed the white tops of her feet, so delicate, like she'd stepped in snow.

We would ride today to the boundary walls, to see the farm. Heirik, Hár and the boys would check and confer on repairs. Betta was to show me the places where we gathered dyestuffs, fungi, flowers for mouthwash and medicine and tea.

I was delighted to get away from the house. Drifa was, too. She pawed lightly at my boot, ready to go.

The walls surrounding the homefield were thick and sturdy, built to protect the most precious crops, the tallest grass, the barley and oats. They were built of sod bricks stacked on a base of stones, about my height. And thick, maybe over three feet deep.

In testament to the walls' effectiveness, a goat chewed on moss that grew on the outside. It stood in my path, a creature I recognized from a child's games and pictures on a screen. I'd seen the goats here from a distance. I hadn't expected the stink, the indifference. It fixed me with a complex gaze, somehow uninterested and challenging at once. It never stopped chewing to comment or move out of my way. Its eyes were alien, the pupils two pulsating horizontal bars that mesmerized me and reminded me of how little I knew. So little about this world, where this creature with foreign eyes would sustain my body in the darkness of polar nights to come.

A hushed rippling sound lulled me, and my thoughts began to drift.

The high, dense grass of the homefield moved in the breeze like the glossy manes of a thousand horses. That grass was so tall, it could close over me without a trace. I knew how that would feel, to be gone, inside. And here I was then, watching from the interior of the tenth century.

I wondered what it looked like to Jeff, what he saw when I disappeared from the lab. Was my body still with him and Morgan in the twenty-second century? Maybe it seemed like I was in a coma and she was holding my hand right now, telling me bedtime stories about a Viking farm gilded with sunlight. Or had I completely disappeared into the tall grass? Was my body gone too, time closed behind me in a neat wave?

I thought of Morgan back there, in her studio with its laughably neat fireplace. The memory was fainter, tinier every time, like we waved across an ever widening valley. My only friend, but not a good one. Could I recall something she liked? Clasps and awls and arm rings were all I could come up with. The color of metal.

Betta favored the ochres and apricots she could draw from her lichens.

I flicked at the stirrups with my outstretched toes, and my legs felt lean and strong. Riding without a saddle—the way Heirik always did—would be a dream. I thought maybe I could do it. I could learn, and then we could ride together that way, the chief and I. I would be beautiful and sure beside him—the two of us and our horses walking the farm. Heirik and I quietly sharing thoughts of work and home. Or running with fearless joy. Drifa and I would race him and Vakr, my red skirt flying as we crashed through bright streams. I imagined catching him, Heirik laughing, bringing my arms up around him, my hand finding the back of his neck, fingers tangled in his hair, pulling him close.

"Tell me your dream, Woman." Betta's horse bumped Drifa's behind.

I blushed and sputtered. The daydream was vivid in my blood. I couldn't think of a lie, and so I stared, guilty.

Betta smiled slyly, her teeth hidden. "It's true then," she said, excitement and satisfaction contained under her cool exterior.

Oh. She could tell. My stomach twisted and sank.

Thoughts came fast and sharp as beaks. Betta knew about my crush. I was so infatuated, I'd forgotten to care whether anyone else could see. And she could. Obviously. Every moment I'd felt dreamy or dumbstruck came back to me in a flood, wondering, Did she see then? Or then? Who else could tell? Everyone? Right now, Heirik might be pretending he didn't notice, just to spare me embarrassment. Oh, gods, I felt sick. I cast my eyes around to find him. Riding ahead of us, the chief was implacable. I couldn't tell.

My whole insides cringed, and I wished I could become the smallest dot in the landscape.

"Never mind, Woman," Betta said evenly. "No one else can see."

Desperate hope surged in me. "Are you sure?"

"They are blind," she told me. "They see only what they already know." She reassured me, but there was something unsettled in her voice. Preoccupied and very unlike her.

"Ginn," Heirik called from up ahead. "Ride with me."

His voice drove Betta's spine up straight. Her eyes flicked up to him and Hár, then she looked at me where I sat stricken with embarrassment and lust.

"Hurry," she told me, an intense whisper. "The chief doesn't wait."

She was a mystery. So strong and secure in herself, so logical and even, and yet scared—or not—of Heirik. I couldn't tell.

He looked patient, actually, like he could wait for me forever. So relaxed and free, at one with the fluid motion of his animal and the peace of his sky. He didn't look back to see if I was coming. He knew.

When I came up behind him, he gave me room on his right.

It was infused in every small interaction—the way he turned the left side of his face and body away. He listened with one ear turned, folded his arms to avoid the awkwardness of unwanted handshakes. He must feel the lack of a friendly jab or gentle brush of fingers on a wrist. A casual tap on the shoulder. Surely he saw everyone else doing those things a hundred times a day. I wanted to give him those moments, to simply touch my hand to his.

My fingers tightened in Drifa's mane, and she writhed a small complaint.

The world was saturated with every kind of green, from the emerald glaze of tall grass to the chartreuse of lichens and gauzy mint of moss. The impression of green seemed ready, though, to turn at any moment to an allover gold. The land was on the cusp of something. The promise of fall coming right on schedule made time itself seem so steady and reliable and slow, passing season by season, not in a crushing blow of 1200 years in a flash. My horse drifted closer to Heirik's. He didn't draw away.

We turned to follow the long curve of the forest. It was deep with knee high greenery and shadows, filigreed with angelica tops and light. A thousand wisps of papery bark curled to reveal blush and orange and copper under the trees' white skins. The wood here was threaded with a crystal stream. I closed my eyes and could imagine Saga and Odin drinking at its tiny banks, somewhere back in the tangle of trees and wildflowers. Tasting the water of time in their cups.

Slow and comfortable moments passed. I looked at Heirik, and I thought maybe I felt a kind of gravity between us. Not only my attraction to him, but a pulling together. He lowered his dark lashes, then, as though with reverence, perhaps for the stream or trees. Did he think Saga was here, too? Or was it just for the stillness of this moment? Even amidst the buzz of the world and the people behind us, I thought maybe he felt we were alone. He smiled in his one-sided way and it was not quite as fleeting as usual. It broke me open with its charm.

He turned into the sun, and his eyes lit up gold and cinnamon before he raised his hand to shade them. He returned, then, to being chief. "We keep the homefield. The walls below will be in disrepair."

It was a simple fact of weather and men and material, and I could see that he'd forgotten snowblooms and stream and was already assessing the solutions in his mind. Which walls, when. His eyes were on the horizon, and I might no longer exist. One moment I felt he was open to me, the next he was a closed gate.

THE PERIMETER WALL WAS BUILT IN THE SAME STYLE AS THOSE around the homefield, but weather had eroded the top and sides, and in some places the wall was worn to a hump-like shape, a huge snake slithering toward the horizon. I dismounted Drifa to walk beside it, running an easy finger along its surface. Assuming Heirik fixed this section of wall every year or two, the effects of lashing rain and whipping North wind were frightening, a pointed reminder of the harsh winter I was bound to live through without snowsuits or heated buildings. I struggled to picture myself enduring the slogging, frigid dark. Without hot chocolate, I thought, and laughed at myself. Was that what I would miss?

Right now, the sun was the hottest since I'd come here. It touched the bareness of my neck and wore away at thoughts of winter. It warmed the spot where my tattoo would have gone. My raven. Now that I knew Heirik, I wanted it again, fiercely. I gave up the relief I'd felt at the bath and wished instead for a blue swan that everyone could see. I wondered if Betta could do it with a needle and dye.

I stood on tiptoe to peer over the wall. Half a foot taller than me, Heirik could easily see beyond. He crossed his hands on top of the sod and rested his chin. Then he looked down at me and noticed I was too short. He drew Drifa close. "Get up," he commanded me gently.

I was being shown the farm, its shape and features, where I was on earth, where the best foraging was for the things we collected, herbs, roots, leaves, lichens. On the surface, this was a simple necessity. I needed to see the places I might be called on to go. But I wondered why the chief himself was spending the afternoon checking out the simple facts of walls. Why he had drawn me close to his side to see what he saw. I felt like somehow he'd come along for me. Some part of him wanted to make me know he was good. The abundant sweep of land proved he was important. The sturdy walls gave me security. This was a prosperous family, and he was head of it. Or perhaps I was wrong, and he simply wanted me to know my place.

He took Drifa's lead and brought me near to his side, closer than we'd ever been before, and now I was sure I felt it. Something lit up between us. His hand closed on the reins, and I felt a luxurious pleasure at being so close, a longing to be even closer. My leg almost brushed his shoulder. I took a deep breath and looked out.

Mountains stood purple and white against a rich blue sky. Planes and curves of heartbreaking colors—slate and ice and green and black—carried to the horizon. Otherwise, the tough grass outside the wall looked similar to that immediately within. And though it was as gorgeous as all the island, this patch in particular was plain and still. Nothing moved, not even a puff of clouds to give the light any shape or direction.

But Heirik watched. He didn't just take in the view. He looked with a wary attention, like one of the dogs who'd lifted its head from sleep. It was eerie. And even more chilling a moment later, when three dark shapes rose small but distinct on the horizon, as though his wolfish attention had conjured them.

He waited calmly and without a word. Soon they were close enough to talk. "Yfirmaðr," one man called, using Heirik's most formal title. My liege. He raised his hand in greeting. Heirik dropped Drifa's reins and stepped away from my side.

"Same thought," the man said. "A good day for checking walls, I guess." His voice was cracked as though his windpipe had been damaged. The air moved laboriously in his throat. A voice like none I'd heard before, a rare treat. He slid from his animal and walked closer until he and Heirik stood with just the wall between them.

When he got near, my curiosity about the man's voice chilled. His shoulders hunched forward as if he carried pain in his chest, so that he was an inch or more shorter than he ought to be. His close-trimmed beard revealed a subtle sneer, an eloquent twist of the lips. I wanted to smooth his cheekbones and eyebrows, iron the creases of anger out them with my thumbs.

"Ageirr," Heirik greeted him with acceptable warmth, but not much.

So this was Esa's brother, the goat in the night. The man whose gloomy and declining house had joined our farm.

He was grieving. His whole aspect showed he had been for a long time, and I could actually imagine him as a lowly animal, aching, leaning his horns heavily into a sod wall in defeat.

Heirik told him, "This is Ginn. A guest of our house." Ageirr turned his pinched face to me and seemed to waken just a little, taking an interest in me. He raised one eyebrow and smiled, devoid of feeling.

Bowing his head slightly, he was through with me, and he turned to Heirik and began talking of the coming hrettir. Roundup. His blasted-out voice, and Heirik's rich one, receded as they walked down the length of the wall. But I still felt Ageirr's attention on me, as though some part of him remained behind. I couldn't shake off how he'd smiled at me with no soul.

Setting out for home, Heirik picked up Drifa's reins and matched her step. He walked outrageously close to me. So near, I thought I felt it again from him, an answering. A desire that called to mine.

It was as though we'd always done this, walked side by side, me on my horse and Heirik on foot. The top of his head was just below my shoulder, and I wanted to turn and touch my nose to his shining hair, breathe in iron and fire. I almost brushed him with my leg. I could right now, yes.

He let go of Drifa. He mounted Vakr without looking back, and he and Hár took off fast, leaving the rest of us to amble home.

The ride back to the house was luxurious. The sun was almost always bright in summer, and I had no reference for how long we'd been gone. I saw the men far ahead, their bodies and the way they held themselves so similar in silhouette. Behind me I heard Betta, Magnus, and Haukur, the foster boy. Their murmurs were just out of reach, and I listened not for the words but for the rhythm and feel. The melting tones of shy flirtation, the surprised laughter like scattered birds. Such sweet young men.

Everything green was rimmed with gold now, and I let my eyes lose focus. I was floating, listening to voices like bells and butter, when Drifa stumbled. Jolted awake, I shrieked and grabbed her mane. She shrieked too and shook her head and I was canting forward, falling face first into the ground. Magnus was by my side, vaguely helping me somehow, lifting me up, Haukur was helping Drifa. All in a space of a few seconds we were put back together.

She'd gone down on a rock. It wasn't just a little twist of the ankle. She'd gone all the way down onto one knee. I shook with the thought that she could have broken her leg. My lovely girl.

Magnus said she was a strong and steady little thing, he wouldn't have thought she'd ever stumble. He searched her face warily, as if she might be an impostor, and it made me giggle.

Magnus smiled broadly then, and he laughed too. Betta's horse came up behind Magnus and inserted her nose under his armpit, curious and worried. We laughed more, and it covered up the racing of my heart and an unsettled feeling.

It wasn't until we got near the house and I heard the chief talking to Hár that I fully relaxed. I felt the safety of him speaking, no matter the words.

I dropped a kiss on Drifa's forehead, meaning it for him, and went inside.

SATURDAY WAS ALWAYS WASHING DAY. THRALLS WORKED ON OUR clothes by the river, and everyone made a point of bathing. I didn't want to make a spectacle of myself getting in the pool and washing my hair more often than everyone else, and so I waited a few days at a time. By Saturday, I felt grimy, hot and disgusted.

I didn't understand why we couldn't bathe first thing in the morning. The pool would be lovely right now, reflecting the massive, cloudless morning sky. I'd sneak a break now, while I could enjoy it alone. I'd dip my toes in the water and watch its blue and purple ripples. I grabbed a wool blanket to take with me, to dry my hair.

The tunnel was fairytale sized and scented with freshly swept dirt and roots. A place where trolls could travel, certainly, hiding from the light. Solitude echoed, along with my footsteps, but it was a brief moment alone, just two minutes' walk. As soon as it seemed too dark to go on, I saw the square of light. I was about to push the door open with my hip, when he rose from the water. I froze, too stunned to breathe.

Heirik was bathing alone. He stood in the center of the pool, looking down toward the sea. Thigh-deep in spring water. It was running off his hair, over his skin. Fine tendrils of steam curled and drifted off every bit of his back and waist and hips. His muscles were both lush and solid as iron. The swells and hollows of him were lit everywhere in tones of palest rose and darkest brown blood. I said thank you out loud. It was the barest whisper to any goddess nearby, for he was fiercely and divinely made.

His birthmark stained his left shoulder and arm, ran down to his waist, followed the curves of his lower back, and further. *Oh.* It was ominous, yes, and inescapable. It ended there, where another kind of scar began, a ragged white gash from a wound. It was not the thin line of a surgically stitched cut. It was thick, healed over in big white twists that disappeared from view below the surface of the water.

My blanket dropped soundlessly to the floor.

I knew I should walk away. I should respect him, should quietly leave him alone. The wall and door felt cold under my palms as I thought about it, about turning around and leaving. I took the barest sips of air, and I watched him.

I saw him in his solitude, and something that had been dozing in me, slowly waking in my gut, now came completely alive. Something far more animal and ferocious than a sweet crush. I imagined standing in the hot water behind him, sliding my palms down to the hollow at the base of his back, reaching around to trace the bones of his pelvis. I touched my own chest, my palm pressing against my breast. I was hungry for him.

And oh gods, I shouldn't watch him, but I did. I couldn't go. I wanted to look forever. I felt a wave of love and knew it had been coming since the day we met. Since the moment I'd looked into his golden eyes. Could I fall in love this way, alone, quietly hiding in the dark? Could I fall in love with Heirik without a hint of permission? It was wrong to look on him in secret. Wrong to take in his body when it wasn't offered. To devour and adore him without his knowing I was even here. But yes, oh yes, I could. And I fell and fell and fell.

I leaned against the tunnel wall, all thought and sense forgotten like the blanket at my feet. Peering around the corner of the window sill, I saw him slick his hair back, wet and long. He smoothed it, pulled it into a tail in his fist, and drew it over one shoulder.

Then he turned my way. And I ran.

I stood in the mudroom panting, my back pressed to the wall. I was barely composed, and had just picked up a bowl to look like I was doing something, when he ducked out of the tunnel, his hair tousled now in blackest waves that clung to his damp linen. I'd never seen his shirts left open at the collar. He wore a pendant, a crude flat silver T. Thor's hammer. It looked homemade. He wore it tied tight with leather, and the metal rested in the hollow of his throat. Somehow this slight glimpse was more erotic than his whole nude body.

His brows drew together sharply when he saw me, just for a second. I felt lightheaded from adrenalin and the vision of his thighs and a sudden odd desire to lick the silver at his throat. I could tuck myself into him, put my forehead against his damp shoulder.

He said hello, and the sound of his voice made me sway. I reached a hand out as if to touch him and saw gray close around me, my vision narrowing.

Betta slapped at my cheek. I opened my eyes and she and Ranka loomed over me. The little girl's braids fell, ropy, against my face. "Please wake up, Lady."

We were on the floor of the mudroom. Betta helped me sit up against the wall and pulled a wool cloak off a hook to throw over me. Ranka had a cup in her hand, and she pushed sour whey at me.

Heirik, a steaming apparition, was gone.

"Pay attention, Woman," Svana laughed at me. "You'll stick your pretty fingers in the lye." It was my turn to stir the pot of ash and melted seal fat. A lazy job, soap could've been made by one of us, or more likely by the thralls. Doing this together was a luxury, a break sitting in the sunny grass.

I stirred languidly with a stick, musing about the chief's body, and experiencing a familiar tightness in my chest every time I recalled the wool blanket I'd left behind. He must've had to step right over it. Oh gods, replaying the scene in my mind didn't ease the embarrassment. It was the opposite. When I thought of him returning from the bath, hot and wet and having surely seen the evidence, I felt my face flare.

The soap was a foul gluish mess, dotted with bits of wood ash, and I watched it intently as it did nothing, changed not at all. I pretended it was fascinating.

No one noticed my mooning, I thought. Svana sat in a puddle of gauzy, peach skirts, utterly occupied with herself. She languidly crushed dried angelica root and a few needles of precious rosemary. The scents bloomed on her fingertips and filled the air, clashing with the stink of the fat. She rubbed her slender wrists together, then pressed them to her temples and made tiny circles there—a small animal cleaning her face.

Betta was lying on her back in the grass, sucking honey off her fingers. She'd been dipping them in the tiny bowl that was meant to get mixed in to our soap. The hunks we bathed with would have a chaotic scent, I thought, ranging from the salt of the sea to honey and fresh-baked rye bread. It's what Heirik's hair would smell like, if I got close enough to know.

I heard my name.

"Ginn might be good for Eiðr," Svana mused. "He is ugly, but smart."

I sat up straight and eyed her with alarm.

Betta laughed. "Svana, do you think of anything but marrying boys? Ginn needs a man." With her pinkie she glossed her lips with honey and looked sideways at me. "Like the chief."

My stick got sucked into the sluggish whirlpool of the soap.

Was Betta testing a theory? Or could everyone tell? She gave me a dark look, and she held her sticky fingers up in front of her lips, facing out, and with a little push she shushed me.

"But ... Woman ..." Svana sputtered and blanched. "He would ..." Her heart-shaped face turned from white to pink, and she blurted it out. "He would turn to Ginn!"

I pinched the tiniest bit of clean stick and eased it out of the sludge. He would turn to me. The phrase was familiar. I rifled my memory of poetic Viking phrases and in a second I had it. I blushed for what felt like the hundredth time this week, probably a bloody crimson. Little Svana was warning me that the chief would demand sex if I became his wife.

I heard his voice suddenly in my mind. *Turn to me.* He'd said it the day I was scared of the birds. He was so embarrassed at his accidental words, and now I realized why. Instead of saying "turn around" he'd told me to come make love. I tried to remember his voice exactly. I imagined how that phrase might sound in the muffled dark of his bed, when he meant it.

"Já, Little Girl," Betta laughed, bright and plain. She teased Svana, who was just three years younger. "That is the idea."

I tried for casual, uninterested mirth, and laughed a little along with Betta, but I sounded unconvincing. It didn't matter. Svana was absorbed in the horror of sex with the chief. She couldn't even see Betta's glances, my flush of embarrassment. Even if she did notice, she wouldn't be able to fathom the real reason why I was dreamy and slow as the sludge circling our bowl.

"Stop it." I smacked Betta. "We shouldn't talk about the chief that way."

Right, yes. We shouldn't. But I couldn't help it, then. His wet body came to mind, and a fluttering of questions. How would it be with him? He was so singular, so unknown. What did he want from a woman? What did he like?

Oh. I tripped on a thought that was so obvious. I'd fantasized about his body entwined with mine, his mouth, his heat against me. I'd lain on my hard bench night after night, watching Betta's slow breathing, and I'd dreamed of his kiss. But I hadn't thought about the reality of sex for him. Namely, it didn't exist. He didn't know the unutterable softness of a lover's lips, the pulse of life in a beloved wrist. He hadn't known a woman's curves and sweet spots and scents. Had never kissed.

Did he imagine it? I supposed he would, like anyone, think about sex. Then the logical and unspeakable idea came to mind, and I swallowed, my throat suddenly dry. Heirik must touch himself.

I lay down beside Betta and gave my breath up to the navy blue sky, my stick forgotten. Svana made a becoming little squeak as she fished it out, the soap touching her lovely fingertips. She took over stirring.

"He does not, by the way," Betta broke into my thoughts.

I turned my head to look at her with horror. How could she possibly know my thoughts? Worse, how could she know about Heirik alone and needy? What he did and didn't do? But it wasn't what she meant.

"He does not ask a thrall to do it," she continued. "Many of them would, at his word."

I turned my face back to the sky and closed my eyes to absorb the waning heat. Betta's words chilled me. I was so ignorant here, over and over again. I knew about this place and time as in a story-book or an arc on a screen. Far down the hill, a half dozen thralls spun and washed clothes all day so that we could have afternoons like this. In the weeks I'd been here, I'd come to think of them vaguely as servants—people who worked for the chief, who brought up wood and thread for dyeing. Really, Heirik owned them. Of course, he could feel a woman's touch if he chose to.

I sat up and looked across the yard and the house sat, too, like an animal with haunches and outstretched paws.

It was a dozing wolf of a house. But in the steeply angled, dark orange light, there was something alert and wild just under the surface. With a start, I noticed Heirik was beside it, crouched low to inspect the place where the walls changed from rock to grass. He sat up on his heels and lifted his head to me, as though he'd heard me calling, and his lupine eyes picked up the gold from the wildflowers on the turf.

A cloud passed over and Svana hugged herself.

I sat up and criss-crossed my legs. Betta stirred the soap now. "Who knows?" She smiled. "I think the chief has wolf's eyes for Ginn."

"Nei!" Svana gasped. And then a whisper, "Nei. He doesn't see women that way."

"Já, well, if that is so …" Betta didn't bother to finish her thought, she so obviously didn't believe it.

Svana didn't answer. She sat breathlessly entranced, no doubt playing out in her mind the horror of a kiss from Heirik, his fear-some face so close, his breath on her. Almost subconsciously she whispered, "Ma says so."

Betta raised an eyebrow at me.

When Svana spoke again, she sounded just like her mother admonishing me. "Where the wolf's eyes are, the teeth are near." It was almost familiar by now—the stab of anger I felt at Hildur when I heard such cruel pronouncements.

Betta must have seen me bunch up with animosity, because she snapped her teeth at me playfully like a dog and made us both laugh. Svana didn't join us. Her eyes were running over the landscape, searching for something, her mother maybe? Some kind of assurance about the chief? That he would never marry, never have a child, never with her.

Her words stayed with me—*Ma says so*—and the more I repeated them to myself, the less I liked them.

Dirty, delicious thoughts of the chief were like dogs at my heels.

It had been almost a week since the day we made soap, the day I first thought about him alone in his longing and wondered if, or what, he did in the solitude of his room. Now the idea kept following me. At first, I forcibly pushed it out of my mind. It was wrong, disrespectful to such a dignified and private man. But the thought would creep up on me, so that sometimes I was consumed and let wicked scenes play out in my mind. Sometimes in the midst of these fantasies, I'd look up to see him, in the flesh, suddenly near me. Disoriented and mortified, I'd look away.

The season was almost upon us when none of it would matter. The fall would be quick, and everyone would be consumed with work.

In this time, all the seasons were warmer than in the future, but the earth tilted and turned just the same. When the light started to change, it would change rapidly, night consuming the light noticeably earlier every day. The girls said we would need to work quickly, bringing in and storing hay, bringing down the animals, shearing them for fall so they could grow their new coats in time for the first storms.

Then, when the house curled up to hibernate, accepting the world's great and silent weight of snow, there would be nothing but time. The work would come to a rushing close and we would sit and play games and stare at each other most of the time until the light came.

I wished that by then I'd be spending all that time in his bed, no longer caught in this agony of dreaming. The furs would be warm against our bare legs, my breasts warm against his chest. In his arms, I would never be cold.

It was a winter dream, as sweet as the ice skates he'd promised me. I didn't know if any of it would ever come to be, but I liked to imagine.

One day it was just a little too cold outside. I stood by the poles in the yard, hanging damp skeins of apricot thread. Even though they had cooled in the pot, steam came off them in languid clouds. My skirt lifted and whipped in a sudden wind. A thousand land wights exhaled ice, and it rose around my ankles like a stream.

I was lost in the wool.

The wind had knocked one of the poles over, and I got snagged and bundled up in damp yarn. It's smell enclosed me, almost smothering, as sleepy and brown as the coming of autumn. I struggled to get free, to put the pole right, but the strands of yarn and lines of string were tangled in my hair and across my face.

"Some help?" The offer was almost lost in the rushing of wind. A man's voice.

"Já!" I laughed, struggling to stand the pole up, and then I looked out from among the strands and saw it was Heirik himself.

He was there in a second, somehow extracting the pole and yarn. I pulled free and smiled in thanks.

He stared at me for a moment, open and awkward. "You have a space in your smile."

As always, he seemed surprised he'd spoken to me. As if he didn't know he was going to do it until just then, when the words left his lips.

I was suddenly conscious of my own mouth, my mind tumbling from there to the thoughts I'd been indulging in just before the wind came. Before he came. I pressed my lips closed, and I looked at his hands, so recently featured in my fantasies. His skin was rough, darker on half of his left hand, and his scratched and beaten bracers were tied with the usual strange knots, not like anyone else's. I was seized with guilt.

"Nei," he said. "Do not hide it."

He was holding the pole upright, already putting it back into the earth, and so I didn't catch whether he smiled, too.

He looked to the sky. "Evernight will begin soon."

A particularly Viking phrase that didn't translate to my own previous language, *becoming night* one elegant verb, *ever-night* another picturesque phrase that built on and within it. He was talking about the winter, when the sun would rise only to graze the horizon and then slide away again, leaving just an hour's glow on either side of midnight.

Oh. Right.

A thought so dumb came to me, I stood still, as embarrassed as if Heirik could see everything in my head. The naive and snow-trimmed skating party in my mind always took place in bright sunlight. The fantasy of my cherry dress was brilliant against shimmering drifts and shiny solid water frosted with white breath. A scene that could never be. The winter sun would be subdued, indirect, and no artificial lights would spark against this ice.

"Will we really skate?" I asked him. My voice was hopeful, and I hated how little I sounded. Like a petulant child, I had asked this more than once.

He sank to one knee to make sure the pole was solid in the ground. Quickly satisfied that it was strong, he rested an elbow on his knee and looked up at me. And though he was only kneeling to fix a clothesline, he looked just like a knight from one of the sims. He picked up his ax from beside him on the grass and planted it, blade down, before him.

It was eerie how his words echoed the image. "I swear, you will skate." And then he laughed, and I laughed too. He stood and brushed himself off.

"We will shear soon or we'll have no winter wool." He raised his eyes to the highlands and soon became lost in thoughts, probably of animals and time and seasons. "First we hay," he added, as if realizing I would be ignorant of the order of things. "We start in a half month, já?"

He told me as though he wanted to confer with me. But it was Hildur he needed to speak with. I had no sense of how to prepare, to set people and tasks in motion. He smiled at me, anyway, before turning to head toward the stable.

"Takk!" I called after him. *Thanks.* And he turned and walked backwards for a step or two, watching me as he left.

THE SWEET SCENT OF FIELDS SPREAD EVERYWHERE AROUND AS Betta and I walked the mile or so to the nearest edge of the woods. We would collect lichens and mushrooms. My hand upturned, a basket swung against the softest part of my wrist. A skin of cool water gently bounced against my shoulder blades.

Betta cut into the silence with a force like she'd been holding something back.

"You should shield your eyes, Ginn." She eyed me sideways. "Don't let Svana or Hildur see more of your heart."

An icy trickle suddenly ran down my spine.

"Not anyone but me," she finished. "Please."

My answer was sharp. "What's wrong about wanting him?"

Truly, what was so wrong about desiring an unmarried, unpromised man, a strong man who was gorgeous and kind to me? The concept of wanting wasn't foreign, I knew. There were so many words for desire in the old language they passed through in my mind as if on a breeze. Words that in the future had come to mean *craving* and *mind*, even *prey*. Savage words for desire, perfect for how I felt.

Betta pressed her lips together for a second, as though considering and discarding several things she might say.

"I can feel it's dangerous," she told me.

I swallowed a frustrated breath, anxious words.

She went on. "Because of my gift."

She dropped this conversationally, as though having a gift was a mere nothing. She had a gift? A gift of perception?

It was a nonsense reason for telling me I should hide my attraction. Frustration drove me, boiled over into exasperation. "What does that mean?" I burst out. "Heirik is not dangerous."

Betta stopped walking and stared openly at me.

"Já," she said, even and serious, without any hint of superstition. Just fact. "He is a dangerous man."

I opened my mouth to blurt something, anything defensive and possessive and mad, but she cut me off.

"—He takes his due easily, Ginn. And he gives elegant justice."

Then she softened toward me and explained with a kind of sweet sadness. "You see him here in his house, where he is cold enough. You haven't met the chieftain." She used the formal word, yfirmaðr, liege lord and god of her known world.

Clouds moved away like slow animals, and in the sun our mood slowly lifted and changed, snappish words forgotten. We gossiped about the few other people we knew. We talked about Kit, pregnant again after losing one sister for Ranka and just birthing a boy in winter. I heard more of the story of Hildur, how she came to be a sort of servant turned housewife—a singular and bizarre solution for a strange family. We talked about the girls needing to be married soon and where they might go. Three of them were fourteen or fifteen. This was their year.

Betta seemed to be sidling up to the subject of herself, talking about marriage, but in the end she didn't bring up her own situation. She was hopelessly old and probably passed by. Daughter of a second generation thrall, she was a free person. She would live a posh life in the chieftain's house, dyeing cloth and caring for children, but without her own husband. Without love and affection.

I tried for lightness, for sarcasm. "And who could possibly deserve Svana?"

"No one," Betta summarized, laughing a little bitterly. Then she changed her mind. "Nei. A man with power and a fine household should be hers. Plus a good body and lovely face. The svakalega." *Gorgeous ones.*

"Where?" I looked around in the trees, as though some different men other than Hár or Arn might be there to admire.

Betta laughed. "We see men at roundup, shearing, you know. We meet the boys from around these lands. Some others."

The size of Hvítmörk grew in my mind every time I heard about such things. Heard that enough eligible young men would come to roundup that the girls could consider which ones they liked. Did a hundred people follow him? How many houses and huts sat on Heirik's land, every farmer sharing the highlands and byways and Heirik's generosity? In return for what? Fear, and a portion of their goods? Gods, my vision had become so happily narrow, my crush so precise and blinding. This new family spread out for miles all around me, but I saw only one man.

"Heirik has no reason to keep Svana. He doesn't want her for himself. She'll be a good trade."

Betta's bitterness shocked me. And her talk about Svana as a commodity. But more than that, it was hard to hear that Heirik could have chosen Svana if he'd wanted to. Still could, even now. The thought was ugly. Could I live here if one day he came to his senses, gave up superstition and took a wife? Every woman was afraid of him, but many would be tempted by the power and luxury of his house.

Já, he still could choose Svana. I spread a palm over my stomach, a sick feeling there. Even with no promise of his loving me, I didn't want him to take anyone else.

We reached the forest and ducked into the first few feet of dense trees. I let the basket and water skin drop to the ground and slid a small knife out of its leather sheath. I got to work on the lichens that would become tea and dye and medicine for Bjarn. The trees dripped with them. As I scraped and cut them away, the smell of bark sprang up rich and dirty.

I wished Betta could just tell me everything I needed to know to make it here. To live. Flat out tell me, comprehensively.

I worked on lichens and listened to the shushing of leaves. The cry of a bird far away, like a thin line. The work began to lull me.

What did Betta think of her situation? She was a woman, já? She must have had desires of her own, and even worse, knew they were hopeless to fulfill. I wondered if she pined for love, perhaps even someone in particular. What man could possibly snare the heart of such a solid, courageous, wary, shy creature? So complex, and with her wry sense of humor. Betta was not pretty, but she had an intensity of spirit, and a voice, that were sensual. She was of impossibly low status, but it was hard to imagine a man truly equal to her. A pang of fear hit me. If she married, she would leave here, and I didn't want her to go.

I looked at her sharply braided head bent to her work, and I loved her.

"I have a secret," she offered, never looking up from her lichens.

I shook myself. Maybe she did have a gift. She seemed to know I was thinking of her hidden heart.

"Já, I suppose you do." I said playfully.

"What do you mean?" She looked up with piercing eyes, suddenly on guard.

She had smiled slyly at me more than a few times this week, teasing me for my devastating crush. It was finally my chance to laugh good-naturedly at her. "It doesn't take a gift to see that you're a young woman. You must have someone you think of. Some one person," I tried to ask it casually. "A man?" Allowing for so many unknowns with Betta.

"Já," she let her guard down and turned to liquid, and her cheeks lit up with shame and pleasure. "A man." Her voice was a breath of fascination, the very essence of yearning. The words could not have been more beloved. *Oh.* I raised an eyebrow, and she shook her head, almost imperceptibly. She wasn't going to tell me. She smiled her secret and turned away.

We scraped.

When she spoke again, her tone had shifted like a dark cloud. "I have the sight," she said, gravely. I waited, and she went on. "A little. Not the sight of the future. Of today."

"But …" I wanted to lift her heaviness. She made no sense. "Can't we all see today?"

"Hah!" Her laugh was a bark, amused and wry. "You are naïve sometimes, Woman."

That much was true.

"Undercurrents," she explained, and she spread her hands out, palms down as if she could draw the thoughts up out of the earth. As though she could feel their contours and waves. "Things that people don't yet realize, or admit."

She turned her hands over to look at her palms, searching them with clear eyes. I tried to see the shapes of musings there. It came together, why she always seemed to answer my unspoken questions. Why she knew I was so bewitched by Heirik, almost before I did. She must be especially attuned to the smallest, involuntary glances, the flutter of hands, longing eyes, flushed skin, the scents and tensions of desire. She probably just saw all these things when they were tiny, before they hatched. Being hyper observant had always been one of my faults, but what if for Betta it was more than that? A real, extraordinary sense? I wasn't an especially easy person to read—not overly difficult either, but she saw all of me as easily as she breathed.

"I don't desire the chief," she assured me bluntly. He wasn't the one who made her heart beat. "But I'm a woman, já? With half a brain. Of course I've wondered." I didn't answer. I swallowed hard, singing in my mind to block out the many images that had been dogging me. She continued. "Thought about what he would be like."

Gods, I gave up. I let the images in, like a tidal wave from behind a door. I opened it, and was subsumed. In my wild mind, I saw him leaning against a wall in his room, eyes closed, caressing himself through his clothes. His hand moved to his waist, to slip inside. What had Betta seen in her mind's eye, when she had wondered about him?

"Were you afraid?" I asked, my eyes tightly shut. The women were all so scared of his body. Betta was so afraid of the chieftain. "Was it awful?"

"No," she said so matter-of-factly, and she might have been telling me whether she'd liked her dinner.

"What I see of him, because you are wondering," she eyed me shrewdly, "Is that even though he won't touch a woman, he wants to. Freyr is still strong with him. He does not feel cold."

I didn't doubt her gift, not for a single second, and her words about Heirik relieved and excited me. It was possible. He wanted to touch a woman, hadn't resigned himself to the years ahead like a barren expanse of ice. Betta hadn't even said he wanted me in particular, but if it was possible, just maybe, then I could continue to inhale and dream.

"And no," she added. "I don't see exactly what he thinks or does, but I can see what's in your head right now as plainly as your smile." She winked. "And if he didn't do that before you came here, he does now."

Oh. It came unbidden again, a vivid picture of Heirik removing his clothes. I saw him from behind, as in the pool, because I couldn't even begin to imagine the rest. I could see his shoulder blades moving as he touched himself.

The lichens had such intricate, coralline shapes and gradations of color. The rust and palest green and peeling bark made a gorgeous mix, and it was no wonder these crusts would dye cloth like amber, like the sun.

"There are some trees we haven't touched yet, Ginn." She thrust her chin over her shoulder to point into the forest. "That way. Are you alright to go alone?"

Lichens were scratchy and abundant under my fingers. I looked up and down the length of the tree, and it was covered with them. Every tree around us was encrusted. Why would Betta send me off alone to look for more? And then it dawned on me, with a rush of embarrassment. I was mortified, but I nodded and picked up my basket. I quietly walked off, underbrush rustling with the movements of my skirts. Betta was more than astute, more than mature for her age. A very generous and witty soul. She'd just sent me off to touch myself.

I found a place, alone, not too far but far enough. And then I realized I couldn't really do it. It was one of my only chances, the house so clogged with people. But I couldn't. I leaned back against a tree, the tough bark cool on the back of my neck. I would just let myself think of Heirik doing it, free from guilt. That would be nice. I'd lean against this tree and think of him in just the same position. I let gorgeous, dirty thoughts fill me, images of him alone, and I pretended he was thinking of me. His eyes were brilliant with the pain of wanting me. My skirts were like clouds, bunched around my wrists where I'd hiked them up. I dreamed of his black hair against a tree like this, snagged in white bark, his eyes closed. Opening at the moment of release. Like mine. Oh, like mine. I opened my eyes to the dark blue sky through a canopy of birch leaves, my breath coming hard and fast, my hand slipping down my thigh.

We took a long, leisurely time to fill our baskets, talking about dye and beads and trade, Betta's dreams of traveling across the island. I wanted to tell her what was there. I'd read in the arcs about vast fields of pumice, waterfalls, and fiery, spewing mountains. Baths that boiled so hot you could cook in them. I thought maybe my glacier was not far from us, and then the giant one that used to lay beyond. Or that did lay beyond, now. I thought of cold buildings, stretching to the sea.

"I think it's all ice," I told her.

"What is?"

"The island. All of it."

"Nei, Ginn," she told me. "It is beautiful under the stars. The men set up camp and they lay back and fall asleep watching Frigg spin the clouds."

We walked home as the sky started shifting. It wasn't getting dark—that wouldn't happen for some hours—but something suggested that the light had peaked and was on its way down the other side of a great hill.

A lumpy knot in my dress flopped against one leg, holding my skirts up so I could walk easier through the grass that waved so tall now. Blades brushed, slim and sharp, against my calves, and they itched above my boot tops. The cadence of the knot bumping my leg, forward and back, forward, back, soothed me. Out of the corner of my eye, I could see that Betta looked similarly quieted. Our steps started to match each other, the shushing of the grass a lullaby.

It was then we stepped into violence. The grass parted around a dead horse, its throat cut.

A jagged rent more than a foot long split his flesh, and he laid bloated and clotted with drying blood. The horse's teeth were bared, tongue swollen, one eye open and lost to the sky. I felt like my organs had been sucked out. Hollow. I retched and stumbled, almost falling hands first into the corpse, but Betta caught me. I closed and covered my mouth, but my eyes were wide open. They wouldn't stop looking, wouldn't stop seeing it.

It was the golden horse Fjoðr, named for the wind. Brosa's horse that lived unridden until his master came home. A gorgeous creature, a loving companion and wild spirit lying in a bloody heap, dotted with flies.

"Gods, why?" I mumbled through my fingers.

Betta grabbed one of my elbows and drew us both back and away.

"It was Ageirr," she stated without question. The man who grieved, the one we'd met at the walls. Why would he do this?

Betta loaded both our baskets on one forearm, and with her other hand she held onto me and started trudging toward the house. With quick, serious strides, she pulled me like a little sister, bumbling behind. The blood kept coming to mind, the gash in Fjoðr's throat, and at one point I stopped and tried to throw up but couldn't. She dragged me along.

I felt about four years old when I asked, "Will Heirik kill Ageirr?"

Betta stopped walking. "Just go kill him where he stands?" She asked as if I were dense as a rock. "Nei." She shook her head and started walking again. "Worse," she added. "The chief will think."

"Think?"

She stopped again and looked at me openly, searching, probably finding that I was truly ignorant. She grasped my wrist hard. "Woman, please, believe what I say. You don't know him."

Her words stabbed me. I felt like I was the only person who did know him. The fact that she had lived with him for a decade dawned on me, and jealousy filled me up, stupidly, reddening my face. How did she know him so well? I wanted to shout that nothing he'd ever shown her was real, that he showed me his true self.

"It's not just his face that scares people, Woman," she told me, and she might as well have said duh. Of course it wasn't. Fear of a simple mark couldn't be sustained across decades and a clan of a hundred people. There had to be more. Betta didn't tell me what it was.

Her voice turned affectionate. "You see his heart," she said. Her words were tender, but clear. "You don't know his logic. What he's capable of."

My skin tingled and my head turned airy and light.

"This," she turned to look behind and around her feet, as though we could see the very dread we were tramping through. As though Fjoðr was there on the ground all around us. "It is bigger than a horse"

We walked on for a few minutes longer, getting close to home. Emotions and thoughts came in great, rapid waves. Protectiveness. Heirik would be devastated by this, his brother's horse. Defensiveness of my bond with him, as fledgling as it might be. Unformed apprehension, Betta's words like a swirling mist. What he's capable of. The bloody horror of the horse, flies stepping lightly on its face. Confused with jealousy of a past I could never have, of Betta watching Heirik grow from boy to man.

She stopped short just before the final rise to the house and tightened her grip. The bones of Betta's fingers ground into me.

"We have to tell him," she said.

I hadn't pictured actually delivering the news.

It would savage Heirik's heart. Fjoðr had been a sleek runner, his sun-streaked mane gloriously flying. No one was to ride him until Brosa returned. I'd seen Heirik speaking to the animal, walking beside him and talking as though this blond and shining horse and his little brother were one and the same. This would be a portent. Somewhere—at sea?—his beloved brother was dead, too, as swiftly and thoroughly gone as his animal.

"I'll do it." I said. Betta's fear was palpable, and I didn't blame her. The cruelty was so calculated, so sharp, it wasn't something I ever wanted to see let alone have to report. But she feared for herself, as messenger. She feared the fallout, the chief's terrible logic, whatever that might mean. I feared only for Heirik and how his heart would break.

We both looked at the house for a long moment, steadying ourselves.

Betta broke in with a small voice and her thoughts—so far from horse and blood—startled me. "Do you think you had a husband?"

"I didn't." I said it so quickly, so confidently, that Betta was roused from her fear and she seemed to become interested.

"Do you remember?" She asked slowly, testing thin ice.

"I just know," I said. "When I see Heirik, I know that he is my husband and no other."

"Já," she said, and it was an eloquent little syllable. It conveyed all the wonder and disbelief that I might feel that way about the chief, and yet, also resonated with understanding. "My mother told me they would say 'ah hushla mo cray.'"

It took me a moment to work out her pronunciation. A chuisle mo chroí, I thought. It was Gaelic, and one of the most lovely, romantic phrases of all time. *The pulse of my heart.* She never spoke of her mother. It felt good that one of the things she kept was this phrase.

We saw the house now. It stretched out lazily in the expanse of late afternoon, unaware of what we'd witnessed.

"Please." Betta suddenly grasped my hands. "Tell no one about me. I'm ...," she looked around at her own hips, her hands. "I'm plain. To be odd, too, I'd never be given to him." Her voice dropped with the last few words.

Her precocious maturity was gone, and in that moment she was a girl, sad that she wasn't pretty, hoping she wouldn't be left behind. My heart ached for her. For her simple wish. I didn't know who it was she pined for, but I silently vowed we would get him for her.

"Of course I won't tell anyone," I told her.

And even in the darkness of lingering death, a lightness and happiness rose in me. I held her hands tight and drank in her worried face, her tense braids and eyes, and all my staggering loneliness lifted. My heart soared. I had a friend! I had a person to be close to, to care about. She was mine.

I squeezed her hands in return. "You are my best friend." I'd never said it to anyone before.

I DIDN'T KNOW WHAT TO CALL HIM. I HAD NO PERMISSION TO CALL him by his name, but the word "herra" stuck in my throat, a formal stone. The Norse word this family used for chief. It was like calling him Sir or worse, *Lord*. All the wrong things for this moment. So I just waited until he looked up from where he sat on a stump next to the forge, sharpening his ax. The gorgeous one that he seldom used.

When he saw me, he raised an arm to wipe his forehead, smearing dirt and black hair.

"Hello." It was all I could think of.

He nodded, obviously wondering what I was about.

I hadn't thought this through. Convinced that my heart would know what to say, I'd just walked up to him. I hadn't practiced.

Slitasongr gleamed in his hand, the metal edge like a strip of ice-blue against the iron head. Just now, I realized that telling him this news was dangerous.

My voice sounded rough. "Your father's ax," I said.

He nodded to himself and looked deep into the steel edge as he spoke. With his whetstone, he brushed away some imperfection I couldn't see. "I wanted to care for it today."

Betta's words played out in my mind. *You don't know what he's capable of.* My throat dried and constricted, and I sounded hoarse when I asked, "May I?" I reached a hand toward the ax.

A cold breeze dried my palm while I waited for Heirik to decide if he'd hand it to me. Did anyone else touch it? Maybe Hár.

He flipped it over easily so that the handle pointed toward me.

It was very heavy. So much weightier than I expected, the weapon dragged me down for a moment before I hefted it up in my two hands. I was amazed at how he swung such a thing so effortlessly by his calf when he walked, the pounds held as though they were nothing. The handle was worn and silky in the places he always gripped, and I matched my palm to a spot where his had been just seconds ago.

The wood felt hot from his hands, but the ax also burned with its own fire. It felt alive and inquisitive, as if searching for who I was. A memory came, of one of my early lessons, placing my fingers on a classmate's throat and feeling the vibrations of speech.

"It feels like it a has a voice."

"You feel that?" His inflection gave away surprise. He recovered himself and then stood to show me, careful not to touch my hands. He stood so close, I smelled his scent of sweat and metal, felt his height and size. If he were to lean in to me, just now, he could press his lips to my forehead. We would fit like that.

"It is called the throat of an ax. Here." He ran his fingers down the long, curved handle with such tenderness. I imagined he was trailing them down the inside of my forearm. I shivered, from his fingers and the life in the ax. "The shoulder," he said, and rubbed his thumb over the thickest part of the iron. Gods, could he possibly know what he was doing to me?

Nei, Heirik did not flirt. He had no idea how. And if he felt anything right now it wasn't detectable—no rapid breathing, no blush of skin to match mine. He was just talking about his ax.

I let the handle slide through my fingers until the iron head rested on the ground by my feet. It was comfortable, its throat under my thumb.

A horse whinnied down in the valley and I came awake and remembered why I was here. I promised myself I'd be brave. I wouldn't cry. I choked the ax in my fist.

"I have to tell you something awful." There wasn't a good way. "Fjoðr is dead."

There was a great sigh from the land all around us, and all the grass lay down as one—a flattening that stretched from our feet across the yard, to the house, the highlands and the valleys that led to the sea.

Heirik sat slowly, elbows on his knees, and hung his head. I sank down onto the ground in front of him, in a rude clanking of needle case, shears and beads. I pulled *Slitasongr* into my lap as though the ax was a child and looked at it until Heirik was ready to speak.

"When he was nine, my brother followed me always." He talked without seeing me. "He wanted to do what I did, eat what I ate, say what I said."

I had no picture of Brosa in my head, and none of Heirik as a boy either. They were part of a vague scene—a dark haired boy and a smaller, golden one here in this yard. I imagined Vakr turning back to bite with irritation at Fjoðr, as if to say leave me alone.

"I was exhausted from it," Heirik continued. "I told him that to be like me, he was too pretty. He would need to be ugly." He shook his head and half smiled. "He took a knife to his own face."

I blanched, felt my mouth open. "You couldn't have known," I murmured. "That he would do such a thing."

Heirik looked at me as though I was daft. "Of course I did," he said. "My brother would do anything I asked." He spoke with rueful pride, and with sadness, just beginning to believe that his brother had died. Had passed him, and was gone like a morning mist.

I tried to adjust to the idea of a boy who would do such a thing, cause himself such pain and risk so he could be like Heirik.

"Brosa will come back," I said gently. "Fjoðr was a good horse. But he was not your brother."

"Já?" Heirik looked to me, desperately hopeful. "Well ..." He seemed too bewildered to finish.

His hair was a mess. I realized I'd never seen anyone cut it shorter. The women cut the mens' hair, most of them keeping it around chin length. Heirik's was long now, pulled back on top with a leather tie, the rest trailing everywhere down his shoulders, down his back.

Right. No woman would cut his hair. Probably Betta's Da would. But what man would want to ask Bjarni to groom him when everyone else was tended by pretty maids and wives?

"They told you that you're ugly." I said it before I'd even thought the words.

His eyes flashed anger at me, a warning, but he didn't get up or leave or say a word.

And I told him, "Nei." It sounded so tender, the word almost lost in my breath.

I shook my head slightly, and I smiled and let him see that he was beautiful to my eye. I hadn't told him how I felt in so many words, but now I'd said something out loud, and it hung between us for a moment. I looked up at him like he was the most divine thing—everything good and lovely in this world. I was confident and sure.

I watched, but he was unreadable. He'd closed down—something he'd practiced his whole life. A sudden realization broke through his wall, though, and he stood in a burst of intensity, towering above me. He snapped, "You saw Fjoðr."

"Já," I said, standing too, *Slitasongr*'s blade narrowly missing my ankle and then settling on the ground there. My thumb found its throat again, and it was solid and warm, and in my hand, not his. "Betta and I found him. In the grass on the way back from the woods."

Heirik was focused, grave. "How was he done?"

Courage, I told myself. Just say the truth. "His throat was cut."

The ground looked foreign and hard, and I concentrated on it, unsure if I should walk away, if I was dismissed, or if it was the opposite, that I was needed. Needed fiercely. I wavered, choked the ax.

"You came to me," he said, incredulous, and then his voice melted into warmest evening. "Brave thing," he said. I didn't know if he meant it was a brave thing I'd done, to come and tell him, or if it was a sort of name for me—*you brave little thing*. Gods, I wanted him to call me something sweet like that.

He crossed his arms, and ducked his head to look under my hair, to find me in here. If he were willing to touch me, he would've lifted my chin. "You are alright?"

"Já," I said. My dress caught on my calluses where I smoothed it, down my knee. My other hand gripped the ax. "I'm alright," I said again. And then I started to cry.

His hand clenched nothing, and I thought he wanted to reach out to me, to wipe my cheek, hold me and rock me in his arms. Instead he moved with swift and terrifying grace. He took the ax from my hand and flipped it so that he choked it just below the head. In an unguarded second, I'd given him *Slitasongr* after all. I'd lost it.

I watched him closely and didn't flinch. I thought, or maybe dreamed, that underneath the quiet fury I saw something good, some protectiveness and concern.

"Look," he said smoothly, his voice dark like black sand. "Look at the blade, here. Put the sun behind you."

He came around to stand beside me and hold the ax up, so we were looking into its cutting edge. "A sharp blade reflects no light."

In the quiet, I felt the brush of his breath on my temple. It stirred my hair, and I wished he would press his lips there, smooth my hair back with his fingers, tell me to hush, that it would be alright. But instead of these impossible gestures, he showed me his ax. The blade was dark, not sparked with light. It was perfectly honed.

"Ageirr thinks he goads me," Heirik said evenly. "He only feeds my power."

A sense of impending violence curled like a cat in the corners of the house. It seemed to stretch itself, then settle down again and fail to stir for hours. On the day Heirik went with Hár to bury Fjoðr, the tension rose, unspoken, around all of us. I was relieved we didn't eat the horse.

AN ACRE

Harvest

SOMETHING SHIFTED, AND THE AIR TURNED TO FALL WITHOUT saying so. It was simply here one day, a cold undercurrent, a shortening of the horizon. Our lazy afternoons picked up a hint of urgency. The dry, warm days would end soon, and when they did, we needed to have as much thread as possible ready for weaving, the most possible fish and roots and berries dried and stored. The pantry full of butter and cheese and skyr.

Fjoðr's death was curiously set aside.

But at times I saw a wild anger in Heirik, barely contained. A hidden desire to kill something.

We worked at putting things away. And as we worked, Betta told me things that weren't entirely useful. She said that Hildur had some beliefs about the chief, and the idea that his brother would be more of a man. Betta also said that vengeance was more satisfying the longer it was drawn out. She looked around, nervous and furtive, when she talked about the chief. At the same time she told me not to pay attention to anyone's fears.

"They're little girls," she stated simply, "Svana especially." Then she added with disdain, "And Hársdottirs."

They were, by my 22nd century standards. Svana and Thora were around fifteen years old. At seventeen, Betta was more mature, by far, even than Dalla Hársdottir who was already a mother four times over. Betta could be more mature than me at times, even though I had so many years on her I would never tell. Not only the thousand and two hundred, but my own twenty-four that I'd actually lived.

"They talk stupid to soothe themselves," she said, "when none of the adults are around."

I laughed brightly at that. Heirik was just over twenty years old himself, and Betta seventeen, but they were truly adults, and Svana was a toddler in comparison.

"What is Svana afraid of?" I asked.

"Her own fascination, maybe," Betta said. "I've seen her wonder about him."

I didn't like that, and I said so.

"Don't worry, Woman. She fears him completely. She's just vain enough to worry that he might break his vow and take her as wife."

She placed a hand over her heart, dramatically, and one between her legs, looking around as though the chief were coming for her. I cracked up—actually rolled on the ground. But something nagged me every time she spoke of Svana. I pictured the girl's tiny teeth at every mention of her name. In a tidy row, pure and dangerous.

The ancestral ax, and the sense of doom, were put away when haying began.

Men gathered in the misty glow of pre-dawn, standing or sitting on logs and rocks, honing blades and breathing the cold breath of morning. A cheerful shink-shinking song of a half dozen whetstones on steel surrounded the back door.

Every man on the farm, from the lowest thrall to Heirik and Hár, had been working every morning from just before sunrise, dropping from exhaustion, getting up and doing it again. They stank. They ate. More than I imagined human beings could eat. They couldn't keep their eyes open any longer than it took to devour what food and ale we gave them.

The women worked too, and any children who were big enough to rake. Dalla and Kit took the tiniest babies tied on their backs. They followed behind the men to sweep the grass into windrows, back and forth each day, turning it until it dried in the sun and could be piled onto horses' backs.

Or so I was told. Betta and I had been left behind, with the little children. For days, she and I didn't work in the fields, and our lives became a continual process of exchanging clothes and turning fish and butter into men. Thralls did laundry, and Betta and I kept the house. We sat outside and made socks in the chilly sun.

Today was the ninth day, and possibly the last.

The stone foundation of the house pressed hard against my back, but the sun was gorgeous and I wasn't going to move. Some part of me felt the light changing, the angle and approach of it, felt the narrowing window of daytime, and instinctively I wanted to keep it. To soak it up and store it like an animal before winter.

Today, the shush of grass moving overhead, and the clack of dry fish like wind chimes made me drowsy. The needle binding in my hands seemed far away. My hands themselves a hundred miles from my mind. Everyone was far down in the valley, the men cutting down fields of grass, the women and bigger children cutting barley or raking, always raking, making hay.

A single wooden pitchfork stood against the wall beside me, a silent companion, left behind while everyone else worked. Perhaps just as grateful for this sleepy moment. I smiled with the irony of traveling to a hard-working farm in order to really take this deep, sun-soaked rest. Outside, amidst the varied sounds of yard and house, not the hum of a refrigerator or bleep of some small technology that spoke up when I was just on the cusp of sleep. I thought of the chill of climate controlled naps. Remembered the sounds of small engines. My mind drifted to a memory, a fight in the tank. The thick, dark ocean in 1900s Atlantic City. Ladies' long dresses whipping the wind. A sharp jolt shot through me, followed by endless falling. I cried out, scrabbled at walls, something to hold. But there was nothing. Only a rending and tearing of something fragile. Sharp steel slicing in my head.

I was returning.

I heard the sizzle of the tank's effort to take me, felt it prying in my brain. Felt the opening of a single moment like an unfathomable flower. I heard someone calling me. Morgan? I heard in my mind, "I'm going home," and the whole idea of home stretched over a thousand years, brilliant and meaningless. I longed for Betta, for Heirik, but they were beyond my reach. I saw the lab, the blinding white of artificial lights in my eyes.

The sadness was brutal, and the acceptance, pining for something already gone.

Nei, I wouldn't accept it. I struggled against the pull of the tank. I thought only of my gorgeous farm, my streams and elf hollows and hay. I reached for them desperately with my thoughts. I didn't want home. I wanted here. This house I sat against.

This house.

An insistent stone stung my spine.

I opened my eyes, and a chicken regarded me, black and yellow and curious, its head jerking around worriedly. Another came, as if to confer on my case. Panting and whimpering, I put a palm to my chest. I felt the hard beat of terror.

Betta rounded the far corner of the house at a run, shouting my name. Her skirts swung out, and dried fish spilled from a basket. Lotta came, falling far behind, little braids swinging. Betta fell to her knees beside me and took my face in her bony hands. Her eyes searched. "Are you alright?"

I wanted to say it was just a bad dream. Já, that's what it was. But knowing where I'd come from, and how I'd gotten here, it would always be more. The missed step I felt upon falling into slumber used to taunt me. When I first came, I wished it was the tank. There were days I'd woken and tapped out over and over to nothing. Now, the falling would feel like an alarm. Every nightmare would be, just possibly, the real thing. My greatest fear, to see the faces of my friends and colleagues, triumphant, the tank come to claim me. I threw my arms around Betta and cried.

"I don't want to go."

"Nei, Ginn." She shushed me and told me, "No one will make you go. Shhhh. Shhhh." She pulled back to look at me with her water-colored eyes. "The chief would not allow it."

"But I'm not even useful." I sniffled. I was fairly bad at every kind of work except the most basic, carrying or scraping things, picking up leaves. "They don't even want me to help rake." The word for *rake* was a howl, bitter and babyish.

Betta sat back on her heels and looked at me frankly. "Honestly, Woman."

I sniffled some more.

"You don't know why we've been left here these nine days?"

Já, I was unfit for real work. Betta must have been assigned here to be with me, to keep me company, take care of toddlers and prepare food for the family, who returned sweaty and filthy from haying. In other words, the work for weak girls who couldn't rake. I wasn't strong and solid like Hár's daughters, not sinewy and tough like Hildur.

Betta shook her head at me. "The chief ordered Hildur that you must stay at the house. You're not to be made to do field work."

Oh.

I looked at her blankly, and so many thoughts reeled and circled. I wanted to live here forever, to live my life with these people, die here someday. And though my heart had known this for a long time, my mind was working to fit this new knowledge in like a boulder through the front door. Heirik had commanded that I not work in the fields. Was he favoring me because he felt close to me, wanted to protect and honor me? The idea of his concern and affection grew warm in my chest. But I could easily be wrong. Maybe he saw me as a guest, living not in our shared home, but in his. Or maybe he just thought I was weak.

That idea made me feel truly worthless. Heirik didn't think I could do it. Didn't he know me? Know that I could be strong? Suddenly I wondered. Could I?

The buzz of flies at the stable came to me, ominous and angry. I could do the work, no doubt better than delicate Svana or wan Dalla. To keep me from proving it, to keep me here at the house, was unfair. I wasn't a princess or ... something weak ... a kitten. I rubbed hard against my eyes and nose, and it stung. My face was sore from crying and must've looked raw. Flushed with indignance. I stood and brushed off my clean skirt for no reason.

All three of us—Betta, Lotta and I—looked up at the sudden sound of hoofbeats. Heirik and Hár came flying so fast on Vakr and Byr, we hadn't even noticed them coming from the field. They skidded to a halt dangerously close to us, full of the pleasure of wind on their sweat-soaked faces and in their hair. The horses' breath came in great snorts, and the animals tossed their heads, the ecstasy of running still upon them. The men dismounted, so deftly and beautifully for such large, and in Hár's case gruff, creatures. They were hot from working with scythes for eight or more hours, clothes sticking to their shoulders, arms, everywhere. They walked toward us, smiling, and I could see a change come over them when they noticed my crying face.

I met Heirik halfway and looked up to meet his gaze. I almost lost my will in the heat of him. He gave it off like a big, radiant heartstone.

"How big is an acre?" I demanded.

His eyebrows drew together, and I steeled myself to ignore their charm.

"Show me here." I gestured toward the valley. Then I saw the coldness begin to settle in his eyes, and I softened and added, "Please, Herra." *Sir*, I called him. *Chief*.

Too late, I realized that was worse. His face closed completely. He was wet and alive and smelled like grass and perspiration and sun, but his face went dead like a stone. A single fly buzzed now, far from the house. Heirik turned and looked in the direction of the homefield and without looking at me, he said "Half the barley." That was an acre. Stiff and formal, he spoke no more words than necessary to answer my question.

It was a vast piece of land to my eye, stretching green and solid and subtly grand. But it was definable. Not entirely too big.

"How many acres does a man cut in a day?"

Heirik glanced at Hár, throwing the question his way, and turned from me. He went to soothe Vakr, removing his saddle and telling him unknown things, thoughts, endearments. I envied the horse, the low murmur of Heirik's voice in his twitching ear. I wanted to know what Heirik told him, when they were like this. I wanted the chief to talk to me that way, gentle and sweet.

He wore two shirts, like always. Seeing him sweat-soaked, it hit me—the reason why—and my heart broke. It was to hide himself.

I remembered I was angry.

Hár answered me. "Depends on the acre." His voice was like rocks, dry and crumbly. "And the man, já?" He winked, then told me seriously. "In good grass, it's a swine's own piss of a job. In sparse land like we did today, an acre and a half, maybe two." He was peeling leather bracers the size of small tree trunks from his sweaty wrists, leaving trails of filth on his skin and shirt. He held them out by the laces, toward Betta, and she took them from him gingerly in two fingertips.

Hár spoke thoughtfully, under his breath, "A long day."

Longer than twelve hours, and even then an acre or two seemed like a lot, like an unfathomable area for a man to clear. These were strong men like none I had known, perhaps not taller, but bigger by far. They could do brutal work. I looked out over the land that rolled away at my feet, and I pictured Jeff out in that field, the one Heirik had just shown me, working with his body instead of his mind. I saw his lovely blond hair pulled back, his tall frame—taller by far than any man here—out in the high grass. He spent his time in icy seclusion or a cozy cafe. But in fairness, I thought he would, yes, he'd be able to cut a field. It was amazing what we could do if we had to.

Or if we were challenged.

Betta looked at me sideways, a growing wariness in her features.

Hár patted Byr on the rump and the horse trotted off to find its own rest. Then he barked at Betta. "Woman, is there no drink?" With a swirl of skirts, she turned to hurry ahead of him and they disappeared into the house. I was alone with Lotta.

"I guess we should feed them," I sighed.

Most of the family and all of the thralls labored all day, but Hár and Heirik had come back early. I supposed they could quit anytime they liked, being such powerful men. Then I realized how uncharitable my thoughts were, and how angry I still felt. These two men gave their blood and flesh for this family, the work of their bodies. It was fair that they should come home, should spend some time reflecting, feeling the warmth of the bath on their stiff, exhausted bodies. Even now, they probably conferred about how many animals could live this winter, how the people could possibly be fed. They held our lives in their hands just as they might hold a scythe blade, turning it over and considering and caring for it.

Still, Heirik did underestimate me. And still, I simmered.

After giving the two of them an unthinkable quantity of ale, Betta locked up the pantry, and she and I took our work outside. Betta looked up at the sun, expertly judging hours and conditions. "We have some time," she said, and she sat down in the cool of the house's shadow and took out her binding. The littlest kids were crossing sticks, smacking them and warbling, tuneless in the breeze. A long-ago memory doing something similar came to me, a glimmer of a former life, here in my hands, but I couldn't catch it.

Betta and I talked about nothing at first. Then small things, like the laundry women and how the dairy was producing. Who the dairymaids were this year. One of them was lazy, she thought, but Hildur never reported it to the chief. The woman would have nowhere else to go, and the season was waning. She wouldn't be hired again next year.

I looped the wool around my thumb and pushed the bone needle. Forward, under, tighten, again and again. Slippery lanolin shone on my thumb where I pinched the yarn. The flies were all buzzing again, and the sound rose like a chant, blanking my mind. Wool on fingers was all I knew. The slick, blunt needle. One of the dogs came and sat nearby, then dropped to its side, four legs stretched out straight in the grass. Its chest rose and fell with big, doggie breaths.

Betta made a choked little sound, and I awoke. She was staring at something, down the slope away from the house. I followed her gaze and saw what she saw.

We were sitting in that spot, where a trick of the landscape revealed the bath, like a sea-green bowl at the bottom of the hill. Heirik was in the water already, sunk down to his shoulders, his sweaty clothes soaking where he tossed them into the runoff to rinse. Hár stood by the water, peeling his filthy shirt off over his head.

Betta watched with wiry interest, strung tight, and I realized she was probably not very familiar with the adult male body. She'd seen boys, já, and probably some men in such close quarters. But now she craved it and studied it. And Hár was an interesting subject, unlike any man I'd ever known. A character from a Viking fairy tale. I could imagine him in armor, a battle cry on his lips, setting fire to some hapless village or abbey. I watched too, mesmerized, as his shirt joined Heirik's in the stream.

He reached to untie the drawstring around his waist, and Betta and I instantly turned away, as one, so fast it was comical. It was quiet for a second, both of us like children caught at something, waiting, and I heard her swallow hard. Then we looked at each other and burst out laughing. There was mischief and amazement in her eyes. She looked delighted and shy, and I wondered how much she knew, how much she had touched or seen of whatever boy she snuck away with.

"A man's body is a wondrous thing, já?" I asked her.

Her eyes widened. "You have seen a man ... that way?"

My stomach dropped for a second. I'd forgotten to be unsure, to pretend I didn't remember.

"No, just at the baths ..." I stumbled over the familiar guilt of these small lies. "I've never seen anything like ..." I trailed off. There was a bit of truth to it. I had never seen anything in the world like Hár. Betta didn't notice my fumbling. Her eyes were five minutes in the past, watching again as his clothes came off. Almost inaudibly, she agreed. "Fearsome, já."

ALMOST EVERYONE WAS ASLEEP, THROWN ACROSS THEIR BENCHES with great abandon after a grueling day's work. A few of us who hadn't worked so many hours—or those of us who'd cooked and watched children and done nothing as hard as haying—lingered by the heartstone after evening meal. Even Heirik, who sat back away from us, sharpening a two-foot-long blade like a silver curve of death.

I'd proposed a bet, and people talked in warbling tones of rising excitement about it. It would be like this. It would be like that.

"Please, I want to do it," Ranka begged.

"You're too little, Child." Betta told her. "The blade alone is as tall as your chin."

"Já, young maid," Hár told her. The he widened his eyes with exaggerated concern and leaned in to grab her braids in one big hand. "Girls your size have been known to cut their braids clean off and leave them for the cows to eat." He tugged on them, and she giggled with bright hilarity.

"Nei," he went on. "What you ladies need for the job is someone delicate. A tiny bird like my Thora." He cast his eyes to where his unwitting daughter slept. She and Grettis hadn't even taken the time to close their curtains. They lay sprawled in a plump, snoring tangle of blond hair and dirty linen. Thick ankles seemed to poke out everywhere.

"Nei matter," I broke in. "I'm the one who will do it. It's my bet."

Hár turned serious, and he spoke to me like a caring uncle, gently breaking bad news. "It is no real bet, Woman. It just is not how we do it, if we can—"

"—The maids will cut the grass." Heirik's voice was even and low, but it cut through our chatter with the ease of a thrown knife. We all turned to him. He sat a few feet away, swiping at his blade, setting off rich sounds of whetstone on steel.

"Ginn and one other," he stated. Then to me he said, "If you cut an acre by noon, I will work for you the rest of the day."

In the shocked stillness, my head swam with thoughts. But my voice didn't waver.

"Good," I said.

I didn't betray the gorgeous feeling it gave me, the notion of Heirik doing my bidding, the idea of him being mine for one afternoon. Grave doubts came, too. Would it be too hard? After all my courageous talk, could I really do it? I had no idea how to cut grass.

Heirik offered more. "If the rest come behind you and rake so the hay is drying by nightfall, I will give a party." His eyes flicked briefly to his uncle, his smile a brief trick of the light.

Voices rose again around the fire. Other terms were discussed, having to do with Hár making dinner and washing Thora's socks. I concentrated on nothing else. He'd said yes.

It was just a half hour later when I went to the mudroom, searching for an extra cloak for sleeping. The wool was all stiff and cold, and a miserable chill seeped into the soles of my feet, right through my socks, climbing my ankles. I reached for a sheepskin and started to turn back into the house when a big weight slammed against the back door. I jumped and clasped a hand to my mouth, stifling a yelp. I stared at the door, frozen in place, the sheepskin clutched to my chest.

There were voices then, Hár and Heirik. They were fighting, and not just arguing. Someone had been thrown against the house.

Hár's words were like knives. "That one does," he said forcefully. There was a long space of quiet, and I imagined them both catching their breaths, gazes locked. My own breathing was ragged, my eyes riveted to the door as though I could see through it and into the heart of their argument. When Hár spoke again it was almost tender. "Take her somewhere," he said. "Away from here."

Her.

He had to mean me.

Hár was telling Heirik to send me somewhere away from Hvítmörk. And though it was in a loving voice, it was very much a command. I'd never heard anyone talk to Heirik this way. I had to know his reaction, but the chief didn't answer in words. In the thick silence, behind the muffling heaviness of dirt walls and wood door, I had no way of guessing what he thought. If he nodded in ready agreement, if he smiled or glared or stalked off into the night I didn't know. Neither of them came inside.

Later, huddled under cloaks, I told myself that Heirik wouldn't do it. Betta had said he wouldn't make me go, and she knew these things about him.

I rested my forehead on her bony back and forced myself to believe.

Hár handed me the scythe. I let it settle in my hand and tried not to stare at his black eye.

The wood was almost plush in the crook of my thumb, where many hands had held and swung this tool before. It had a strange, uneven weight. But even as it was odd, it was elegant too, and lighter than I expected. Magnus showed me how it worked, how its awkward shape was made perfectly for its single task. I stood it on end, and the blade curved just over my shoulder.

"Not near your face, Maid." Hár told me, gruff and irritated. "Unless you want to live with one ear."

What did he care? He wanted me gone.

I looked for Heirik and found him standing at the top of a small rise. He talked to the boys, his arms crossed, unworn gauntlets hanging from one hand. From far away, I could see his shoulders slightly raised and hunched forward in frustration. When he turned and his eyes caught mine across the distance of field, he didn't melt into a smile. He looked through me.

His open sleeves moved in the breeze, and the grass spoke all around me like a thousand whispers. *Take her somewhere.* I remembered Hár's words from last night. *Away from here.*

My skirts swished around my ankles as I walked up the hill. I watched the swirl of bone-colored linen billow out and return with each of my steps. A house dog nosed at my hem. It walked beside me, oblivious, panting. When the dog and I crested the hill, I saw the field we would cut.

The grass spread out tall and uneven below me, reaching until far away, it ended with a ragged edge defined by a stream. Beyond that sprawled a rocky strip, and then the forest's edge. It was somewhat sparse, but not embarrassingly thin. Heirik had chosen a loose and natural acre for me and Thora. An acre that would be honorable to cut down, and yet feasible over the next six hours. A thoughtful choice for a man who was so angry and vicious today.

A dark bruise mixed with his birthmark along his jawline, not quite hidden by his beard. He didn't even speak to me, just pointed with his chin at the field and turned to go somewhere, I had no idea where. He wasn't going to stay.

And so I cut the grass.

I did what Magnus had shown me, stepped into the field and moved the scythe with my hips. It was awkward, and after a few swipes my shoulders bunched up around my ears. "You're cutting with your arms, Woman," Magnus told me. "You'll tire yourself out. Let your back loose." Poor Magnus was always trying to get me to lighten up. While I clutched desperately to horses' backs and scythe handles, he walked beside me and told me over and over to let go. It made me snicker and smile, and my shoulders relaxed just a little. My hips took over more of the job.

Soon the light scythe weighed more than a boulder.

Thoughts drifted by and away, of men and machines, drawing me out of the physical pain. Images of the grass house turned to the white and gleaming lab, the towering buildings that would rise right here where I toiled, and stretch all the way to the sea. I couldn't shake thoughts of the stark future. I wondered if I'd see that world again, against my will.

I ducked my head to wipe my sticky forehead on the shoulder of my dress.

I breathed in farm smells, the land and plants and dog. So familiar now. I focused on my breathing and after a while a great pressure eased and the rhythm of hard work began to soothe me. The lab vanished, and I saw the heartstone, the emerald hills and birds in the hollow. Memories of the rushing stream. Finally, I let myself go. Once my mind stopped circling so tightly, I felt my body instead. I felt the sense of using the powerful muscles of my legs, felt the ease of fluid motion, and I knew that somewhere up on that hill Magnus could see that I'd gotten it. I had changed.

Sharp blades of grass whispered around my shoulders in some places. In others, the spears gathered child-high around my waist.

I fell into a dreamy, sensual rhythm. The sun climbed higher and kissed the back of my neck, and I found my eyes closing even as my body continued to work. Finally, I thought of nothing but the song of grass and flies and a snuffling behind me. I broke my cadence to turn and look, and the house dog was with me, smelling the newly fallen grass. Behind him, Ranka and her mother followed with rakes. In the stillness of the field even Ranka didn't speak. I turned to my task.

Maybe an hour later, maybe a lot less, I started to really hurt.

Pain came to press like a palm against the small of my back. A suggestion first, like a lover guiding me from a room. It grew until soon I could think of nothing else. I raised my eyes to the gray and lavender sky, listened for simple sounds, but the fire in my spine got worse. Blisters—or the places they would come to be—seared my hands. Dry, red spots burned where the wood twisted as I swung the handle. I shifted my grip and messed up everything, my rhythm, technique, my will itself. I didn't know how I would finish.

I would, though. There was no question. So I cried a little and kept on.

The men had done over a week of this, nine long days of muscles howling with pain and only the prospect of more and more and more. Now they were done, and watching us. Many of them sat on the hill with cups of ale, and I could feel their amused and doubting gazes. Screw them, I thought, and laughed at myself.

I came to water.

The sluggish brook stood, almost still, across my path and down the slope of field. It came so suddenly, I stopped and stared at it. Shoots grew tall and thick from its banks and its sludgy bottom.

The soggy roots made cutting difficult, a sopping mess, everything bending and folding and swaying but never coming clean off. I put my back into it harder, and my whole body sang with pain. But I could see the edge of the field now, not far beyond the brook, and I bent in deep and solemn concentration. I would get there. I gathered big bunches of waterbound roots, cradled them in the arc of the blade and pulled, dragging everything out. Clearing out the water. It began to trickle and move, and then flow again. I cut through everything, and when I was done I stepped over to the opposite bank. With one last big swipe, I came through into a vast space.

No grass waved beyond my feet. I'd reached the rocky swath at the other side.

The land was dark gray here, scoured by time and weather and strewn with pumice. I looked a mile out, my eyes struggling to adjust to the distance after staring so long at my own hands. There, just beyond the windswept nothing, the white woods began in all their misnamed, colorful splendor. Apricot, bronze and black glowed against white papery peels. Green leaves rustled, and dusty juniper crept underfoot.

I wanted to go to it. I wanted the forest. I dropped my scythe and started to walk away from everything, into the land.

"Woman, where are you going?" Thora's voice called me back.

Our task was done. I liked the silence and completion of the moment, so I let Thora return ahead of me. I stayed and watched the woods, and I thought for a second that I saw the movement of animals there in the short brush, maybe a tail, a flash of silver. I felt the breathing of fox and bird, but I didn't see anything. After a minute I turned back, to walk through my cut grass and back up and over the slope toward home.

Sweat turned clammy and cooled between my breasts, and I plucked at my dress. I stood up straight to try to ease my back, and it spasmed instead, stealing my breath. I walked on. Soon I could hear voices rising, men and boys shouting, women's scattered words higher and brighter, boisterous laughter.

On the rise, Hár stood like an amused mountain god, arms crossed tight, mouth upturned under his bushy gray beard. Away from his uncle, Heirik crouched down on his heels, gravely watching me come up from the field. In the peace and solitude and repetition of the cutting, I'd forgotten both men. I'd forgotten the crimson and blue that bloomed under Hár's eye and lined his nephew's jaw. The old man's words in the night rushed back. Now, both men watched me.

I walked with even strides, the scythe flung carefully over my shoulder like the body of a felled animal.

I won. I owned this field. My skirts dragged behind me, rustling and snagging on the fresh cut stubs of grass that I had made. By the time I reached the family, I felt no exhaustion or pain.

I uncurled my hand from the scythe where it gripped like a claw, and handed it to Hár. I ducked my head, a sarcastic bow to the great man. He took the blade, stared at me for a moment, and then burst out laughing. Uproarious, amused, happy.

I walked away fuming, and suddenly right before me stood Heirik like a turf wall. I couldn't get away from them. The men of this family were everywhere in my path.

"You did well," he said, and even his voice didn't soothe me. Even his praise—the words I thought would feel so good, the words I thought would make vindication well up in me like a warm sea—just washed over me. Grass stained my red hands. I could feel green on my face and in my nose and lungs, mixed with dirt and dried sweat. Blisters rose. Pain flared in my spine. And I was satisfied and strong. Whatever he said didn't matter.

"I am yours, then."

Except that, maybe.

He didn't look inviting or wicked or even kind. But gods, those words! I was like butter over a flame.

"For the rest of the day," he told me. He raised his hand as if to touch my hair, tuck it behind my ear, but he stopped himself and crossed his arms.

I sighed, a single syllable taken by the breeze. And in a moment all of it—the work of so many hours swinging the scythe and cutting and moving, always forward, always onward through the massing of green on every side, the thoughts of the future, fear of leaving the farm—it all settled in my legs and they went out under me. I sat undaintily in a heap at Heirik's feet. I looked up at him and shielded my eyes from the sun that came from above and behind him. I saw nothing but the shadowy features of the chieftain, quiet, unknowable. Mine for the rest of the day.

I looked out at my field instead. My acre. Sparse, inexpertly done, but all cut. Women and girls made long rows of grass, their rakes a far off scraping.

"That's right, Chief," I told him. "You are mine."

Drying grass fell from my forehead when I dropped my hand. It was everywhere in my braids. I shook my head to dislodge the greenery and confusion, but thoughts of leaving Hvítmörk wouldn't stop. I could no more ignore them than I could the burning of my split palms.

FLOWERS & FLAME

"If you want the men to have good breath this winter, you need enough roots."

Heirik said this with finality, as he piled a saddle and empty baskets on Drifa's back. He would work for me for the rest of the day, but he had chosen the job and ordered me to come with him to harvest snowblooms, away from prying eyes and joking men. My pure desire and delight at the notion of being alone for the afternoon was tempered by the throbbing pain in my back and his terrible mood. I felt damp and stinky. He hadn't given me any time to do more than wash from a bowl and loosen my hair. I had on Betta's clean dress, and it swept the grass, an inch too long on me. My stomach felt like something was slowly listing and sinking inside it.

"Fine, Herra," I said. *Chief*, I called him. *Sir*. And then I bent to whisper nonsense to Drifa, to calm and settle her. In the way of animals, she'd absorbed Heirik's tension, and her white tail twitched. She took a few steps in place, adjusting herself whenever he touched her. He stopped short of picking me up by the waist and planting me forcibly on her back.

He went to get Vakr and I waited, unsure of whether I should even move. In the silence of my indecision, I heard Magnus whisper, inside one of the animal stalls. "The chief is eager for an early snow." I heard a girl's voice, an urgent shushing. Was it Betta? Hidden with him in the dark? Was he her secret crush? Nei, he wasn't old enough for her. And besides, she wouldn't sink to taking kisses in the stink of a stable. Not Betta.

The chief came alongside me on Vakr, then. "We'll go," he told me. I barely caught him as he rode away.

Dead silent, we walked near one another and yet apart. I could count the sighs and footsteps of the horses. The only sound that joined them was the satiny stirring of the leaves where they curled on their branches. It was a rushing sound like water, and yet dry as fall.

With long moments to think along the way, Magnus's words caught up with me. An early snow? He was joking, somehow, about Heirik taking me to the woods, but I didn't know what he meant. I glanced at Heirik, and thanked the gods he hadn't heard the boy. In his mood, I imagined Magnus would be walking around without an arm.

We rode for more than a half hour, around the far side of the woods to a place where none of us ever went to forage. The trees were thicker here, the snowblooms opening around each one like a knee-high skirt of white and electric green. The blooms ran wild and untouched, thriving, each cluster of blossoms almost as big around as my head.

Heirik tramped on them with ease. He left Vakr by the edge of the woods and plunged in.

I left Drifa and followed him, pushing through the densely packed birches at the forest's edge. I thought he would deftly turn and duck to move like a quiet animal through the forest, but nei. He attacked it. He swatted big branches—the size of small trunks themselves—out of his face, and let them whip back once he passed. A papery rain of leaves fell on me as I came along behind.

His ax, *Slitasongr*, rested at his side, secure in his belt. He was the one who'd picked this lonely place. Ill and silent dread came as I looked at that gorgeous ax. I wondered, in the way of strange, sudden thoughts, what it would feel like if he killed me. Alone here, miles away and twelve hundred years from help. There were times when I watched him and spoke with him and he was so familiar. I often felt like he was no different than me, or more, sometimes like he was part of me. Then something would remind me of what he was. A creature so wholly different.

Heirik turned sideways to push through the spaces between trees, while I walked through with ease. The birches reached several feet above Heirik's head. Still, they felt sheltering and sky-high. Their leaves filtered the light and formed patterns on his gold and brown wool. Shifting dark smudges against the soft yellow tones. Sparks of light caught his hair. We came to what he must've thought was a good place. To harvest, yes. We could have done it anywhere, but here was where he ran out of steam and stopped. He dropped baskets on the ground and shears fell out, lost among the brush.

The angelica sprawled here, searching for sun, rather than towering in thick stands like it did in open land. The forest felt cool in a lovely way, under the canopy, not cold but fresh.

Where we usually harvested, closest to the house, the women showed me how to keep the plants flowering, always just one more time before autumn, when we would let them go to seed and collect the tiny brown kernels for even more uses. In fall—now, I thought with a start—we would take the seeds and roots. I supposed it didn't matter out here in the far woods. There grew enough blooms to make mouthwash for a horde of Vikings. But still, I knelt among the flowers gently and showed Heirik how to cut the tops where the branches met, so the plants could live over winter and bloom again in spring.

He crouched down in the brush. He took his knife from his belt, strangled a thick handful of plants and beheaded a dozen at once.

"Slow down, Chief," I said playfully. His eyes darted to mine, angry, like he intended to reprimand me.

The intention died, though, when he met my eyes. After a long morning of tension and acrimony and confusion, Heirik finally really looked at me, and he gave something up. Something that had been gnawing at him all day. He was so tired from it. He seemed to fall into my eyes like a child into a nest of blankets, and I gathered him with my gaze. I wished I could gather him in my arms, too. I swallowed, gripped my knife handle.

Looking around, I finally saw where he'd brought me, alone among the twisting branches and rambling autumn snow.

It became hard to talk. "They won't flower again if you do them that way. For two years." I showed him, again, the little vees where the stems branched off. "Cut above." I held one stem and pointed, and he took it from me. Our hands were close together, our knees almost touching where we knelt.

"You don't remember anything," he stated without looking at me.

My heart stopped for a second. Whenever anyone questioned me about my past, the word stranded sprang to mind. It became harder and harder to lie. The chief could keep me or send me away as easily as changing his shirts.

Today I was more scared than ever, the horrible crunch of bodies against the back door still vivid in my mind. Hár and he had fought about sending me away.

Oh.

They'd fought.

A tangle of logic that had been confused in my gut all night and all morning started to come undone. So slowly, I could almost feel it unwind. Hár had told Heirik to send me away, and Heirik had fought him. He hadn't agreed. He wanted me to stay.

Heirik wasn't mad at me. He was mad at his uncle.

Relief felt luscious, stealing over my skin like silk. I felt so stupid for being afraid, felt remorse for that tiny part of me that watched his ax, as though he might ever hurt me. A realization came, that maybe he'd never been alone like this with a woman. Maybe he wasn't angry at all. Just terrified.

The pain of lying to him was always quick and brutal. "I remember scents and colors," I offered. "Sometimes."

"Já?" He seemed surprised. I hadn't mentioned such a thing before.

I treaded lightly. "The color of a dress, my hands in water." I looked down at my fingers and thought of vents moving cleansed air. They were true memories, sure, but with each one I spoke I felt dirtier, a liar. I couldn't tell him what I did really remember. A great many things. Blinding light that shone even in the evernight. Buildings so tall you could live on top of a thousand other people. Farms as flat as wall screens. Writing behind my eyelids. So many changes of clothes, you didn't wear the same thing once all week.

With drawn brows and silence, I must have looked upset. "It is alright, Ginn," he said. "You don't have to remember anything." His voice promised me safety, a shield against the vast unknown.

I wanted him to hold me. In the cramped longhouse, people touched me all the time, but not with affection. Only Betta really hugged me. I wanted Heirik's arms around me, just tenderly, let alone with desire. I thought of him living with that same absence and longing, for ten years or more. Since his mother's death. A lifetime.

"What do you think about?"

He spoke like he was coaxing me, drawing me back.

It was an interesting question. Without a past, what would I have to ponder or dream about? This morning in the field, I'd thought about nothing for big swaths of time, and it was so satisfying and good. It would be easy to live that way, if I really had nothing to reminisce about or regret. Sometimes like today cutting the grass, or sometimes when I rode on Drifa or slipped a needle through greasy wool, I gave in entirely.

"Learning what's in front of me," I told him. What I thought about was just that—doing each one thing.

And him. I thought a lot about him.

I'd had the feeling before when I was alone with Heirik, that I could tell him the truth. He would know me, and he would believe and forgive me. But when I opened my mouth to start, I was overcome with the fear of losing him and everything I had here. If he thought I was insane, what would happen to me then? What did they do with crazy women here, in this time and place? I might lose my home, let alone my tenuous hold on his heart.

Heirik was fast becoming precious to me. More profound than that, it was like he was becoming my house itself, my home, my blood. He was so known to me, from the moment I saw him, like knowing my own body. And I wasn't even giving him the chance to really know me. I wasn't brave enough to tell him who I was. I hid myself every time we talked. Now, I wanted to give him something. Some safe piece of my heart.

"I think about voices."

He stopped cutting and stared.

"Voices." He thought a moment. "Anyone's?" He asked gingerly, testing my sanity.

"Mmm, all of them really. Sometimes the whole wash of them." I was forehead deep in stems and thoughts of the field came to me, the entirety of the voices of the longhouse making a path like my scythe blade. "Just … how we all sound when we talk. The men coming in from the fields, from far off sound like sheepdogs."

He gave a soft and amused "já," clearly thinking about it for the first time.

"And then when you think about a single person's voice …" I hadn't shared even the most basic thoughts about speech with anyone. I hadn't talked about anything I loved in so long. I started bubbling like Ranka. "A word can be the same. You and I can say 'hestur' já? But our voices add depth and meaning …" I was talking so freely about words coming from another's chest. He and I could say anything, and it would never be the same. He was a man, half a foot taller than me, with Viking bones—the whole instrument on a different scale than mine. "Our bodies," I started to explain. "Our mouths …"

I saw him and trailed off.

He was sitting up on his heels in the plants, watching me from under dark lashes. His hair was tangled across his forehead. It was hot in the woods, and I wanted very much to take his hand and press his fingers to my lips.

"Munni?" The word for *mouths* slipped from his tongue, a burning ember.

I continued, trying to recapture the conversation. "How we hold ourselves," I said. "What we do with our hands."

Gods, everything I said seemed lascivious. I bent to my job, turning away from him to sever a dozen heads.

When I turned back, he had stopped helping me entirely. Not that he'd been doing much anyway. Now he leaned back against a tree, sitting on a crush of underbrush, his shirts loosened at his throat. He had one knee bent, his wrist resting on it, knife dangling casually from two fingers. He looked off into the thickness of trees.

"Your voice …" he said. He tested the knife's balance, shifting it between his fingers. Hesitated for just a moment, intent on the far woods. "Your voice is deeper than it should be."

I whispered back, my heart beating hard. "Than it should be?"

"A strong voice for a small one like you."

The way he said *small one* sounded like a love song. Like a hundred confessions. The way his voice descended, softened, cradled the words. He'd been listening to me, looking at me. I stood inches over the women of his family, and still he found me little. The way he said litla, it was like he held me gently in his hand and was in awe of me. Small but strong.

He lowered his eyes, seeming surprised by himself. I could see his realization dawn. How very much he had revealed and offered with those simple words. Then he looked up, direct and challenging, and I wondered what he expected. For me to cringe, or bolt. Or perhaps he hoped for the same from me, yes.

"Your voice …" I told him. But in a thousand years I could never describe the voice that had soothed me, steadied me amidst constant fear, that I listened for every morning and fell asleep to every night. The voice I responded to with a rush of blood, my lover's voice. I could never explain what it did inside my chest, throughout my body every time he spoke. "Your voice changes," I started. "It's rough like black sand, and then it turns warm and smooth like melting butter."

"Butter?" He laughed. Rare big laughter like a flash of wings disturbing the brush.

"Mmm hmm." I casually watched my own fingers and shears working, not meeting his gaze. I wanted to give him more than that, more than an image that made him laugh. I wanted to return just what he'd given me, small one, the sound of his heart. My voice became very deep, hoarse. "Sometimes when you say certain things, your words turn to honey."

He asked immediately. "What certain things?"

I'd worked myself into a thicket of snow blooms, and my hair tangled in them. What certain things should I admit? The umbels made lace shadows on the backs of my hands. I felt a little lost.

"Ginn?" He called me back.

"Já," I looked at him, still a little gauzy headed. "That …," I told him. "When you say my name."

The woods had finally relaxed him, and his big body was natural and poised now. The deepest blue ran through his hair, encouraged by filtered sun and shadows. He watched the knife turn in his fingers, then let it slow and stop.

"You are all flowers," he said. I was confused, then realized he meant my hair. I reached a hand up and found that stems and bits of blossoms stuck there.

"Oh." I picked out sprigs.

"—Leave them." He demanded, and then he softened as he always did for me. "Like the grass was, after the field."

Gods, he had been watching me, closely today, liking and memorizing what he saw. A gorgeous reaction to this came from deep in my body. I sat, settled in the brush like he was, my foot just an inch from his. I shifted, and he did, and our boots touched.

The pendant at his throat captured a bit of sunlight and I tried to focus on it.

"What is that?" I gestured at my own blushing throat.

"This?" He touched the silver, surprised, and while he answered he slipped his fingers absently under his collar and left them there. It was so raw, him touching his own body, I wanted to cry.

"You don't remember Thor's hammer."

I did, but it was easy to shake my head dumbly, unable to take my eyes off his open shirt and hand.

"Every boy makes his. In our family."

I conjured a vague picture of young Heirik, eight years old, hammering away at a hot piece of silver. "It's beautiful," I murmured without meaning to.

He laughed. "I wouldn't say that much."

"Okay, then," I said, laughing too. "It is … well placed." I blushed at my own words and hung my head.

His voice drew me back. "Don't go," he said, hushed, but urgent.

I looked questioningly at him, and he went on. "You will stay at Hvítmörk, já?"

Of course I would.

I got smoothly up on Drifa, feeling graceful, like I always did when I rode her. She smelled furry, her hair pungent in the waning sun. A good smell. Not like the sharp tang of a goat. I lay down along her neck, my face turned toward Heirik, where he stood speaking softly to Vakr.

I didn't want to leave the woods behind. I wanted to stay lazily draped over Drifa's body forever, watching Heirik talk to his horse, the orange light of day's end filtering through the trees behind him. Vakr was one of the only living beings he touched with affection. He was part of his soul, in that way that only an animal can be. Heirik's whispers to him were a private moment, and he'd allowed me into it.

I'd taken some flowers, not for tea, but for prettiness. A bouquet of long snowbloom stalks hung from my hand, resting along Drifa's leg. When Heirik looked up, he saw me and froze. He looked disconcerted, almost scared, and it worried me. Again, I'd done something weird. When any of them looked at me that way, I never knew what it was, but it was always something slightly off, the way I tied my shoes or didn't know how to hang a fish from its head. Was it the way I rested so languidly on Drifa? I sat up.

Heirik shook the look from his eyes, and in one fluid motion got up on Vakr and pulled alongside on my left. We rode home in a honeyed silence. With a slow gait, as if neither of us wanted to get there.

The sun fell rapidly as we walked, and it was evening when we rounded the woods and were almost in view of home. My heart leaped with sudden fear—a giant billow of gray smoke smudged the sky. There was a fire!

Heirik was not worried.

"Wood's bane," he said with a note of resignation. *Fire*. "Many are here, then." He faced me with an unusual gleam in his eyes, apologizing, anticipating. "We stayed out as long as we could."

Many people were here? Around a fire.

And then it dawned on me, and I felt dumb and a little used. I was nettled, and my words flew out in a mix of future- and now-language. "You were throwing a party anyway," I stabbed at him. "Whether we cut the field or not."

"Já," he smiled at me, then laughed a little, then more. "You are like a lamb after its first shearing." I did feel lamblike, peeved, naked. But he was so amused, I finally smiled and laughed too.

"Throwing a party," he said. "I like that." His voice took on the smallest note of bitterness, like a tiny sour berry between his teeth. "A spear at my own people."

I gazed out at the smoke rising from the yard in gray billows against the dark sky. "It won't be fun, then?"

"Oh, já, wild," he told me with a small, strange smile. "But for me, heiðr."

It was a simple word, but he said it with a nuance I hadn't heard in my sterile language lessons. It meant honor, in the sense of duty. It was his job to be generous. That was what I knew. But hearing it from him, in the voice of a real Viking chief, it meant far more. It encompassed all the people who gathered just out of our sight, where that smoke originated, all waiting to revere him. He was honor bound to give a party. But he would also be honored. And it was his due. Betta had said he took it freely.

He should, I thought. He worked hard and got little in return.

Drifa moved closer to him, so close that I felt we were together under a great wing. I viewed the house and party the way I thought he did. I started to understand something I'd seen and heard before, but hadn't got. An honor-feeding. A generosity that in itself was a reward, for all that he forewent and did for these people.

Men stoked a big fire. They gathered in the yard, boys and young men I'd never seen before, two dozen at least. Close to the blaze, a few poked at it with what looked like spears. The pyre reached as tall as some of the men themselves, and pieces of flaming wood fell dangerously at their feet. Older, bushy-bearded men stood back from the crackling fire, drinking from horns and dark metal cups. All smiling and laughing, demonic in the flares and flashes. The house reflected the fire, its grassy walls rendered colorless gray.

A few women gathered outside the door, one with a lamp shielded in her hand. It flickered softly on her face and lit up her dark blond hair—a cascade that belonged to an angel. She looked like a fairytale princess. It was Dalla! A dark dress lay snug across her bosom, then fell long and loose from just under her breasts. It moved around her legs like water rippled with a breeze. The lamp's light dipped and danced and she cupped her hand tighter to protect it.

She looked up and stared at me and Heirik, and her face changed. Her sisters and Svana stood around her, and they lifted their heads. Alert little animals with ghost-like eyes. Every one of them stopped to watch us ride into the yard. Around the fire, the men's voices stopped. Bonfire and lamp light raged on their frozen cheeks.

I turned to Heirik for some explanation, and he was a different man.

He sat on Vakr's back with a different confidence, tinged with self-importance. Almost arrogant the way he held himself.

He rode slowly into the yard and nodded to the men at the fire, to the women by the door, and in the space of a breath and as if they were one, they dropped to their knees. Everyone, even Dalla. Even Hár.

Oh.

Betta's words cut through my shock. I'd known Heirik only here in his own home with his nearest family. It was true, I had not met the chief.

Drifa walked slowly among men and women. So far above them, I noted each man's messy hair or balding head, women's braids and kerchiefs. I could feel their awe and curiosity reaching for me like fingers. And as we passed by, each of his people were released. Like a great wake closing behind us, they began to stand and rustle about and murmur questions.

Dumbstruck, I slid off Drifa. Heirik motioned to a boy who took our horses and saddlebags with the few leaves and flowers we'd cut. The chief nodded to me and was gone, as he so often was, into the back mudroom, taken by the dark of the house.

I had not bowed to the great man, but instead had ridden by his side. He'd led me to this yard without warning. He didn't do things accidentally. He wanted to show me this.

Like hurled rocks, it hit me—a feeling that just moments ago I thought I'd understood. Now, I felt it truly. Beyond the responsibility and loneliness, laid a sense of entitlement and superiority. He wanted me to feel what it was like, hovering over this big family and being adulated.

I curled up inside, confused. I was glad that for this moment, the chief was respected. Maybe even in some twisted way, he was loved. But for now, my private Heirik was gone.

With Heirik's passing, everything erupted. Shouting, drinking, fluttering around with lamps and jabbing with spears. Gruff singing began around the fire, crazy flames leapt. Sounds and images whizzed past me like terrible birds. Giant men roaring in the yard, plain women rendered gorgeous, my cozy house gone mad.

I was a mess, in Betta's everyday dress sweaty from haying, smudged and sprigged with bark and flowers. I bunched it in one hand, and lifted it up so I could walk with dignity from the stables to the house. I felt the sting of scrutiny. I felt exposed, raw and inadequate.

I made it to the back door and roughly pulled Svana aside. "Why do they stare?"

She pulled back from me, as though I were deranged. "The chief is home," she said, as if that were explanation enough. It was clear she was hiding something.

"Nei, what else?" I kept at her.

Demure and pale, she answered. "You rode with him." She pointed at the flowers in my hand, where I'd forgotten I clutched them. "You looked like his bride."

I stepped back from her, stunned.

I'd assumed people stared at my wild hair and messy dress, my inappropriate filth. They must have been confused by the ugly, messy stranger who dared to even speak to the chief of this superior house. But his bride?

"A woman carries them at her wedding," Svana stuttered out. "She rides her horse with snowblooms in her hand. For many babes." In a second I understood. It was a fertility plant. I blushed in the dark, hoping she couldn't see how very much that idea moved me. She was moved by the notion, too. The fear of such children—and what had to be done to get them—was plain in her light blue eyes, so pale they were lost in this light.

"Not just for children, Little Girl," Betta said breezily, approaching from behind Svana. "For passion." She winked and as always lightened the mood. *Passion* was laced with innuendo, not entirely the same as the future word, and when I got it I put a hand to my forehead and closed my eyes in mortification. The flowers weren't just fertility plants, they were aphrodisiacs too. Was Heirik more devious and less shy than he seemed? He'd been driven by something today. Agitated and forceful and mad at Hár. And then, oh Gods, he'd taken me out to join him in a bed of white suggestion. I'd dropped to my knees with him there and cut the flowers all around us. I remembered Magnus's words, then, about the chief's eagerness for snow.

Betta had warned me to hide my heart, and I had miserably failed.

I was suddenly sick of it all. Of Betta's pronouncements. Of prying eyes. Sick of every person who knelt before me when I entered this yard at Heirik's side, and now undoubtedly talked behind my back.

Something transpired in the flowery wood, between him and me. Heirik confessed he was drawn to me, just as much as I was to him. We had felt the flowers' call, and we'd ridden home in a sex- and hope-infused quiet. We'd stood together sharing thoughts of duty and home, before braving this yard full of honor-feeders. I would never be sorry for going to the woods with him. For coming home looking like his bride. Under the grass and dirt that stained my skin, I glowed with satisfaction. And anticipation for what would come next.

It wasn't exactly what I'd expected. It was Hildur I heard next, and her voice drove away all sensual notions.

"See that she stays here until she's dressed properly."

She. Meaning me.

I entered the weaving room ready to argue, and I was frozen by the sight. Hildur stood in the center of the room, tight lipped and glowing with fierce pride in a house well prepared. Her hands were folded at her waist, and she was the one who looked like a bride, gleaming tables arrayed around her like a gigantic, flowing dress. She turned in the center of it all, turned to look at Heirik's seat. It was higher than the rest and heaped with sheepskins. And furs! So many lush furs in brown and white and silver.

Benches had been drawn in close, and the big tables taken down from the ceiling. All the seats near to his were laid with furs and skins. Oil lamps lined the tables, casting a surprising amount of flattering light. It was becoming to Hildur, her profile lit with peach-hued satisfaction. Then her eyes found me, and her counte-nance turned sharp.

She didn't say hello. She nodded at Ranka, and the little girl dashed up to me and handed me a bundle of clothing. It wasn't mine. An ice blue dress lay folded together with other undefined things, a froth of linen and something else soft and white. I took the pile of clothes mechanically. This day was too much, and I felt myself starting to slip away. I needed to rest my head and my body.

"The chief will be up from the bath soon enough," Hildur said.

Ranka nodded with importance and led me to a bench. "We will wait here, Lady."

Besides us, the room was empty, barred from the guests just yet.

"Okay," I told her, and I sat heavily and let my mind go blank. She sat next to me and swung her little legs.

While we waited, Ranka took the bundle from me and put it between us on the bench. "Look!" She gave me an orientation to what was included. The dress had a slim waist and long bell sleeves, and the color was unbearably soft, of birds' eggs and newborn ice. The dye was from somewhere else, Norway or farther. The frothy cloth turned out to be a brand new underdress spun of the very finest wool threads, so fine, like a garment made of mist. It had long sleeves and a low cut neck. A wispy and lusciously clean thing. I held it to my face and cried in it, just a little.

"You don't like it?" I looked out from the cloud of fabric and Ranka was watching me, her lower lip actually trembling.

"I love this dress," I told her seriously, with my whole heart. "It's the best dress in all the world."

She smiled then, relieved and beaming.

"I sewed the hems," she said, with a hint of Hildur's satisfaction and pride, and she turned up the edge of the billowing underdress and pointed at her jagged little stitches. "Ma made the blue one longer for you, here."

"It's wonderful," I told her. "I'm just so, so very tired. So confused." I let the fabric run through my fingers.

"Já, well, you are tall, Lady." To her mind, this explained and encompassed everything in the world. To me, it led only to more questions. Were these clothes made just for me? Why?

Then Ranka showed me a piece of fabric like none I'd seen here, made of something other than flax or wool. I ran my fingers down it, wondering if it might actually be cotton. "It's made just to dry yourself, after your bath," she informed me. A towel! Thin and too small, but the only one I'd seen, after months of drying off using my dress itself. Feather-soft and welcoming, it seemed to pull at me, invite me to wrap up in it. It could hide me, like a nest surrounding my new eggshell dress.

When it was safe—that is, the chief was through—we went to the bath. Once I was in the water, Ranka made sure I had the soap and then ran off, leaving me finally, blessedly alone.

The bewildering, back-breaking day had become gray night. I could see more than five stars! Even without full dark, I could make out so many more than that! They massed in the sky, a long held dream. I wanted to rest in the water all night and bask in their sparkling indifference. I wanted to spend luxurious time reliving Heirik calling me small, his words so dark and sweet, his boot brushing against mine. His urgent question—would I stay?

The hot water held me close, and I tried to avoid understanding anything. I tried to just absorb it all and let it go. Hár's frustration, their fight, my triumph cutting the field, Heirik turning comfortable and free in the blooms, flowers of sex and snow all around us. And then the press of people, kneeling before us. I let each thought pass and discarded or savored it in turn.

"Skyndi, Kona!" Ranka startled me. She'd come back from the house.

Her scolding sounded just like Betta, telling me to hurry up. Her hair fell loose, and a little crown of flowers wreathed her head. She held a small torch, and in her other hand she cupped something precious. Her fingers were chubby and tight around whatever it was.

I stepped out of the bath into whipping cold and snatched up the towel. My new shift went first over my head, and for a moment I felt even colder, clammy and miserable. I pulled on the new underdress and then the frost-blue wool. I shivered and counted the seconds until the clothes started to warm me.

With a shaking voice I asked her, "What do you have here?"

She opened her tight hand and in her palm sat dark little shapes, three long ones like tiny spears and a few rolled up, indistinct balls. I ducked to look close and smelled pure summer. The aggressive scent of rosemary and the overwhelming powder of lavender flew up from her palm. It was shocking. I'd come to love the reedy, dirty fragrance of the farm, and this floral blast was like candy.

"You rub it in your hands," she instructed, "and then you put it here." She touched her own temple to show me, and the precious needles and dried up blossoms fell to the stones.

"Nei!" She burst out crying and went to her knees, immediately searching. The little torch wobbled, and I knelt and took it from her.

The poor child was as overstimulated as I was, emotions hanging by a thread.

"Ranka, listen." I lifted her chin. "Shhhh, listen."

She gulped and sniffled. A tear traveled down her cheek.

"We'll find it."

I brought the torch close to the ground and searched while she talked miserably. "They said I could bring it to you if I didn't lose it." Her voice hitched. "Only the ladies can wear it. Only a few pieces. We don't have so much and we don't know when we'll get it again and …" She started to warm to her subject, and soon her tears were almost forgotten. "It's from Alba," she said offhandedly, as though this were the supermarket downstairs from her apartment, not a kingdom so far across the sea that men gave their lives to bring home things like these herbs.

Brosa, the chief's brother came to mind. The indistinct image of a man on the sea, alive and well and heading home.

I saw all three rosemary needles in an instant, slightly darker spears against the night stone.

Ranka combed and settled my hair into two long ponytails that she drew to the front, falling over my breasts and beads. The ends of my hair looked stark white and longer than I remembered, the color almost ethereal against such pale blue. I tried to remember my own icy gray eyes and imagine them reflecting the color of the dress. Strange, I hadn't seen them in so long.

Ranka drew something—a ribbon?—from her belt. It was a fillet for my forehead. Dark blue like the night itself, it shimmered slightly with a single starry thread of silver. She secured it around my forehead just like her own crown, and then she pinched my cheeks hard.

"Ow! What are you doing, Girl?"

"It makes you pretty," she said, and did her own cheeks too.

She headed back into the tunnel and begged me to follow. I told her I'd be right there. I wanted one more moment. I held my hand up to the sky, just to look at myself. The impractical, flowing wrists of the underdress foamed from beneath the woolen sleeve, and wisps of steam rose from my skin, still warm from bathing. I felt like a princess.

IT WAS LOUD AND WILD IN THE YARD BY NOW, AND I PICKED MY way through the grass, anonymous in the chaos. Focused on holding up the silvery blue and ivory dresses, I tried to forget about stares and questions. I trembled with the effort to not stumble, not dirty the hems. The little lamps with their twisted handles were stuck into the walls on the outside of the house tonight, and I came around the corner and almost ran into one.

"Easy, Ginn." Heirik's voice was sudden and dark, almost inaudible under the shouts and songs of the yard.

I looked up and was stunned.

He was Hildur's nightmare come to life. His clothes were the dark blue of ink and wings, with black pants tucked into even blacker boots. His wool tunic swept his knees, long like a kilt. Against the depths of his hair and clothes, his face looked like blood and moonlight, framed by a fur he wore thrown over one shoulder. The lamp highlighted threads that wound through the wool trim around his neckline, where a snow white shirt stood open over a priceless silver torc. Two raven heads met at his throat. Their eyes were of silvery stone like mercury, their beaks open, one biting blood.

A deep black leather belt held a single knife—a short sword that hung across his waist, with bits of silver worked into its black leather scabbard. Not one tool or cup or carving knife hung there. The blade of *Slitasongr* nestled comfortably against his side, the handle hanging past his knee. It brushed against his knee-high boots, crossed and tied with leather bands.

"I …" I couldn't speak.

I retreated a step, the house at my back. "I …" I said again, and then finally forced out a single word. "Hi."

He watched me without speaking, waiting for something, and so I stuttered on. "I don't know where this dress came from." I looked down at myself, touched my bare neckline, and his eyes followed.

"The women of my family," he said. *Oh*. His mother wore this dress. He tossed the words off, trying to sound as if he brought it out for girls to borrow all the time, but his eyes were full of emotion—loss, hope, things I couldn't see or make out in the bonfire. He looked strange and uncomfortable without a knife or ax in his hands. He rested his palm on the hilt of the short sword.

"It is good to see it again," he said, and then added shyly. "On you."

On me.

I was dreaming his words, I had to be. I swayed and fell back against the house.

"Ginn?" He took a step toward me, as though he might reach for me, but he didn't. He reached for the fur instead, the one on his shoulder. He held it out to me, and I took it and wrapped it around my shoulders, pulling it tight. A few hairs moved with my breath and tickled my nose. It had an earthy smell, so different from synthetic flur.

"I'm just so tired," I said. "All these people. I just want to sleep instead."

His brows drew together and his voice became strained. "You will be here," he ordered me. "At this party." Stiff and turning cold. What had I done?

Stupid, stupid, I thought, and I literally put my face in my hands.

He'd dressed me tenderly and lovingly for this celebration, one of the most important nights of the chieftain's year. A party for hay, for fall, for sustenance and plenty. He'd dressed me. Made me pretty. Told me he wanted me to be seen in the clothes of his beloved, lost family. And I'd asked like a child, Do I have to go?

Like a rush of wind, understanding blew in. I saw him honorable and tall in his beautiful clothes, his rich silver neck ring, no need to carry his own cup or tools. He would be served completely, and only needed to adorn himself with his most gorgeous weapons. In a life full of loneliness, this formality was a blessed relief, a pleasure. At every other moment, the family didn't love him. This kind of night was how and when he was adored. And he wanted me to see it, to be part of it. He was shyly proud. Gods, it was charming.

"I'm sorry," I said, and it felt tender and raw. "I am so glad you want me to wear these clothes." I told him clearly, so he would never mistake my meaning. "I feel beautiful in them."

He looked. At the fillet across my forehead, the neckline of my dress, now framed in fur, my arms, the sleeves at my wrists, and down to the puff of underdress peeking from beneath the blue hem at my ankles.

"Já," he said, a faint brush of a word, almost lost in the shouting of men and boys.

He had really looked. I wondered if he knew what he'd done, eying me that way, wondered if he'd ever devoured a woman that way before. It drew me, away from the house and toward him. We were close together, now, so painfully near I thought I could feel his heart beating. His eyes were unreal, the color almost disappearing in the burning of the yard, everything on fire, all around us.

He shook himself.

"Toasts and blessings," he said, and he raised his chin to indicate the house and people.

THE PARTY WAS LONG.

There were more people than I could fathom fitting into the back room, so many honored guests, all touching shoulders. I sat close to the high seat, crushed between a man who stunk powerfully of sweat and a sturdy woman who'd rubbed a handful of rosemary all over her throat. I was introduced to so many men and women, the most important ones from among Heirik's followers, and more, from beyond Hvítmörk altogether. Farmers on their own land, with their own generations of young men and children, their own families and much smaller tribes in tow.

Blond and ruddy and strong, the men wore close-cropped beards and chin-length hair. Their wives wore braids piled in coils. The littlest children were stuffed in the crannies between their parents and grandparents, pieces of bread clutched in their hands or disintegrating in their sleepy mouths. Small girls had braids like Ranka's, falling long over their aprons, the ends rolled up into adorable O-shapes that bounced when they squirmed on their mothers' laps.

And there was Heirik, utterly changed.

I'd never seen the high seat used before. It usually lurked against the wall in the back room, near the big loom, but tonight it had been drawn out and placed at the head of the long tables.

A big wooden bench, its magnificent, high back rolled like an ocean wave, its two armrests carved into polished swells like prows of twin Viking ships. They ended in snarling wolves' heads—the animals most loved by his father's father. The bench was piled with cloud-like, precious furs. The seat was big enough for two people to sit side by side, but Heirik sat alone and literally above us. He scanned the crowd with benevolent arrogance. One of his hands rested absently on a wolf's head.

Even more separate than ever, he was also more assured than I'd ever seen him. Not a hint of shyness remained. It wasn't cold. Not like his usual lock-down of features and heart. He was simply in his rightful place, accepting the adoration and obeisance of everyone around him.

Those who sat very close were the chosen few he spoke with, and he talked easily, without the hesitance I knew. Beyond them, he watched.

The room grew silent.

Dalla carried Heirik the first official drink of the night. She set a glass in front of him on the table, the light wobbling and reflecting in its thick sides. Svana had shown them to me, when her Ma had her clean them—the hrimkaldar. *Frost cups.*

Dalla poured ale from a dark metal pitcher. "Drink of this cup, my chieftain, breaker of rings." She sounded lovely and assured in a way I never could have imagined—an elevated and proud hostess. Though she continued to speak to Heirik, she glanced with terrific grace to include the stifling crowd. "For the good of us gathered here, be generous and mindful with these gifts. Show us strength and desire." The word for desire meant something like *motivation* and *hope.*

He nodded and lifted the cup.

"Herra," she said simply, and with a ripple of watery dress she moved on.

Heirik was already looking elsewhere, listening to the man next to him. He absently made a mark with his thumb against the rim of the glass, like a letter T, and then sipped the ale. I noticed Hildur in the shadows. She nodded firmly to herself, just once, and smiled with satisfaction and pride. Complete indifference from the chief must have meant that the ale was good. He was a contradiction so intense and complex, my head felt full and heavy.

I drew a shawl around me and watched Dalla pour a drink for Hár, and then she and her sisters worked the crowd in some complex descending order until a dozen men had been served, before everyone else broke into a party and started dipping into buckets of ale with their own cups.

Heirik made toasts and thanks to gods, and people sat enthralled, every man, woman and child lulled or shocked into silence by his voice. And I would have watched and listened to Heirik all night, but like a child struggling to stay up too late, my eyes kept closing. Then others toasted too and made speeches until I nodded with tiredness—so, so many things men had to say. Halfway asleep before the party really began, I heard the chief's words again, just their tone and cadence. The answer of cheers, the rise and fall of dozens of voices in a crowded room, raucous, cramped. Words floated free—*fox* and horse and *baby boy.* A sea of language rocked me, and I was held as in the curve of a boat.

I opened my eyes.

There was meat, and I didn't know what it was, but I ate it with vicious appetite. My hunger roused me for long enough to eat chicken and flat bread and dried berries and goat cheese. I drank ale and smiled drowsily at people. I thought maybe I would get up and slowly make my way to my sleeping alcove, crawl in on all fours, press my face gratefully to a sheepskin.

As if I'd called him, Heirik turned to me right then. His gaze was like a hand to my chest, pressing me back into my seat. *You will be here.* I knew this man, and yet Betta was right. I hadn't met him before. He basked in a required kind of love, and took it. Smoothly and gracefully. His fingers brushing against a wolf's teeth.

Between naps, I'd jolt awake and remember to watch Betta. This was my chance to find out who she pined over. Somewhere at this party, there was a young man she wanted. With so little time together, she would have to be with him, smiling with her big teeth, tender and near. But I never caught her talking to anyone special. Not anyone unusual at all.

Ageirr was there. He sat at a fairly prominent place, but I never noticed Heirik look at him. Despite the chief's outgoing and generous expansion, he never included Ageirr or his brother Eiðr in any of his talk of land and laws and far away places, of animals and gods and the coming blanket of snow. The two men ate like all of us did, and they sat in Heirik's circle. Nothing was denied them except for the chief's own gaze. The goat and his ugly little brother closed in on themselves, alone in the midst of everyone else's camaraderie.

I almost felt sorry for them. Almost forgot what they'd done. Especially Eiðr, who seemed like a little boy drawn in the wake of his big brother's stupidity. But images of Fjoðr came to mind, such a wild and blameless beauty, cruelly destroyed, and my throat closed in disgust.

Betta came to my side, and bent to speak in my ear.

"Woman," she said to me, "He's really got you by the throat."

Her violent echo of my thoughts made me cringe. "What?"

She glanced at the rosemary-scented woman, then took my hand and drew me away to the back mudroom door, at the edge of the party.

"The chief," she glanced his way. "You can't take your eyes off him."

I ducked my head, embarrassed, but no one else could hear her. Sounds whirled around us—laughter and chatter and barks and songs—and our conversation was as private as if we'd put our heads together close in the deep woods.

"Really?" I honestly didn't know I'd been staring. "He looks so ..." I pressed my forehead to her sharp shoulder.

"Fierce," she whispered.

"Handsome," I murmured at the same time, and I giggled.

I raised my head and found her looking at me with those clear eyes that changed course as quickly as water, one second insightful and sly, the next incredulous. She shook her head slightly. "He is not a handsome man, Ginn."

"Stop," I told her, and pushed back a sudden sadness in my throat. She pressed her lips together and ducked her head, an apology. In the awkwardness, I changed the subject. "I don't see you looking at anyone."

"That's because you are half blind—" she began, but I'd had enough of hearing about my own infatuation.

"—Nei," I said. "I've been watching you. You haven't talked to anyone special."

Her lashes swept the soft skin under her eyes, and she smiled a close-mouthed smile, secret and pleased. "You look only for what you expect."

"That's not fair!" I nudged her hard in the ribs. "Tell me who he is."

"Shhhh," she hushed me urgently, then moved the subject, always, back to me. "You know, the chief sees you, too. He wants to watch tonight."

"He wants to?"

"You are truly dense sometimes, Woman," she said.

"I am asleep." I swayed with exhaustion.

"Well, you don't see yourself. You look like a handmaiden of the goddess." She brushed a strand of hair out of my eyes. "Your snowy hair, your eyes like driftwood ash. You wear his mother's dress. And Amma's crown." She ran her fingers across the band on my forehead, and her wistfulness hit me like a wave. She motioned toward Heirik. "You should be sitting in that seat next to him."

I glanced at the empty seat by Heirik's side, and her words warmed me all over. I tried to imagine sitting next to him, his wife.

"He can pretend you're just a guest without proper clothing." She went on, telling me no one would comment out loud. "He's careful not to look at you too much. He watches everyone else, how they treat you, where the threats lie."

The threats.

Oh. I looked again and now the empty seat by his side was not as welcoming. The rare lavender he'd given me, the precious clothes, weren't as tender a gesture as I'd thought. I was on display. I stood straighter, anger rising hot in my cheeks. "He's using me as *bait.*" Nettled and surprised, I said it in English.

"*Bait?*" Betta was curious, her lips pursing to push out the foreign word.

"Luring the animals to his spear," I told her. "Drawing them out of the woods."

"Já," she said. "That is exactly what he's doing."

"I don't like it." I felt naked and freezing despite the suffocating press of bodies. Now I saw how every eye shied away from me when I looked, determined to prove they meant no harm. The herb-scented woman had seemed completely uninterested in talking with me. Now I saw that she'd been leaning away, evaluating me out of the corners of her downturned eyes.

Betta maintained the chief had to do this. "There are many here who would be … upset … to see that seat filled."

I drew my shawl tighter. "What if someone does take the bait?"

"Já, well, I imagine you would find Magnus and Hár at your side in a heartbeat."

I followed her glance. *Oh.* Even now, the old man sat so close he could grasp my wrist without turning. Cold crept up my spine. I had no idea all this was happening around me, focused on me, and I felt dumb and self-conscious, imagining how I'd looked all night. Obliviously wolfing down chicken and cheese and dozing in my seat.

"Hár wouldn't save me," I said. "He'd sooner take me to the heart of the woods and leave me."

Betta's brows drew tight together and she shook her head. "Nei, what do you mean Woman?" She was truly surprised. "Gods, he would never!"

But I knew what I'd heard, and the great fear that had been dammed up since last night finally flowed out and I told Betta about the fight I'd heard, the heavy body hitting the back door. I repeated Hár's words. She shushed me and said that I was wrong, that the old man was happy his nephew had someone who cared for him. He wanted Heirik to do just what he had done today—take me somewhere, away from here.

Could it be? That Hár had meant for Heirik to take me somewhere so we could be alone, a man and woman together in the woods?

"Ginn, you must know, this is all new. No one ever thought ..." I let her voice wash over me and tried to believe. All the while, in the back of my mind I pictured me and Heirik the way we could be together if we were nobody special, walking hand in hand in the evening light, feeding each other bread at one of these benches, handing a chunk down to our little son who sat between us. If I was from here and now and he was just a simple farmer.

"I'm sick of people caring what Heirik does," I said, a petulant child.

"Shhh," Betta told me, with that small push of her fingers, a shushing motion. But no one could hear us in the roar of party.

"Woman, listen well." Her whisper was grave. "He is chieftain. Everyone will always care what he does. If you succeed, they will care what you do, too. They'll watch you move and eat and breathe. They'll watch you carry your blood-cursed raven's children, and you will learn to guard your back, and shield your eyes and heart."

I shivered at the center of this cruel and strategic place, a saga come to life.

"Like he does," I whispered.

"Já," she touched the fillet on my forehead again. "He is good at it."

I nodded and sniffed.

"Watch," she continued. "That's still the cup Dalla poured for him."

I forgot sometimes that Betta saw everything, every fine detail and intention. Heirik held the cup absently by its rim, as if he'd forgotten it was there, and through the thick glass I could see it was still half full of murky ale.

"Já well," Betta said at full volume, making a point of no longer whispering. "Too much ale and a man's heart is laid open for all to see."

The men nearest to us laughed at her words. One of them was Hár, who turned in his seat and smiled, a great beautiful smile from behind his silver whiskers that confused me more than ever.

Later I realized how deftly Betta had moved me off the subject of her own heart.

THE MORNING CAME, SOGGY AND SORRY. EVERY WOOLEN BLANKET and cloak, every sleeping body, every beam of the house itself stunk of stale beer and the tang of sweat.

I half crept, half stumbled to the front door to get a blessed breath of air. I picked my way over heaps of sleeping people, women and children lying right on the benches where they'd eaten last night, or sitting up against the walls, leaning on one another. I bumbled across one woman's legs. She started and woke with wild eyes, stared at me for a long moment, then closed them again and pressed her cheek into the wall.

Outside, men roamed the yard and gathered in small groups, grumbling or sitting in stoic misery. Some still slept in the grass, near to freezing, curled around their weapons and drinking horns. A black pit smoked sluggishly where the bonfire had been, and two boys worked at rousing new flames. Lost knives dotted the landscape, and the bones of small animals were strewn across the yard. Bjarni tended to injured men, two who were bleeding, one with something gravely wrong with his arm, another holding his jaw, waiting with his head thrown back against the house.

I'd changed out of the precious clothes last night. I lifted my everyday dress and skirts in my fists to step over weapons and carnage, and as I passed by them, the men and boys stood up taller, nodded to me. They acted deferent and even a little scared, and I tried to imagine my strangeness. Tried to imagine a woman from out of nowhere, spewed forth by the sea and upsetting their universe. I must have looked like the harbinger of doom in that ice blue dress last night, the mother of impending death.

I made my way to the forge. One of my favorite spots, it sat forgotten this morning, high on its rise above the valley. I breathed gratefully, deeply, and looked far out over the woods. This was where I stood the first time I saw Hvítmörk. The first time I looked at Heirik and lied and said I had no story, no why or how. Today, the miles of golden leaves rippled, then began to toss and sway on a breeze that picked up and changed to wind. My dress billowed and tangled around my legs and my hair flew forward and whipped around my face. My eyes teared with the lashing wind and the beauty of the forest.

The chief will think, Betta had said. I saw it now, how for days he'd known he would do all of this. He must have ordered Hildur to get those clothes ready for me. He'd seen an opportunity when I wanted to cut the grass. He took me to the woods to get away while the party gathered, then brought me out dressed as the image of his mother, the lady of this great house, naive, a target on my back.

When we were alone, I knew Heirik wanted me. Now I was certain. But here with people all around, the chief was someone else. By the time the night was through, I couldn't tell whether it was me he wanted or whether by chance I'd offered a change of perspective—the notion that he could take a wife and have children after all, curses and vows be damned. It might be possible, if the clan would let it be. He tossed me out in front of them like a chunk of wood on a fire.

Did it matter whether he wanted me, or he simply wanted a wife?

I sat down on my heels and clutched my stomach. Nei, that wasn't right. I didn't want a practical Viking marriage. I wanted him to love me.

I stood stiffly and said a small goodbye to the woods for now, turning back to the house to help put it in order. I would clean up the yard and feed the hungry people. From up at the forge, the men looked like a straggling mess of dogs, wandering out to sniff every inch of ground, stopping to scratch and barf. Their wives and daughters made their way out of the house now.

It was a Viking farm in the wilderness, a land of gods-driven, ax-hewn justice. I considered taking Drifa and running for the sea, trying to go back to what I used to call home. I thought about riding her with the wind in my hair, thought about the relative safety of the future.

Heirik stepped from the house.

Clean and awake, he was dressed in his work clothes with his hair pulled back neatly off his face. Nothing lingered from the night before, not a hint of revelry or regret.

With his appearance, everyone seemed to stand up straighter, to shift and move toward the stables. Heirik watched them with an unreadable gaze, and with one hand he tightened the laces on his bracer, working his thumb against one of the odd knots.

Those knots—I'd wondered about them many times. I couldn't believe I hadn't seen it before. They worked one-handed. Heirik had no one to sew up his sleeves for him or tie his laces in the morning, no one he would involve in such personal things. Too stubborn to wear something different, he'd found a way.

I imagined him in the dark of his room, doing this small, daily thing, and I felt a great longing. I feared and hated him for last night, and yet a love so great bloomed under the surface, rushing up through my guts and bones and lighting up my skin. I felt the wind push at my back, urging me toward the house, toward him.

In my mind, I saw myself helping him dress. Not in a romantic way. Nei, I saw it the way others might. A powerful and frightful man made even more so because of me. And I understood some of what Betta was trying to tell me last night.

What I wanted was something simple, and yet greater and tougher than anything in the world. I wanted his heart and home to be mine, too. I would grow strong, I told myself. Strong enough to handle the chief and anyone else in this yard.

Right then, he looked far up the hill as if to judge the sky. But he was looking for me, and when he found me, he nodded. Just once. Yes.

THE MEN HAD GONE—ALL OF THEM—ON TWO DOZEN HORSES that took off in a great, dusty cloud. With their departure, the women settled into an easy camaraderie that didn't include me. They lazily straightened things and wandered outside, while thralls began the real work of cleaning. Shouts filled the house, and as they raised the tables, the wood let out a tremendous scraping and groaning, like ships grinding together.

I escaped to the yard.

The fall air was cold, and the light was already falling, cutting a sharp angle across the rocks and grass. The hours of daylight were much fewer now. All the trash had been carried away, and women roamed the yard now for pleasure, taking in the sun and clean air with their children racing around them.

Betta stood lit from the side, her hair almost copper. She lifted a cloak high over her head, and it rippled in the wind.

"The women will go to roundup today," she told me as I neared.

"Not me," I said, still feeling my singular strangeness.

"Nei, probably not." Betta agreed. "Nor me."

The air moved at a tremendous speed and then slowed alternately, and the shaggy house ruffled and shushed.

"Magnus won't be going either then, já?" I asked

She laughed. "You are finally understanding a few things," she told me. "Já, Magnus will probably stay with you."

I looked off in the direction the men had gone, wishing I could talk with Heirik and find out what that nod had really meant.

Betta went on. "A few of us will stay, not just you. There are more parties to come, and I'm not …" Her voice broke on the truth, that she was not important enough to go to roundup. "I'll stay and get food ready."

I gave her a sidelong glance to see if tears stood in her eyes, but I found her watching me with wonder. "I never thought I would see such a thing." She said it softly, a hint of wistfulness in her voice.

"What?"

"You change everything," she said. "The whole world."

She folded a giant cloak over her arm and smoothed it.

"No one thought of him this way before. He had this great house. Power and beautiful things." She punctuated her words with great swipes of her palm over the wool. "But he was not for marrying. Not Rakknason Longhair." She tossed this name off, as if to shed all her emotions with it. She stacked the folded cloaks on the ground, picked up another and let the wool unfurl like a sail overhead. It snapped in the wind. "Now he is a man, já?"

I'd never heard the nickname before. I'd never even heard Betta say his name at all. "Why is he called Longhair?"

"Oh," she said easily, as though everyone knew. "Because he cuts his own, and so he waits too long. Down his back now." I thought she might kid with me as usual, about how I loved his hair, but she was serious. "The black is beautiful. I'm sure you've noticed."

Já, of course I had noticed its gorgeous depths. But she had, too? I didn't think anyone, even Betta, looked at him that way.

I had no time to contemplate it all. We came around the corner and Ageirr and Eiðr laid there, slumped against the grass walls, deep in sleep.

"Uck," Betta said and jumped back a foot as though she'd stepped in something questionable.

Another woman noticed, and then another, and soon a small flock of us stood around Ageirr and his little brother, watching them slump and snore. Betta stood with her arms crossed, her stack of cloaks resting on the ground, as high as her knees. My bowl rested on my hip. Another woman held a knife in each hand, letting them hang casually by her sides. A child gripped her skirt and hid halfway behind her leg. Svana came too, hesitantly, like a little animal testing for a trap. I had the image of us as a ragged band of Valkyries, come to herald the death of the mens' dignity. It made me laugh out loud, and Ageirr stirred. The woman next to me was short and twice my width. She cleared her throat and kicked at Ageirr's foot.

He sputtered awake.

He raised a hand to shield his eyes from the harsh afternoon sun, which did nothing good for his scowl. I could almost hear his thoughts grinding and falling into place as he noticed the angle of the light and the gaggle of women and children, not a man in sight. He elbowed his brother, who groaned and rubbed his eyes.

Ageirr was already standing and brushing off his pants. His voice scratched, "Where are the men?" Suspicion and resignation were threaded through its screechy tones.

A girl of maybe sixteen whispered, loud enough for all to hear. "He had no excess of wits to spare on drink, já?" A scattering of laughter made Ageirr furious. He growled and turned on the girl.

"Where are they?" He towered over her and she shrank back.

"They're in the hills, Fool," said the wide woman, placing herself between them.

I saw Ageirr get it, saw him realize that he'd been left behind. And then I saw that he was reaching for his ax. Time seemed to slow and stretch as in one of Jeff's wrestling sims, and yet I had no time to do anything. No time at all. I watched him draw the ax and turn away from the women. With savage anger, he buried the blade in the house. He wrenched it free and swung again.

"Nei!" I shouted, and with my sharp command time seemed to start again. "Not the house," I said.

Ageirr stared at me, stunned, his ax swinging at his side. I was just as stunned, my heart racing, face tingling with a rush of adrenalin. He was armed, but some twisted wash of possessiveness made me unafraid. No one hurt my house.

Eiðr was staggering to his feet, grabbing at his brother's ax handle, but Ageirr had already given up on me. He held my gaze, but not in anger. He just couldn't let go. I felt his sadness like a physical force. I felt how lost he was, how alone, mortified and left behind.

Finally, he broke my gaze, shouldered his ax in a final threatening gesture and shoved past us all.

The two men retrieved their horses and in moments they were ready to leave. Just before they left the farm to ride to the highlands, Ageirr spent a moment talking with Hildur, too far away for me to hear. She handed him up a bundle of food and a cup, which he drained and handed back to her. Then he nodded and took off, his brother trailing along in his dust.

The farm was left in a serene silence, broken only by the snuffling of a dog around the ground where Ageirr had slept. The diversion ended and the women wandered away, but I stayed frozen in place, trembling now that it was over. Betta put a hand to my back and said "Shhh" and "let your heart calm, Woman."

Calm, yes. On the first day I resolved to take this house as my home, someone buried an ax in it.

Heirik knew down to a man exactly who was with him and who was not. He'd nodded to me, and left me here, trusted me with Ageirr. *Brave little thing.* I'd passed the test.

Betta must, like me, be thinking of Fjoðr dead in the grass. That day at the forge, Heirik's words were clear, and if Ageirr thought he'd been forgotten, he was wrong. This moment of quiet surrounding the house was like a fog made of ale and hay and dwindling daylight that would lift when roundup and shearing were done. I recalled looking straight into the edge of Heirik's ax, expertly sharpened. I remembered what he'd said about Ageirr—*He only feeds my power*—and I knew Heirik hadn't forgotten a thing.

INTENTIONS

I WAS RIGHT. MAGNUS AND I BOTH STAYED HOME FROM ROUNDUP. He lurked around the house, an unobtrusive but always present guard. Every hour or so, his eyes would brush over me respectfully, diligently, making sure I was still here. He seemed both capable of protecting me, as if such a wild thing would really be necessary, and also very worried. He tapped on his knee all the time, sharpened things. Everything in the house gleamed with a fine edge.

Now I watched out of the corner of my eye, lulled by the gentle scraping of his whetstone on some little pieces of iron, dainty, almost disappearing in his big hands. I didn't get the impression he was bitter exactly, for being left behind, and now I finally placed his emotion. It was fear. He was anxious for his life, or something just short of it anyway, if Heirik returned and found me hurt in the slightest way.

He came to me and dropped three sharp sewing needles in my lap. I picked one up and took extra care not to prick myself.

On the third morning, Magnus sat on an upturned log in the yard, just a few feet from where I sat and sewed on the stable wall. An already-sharp knife hung from his tired fingers. Suddenly he slapped his thighs and stood. "Woman," he declared. "Come down from that wall and ride with me."

We didn't go far, just a slow ride around the homefield. It laid under the cold sun, a lonely stretch of cut stalks. Its brilliant emerald had turned to remnants of hay and dust. Still, it was full of promise.

"My grandfather was Magnus Heirikson," he said with shy pride. "He carved out this field from the cold ground. Built this farm." He took a deep breath, and I could see how good it all felt to him—the homefield and walls, the fresh air, his home. I saw the roots and tendrils of ownership taking hold, a chief's view of the farm growing in him, and I liked him even more.

His grandfather was Magnus. And his great-grandfather had been Heirik! Names were passed down like that, in this time and place.

Heirik Rakknason. The chief used his name so infrequently, it didn't often come up, but when it did, something nagged at my thoughts. Suddenly it came clear.

"What is your full name?"

"Magnus Hárson," he said. "Of course."

I'd become used to the wary looks I received when I asked dumb questions. "But the chief is Rakknason." I said. He should have been called after his father, Ulf.

"Oh!" Magnus seemed relieved, as if my question was sane and easy. "Rakknason is for his mother, já?"

"Signé?"

"She was called Melrakki." The Norse word for arctic fox. "They say he was so much hers."

Gods, he was named for his mother, the one whose curses and blessings ruled over the spiritual life in this house. It was a byname. A Viking way of recognizing someone who was well known, to give them a nickname.

I pictured a woman whose face was vague to me, looking regal in the ice blue dress, silver haired like a rare, "blue" fox. She must have ridden these walls, just as we did now. Must have held little Heirik before her on her horse. I stared out at the dry stalks in the field and imagined it.

Heirik wasn't a wolf pup after all.

A little voice shouted from up near the house, then another. Children were calling out, "Sheep!"

Magnus and I turned our horses, and as we rode back to the house, I saw them come spilling down from the high ground. When we got closer, we heard them, so many cattle and sheep that their voices melded into a great moaning that rolled off the hills and down to the house.

People from all over Hvítmörk came for shearing. Dozens of animals spilled down the hill like dirty ocean froth. They moved ever onward. Confused and vaguely restless and yet compliant, walking almost in a dream, each cow or sheep followed the ones in front of it. The smell of so many animals came smothering and heavy down the hill to where I stood. Dogs barked and ran at them, but the cows fanned out to chew, mildly interested in the new tastes of home.

My heart stuttered when I saw the chief, so beautiful riding Vakr. He shone among all the messy, slouching men and boys. He saw me, too. He looked to find me, in that way he had of seeming to answer a silent call. Over the sounds of a vast, chaotic sea of animals I smiled at him, feeling perfectly here and now.

Thirty cows and two dozen sheep changed everything, and Heirik was lost to the labor. A few of his animals still roamed, and the chief was absorbed in the facts of errant sheep and wild-smelling horses and men. On Vakr, he went out beyond sight all day. He came back late with the last few animals, falling down tired.

I wasn't waiting for him, nei. I only happened to be sitting against the house outside, and so I saw him as he nearly stumbled with exhaustion from the stables to the back door.

I ducked quickly inside, where Betta was preparing food. I quietly begged a handful of dried fish from her, brittle like crackers in my fingers, and stashed it in the purse at my belt. I would give him this one small thing, along with a handful of dried berries. I walked casually through both rooms of the house to the mudroom door.

It creaked when I opened it, but the sound was not enough to stir Heirik, who sat on the bench just feet from his bedroom door, dead asleep.

His feet were planted far apart on the floor, one of them covered with just a sock, and his dusty boot rested across his lap. His shirts were untied and sleeves loose, his belt, knives and firestriker on the floor. A cup had fallen from his belt and rolled across the room. It rested at my toes.

I looked behind me into the dark house and no one had followed me, so I stepped through the big door and let it close behind me as gently as I could.

I stood, soundless and still, and drank him in. He was a big man. He didn't tower over me when we stood together, nei. He was built differently from people in my time, not tall like Jeff, but far more substantial. Compared to his shoulders and hips, his waist was lean, and yet it was so thick I could never get my hands around a quarter of it. Watching him sleep, images came to me of his grace, how his hips moved with the elegance of water despite his size. I'd thought so many times about what it might be like to feel those hips pressed against me, while I reached my arms around his back and traced the curves I'd seen at the bath.

I had dreamed of seeing the openness of his face in sleep, no concern, no hiding. And here it was. I took in his long straight nose and broad cheekbones, the hollows beneath them licked with moving shadows. I adored his dark lashes, the hair falling in his face, the color of blood that was part of his loveliness. His lips were parted like a child in slumber. I watched the tide of his breath, and I drifted closer to him, crossing the small room, standing almost between his knees so that my skirts brushed him ever so lightly.

Betta and Svana were wrong. He was a handsome man.

Nei, he was gorgeous. And I desired him. So much that I didn't think I could wait any longer. I couldn't wait for him to be ready. I needed to touch right now, to steal a brush of fingers against him, any part of him, even his shirts. I knew I shouldn't. It wouldn't be right. But I was so close, wanting, reaching. His filthy boot was warm in my hands. I turned it over, watching my own fingers against the leather.

He stirred and I dropped the boot into his lap. I jumped, and nearly flew backwards toward the door.

Heirik sat up in confusion and opened his eyes to find me standing still and breathless, just two feet away.

"I …" I said. "You were asleep." Brilliant.

He took in his surroundings and then sat up with a start, suddenly alert.

"Don't worry," I told him. "No one else has seen you."

"Já," he murmured, wiping his cheek and chin with the back of his hand. "Good."

He looked at the boot in his hands, then at my skirts. A big swath of dirt streaked across my apron. I bent and picked his cup up off the floor and held it in both hands.

He looked like he was going to speak, then stopped, and looked up like he would start again.

"Tomorrow," he said, and his voice was dark and smoky as the heartstone.

He turned his boot over in his hands.

Tomorrow. As if it would be the day that something would finally happen. He'd touch my palm, might kiss the hollow of my hand. I imagined his lips would be chapped from sleeping in the highlands. His beard would graze my wrist, ticklish and good. *Kiss me, Heirik,* I thought, and I felt my gaze blur, my lips open so slightly, uncontrollably. It would be so simple.

"It is a day for intentions," he said, removing his other boot.

I drew my brows together. "What do you mean?" My voice was hoarse, the cup pressed hard between my hands.

"The shearing," he stated, pretending to focus on untying his bracers, and I thought he was practicing indifference. I'd watched him carefully enough these past months for me to know when he was hiding emotion.

"The shearing," I repeated, dense.

He leaned forward, placing his elbows on his knees, long ties hanging. He asked, and it was a gentle query. "You don't remember?"

"Nei," I said, and this time it was the truth. I'd never seen a sheep sheared, and I didn't—couldn't possibly—remember a thing.

He smiled, stood and took a lamp from the wall. He flipped the latch on his bedroom door. "I'll bless the harvest, and the viljandifalne will be plentiful," he said, and this time the emotion was clear. Bitterness like a hard berry, spat out, a word I'd never heard. The *willingly slain*? I just looked at him.

The lamp lit his face from underneath, and he closed his eyes for just a second, shy, lost in something, as if his voice failed. But it didn't.

"Sleep," he told me, as soft as a kiss, and then he ducked into his room.

"Goodnight," I said after him, just before he shut the door.

THE COURSE AND CRASH OF WATER ECHOED IN THE PRETTY ravine, louder than I remembered. Louder than I thought possible, as though the stream, at fifteen feet wide, was a lie. It was actually a raging river. Its volume drowned out all sense.

I'd ridden out in the early morning to the little waterfalls. To the edge of the fast-moving water, where Heirik and I had once spoken of birds and elves and Hildur's superstition.

A big day ahead, everyone was ready to shear the sheep and celebrate the year, the coming winter, the growing world. A crush of people still slept in tents in the yard and in every crevice of the house. I thought of the party as rolling over days and days like that bank of clouds, huge and slow and inexorable.

Most everyone was thrilled with having different people here to chat and work and be near, and weeks ago I would have guessed I'd feel the same. But I left that idea behind after the first night of the harvest party, and I was glad that today, after shearing and more drink, the celebrations would end.

Now I sat on the bank, my skirts tucked under my crossed legs and cloak gathered around my shoulders. My gaze passed aimlessly over the water and settled on the tiny island. The foundation of Heirik's stone fort still stood there. A few black and pumice gray rocks were a small testament to what happened here. At first, the chief had scared me, but then we splashed and smiled, and without my knowing it something had taken hold.

I let my eyes wander over the opposite bank, the man-sized caves and steep, rocky slope up and away. Clouds moved above it, separating and joining and drifting for miles.

In the city, there had either been clouds or not. The buildings stretched so high, we saw a tiny section of the sky, a slice only. Until I came here, I hadn't thought about the possibility of lying low to the ground and seeing the clouds move, watching them roam the sky. Here I could see a mass bigger than the glacier itself, moving like a slow beast, slinking away. Its ominous, black bulk moved off, and as the sun rose higher it left only fluffy white scuds. Pink morning.

Images of the harvest feast came—memories of heat and body odor and warm ale. Of ice blue fabric slipping through my fingers, and anger at Heirik for throwing me into a bonfire without warning or explanation.

I lay my head gently on the rocky bank. I let my hand fall to my side, palm drifting open. My fingers broke the surface.

What would today be like?

The current tugged at my hand. I let my anxiousness go with it, remembering Heirik's gentle words, the kiss of a single word, *sleep*. All hesitance and worry went with the water, calming my head, and—freed—my thoughts suddenly fell to the vision I'd had of nine-year-old Betta, and now I remembered details that I hadn't before. A man, blond and shining, bent down to hand her a toy. It was a wooden doll he'd made, his carving knife still held in his other hand. She took it and twirled away with a flare of skirts, then ran down the hill toward the valley. I still couldn't see young Heirik. I saw him as he looked last night in the mudroom, fully grown. He reached a hand to my brow, caring for me as if I were sick.

I jolted awake to a blinding fear.

A driving storm of white steam surrounded me. Opaque mist, streaming faster now, blown by a sudden, hard wind. The coursing steam was violent and beautiful and it pressed down on my chest like a snarling animal. I felt pinned to the rocks. This part was no vision. This fast-moving mist was real. And though it was abrupt and odd, it felt familiar.

This was what it should be like traveling through time. I should have been able to feel it pass like this ferocious jet of steam, driving hard into my eyes and nose and stealing all my senses. Pulling on me mercilessly, like this watery wind. This would have been fair Not just a metallic ripping followed by being plopped on a beach.

Any beach. Here in 900s in Iceland, or 1900s Atlantic City.

I gasped and yanked my hand out of the current.

I hadn't thought of it before. I could have been stranded somewhere else. In the Gilded Age.

My fingers dripped and water ran down under my sleeve in miserable streams.

I could've been living in 1900s America right now, trying to get by in a world of bustles and straw hats. It had really happened, that night in the tank, hadn't it? Something had pulled me back, brought me back, so I could go into the tank the next morning and land here instead.

My heart beat hard. *Saga, thank you*, I thought, and I felt an answer return to me, not like an actual voice, but a lifting of the steam to let in a sharp blade of light. And with it a thought came so clear and bright and substantial it couldn't be ignored. Something that happened once in a million lifetimes—or maybe once ever, in all of time—had happened to me. And it happened just right. It didn't work when I went to turn of the century Atlantic City, because I was only meant to travel here. My right place and time.

I sat up in the fresh air, the steam gone. The stream still rushed by my side, forever and ever. This stream that still ran under the ground so far in the future, maybe right underneath the lab.

I'd been bumbling around hoping to hide my secret, trying to get by with my poor spinning and mooning wishes for the chief to like me. Waiting so dumbly for something to happen. But being here wasn't a disaster, and I had no reason to wait anymore. I would touch and take Heirik today, somehow, if only by the hand, and it would be a start. That much of him would be mine, and the rest would follow. Yes.

Betta's secret would be mine, too. I would find out today.

It was a day for intentions, he'd said. I didn't know anything about it. I didn't know what it meant to be willingly slain or what any of my own intentions had to do with cutting sheeps' hair. But I was ready.

It turned out there was more waiting and work to do first, and the passion of my intentions dissolved into a morning of food preparation and bringing out a dozen more cups from the very back of the cave-like pantry. A few of the thralls had come up from the lower house and were setting up food and drink under Hildur's strained and beady gaze.

It wasn't as formal or huge as the party several nights ago, but it was abundant. I drifted slowly around the tables in the back room, fingers trailing over the blond polished wood. I reviewed the food and drink, noted the big bowls of ale, metal ale geese hanging on their rims, their long hooks like beaks for dipping into the drink.

Outside, a small crowd of farmers and wives and children were gathering around the circle of stable walls, kids and men climbing over to step inside with the sheep. The shepherd brought in a few wanderers, then lost another two before closing the wooden gate. I counted men, women, kids, then ducked back inside the house and looked over the tables once more. I did the math in my head—who was here, how many, what they would eat and drink—and the experience of the steam weakened.

I'd felt Saga's presence so sharply this morning, like she'd snapped her fingers in my heart, and I knew without a doubt that today I would pry Betta's secret free, would touch Heirik for the first time. But after an hour of considering the facts of cups and ale and food, I wasn't sure what I had left.

In my alcove, I sat with legs crossed and pulled a comb out from under the skins. I wanted to stay in my cave for a little while, so I could miss Heirik's entrance, everyone honoring him with bowed heads and bent knees.

I drew all my hair over one shoulder and combed out the frayed ends. I had no way of knowing what I looked like anymore. Probably a confused mess of determination and desire, like a woman with well-brushed hair and no plan.

I stayed in my alcove with the curtains drawn, listening to people come and pour drinks and go back out, and when the rush of people slowed, I emerged. I went to peek around the back door frame.

Heirik was already at the stable, a few men standing around him talking. It was safe. And so I got a cup of ale for myself and went to hop up atop the curving stable wall and watch the shearing.

Several women sat here, and all around me they cooed and laughed and whispered behind cupped hands. Everyone reveled in this break, a party, the sun, so different from spinning and cooking and squinting at looms in the half dark.

Three dozen people or more milled around the stables and yard—the whole family, Ageírr's family too, his little brother Eiðr, all the thralls from both houses. Children and random animals ran in and out of peoples' legs. Little boys and girls fought with wooden swords and shields, a puppy jumping and snapping between them. Older boys stood near the forge, joking while one of them sharpened iron shears on the big whetstone.

Ranka's Da grabbed Kit's backside firmly. She swatted him away with a smile, but he stayed close, standing behind her and nuzzling at the crook of her neck. A tender moment that felt cozy and familiar. I was safe with these people. I closed my eyes to feel the sun.

Svana broke into the moment, jumping up onto the wall beside me in a satisfied flounce.

"Do you remember the shearing?"

I told her nei, thinking of an arc on a screen. I'd watched it over and over, but it was no real memory.

"Then you don't know, já?" She grinned. "Why everyone is like this?"

She thrust her chin toward Arn, who still clung to Kit, encircling her from behind. They were slowly swaying together, an unconscious dance, sex-infused and true. I looked around and found other couples talking close. Thora looked up from under her eyelashes at a boy who was half her width, women watched the men and whispered, a husband touched his wife's nose.

I looked for Betta and found her talking to Hár. He sat on the ground against the house, one knee bent. Betta stood over him talking, her hand shading her eyes, and when her skirt moved in a small breeze it caught on his knee. He left off carving a small block of wood and looked up at her, charming and potentially immoral. He was flirting as though he talked to young women every day.

And then it hit me, fast and hard, like a blow to the head. Gods, there it was, a spark of sex between them. Her skirt still snared on his leg, neither of them removing it.

It was Hár. Betta's pulse of her heart. She was in love with the "old man." I swallowed ale and coughed my throat ragged.

Images of them came unbidden. Betta smiling at Hár, her big teeth beguiling him, an image of—gods!—Hár's shaggy head bent to kiss her, her tight braids cradled in his giant hand. I saw her looking ravished, her hair messy and free, the night she came in from riding at sunset. Saw a beaming, blond man handing little Betta a toy doll. My brain spun and ale clogged my nose.

Svana smacked me on the back. "Are you okay?"

"Já," I croaked and looked at her hair and eyes and dress before I thought of something to say. "Just thinking of other things." Right. Like Hár's rough hands all over my friend.

"It is proof of a real man," Svana told me, and I almost choked again.

I focused hard on Svana, struggled to listen while the idea of Betta and Hár roared in my brain. He was more than twice Betta's age, já, but still young enough to love her. To be her lover. Oh gods! I couldn't even think of it, and yet couldn't think of anything else.

"To shear a sheep perfectly," Svana said in her scandalized, little voice. "Ears to belly to toes in one piece, and nei cuts on the animal. It is a test."

The men teased each other about it, she said. They would make bets and dramatic gestures. The women would watch lasciviously, and at least one or two would grab a man and take him alone into the little woods near the ravine. If anyone would be so bold, it would be Betta. I could imagine her crashing happily into the birches, dragging Hár along behind her.

While Svana chirped in my ear, I turned this impossibility over and over. Hár was Betta's one, her breath, the man she wanted more than life.

I had to talk with her. Now. To be sure I was right, that this was true. But I knew it was.

Betta came toward me, a smile flowering into a toothy grin. I saw the very moment when she realized that I knew. Her step faltered, she staggered a little, all skirts and ankles, her grin left unfinished for just a second. She drew up her dignity and stood still for a moment until the fabric around her feet unwound, then walked calmly toward me and lifted herself easily onto the wall by my side.

I felt flanked by birds. Svana chattering about sex. Betta folding wings protectively around her desire. She looked as if I might take Hár from her, take her dream.

With a bustling all around us, I could talk freely in a low voice. But with Svana so close, I chose neutral words and hidden gestures. My fingers spread out on the wall between me and Betta. I flicked my eyes toward Hár, where he now stood amidst a knot of sheep inside the stable walls.

"I'm right?" I asked.

Betta blushed with that modesty that she seemed to turn on and off at the drop of a needle. She nodded. And then asked my opinion. "What do you think?"

I took her wrist in my hand. What did I think? I couldn't think at all.

Her pulse jumped under my fingers while she waited for my approval. It warmed me, how she cared what I might think. I was that important to her. I'd never been that important to anyone before.

"What do I think?" I repeated, and I blinked my watery eyes. I was stunned. Disoriented, I sought Hár out to try to see what she saw.

And I did.

He stood next to Heirik, like father and son. And in a flash, I saw Hár as a totally different creature—someone to want, to play with, to watch privately in the firelight.

He'd raised Heirik, and so I thought of him as old, a kind and rough uncle. He characterized himself that way, and I'd bought it, like any five-year-old listening to stories at his feet. Leave it to Betta to find a lover in there. Somehow, she'd seen past that shield, and now I could too.

He was an adventure to look at, his size alone dazzling. He was loud all the time, whether laughing or joking or stamping his boots in the mudroom. He was brave and responsible and honorable and wild. Off-putting, and casually high-handed, but prone to bust into laughter and smiles full of mirth and sin. It was the sin I noticed now, as he glanced back at us, and I heard Betta swallow hard beside me.

His hair, which I'd thought of as messy and gray, was more like ash blond shot through with pewter. It caught the sun now and turned to silver, to match the pair of metal cuffs on his forearms. They looked heavy, hefty, and I thought I might fit both my wrists inside one.

I couldn't name why, but I thought he was just right for Betta. Já, good.

"I think it is wondrous," I said, turning to her, and I was struck by how much she wanted him. It was plain on her face today, almost recklessly so. It made me wonder how much of him she'd had already.

I remembered my intentions for the day. Find out Betta's secret. Make Heirik know how I feel.

One down, I thought in wonder. Now I just had to get the chief alone.

The shepherd had all the sheep gathered in the circular yard, and Heirik walked among them. He always took my breath away, even on a regular day, even for a tenth of a second. But today he was something new.

He walked barefoot through the clean grass outside the pen. I'd seen him once or twice without tightly laced boots, but never outside like this, in front of people. There were a thousand common things I didn't understand every day. His pants hung loose without being tucked and bound; his sleeves were the same, no gauntlets holding them fast. His hair was pulled back on top but otherwise hung long and free. The loop of a pair of shears hung from two fingers, balanced casually as he looked into the animals' eyes.

The shears didn't seem fine enough. I couldn't imagine such a feat of delicate trimming—a fleece in one piece with no cuts on the sheep—being achieved by anyone, regardless of his masculinity. The blades were well-formed, but looked too rough to slip through wool like that. The animals looked too lively. They would never stand still.

"The chief does this first?" I asked Betta, already worried for him. The cloth we made from these animals would let us thrive and prosper through trade, the meat from a few of them would keep us alive this winter, and it was Heirik's place to go first, to bless us, to promise.

"Don't fret," she told me. "There is no man here like the chief with a blade."

I stared at her for a second. With her sitting so close, her body warm and angular and real, the whole thing hit home again.

"Not one?" I raised an eyebrow.

She actually turned away from me, just a little, with a shy dip of her head. When she turned back to me, she was blushing dark crimson.

"We'll talk alone," I ordered her. "Right after this."

"Já," she said, "okay," and she smiled, not with her typical wry or knowing smirk, but with genuine pleasure and embarrassment. It was beautiful.

"You're right, in any case," I said. "There is no man like him."

Not in any way, I thought. But with a blade especially. I'd never seen anyone so attuned to scythe, ax, knife, as if they were extensions of his will itself. Heirik was gifted, I thought, my head already pleasantly vague with ale and reeling with truths. He was powerful, intelligent, exquisite in movement and form. Rakknason Longhair. The waves fell down his back now, free from braids. Unmarked, he would've been like a god, women on their knees around him wishing for a single blessing of lips and tongue. Marked, he was revolting. They couldn't see what I saw.

The shears in his palm were an elegant if primitive tool, a single curved loop of iron, held under tension. Triangular blades at each end came together like scissors. He weighed them thoughtfully, flipped them over in his hand.

He flicked the shears to indicate one of the sheep. A solid old wether, immensely woolly, dispassionately chewing. The shepherd pulled it by its tail, away from the others. It reared up, and he took it by the shoulders from behind, dragging it over to Heirik.

In the quiet, Heirik knelt and took the sheep to him by the fleece at its jowls. He and the animal had a short, silent communication. Then he stood so that he straddled the sheep, the animal's face tucked between his thighs, and he began clipping at the forehead.

The shears snicked, crisper and more precise than I expected. He worked from one ear to the other, now pulling back the sheep's chin with his hand, so he could turn it from side to side. Heirik worked across the back of the animal's neck, letting the fleece roll down, until soon it was a ruff around its shoulders. He followed the same pattern until he was shearing down its back. The fleece was a thick blanket, folding back in one piece to let a velvety, vulnerable creature emerge. Its head lay still against Heirik's thigh. Mesmerized.

By the end, Heirik was kneeling, straddling the sheep on the ground, to finish the haunches and lower belly. Then the animal was bare. Heirik let the shears drop to the ground, and stood and turned the wiggling sheep around to face forward toward us, then locked it again between his thighs. The chief picked up the fleece by two corners. He unfurled it against the sky, its perfect shape lifted high on a breeze. His linen sleeves moved with the breeze, too, and a ray of sun lit up two thick silver bracelets on his forearms. There were whoops and hollers and clinks and dull thumps of wooden cups.

Hildur took the fleece from him, and she looked elated and young, almost kind. We would make it through winter, then, and prosper. For this one moment, she didn't seem to mind that we had a masculine and potent chief. In a little ale-induced trance, I watched his thighs where he still held the sheep. I wanted to climb on Heirik's lap and feel him rise to me, proof that the test was right.

Then Heirik held up his hands, palms up, and the hush was immediate. The air trembled with expectation and the repressed need to celebrate, but everyone waited for something important.

"Freyr," he began. He kept his hands raised, and as he spoke he looked past us all toward the sea. His voice was clear, as though it could carry all the way there, to reach the god himself as he sailed his wave-steed.

"You rule over rain and the shining of the sun. Abundance and pleasure. Fruitfulness of seasons, of unions. We are mindful."

He grasped the sheep's ear, drew its head back, and with swift precision slit its throat. A sure cut, blood flowed fast and free around Heirik's bare feet. He squatted to gather a shallow handful, brought the blood to his lips, then stood and held the cup of his palms up to the sky. A gentle and violent creature.

"This is our gift."

A sudden breeze lifted a red spray from his hands. He dropped them to his sides, and blood ran from his fingertips in thin streams. It pooled around his feet and the body of the fallen sheep. Heirik opened incandescent eyes, and for a moment, he was transformed into the face and soul of the god Freyr himself. Irises of lit amber, hair like black flame. And then he smiled. It was a mischievous half-smile, seductive, smeared with blood. He called "Hár, up!", challenging his uncle to do better, and everyone cheered. The party had begun.

I sat stunned.

I turned to look at Betta, but she was gone. And when I looked at Svana, her pale cream cheeks were infused with a becoming pinkness. She sighed, eyes fixed on Heirik, and it was dreamy and unsettling. Her gaze was hungry. Gods, it was true. A fertility god had been invoked, and it was real. Could even Svana be moved by its presence enough to see past her disgust? Oh, nei, nei, nei.

He came toward her, and I had a brief and gut-wrenching vision of them together. Of this world had I never come. Svana would want this all—this house, this family, and eventually in spite of her fear, this man. And once she reached out to Heirik, he would be drawn to her, and they would find their way. My heart raced.

But he wasn't coming for Svana. He was coming for me.

Heirik walked toward me with intent, and I saw the man I'd seen in the wildflowers, in the woods, times a hundred. He had drunk the power of his god and was lit with it, emboldened and free. With a lithe motion, he made wiping his mouth on his shirts seem like poetry. Then he was standing close to me, his hand against the wall at my side. He leaned into it.

"Ginn." The way he looked at me, sweet and speculative, I would have done anything for him.

"Spin that fleece."

It was the last thing I'd expected, and I laughed. I was moved by his demand, that he would want that from me for this first fleece of fall, the blessed one. His. At the same time, I guessed the wool weighed five pounds. I was aroused by his nearness and playfulness. I'd say yes, yes, yes.

"You don't want me to do that."

"Já, I do." He smiled again, his lips still stained.

"I'm very, very bad at it." I was serious. "You can have the thread for tooth floss."

"Then I will clean my teeth a happy man until I'm with the ravens." He smacked the wall and walked away to see how Hár was measuring up.

Dozens of thoughts beat like wings in my head. Disbelief. Awakening, physically and in my heart. A wistful sense that this is what it would be like, if he were my husband, coming to see me and flirt with me. Maybe someday stand close against my back and nuzzle my neck like the other couples in this yard. Elated and flushed, I wanted another drink. I thought someone would have to wash the blood from his clothes. I wanted to ask him if I could take care of such things for him, with him. But I knew. I knew that his freedom and intimacy would be gone the very next time we met.

It wasn't, actually.

The effect of the shearing and blessing was lasting and strong. It suffused everyone, all over the farm. More than one couple wandered off together, suspiciously close to one another if not hand in hand. Hár and Betta leaned against the back of the house, talking casually, intimately. I had the urge to run over and cover and hide them with a giant cloak, ask them what the hell they thought they were doing.

I felt it myself, like a directive in my gut, a desire to take and consume Heirik. To roll in the grass and comb his hair back off his neck with my fingers and bite and kiss his throat.

Where was he?

And where was Svana? The thought of her made me uneasy, like I'd lost track of a dangerous little animal. I looked around to see where she'd gone.

Scanning the gathering and not finding her or Heirik, I told myself a lot of scattered things. Svana was afraid of him. She wouldn't go off with him, ever. But she was fifteen years old and self-centered, and things were chaotic at her age. Heirik was so young. He didn't speak to women ever. Only me. I wondered if he even knew how to deflect Svana. And yet. It was Heirik's place alone to tell Svana if he didn't want her attention. I had no right to demand anything. He wasn't mine.

Still, something possessive clawed its way up into my throat and wouldn't go down until I'd found her.

She *was* with him. About to turn the corner of the house, I heard her voice, tiny and querulous. "Herra?" she asked.

"Svana," Heirik answered, surprised, his voice like golden light.

It was all I heard before I rounded the corner. I simply stared at them, standing several feet away, and they stared back, a dumb moment. I gasped in surprise when Betta slipped an arm around my shoulders from behind, her timing impeccable.

"There you are!" She drew two other women into the conversation, both of whom wanted to see my beaded necklace.

The girls seemed afraid of me at first, like cats reaching out curled paws. I tried to seem human and normal, as though I hadn't come from the sea, as though I hadn't worn Signé's clothes. They bent their heads to see my necklace, to touch its cunning needle case and winding beads, and I watched over their heads.

Heirik broke off standing with Svana and came toward us.

I thought the two women would fall down and tremble at the sight of him. They used the most formal term of address, calling him their chieftain. Heirik nodded silently to them and to Betta, dismissing them all, then set his eyes on me, and I was very much not dismissed.

"Walk with me."

He smelled like cinnamon and ale and blood.

"Yes, Chief," I told him, with a nod that verged on a bow. He walked away, leaving me to smile goodbye to Betta, and to the tiny women, who stood astounded and sorry.

I went off after Heirik, and he led me past the house and the stables, down to the steep grassy slope where we could sit hidden from the house.

He bent his knees and rested his wrists on them. Without gauntlets, his sleeves hung loose, tinged with blood. Stupidly jealous and filled with lust, I wanted to slide my fingers inside those sleeves, touch his bracelets, feel his pulse. His eyes were still electric, drawing out the autumn gold in the grass.

He wasn't smiling.

"I didn't like that, Ginn."

I drew my brows together. What had I done?

"You bowed down to me. You called me Chief."

I settled into the grass and drew my knees up, too, and wrapped my arms around them. "I've been instructed to call you that and nothing else," I countered with the gentle looseness of two cups of ale.

"I know." He looked off down the cascade of yellowing hills and laughed quietly at himself. "I make no sense. In front of them, you must."

We were still, and then he spoke again.

"You said my name, the first day you came outside."

The first day, when I came outside to meet him. Memories of blinding daylight and fire welled up, his shoulders working over iron and stone. In my gut, I felt an echo of the distress of those first hours in this alien time and place. But also contentment. Back in that quiet moment, squinting into the sun on my first day outside the longhouse, I'd been at home. I'd known him already, before I even heard what he was called.

"Heirik." I gave his name to him now.

"Já," he whispered. The day's fiercest breeze came up, rippling the grass and filling my ears. I could barely hear him. "Again, please," he said. It broke my heart.

"Heirik," I called to him softly, willing him to look, and he turned to me finally. It wasn't just the remaining fire of ritual that lit his eyes. They gleamed with moisture at the corners.

"Don't call me otherwise, when we are alone."

I nodded a solemn vow. I would call him by his name, privately, in all the small moments I could. And I would not say herra in his presence again. If it hurt him, then I would find a thousand ways to avoid it.

We shared the view of the valley in silence, and I longed for him to call me something secret too. "In the woods," I blushed. Pushed myself. "You called me small."

His lip curled up, amused. "You liked that."

Two handfuls of dry grass occupied my hands. I watched my fingers close into fists, heard the ripping sound. Admitted it. "Já."

It was a lover's way of seeing me.

"Já, then, Small One." It was the sweetest sound, in a lifetime of listening to the beauty and nuances of thousands of voices. This one, now, was it.

He didn't say anything more, but I was familiar with his silences. I looked to the horizon and luxuriated in the tension between us. After a while, he talked to me again.

"We'll do three more for winter," he said. "I can keep fourteen."

He was talking about the sheep. He'd considered the hay, the animals, the people. Children, four girls not yet married off, Kit would have another baby in winter. Each animal ate so much hay, yet fed so many people with dairy if we could keep it alive through the polar nights. There were cows, too, so many of them. Some of those would be slaughtered. Heirik knew our food stores, knew our needs. Some was calculable—a cow ate twenty tons in the winter, he told me—and some was not. Variables like weather hovered just outside his reach.

And then, fourteen. That was the answer. A clean, simple answer for such a complex equation, and some diminishing part of the future me would have found it cold. The newer me sat beside him like a chieftain's wife, considering his logic, thinking of the best way to deploy the women in reducing and preserving the dead. Looking at the farm the way he did, somehow we'd come to sit closer. Side by side, very close. My elbows rested on my bent knees, just like his. I felt like two sheepdogs, surveying what we were born to protect.

"Salmon is done for the year. We have enough," he said. "We'll bank more small fish. And shark, before the rain and wind." He turned to face me, and I could feel his breath on my cheek.

"More important," I murmured. "We have enough grain for ale."

I turned to him with laughter on my lips, and suddenly we were a hand's breadth apart, no more. His breath was sweet with honeyed drink and a hint of blood. Loose wisps of his hair brushed my cheeks. We both stayed seated just as we were, then he leaned in so slightly and I tilted my head up to him. So close I could feel the shape of his lips in the air between us. I could move to kiss him. I could open my mouth. I would. I was.

"Rakknason!"

Heirik and I drew apart in a flash.

Behind us, Ageirr descended the hill with long, loping steps. Heirik stood with swift grace and dignity. Not much taller, somehow he towered over the man.

Now I was sure Ageirr's half-sneer was permanent. A moment of pain and anger had seared itself into his features.

He drew his knife from his belt, considered his left hand and started trimming a fingernail. He nodded to me. "Ginn Sjódottir." Sea's Daughter. Everyone knew I was odd, come from nowhere, with no name. The insult sounded greasy on his lips. Incongruously, my sex throbbed from the promise of Heirik's kiss, unfulfilled. I rolled my hips ever so slightly and pressed against the grass to quiet my body.

"Ageirr, my honor-feeder." Heirik used a lyrical kind of Viking metaphor, a word poem. It sounded appreciative, but it was a deft reminder of their places—that Heirik was the one who protected and commanded Ageírr. It was a slick little jab, above reproach, and I liked Heirik for it.

I stood and wiped bits of dry grass from my skirt, and I nodded to Ageírr, as if I hadn't barked at him last time we met. I listened to them talk about fields, hay, cattle, the same subjects Heirik and I had just spoken of, but this time I was not part of them. I became awkward and unnecessary. Then Ageírr mentioned a lost horse, and the mood turned ominous.

A breeze punctuated the quick change. Heirik shifted his body to form a wall between me and Ageírr.

"You've drawn now," Heirik told him with finality.

Ageírr expelled a disdainful "ffft" through closed teeth. "The blood of an animal." He cast a glance at Heirik's reddened feet, then looked in his eyes. "A beloved woman lost. It's not the same." His eyes rested briefly on me. "Is it, Chief?"

A cold calm stole over Heirik's body.

"To the house, Ginn." He commanded, in a way he'd never spoken to me.

I glanced at the knife in Ageírr's hand, noticed with cold clarity that Heirik now held his knife, too. In my muddled head, I was still the chieftain's wife, and I knew with certainty that the way I reacted now would reflect on Heirik. Was I supposed to stand by, ready to fight too? I thought of my own little knives that hung from my belt. A Viking wife might or might not. But I would be ridiculous, and Heirik would be savagely angry at me.

I wouldn't fight, then. I wouldn't run, either. I would remain collected. But I consumed the hill in big strides.

Looking back was weak. I tried to resist it. I watched my boots instead, one after the other kicking out from under my skirts as I climbed. I couldn't hear anything behind me, no shouts or cries. But my love was back there, and knives were drawn, and I'd so recently seen that very knife slit cleanly through a sheep's throat. Tears started to come and I had to turn. I had to know.

Far down the hill, Heirik and Ageirr were talking. They'd put their knives away, and Heirik stood with his arms crossed over his chest, in his way. He wasn't exactly at ease, nor was Ageirr, but they were not lunging at each other and struggling and snarling like dogs.

It took a second to sink in. They weren't fighting.

A gust of wind lifted my skirts and made them billow around my knees, and I wanted to just let my legs fall out from underneath me. I wanted to sink into the grass right there and be grateful. There was no danger. And at that moment, Ageirr looked up and saw me. He smiled, without warmth or joy.

I crested the hill, and there sat the house.

All around it played an idyllic scene, out of an old painting. Pink-faced children chased chickens. Men laughed and sheared sheep, while those who'd already proven their prowess drew women away behind the house. Ale sloshed in metal and wooden cups, and the kids dribbled milk from rolled up cones of birch bark. The grass on the house was long and brilliant green and gold. A single naked sheep stood on the roof eating it.

The house was a massive, living thing. Solid in the landscape. And it was mine.

IT WAS A BIT LATER BEFORE I GOT AROUND TO THINKING OF BETTA again.

Despite my assumption that she and Hár would run off to the trees, they were both still in the yard, separately talking and drinking with people in the late sun.

I drew her away, and we tripped down the hill to sit by the river, far down the front yard. We bared our feet and dipped our toes in the freezing water, and she laid a hand flat on the ground beside me while she looked out into the distance.

Betta didn't realize how lovely she was, with her beautiful ideas and quick, mischievous smile. The seriousness of her gift. Her long dexterous fingers, good at spinning and dyeing. True, Betta wasn't adorable like Svana, but no one was. Svana was a singular little cloud, a puff of sugar. Betta was a woman.

Open to the unexpected, surely. Brave.

Unwise.

He's too important for me, she'd said of her secret lover. And he was. I spread my toes and wondered if she really understood what her relationship could—and couldn't possibly—lead to.

I didn't say anything, and Betta waited a while, in that way she had of allowing the air to become still before dropping a pebble, a rock, a boulder of a question or statement into it.

"Do you remember …?" She started. Drew up some conviction, and then started again. "Have you ever felt a man?"

I stopped swirling the water with my feet and spent a long moment trying to decipher her question. Surely, she wasn't asking about a man in general. She'd seen me touch men incidentally. Then I figured it out and my mouth curled into a compassionate and amused smile. She was asking if I'd touched a penis. I couldn't possibly tell her yes, not only because I had amnesia, but also because it was such an undefinable experience, the first time.

Then my smile faded, as the impact of her question hit me.

"Did you?" I asked delicately at first, but then I just had to know. "Did you touch Hár?"

She smiled and then ducked her head shyly. "Nei, nei," she said. "Not with my hands."

What did that mean? I didn't know whether to be relieved or infuriated at the old man. I made her tell me more.

The first time Hár took her riding was like a romantic brand seared into her mind, dark and moonlit and luscious. She'd saved every detail forever, and had been waiting to tell me for so long.

He'd helped her onto Byr and got on the horse behind her, and she first felt his arms—any man's arms—around her. They rode so fast, she would have been scared, but the feel of his body fascinated her, so warm and sturdy. Something rose in her own body that she'd never known.

He took her to a high hill where they could look out into the moon-stricken valley, and they stayed there for a long quiet time. She was amazed at his solidity, after imagining his embrace and failing to really grasp how it would be. How big he was up close, his breath on her neck and the beat of his heart against her shoulder blades.

He undid her braids, and she let him, her breath suspended. Hár said he wanted to see her that way, to feel her hair in his hands, smooth his palms down the length of it.

He gathered all of it in one hand, placed it over her shoulder, and exposed the nape of her neck. Bent and kissed her there. Her first kiss. His beard was wiry, and then his lips were so unexpectedly soft. He slipped his hands under her cloak, took her by the waist and pulled her closer to him. She told me that he was breathing heavy in her ear, and that's when she felt him, hard against her.

"It was shocking," she said. "But then, not really."

I had a sudden recollection of Betta coming in from the cold weeks ago. Her hair had been loosened and her eyes sparkled with secrets. I was preoccupied at the time—I'd just that minute fallen in love—and so I'd taken her word for it that she had been "out riding." Wind-swept and alive and surprised. It was still hard for me to picture her riding with Hár.

I imagined being introduced to all those sensations in one night, having never before felt a man's embrace, lips on her skin, hands in her hair, and then to feel him against her like that. Betta was such an inquisitive, innocent girl sometimes. Worry gnawed again.

"What have you done with him," I asked. "Besides riding, and … feeling him that way?"

She laughed lightly, and it was like a splash in the sunset river.

"As bold as I am, and the man such a savage, you would think we'd done every act Thora goes on about. But, nei. He will not." Her voice was a wistful mew. "He says one day I will want to marry a man my own age. As if there are any men of seventeen." She looked disgusted, probably imagining the candidates. Then she became dreamy and smiled again.

"He kisses me. He has rolled me around in the grass. He weighs more than a horse." She laughed and showed her big teeth. "And I can feel him, já?" She grew serious, and I suddenly wanted to burrow into the earth and stop thinking about Hár's mouth on hers.

"I know he wants more of me," she said. "He won't take it."

I was relieved at that, and it made me like him. But I was full of sadness over all the lost lust in this house.

ARROWS & SPEARS

I SPLASHED MY FACE WITH FRIGID WATER AND SWISHED WITH A lot of mouthwash in the pre-dawn dark.

We'd eaten quickly and were leaving for the coast in a thick and dusky mist—a kind of dark that was entirely new to me. A lowering of the light, still, not quite completely dark, but enough for the low clouds to obscure my sight. In the city, this kind of gray dusk couldn't exist together with the blaring electric light. Here, it began to linger longer every day.

The idea of full dark scared me, and when I imagined it I panicked a little. At the same time, I desired it, a dream about to be fulfilled. I would see so many more stars. I'd longed to see them, when I read about them at home and saw images in the arcs. Time lapse shots that streaked the sky with their movement.

I'd stood on the glacier, as far as I could get from the steady artificial lights that stretched to the sea, and searched for them, but only the same five were always visible. I'd seen more in the gray dusk of haying. But I had no way of imagining how many would be revealed in this place, when the winter came.

Heirik took a small group of us to make the last trip to the sea before the frigid months. We would pick up eels and shark from the fishing camp. Women would gather late berries and small pieces of wood, shells and bone for spoons and combs and pins. The boys would catch auks and plovers and puffins, and we'd come home loaded down with everything the horses could bear.

In the back mudroom, by the light of two wall lamps, I found a wool hat and pulled it down over my head. It was a work of art, this everyday item that someone—one of the women I knew?—had made. A wide band of dramatic dark brown fur sat like a wreath across my forehead.

I wondered how it looked on me. I hadn't seen my own image in months, and I knew I'd been changing here, with this food and work and the elements. I ran my tongue over the backs of my teeth, feeling the space there in the center, a reminder that I was still me. I could see the ends of my white-blond hair, my familiar long pony-tails coming out from under the hat and down over my shoulders. My hair was the same as always. But my hands were new. I turned them over in the quivering light and they were stark and strong.

I pulled on my wool cloak, and started looking for a good blanket to go over it.

Heirik came out of his room, throwing massive, moving shadows across the light of the oil lamps. Flames guttered in the breeze he stirred up. Colors were indistinct in the mudroom, in this light, but I could see he was dressed in his dark blue wool. His most formal clothes. A lush, silvery fur rested across his shoulders, seeming to glow with its own light.

I thought of him tenderly in these clothes, knowing they were a symbol of the rare times, the events where everyone was compelled to love him.

I also thought he looked flat-out gorgeous. I let my eyes drift shamelessly from his hair, down along his jawline, where his beard was trimmed neatly, wandering past his throat where Thor's hammer hung, and on down his body. Past his black leather belt, littered this time with everyday tools and knives as well as the seax across his waist and ax at his side. I devoured the blue fabric brushing his knees. His boots were tied so tight, I could see the curved lines of his calves. He was handsome beyond reckoning.

His voice was hoarse. "You are cold," he told me.

It was obvious. I shivered, mute.

"Turn," he commanded, with a thrust of his chin. He took the fur from his own shoulders and placed it on mine and it was warm with his heat. His arms very nearly around me. So close, I felt the pressure of knives and tools against my back.

Luxurious, velvety soft fur brushed my chin, and I pulled the skin close around me. It was pale silver, maybe an arctic fox. While it had been a slight shoulder covering for him, it fell halfway down my back and arms. The warmth from his body was in it, and it made my blood rise to meet it.

The animals were ready to leave, tossing their manes, their breath making great puffs that were lit by thralls' torches. Freezing air crept up my legs, and I stopped to tuck my wool bloomers into the tops of my rock-solid socks before I climbed onto Drifa.

The coast was less than a half day away, maybe four hours, I thought. In terms of the whole island, we lived virtually on the beach. We walked in the gray mist, our horses mingling and bumping. About a quarter of the way along, a suggestion of sun began to penetrate the gloom, a lightening that I didn't notice until it was there, faint but steady. Steam lifted and began to vanish, and the sky opened up, brilliant and massive over our upturned faces.

I'd wondered about Heirik himself, in his most beautiful clothes, on a supply run to the beach. It seemed an errand he could entrust to Hár and Hildur.

Now I thought I knew why he'd come. He desired this sky.

The color hovered somewhere between lavender and the edge of an ax. Purple and silver joined and pulled apart and shifted with the serene movement of pewter clouds. The last remnants of mist rose reluctantly to meet them, to be lost in the larger vapor of the enormous atmosphere.

I watched a few of Vakr's sure steps, and Heirik's back before me. His clothes were dark, but he wore another pale fur on his shoulders, his hair falling like a midnight tail. It had grown so much since I met him. When I first laid eyes on him, his hair had curled around his shoulders. Months since I'd been lost.

"Ginn," the chief called. "Ride with me."

I came up even with him, and could see that black wavy strands had come free around his face. I wanted to reach and tuck one back, care for him in that small way. His short beard would feel rough under my fingertips. Under my lips. I opened them slightly, involuntarily, and he noticed. It wasn't quite a smile he gave me, but his features were open and calm, his breathing slow and satisfied.

"Don't be afraid," he told me, and I wondered why. I thought that there wasn't a single part of me that feared this. Never.

And then we crested a rise, and the heads of three haunting giants rose up before us.

I sat, struck viscerally by the crude figures, fear pooling in my gut. Made of stone, they stood at least twice the height of the house. Their bases sat far below us, and I peered down to see that someone had built on top of natural rock formations, with tremendous blocks and boulders. On top of each towering pile sat an oval stone that looked like a head.

They stood in a line, leaning toward us, as if they walked toward our home. We passed them on our right, from largest to smallest. Crude but so real, the two-story-tall bodies were hunched and frozen along their eternal path. They seemed far more ancient than possible, as though they'd been bent into the wind for millenia, always making their way to Hvítmörk.

"The stone sisters," Heirik said. "They show the byway."

Then Drifa canted forward and the world dropped away from under me. I grabbed frantically for her mane with both hands and clutched hard, and she shook her head to push me off. I looked, and a cry stuck in my throat. We were riding straight down a cliff. Every part of my insides battled to get out, any way possible. Acid burned my throat and my intestines felt liquid and weak. I closed my eyes, which was much worse. I opened them again and looked out across the vast open space before me.

The rock face went straight down at a heart-stopping angle, the surface jagged and tricky. The cliff was threaded with the barest hints of path here and there, slippery patches of slate, grainy with dirt. The places where for decades horses had chosen the same footholds.

Now, Drifa followed right behind Vakr, picking out places to step with complete ease. I watched her feet. She was impatient with me, twitching to remind me to let go of her mane, but my hands tangled there like claws. I clenched her sides, and she took great big breaths to try to throw my legs off.

A few miniature plateaus, here and there along the path, gave me a chance to breathe and look out, briefly, toward the ocean. It stretched like a blue thread, visible here and there beyond rows of far hills.

It could have been a thousand miles away or closer than I dreamed. The vast distance seized me, like it did any time the land opened up around me and I could see out. See distances that weren't possible in my original time. Far off, the water waited patiently, dark green and iron under an endless lavender sky. Sun came—a brief, straight ray—and kissed the surface, lighting it up a deep aqua before quickly turning blackish again under a shadow of clouds. For a moment the voices and language I loved so dearly had no meaning. They yielded completely to something big and wordless.

Tiny rocks and gravel spilled away as Drifa skirted an outcropping, and I gasped. I fixed my eyes on Heirik's back and watched as harsh breezes that verged on wind struck and riffled his fur. I trusted him in my bones, entirely, always, with my life. He would not lead me onto a dangerous path.

More than that. We were born to stand next to each other, protecting each other until our last breaths. I would be patient, and one day we would share the passion and everyday beauty, face together the exigencies of farm life and grave decisions he had to make. I would be beside him for those things. I was no longer scared of the steepness.

A while later—a very long while, or perhaps a scant handful of minutes—we stepped off rock and onto flat ground. The floor of a gold and lovely valley opened at our feet, flanked by thick birch forests on either side.

Drifa's feet hit the valley floor, and in a second, we flew. She picked up speed in an instant and was running free across the flat ground. I almost shrieked, it was so sudden and violent. But in a second I was there with her, riding with a complete and contagious joy, at the edge of terror. I leaned into her muscular body, and the wind took the tears from my eyes.

The men rode even faster, their horses' feet a grassy explosion. Heirik took off after his uncle, until they both flew. Magnus and Haukur went by in a hopeful blur, wanting to catch up with them. Soon Drifa's thirst to run was slaked, and she slowed down and down until we finally walked at an easy pace. The men were small flecks of pepper in the distance, already near the sea. The oppressively vast distance between us, the smallness of their lives against such a big place, made my heart flutter. I looked down frequently at Drifa's twitching ears and bent to pet her strong neck.

We traveled at a modest pace now, following a small river that cut a single grand curve in the golden grass. The horses stepped right into it as though it weren't there. Knee high, it shushed all around us and I lifted my feet to keep them dry. My cherry skirt skimmed the surface. So late in the season, the grass burst with colors of straw and golden ale and rust before it would soon slide into dormancy or death.

It wasn't a morbid thought to me. It was a comfort, the steady and normal turning of the seasons.

In another quarter hour, we emerged at the top of a big, gradual slope, with the sea waiting below. The horses stepped through brittle, brown snowblooms as high as their chests, as sure on the shifting sand of this dune as they had been on the rocky terrain an hour ago.

Then the plants ended, and we dropped into the immense, curving basin of the black beach and sea.

We picked our way as if we were the only living creatures among a scattering of the dead, driftwood all around us like bones, in all sizes from tiny sticks to whole trees I wouldn't be able to put my arms around.

The russet and cherry of my dress stood out below my fur and blanket, and I felt like a single rufous bird in a world of pewter and steel. A world that was otherwise uninterrupted by the natural creams and browns of common dresses. Even the dark blue of Heirik's clothes blended with the purple and steel of the sand.

Then we met the water.

Curious, fearless Drifa stepped straight into the pounding edge of the sea. She waded in until she was knee-deep in the violent white foam that exploded against us, sending spray up my legs with every darkening wave.

I wasn't prepared.

I knew I would face the water. But as it came time, now, I wasn't ready—could never have been ready—for its roiling assault. The sound of the sea was deafening. I didn't remember this crashing, over and over, every wave throwing up an angry spray. I drew back on the reins and Drifa backed up, tripping and confused by the pull of the undertow, the pull of my dread. The water touched my boot and I shouted, incoherent fear. I turned her hard to get out of the ocean, away from its sucking desire to take me back.

The waves I remembered were even and relentless. Not like this. This was an autumn ocean, tossing and wild. I was afraid if it found me, it wouldn't let me go.

With a few wind-sucked shouts and barks, Hár split the party up, some galloping off to the fishing camp, just visible in the distance down the beach. Heart racing, I was vaguely aware of women taking baskets, boys heading off toward the high crags, grabbing clubs of driftwood to hunt the slow and hapless auks that gathered there.

I still trembled, looking into the sea. When it clutched my ankles, I felt a kind of desire in it, like it wanted me. The gritty smell of salt filled me, choking off my breath. Like a child looking for a big hand to draw me up and comfort me, I turned to Heirik. And I lost my breath at the sight.

He watched me with those gold eyes. They burned with a slow flame, but it was ready to flare. He wanted me. His eyes said *mine*. Question, plea and command. My heart dropped away, and I let my own eyes show him, yes. I whispered, but so softly it was eaten by the wind. "Are you mine, too?" He watched my lips form the English words but couldn't possibly hear them.

He came toward me, Vakr kicking up foam. Drifa shook her head at him, snorting and complaining.

"I'm okay," I told Heirik, though he hadn't asked. I looked around to find Hár and ask for an assignment, something I could gather or pick, baskets I could fearlessly fill with berries and shells.

Everyone was gone.

While I'd been struggling with the ocean, Heirik and I had been left utterly alone. I hadn't been given a job to do. It was just the two of us remaining at the water's edge. We'd been left so efficiently and completely alone, that it dawned on me, and I thought, *oh. Oh.*

I wasn't here to do a job. I was here to just be with him. He took me on this gorgeous journey, wore his beautiful clothes, trimmed his beard, to have this day with me. This last breath of sky and landscape before the dark came. Gods, it was intense and sweet.

Heirik turned Vakr, and with a shake of tails we rode just a few meters away and up a slight rise. Small, cave-like spaces were set into a tremendous rock face that loomed over the beach and stretched all the way into the sea. An epic wall, enclosing us. The caves weren't deep, just depressions in the rock. Heirik found one that was hidden behind a giant limb of driftwood as big as a boat.

I dismounted and let Drifa move off to eat. I met Heirik by the driftwood and sat next to him in the sand. I settled in as close as I dared, as close as I could handle with restraint. Without touching him tenderly, or trying to complete the sweet kiss we almost shared at the shearing, or perhaps grasping his clothes and pulling him viciously against my breasts and mouth. I sat just far enough from him to control myself, and yet near enough to smell the scents of fur and Heirik himself that I could never parse. They were both so much part of him and one another.

I pulled the fox tight around my shoulders.

"Part of my mother's morning gift," he said, calming me. He meant the silvery, luscious fur. It was his mother's.

"The blue fox is rare," he told me. "My father's arrow bit the animal the day they were wed." As he spoke, he didn't look at the fur at all, only in my eyes. He was checking that I was alright, but more than that. Maybe I was dreaming, but I felt he was falling into me, the way I did him.

"This is where you came," he said gently.

I looked around, unnerved, my heartbeat scattered by fear and hope and lust. "The exact place?" My voice broke.

He prompted me. "You have no memory."

I didn't, truly. It had been a beach, the sand black and wet, but I'd been disoriented and half conscious. I couldn't remember many details of that day, and this could have been any stretch of coastline. I had no idea this was the actual spot.

"Just sand," I muttered, and felt some between my fingertips. "Just this sand."

Heirik tightened the one-handed knot on his right gauntlet. The black leather was stiff from disuse, worn only for feasts and rituals, significant days.

"I remember the whine of the wind," I told him, discovering the memory even as I said it. But I found no way to describe the howling pain, the confusion and sorting of sounds and visions. I settled for insufficient words. "I was so cold."

"Já, you were blue." The knot fell apart, and he absently let it drop. "I thought you would die on the journey."

An awkward silence fell after that frank recognition of my mortality. He'd found me, though. I was alive. Silently, without permission, I took his black laces in my fingers and tied them.

He watched my hands work in wonder, as if an exquisite, tiny bird had landed on his forearm.

When I was finished, I slowly trailed my fingers down along the column of crossed laces. Even the feeling of his leather was forbidden, let alone the skin beneath it. But I took it. And just the leather itself sent a thrill through me that exited through my skin, everywhere at once. I trailed my fingers farther, until we were palm to palm, and then farther still until our fingertips touched briefly and let go.

He dropped his hand to his knee and curled it into a fist. He looked at it while he spoke. "No woman has touched me since I was a child."

I let the words remain in the air, while I tried to absorb them. He hadn't been touched by a woman, not even with the most minor ministrations, in more than a decade probably. No one had cut his hair for him, sewn his sleeves in the morning, nor even brushed fingers handing over a bowl of food or tapped his shoulder to ask him a question. How he must have hungered for even the simplest, most casual of those touches.

He opened his fist, his upturned hand resting on his knee, and he looked at it with detached interest. I moved slowly. I laid my hand in his palm, like a wing gently spread. Hovered there, delicately introducing the idea.

He grasped my wrist so roughly, he could have broken my bones. I gasped, wild-eyed. Thrilled.

It was the first time he'd reached out to touch a woman. And now I didn't just understand the word—untouchable—I knew in my body what it meant. He didn't even know how. How strong or gentle to be. How slow or sudden. Or perhaps he did. After waiting so long, years of thinking about how he would do it if he could, maybe he knew exactly what he wanted. A rough ownership. No chance to turn back.

He pulled me by the wrist, pulled me to him, and pressed his mouth to mine. His mouth. Gods, it was soft and I'd waited so long. I opened up to him, gave him my mouth, my very breath. He was possessive and impatient, wanting our kiss without knowing how to take it. I parted my lips to show him. I let my tongue brush against his, and he pulled back, so slightly I could still feel his lips hovering just beyond mine. He met my mouth again, murmuring a soft sound of comprehension, and he opened his mouth and gave me his tongue.

My fingers followed the leather of his bracer and pulled his sleeve free so I could get my hand inside, moving up his bare arm, skin burning. With my other hand, I felt his long hair, as thick as I imagined it would feel. I pulled on the leather strip and it all fell free, over my hand in waves.

We separated for a second, our foreheads together, breathing hard. Heirik's hair fell forward over me, enclosing me, and he closed his eyes. He captured the back of my head with his hand. His other had pushed up my sleeve, was inside it, thumb pressed into the crook of my arm. He nuzzled the hair at my temple, pressing his lips to the skin there. I kissed him everywhere, his jaw, the corner of his mouth where he smiled. On his cheekbone I tasted salt. I kissed his throat, and he lifted his chin to let me burrow there, where I'd always wanted to devour him. My tongue traced Thor's hammer, and Heirik growled a word into my hair. Incoherent lust and surprise.

He grasped me hard by the chin, too hard, and took my mouth again. And then his fingers moved to explore our kiss. He touched the place where our mouths joined, as though he were blind, until his tongue and lips and fingers were one sensation.

A WORDLESS CRY CAME FROM FAR DOWN THE BEACH. IT WAS A mournful sound, almost lost in the sea, but Heirik heard it and broke away from our kiss. He was on his feet in less than a second, and mounted on Vakr in one more. I sat bereft in the sand, my breath coming hard.

He was lithe getting on his horse, quick like a cold brook. Even as I wondered what was happening, passion still coursed through me, and I thought of taking his hips in my hands, feeling that fluid motion coming into me.

The dream fell away when I saw him draw a knife from his belt. It had a strap he wrapped around his wrist, letting the blade fall and hang there. He looked down the frosted water's edge, and I followed his gaze. Riders approached fast. I couldn't make out who they were, could only discern a half dozen spears like quivering arrows pointing to the sky. A pair of great dark birds circled overhead.

Heirik ordered me calmly. "*Slitasongr.*" I cast my eyes around where we'd just knelt together against the gray stones, black ground, ash-white wood. The ax laid somewhere melting into this blade-colored landscape. I found it. It was heavy in my hand, and I felt the energy in it, its voice. I handed it up to Heirik, and he took it from me without glancing my way.

I stood beside him for a solemn moment that seemed to stretch forever, the riders never getting closer. His palm was on my hair then, his thumb brushed my forehead. "Get back, Litla, away from here."

We both turned to view the long slope on which we stood, the black rock face stretching forever, straight into the ocean. Shallow caves dipped into the rock everywhere, but none deep enough for me to really hide. Pain crossed his features like a breeze, there and gone, and he seemed to clear his face of all emotion. So I wouldn't be scared, I thought. He looked down at my red dress. "Cover yourself," he said. With those words, he took off fast, Vakr spraying my skirts with sand.

I stumbled back to the place where we'd just held each other, an abandoned bower full of furs and love. His gauntlet sprawled there, his hair tie, his mother's fur, and time seemed to slow almost to a halt, while I noted these things one by one. I'd pulled his hair loose to bury my hands in it, ripped the leather away from his wrist to get inside his shirts. Now he would fight with his hair in his eyes and one hand tangled in linen.

I covered myself entirely with my cloak, like a child hiding, and my breath was hot and ragged inside my little fur tent. Hoofbeats fell right outside, and I heard Heirik shout, "Ageirr!" And then the fight came nearer, bellowed oaths and warnings clear now, horses screaming. I thought of Drifa with alarm and almost jumped up to search for her. But the din of men and beasts mingled with the pounding and roaring of the sea and the sounds came closer and closer and pinned me, shaking, to this rock. I melted into it, a thin slime under my cheek.

Heirik had ridden out to meet them, but somehow the fight had come right back here. Right to me.

The clang of iron and grunts of men were no more than two house-lengths away. A horse squealed above the din, more urgent than the rest, a man cried out and the ground shook with a thud that resounded even among the downpour of hoofbeats. There were more strangled cries, and angry words slashing. None were Heirik's. I would know his injured voice from the others.

Would he, maybe, call for me if he fell? What if a spear ran through him, or an ax cleaved his head? I thought of his enigmatic smile, his golden eyes going blank and dead, lost to me before I'd ever truly known and had him. I didn't want to cower with my eyes shut and cheek pressed to the wall while my love was torn up and wasted. I wanted to be present, wanted him to know I was here. I heard Hildur's words about his brother Brosa—*tall as the chief and just as fierce.* I willed it to be true, that Heirik was fierce. I pulled the cloak down from my head and opened my eyes.

My blood ran cold when I saw him. He'd pulled Vakr back from the fight, skirting the outside at an unbelievable speed, and his hair flew out behind him like in an epic poem or a painting from history. Savage and intent, his face smeared with sweat and blood and misted with the spray of the sea. He was the raven, the last sight before Valhalla.

Rearing back on Vakr, he swung his ax above his head in a splendid arc and connected with the wrist of one of Ageirr's men. It was his brother! Eiðr's hand fell to the ground, neatly severed. I retched and doubled over, forehead on the sand, grit in my nose, in my mouth, choking, whimpering. Violence too hard, too near, my body was screaming to run.

Drifa's scent came strong and near. I looked up to find her pressed against the rock wall beside me, crying, a sound like nothing I'd ever heard. She was in danger. I needed to reach her. And she was a way out. On her back, I could get away. All I wanted was distance, to be far from knives, axes, horses fighting with a demented will. I staggered to my feet, lurching for her, and climbed up on her back. I turned to find my way past, and found Ageirr looking at me.

Ageirr's eyes were lost in the trance of fighting, but I watched as they cleared. He came at me, and I turned Drifa and tried to run away, but there was only rock face in both directions. I didn't know how to get past him, nor did she, just a baby, shaking with fear underneath my thighs. Ageirr was upon us in a second. And in the next second, he'd torn me off of Drifa's back and had me in front of him on his own horse. The animal reared savagely, and I screamed. I fought with fingernails, arms, feet, but Ageirr was immovable.

And then there was silence. Time slowed down again, in its odd way of changing and stretching in moments of fear and flight, and I could see the scene laid out before me. The fight was over. Heirk, Hár and Magnus were there, alive, bloody. Ageirr's family had fled. None but he remained.

I stopped struggling and watched as Heirik's head turned toward my cry. A terrible focus moved over his face like a cloud covering the sun. He spoke with an even cadence and low, soothing voice.

"Ageirr," he said.

His voice made me feel secure. Ageirr's horse settled, too, Heirik charming us all.

"Ageirr, what are you doing?"

Ageirr didn't answer, though I felt him shake his head. His horse tripped backwards over driftwood, making it skittish again, wary. It came to me plainly, Ageirr had no plan. He'd grabbed me on impulse, and now he was the only one left. Aggressive, wounded, full of rage and jealousy and grief. His arm tightened around my waist. He smelled like blood and metal and sickness.

Heirik continued to talk to him from a distance. He didn't come forward to save me. I wished for him, remembered his strong hands on me and wanted them now, willed him to come. But he did not meet my eyes, only Ageirr's.

"What do you want, Ageirr?" He kept saying his name. Lulling him, making him feel drowsy and safe. Hár was on the ground, moving slowly to retrieve a dropped spear. Heirik held Ageirr's eyes, so my captor didn't notice when Hár handed the spear to Heirik.

Dreadful realization came. I saw Heirik's plan. He would throw a weapon right at us.

I cast my eyes around, wanting bravery, wanting a way out, and all I saw were discarded blades and a severed hand reddening the foam at the water's edge. I drew my eyes away, my thoughts inward, searching for strength, or at least ignorance. What I found were sims, and I almost barked a sick laugh. I thought I'd seen men fight in the cage, punch and kick and dislocate and wound. I'd seen nothing. Useless memories passed by, of cheering at things I didn't understand.

And then a memory of an elbow to an opponent's head, two, three, four times, and there was cringing and howling from the crowd.

Heirik held the spear loosely, hanging by his side, casually waiting for his chance. I couldn't wait any longer. I had to do something. And so I curled up and then struck out with my elbow, up at Ageirr's chin, harder than I had ever done anything. He grunted and loosened his grip so that I hung from his arm. Far enough away.

In the slowness, I watched Heirik. His face was cold resolution. His throw smooth and easy. A breeze lifted loose strands of my hair as the spear went by. It was that close. Then I hit the ground, my head bounced hard off a piece of driftwood and I was free.

GRAY WASHED ALL OVER AND ABOVE ME, FROM THE GREENEST, moistest clay to blackest iron. The colors of the sky swirled together, purple and dark blue, twisting and crossing. I was lifted from the ground, and things shimmered silver all around, enchanting. There were faces, too, beloved ones. Hár held me on his horse.

Byr picked his way through a sea of knee-high plants, green against the black sand and gray wood, and I let my hand drop to skim them with my fingers. I almost fell off until Hár grasped me. I leaned back into the old man and smiled. This was the second time he would carry me, drowsy with pain and cold, home from this beach.

Heirik rode before us, just like on the first day I arrived, when he was still the chief and I was Jen. He led Drifa beside him. His hand rested lightly on her saddle, mottled fingers closing over the leather where I'd sat, stroking with his thumb.

The peace of wading through driftwood and greens exploded with force as soon as we were clear, and the horses took off on flat ground. Hár crushed me to him, and we flew.

They drove the horses hard, and the wind scoured my face. I felt Hár's long beard on my cheek, reassuring and ticklish, and I thought of my friend kissing him, touching him. My head fell to the side and I watched his thighs hanging on to Byr, his muscles like iron. A thick, red mess was flowering on the brown wool on his leg.

I'd been held by Betta's lover far more often than my own.

It was a single wistful thought, lost to the darkening sky that yawned above and sucked all air out of me. The temperature seemed to drop a dozen degrees in the space of a breath. The weather gathered itself, and the sky stretched out above us, endlessly churning. And in the next instant, it turned to steel and closed over us like a vault. Soon, the stark stone sisters rose to meet the blackening sky, and water ran into my eyes, blurring their terrifying forms. Like condemned spirits, they made their endless way, the shortest first this time. Leading us home.

I dozed off, and when I woke the winter had risen all around us. Hard whipping gusts of wind drove it into us, freezing and raw. The horses—even with wills and bodies like the gods themselves—were driven off course. They bore down, every person, every horse, focused now only on the promise of shelter. I believed in the idea of warmth, I had to.

The notion of going somewhere safe seemed important. But where?

Anywhere but this time and place, with its iron and steel and blood that ran as freely as the men felt necessary. Not here, where hands were shorn and spears thrown. Here where I rode on a gorgeous horse, at the confluence of violence and clear beauty. I sputtered as ice cold rain flowed over my face. Water filled my nose and I pursed my lips and blew against the spray so I could breathe.

A sense of white and glass came to me, big skylights, interiors brilliant with sunshine. The clean lines of a stainless steel coffee table. The smell of coffee itself. A quilt warm from the dryer. It smelled like detergent. The sensation of someone's arms around me. I imagined the feeling of a bearded chin against the bridge of my nose. That was safety. I imagined lying my forehead against a warm chest, the feel of skin and metal and leather. The smell of smoke was safety.

I was sleepy. I kept falling asleep.

I didn't know if Heirik had killed him. I wondered if Ageirr had fallen dead with me in his arms and let me go with his last breath. Heirik would kill someone to save me, I knew.

The grass lashed all over the house. Heim, I thought, já, and trygg. I struggled for the English words, thinking they were important. *Home. Safe.*

I was handed from one man to another. I searched their faces, but they were indistinct, so many. "Heirik?" I tried to call, and it came out weak. I heard a woman's gasp, Hildur's voice. "Child, the chief is right here!" It was a warning, not an answer to my question. Maybe his name? I had used his name? I heard him speak, then, and the words didn't matter because his voice calmed me, even and strong. I clung to that voice, and it followed me.

There was smoke and less light, and the familiar feeling of my bench. Someone lifted my head and put blankets there. Some more were dragged on top of me. The wool welcomed me into sleepy oblivion. I heard a man's voice—it was Betta's Da—saying "Child, wake up," but I didn't.

I dreamed that I'd been injured and Heirik was caring for me. The chief himself, sitting to tend me. My eyes were closed, but I knew it was him because of his scent, like cinnamon and fur. It was mixed with the metallic smell of blood and the scent of juniper infusing a cool cloth on my forehead. I felt a brush of something silky on my face. I found it was his hair on my cheek. It fell like a curtain around me as he bent to speak.

It was a vivid dream. I'd never seen him in my sleeping place, in this space where no color lit his irises. Never seen his eyes so dark, almost brown. He looked worried. I smiled to let him know I was alright, but it felt wobbly, like I'd had too much ale, and I laughed.

I expected one of his sweet smiles to follow, but it didn't come. He sat straight up and asked for someone to find Betta's Da. I missed Heirik's closeness. I didn't want this part of the dream to end. I didn't want to dream about Bjarn instead. I started to feel slumber coming, fast, like a train.

"Stay," Heirik commanded me. He brought the back of his hand gently to my face and brushed across my cheek. The contact burned like fire, instant and fierce. A good burning, so unbearably good. "Stay." It was a whisper this time, a plea. I turned my head toward his hand and parted my lips to kiss his knuckles, and his bones were strong and hard against my mouth. He was speaking my sweet name, Litla, in a voice dry like bark. The curtains rustled and Bjarn appeared.

"Oh," Betta's father said, an awed exhalation. He might have seen a god or goddess in the flesh, his voice was so incredulous, so full of wonder. He drew away, but Heirik stopped him with an order. The dream dissipated and my lover was the chief again.

"Care for Ginn," he said. "And speak to no one." With swift grace, he was gone.

SNOW & STARS

Winter

THE NEXT DAY SNOW CAME, FAST AND DEEP, AND THE WORLD moved inside.

In the morning, it was all we talked about, in tones that echoed differently in the snowbound house. It was amazingly fast, everyone said, how in one night it had piled up outside the doors, up past our knees. Nothing compared to what might come. Stories of past winters were murmured like charms against the elements, tales of houses buried, animals gone. The sudden and complete isolation was shocking. It made me panic, and thoughts of Ageirr came again.

Nei. I steeled myself to be brave and live with the memories of the fight. The way Heirik would. And so I sewed together rips and hems with a spinning head, and followed gingerly after little Lotta. The snow was as tall as her, and she confirmed it by opening the front door over and over. We'd forget about her for a while, and then icy fingers would creep up under our dresses, and I would make my way to the mudroom to drag her back.

The snow muffled everything. It wasn't just my head. I had a concussion I thought, but there was something else hushed about the house, the silent bulk of snow making the voices and gentle echoes different. Besides Lotta's delight, the rest of the children responded with a confused quiet of their own, broken by small cries here and there. It was the beginning of a long winter.

The pantry was always cool, but today, with the new snow outside, the cold stole the smells of the most pungent cheese and sharp fish, leaving behind a clean wholeness to the air. I could relax here, with the door closed. All day, I'd cycled through intense, mixed up visions. The joy and pleasure of Heirik and me together, strong, seeking hands, smiling into a kiss, a hand severed, bone and blood and cries of aggression and panic, Drifa's wild nostrils and scared eyes. Ageirr's grief-stricken hold on me was the clearest of all. And the spear. Even now, I felt it whisper as it passed. So vivid, once I thought my hair actually feathered with the memory.

Here in the pantry, I could blank my mind.

Betta helped me, by opening the door and then returning the keys. No one knew I was in here. Leaning heavily against the wall, I let my eyes soften and my thoughts turn to a flat and open plain, a big blue sky. I let my gaze wander the shelves, and saw the precious box of herbs peeking out from the back of a high shelf. I'd seen Hildur put it away, and now I stretched on my toes and pushed danger aside, along with baskets and containers of lesser foods and sewing supplies.

A wash of fragrance filled the room when I opened the little box. I picked out one tiny spear of rosemary—"ocean's dew"—just a bit bigger than a grain of rice, and placed it on my tongue.

The door opened, and I shoved the box back deep on the shelf.

The silly guilt, and frustration at having so little time alone, both vanished in a second. It was Heirik ducking low under the door frame. He shut the door behind him without taking his eyes off me. He made that shushing motion everyone here used, palm facing me, fingers pushing sound away. He whispered.

"Are you alright?" His voice sounded simpler here, absorbed by the close, earthen walls, but not flat. Still depthless.

"My head hurts," I said quietly, around the bit of rosemary. I added a light laugh to try for bravery, or nonchalance, but it sounded more like a whimper, without any reverb to buoy it. Sudden dizziness sloshed in my head and I bent forward, resting my hands on my knees.

He covered the distance between us in one stride and caught me, and I fell into him without a word. His arms came up around me, awkward, unaccustomed, and it was too much—the spear, the pressure and pain in my head, the fact of Heirik's years of isolation echoed in his too-tight grasp. I cried.

It lasted a long moment, my silent crying, and he held me without a sound. Then I felt the vibrations of words in his chest even before I heard his voice.

"Many times, I have wanted to care for you," he said. "But in small ways. Not like this."

I smiled against his chest, warmed by the thought that his desire matched mine so exactly. That he wanted to care for me in daily moments. That his fingertips fit so well into the curve of my spine. With my nose buried in his smoky shirt and his beard tickling my ear, I'd come home.

His hands came to my waist, and he lifted me onto the high bench. He stood between my knees. Swirls of apron and dress between us, no height separated us now. I looked right at him and lay my palm on his cheek. He sucked in air, unused to tenderness.

"Ginn …" My name sounded twisted and wrong, and I didn't like the sadness in his eyes. I brushed my fingers into his hair, and they snagged there in black tangles. He quickly kissed me, hard. He still had no idea how. It was reckless and new, and I let myself dissolve into it.

Just like yesterday, the force of possession, hands on cheeks, fingers raking skin, his surprised murmur, "Sjordogg," lost against my lips. *Sea-dew.* A taste of rosemary. I slipped my fingers under Thor's hammer. They caught in the leather at his throat, pulling him closer, and then Heirik stopped.

He leaned his forehead heavily into my shoulder, and let his breathing settle, and then he stayed there. It lasted a little too long, felt a little too much like resignation.

"I am going away," he said, and he lifted his head.

"Nei!" I blurted it out, too loud. He would be gone from me? Right now, when this was so new and delicious. Suspicion and fear crept in. Was he going for Ageirr? In a breath, I thought of them fighting, of more blood and bones. A brother's hand for a brother's horse. What in exchange for me?

"For two or three days only, Litla."

Out of all the many warning cries and questions in my head, I blurted out a dumb one. "How?"

"How?" He echoed my question, as if he hadn't heard me right.

I rested my head on his shoulder now, and mumbled into his shirts. "The snow, it's as high as Lotta." So naive. What did I think? That he wouldn't know how to deal with a couple feet of snow? He'd spend the whole winter in his room?

"Já, well, Lotta is not so high," he pointed out. He pulled away from me so I would lift my eyes to his. He surely saw worry, wondering.

"Vakr er stor hestur," he said with a smile. It was like a line from a children's story. *Vakr is a big horse.* I laughed, a birdlike laugh this time, and I bent to muffle it in his shirts.

"Is Ageirr dead?" I asked into linen.

"Nei," he said, with a sigh in his voice, full of relief or regret, I couldn't tell.

When Heirik ducked out, he pulled the door shut behind him, but I could hear Hildur say "Herra!" Her shocked tone traveled like an arrow, right through the heavy wood. Somehow she both submitted to him and chided him at once. "If there is anything you need from the stores, tell me."

"Walk with me," he told her, in a tone that certainly had her clutching at beads. I heard them move away.

I pressed my lips together to seal our kiss before I went back out into the house to see the likes of her. Love was not Hildur's to dole out. And real respect, not the kind born of superstition, was something she would never give.

The house closed in on itself, beginning to stew with heat from the fire, packed in and reflected by the insulating snow. It started to stink right away, and I had to get out. I went through the tunnel to the welcoming, little pool.

The horror of the fight, my new and epic love, my concussion, all kept me preoccupied, and I'd forgotten the sky. When I stepped from the tunnel, I almost fell to my knees with the weight and glory of it. Stars! They pressed down on me, a million of them at least!

The enormity of the sky, its depths, bewildered my senses and I pressed my fingers to my temples, trying to fathom it. The big stars were the same ones that I'd known. But in among them were packed a thousand more for every space I used to think of as empty. A sky of sifted sugar. It was really, truly dark out, and I was stunned.

I floated in the hot pool, my head thrown back on the stones. At first, I felt trapped by the stars' density, their unimaginable numbers, but then my eyes and mind adjusted and the sky opened to me with its depths and distances. So many things here—almost everything—were more heartbreakingly beautiful than I dreamed.

THE WELCOMING, LITTLE POOL BECAME AN OASIS, WHERE I COULD be small amidst the stars and steam. Betta and I took the little girls with us twice a day and floated and told stories about fine dresses and foxes and hawks.

They asked about how I came from the ocean, and I told them a big bird had dropped me on the sand like a stone. I thought they would laugh, but they looked at me with gigantic eyes, and I had to tell them I was kidding, that I just didn't know.

Inside, Betta taught me to play tafl. It was a game of strategy, with smooth, round wooden men and one tiny carved chieftain, who hunched, curled around his long beard and gripping it with two hands. I'd learned the game before of course, in the future, but I pretended not to know. I let her show me how to move, to protect my chief, to take. We played with Magnus and Haukur, and it filled up some of the hours.

On the second full day that Heirik was gone, Hár showed the little ones how to make char with the tiniest bits of linen that could no longer even be mended or used as a cloth. He stuffed them into a tiny metal box with a hole in the top and roasted it on the fire.

I watched the smoke climb to the roof, and I sewed languidly, never finishing anything. I named the new colors that spread through the house and settled in. A dusky plum in the shadows, deepening until the eye couldn't parse it from espresso, moist earth, then black. I thought of espresso fondly, like a long-ago lover. *Doppio con pana.* I put my finger in my mouth as if to lick the whipped cream.

Not as though I'd forgotten where I was. Nei, I felt my home around me more acutely than ever, every hawk's eye on me, wondering about me, probably searching for my reasons to want such a frightening man, because I clearly did. I couldn't hide it. Striving for this rich house probably, to be the mistress of it despite the master I'd have to endure. That was a likely conclusion.

About the lying, they would be right, not in the way they might think.

I pretended I'd pricked myself, regarded my needle with mild betrayal. I went back to my lazy, disinterested project. A hem maybe. I wasn't even sure, and had to look for a long moment to remember the soft, worn shirt in my hands.

Men went to the stables to check after animals. They came back with brilliant sparkles of melting ice in their beards and the fur that ringed their hats. They brought out skið and rubbed them with foul-smelling fat, and again Magnus sharpened every knife in the house.

Children played at fighting with adorable shields and axes, and the girls put imaginary babies to their breasts and then to bed in soft furs. Still Heirik didn't come home.

On the third day, I switched to binding socks, and immersed myself in memories of kisses, my eyes going soft, entranced. I mused about why he'd gone away, wishing and hoping that it wasn't for Ageirr. That it was something else, anything, that would not lead him into danger and bloodshed. I imagined what it would be like when he came back. I wanted to rush to him and greet and hold him, but I knew I would not.

When he did come home, I heard him first, talking with his uncle in the back of the house. My heart sped up, but I made myself appear unfazed. He would come to me, and I could wait until then.

But he didn't. He never came to see me, not even after he'd been home for what felt like a thousand hours. Not even after the evening meal, when the house was settling into night and there was no more chance for him to casually walk into the main room and say hello.

My throat tight and full of questions, I went to straighten up the back mudroom.

Wooden snowshoes stood against the wall, and though the men and kids had taken care to hang up everything they wore outside, most of it was weighted with dripping snow and had slumped and fallen. Cloaks and blankets and boots gathered on the benches and stone floor like knots of birds around crumbs. The ones still on the hooks hung lifeless as though brought home by a hunter.

The room was scented pleasantly with mud and snowmelt. The cloaks themselves smelled of wet wool, a sheepy smell, but processed by carding and spinning and felting, not like the spiky reek of the animal itself. I folded and stacked them, satisfying myself with mindless hand work, trying to trick myself into believing I wasn't watching his door. Nei, I didn't care if he was in there. I didn't long to knock.

I'd always liked to smooth blankets and hang them over the back of my couch, one on top of another until there were more than enough for any dark and frigid day—as if my apartment could ever approach a cold like this. A bone-blasting, deep cold I could never have imagined, much less believed I could live with.

I heard the crunch of footsteps, and in a breathless moment Heirik was filling up the room, stamping his snowshoes and boots, and taking off furs and wool. I took a sharp breath, always stunned by him. He turned, and for an unguarded second, he saw me. He said my name, in that way that turned his voice and eyes to honey. My name was the most subtle and lovely thing he ever said.

"You were outside," I said dumbly.

He sat on the bench to undo the leather laces of his snowshoes. "Já, everyone settled." He pulled off his hat, and his hair fell loose with no braids or ties. Just him. It was more stirring than if he'd taken off his clothes, that untamed hair was so naked. He saw me looking and ducked his head.

"Saying goodnight to the farm, my mother called it," he huffed as he pulled off the big, unwieldy snowshoes. "We would walk all around the outside of the house and stables, counting animals and people. And then go to bed and directly to sleep, I suppose was the idea, já?" His half smile was luscious.

I smiled too, at the thought of little Heirik, this fierce and commanding man a four year old child. But I couldn't conjure a steady image. Without a photo it was hard to pin down. Hard to really understand how this towering person with rough beard and serious eyebrows used to be a little boy with tousled black hair, saying goodnight to the sheep and grass and horsies. How could I ask him, *what did you look like?* It struck me that he didn't know what he himself looked like now, let alone then. There were no mirrors here. There were various surfaces of water, reflecting indistinct and riffled images. Mostly everyone depended on others to know how they looked. Men depended on women to trim their beards, cut and comb their hair, react with longing and flirtation, or not. In Heirik's case, most often with fear or revulsion. No wonder he thought he was a monster. He couldn't see his own divine face.

He sat with his elbows resting on his knees, his capable hands hanging between his thighs. It was too much to look at it. I turned to study the cloaks on the wall, stroking them aimlessly. I drew my shoulders forward ever so slightly, offering my back to the steady, hot pressure of his gaze.

"Do you remember the names of the stars?"

I thought of the five I could see in my original time, and the press of the multitude I could see now. I had a feeling he didn't mean NGC 3576. Flustered, questioning whether I should pretend to know or not, I turned to him and nothing mattered. There he was, and I knew him well. He was unsettled.

He stood. "Come look." As always, confident his word would be followed.

I looked down at my dress and glanced back at the house where my own cloak and blankets lay neatly folded and stacked in my alcove.

"Not through the house." He told me to wait where I stood, and he ducked low into the door to his room. He brought out an armful of silvery fur, and unfolded it for me. Oh gods, it was a breathtaking coat. Made of blue-fox and wool, thick and heavy, but small, a woman's coat. Despite its bulk, it was almost fitted through the waist, and I tied it tight with its leather sash. Straight out of a fairy tale, it had a pointed hood rimmed with fur. Its giant bell sleeves were chased with fur, too, the whole thing falling down past my waist. The coat of a princess.

"My mother's," he explained.

Oh. Heirik was loaning me another beloved heirloom, something that had belonged to the only other woman who loved him. I turned from side to side to show him.

"Put on these blankets, too." His voice was hoarse. He liked me in the coat. "As many as you can."

It was the sleepy time of night when I let my hair hang freely, like his, the long white-blond strands fell all about my shoulders. I felt like he and I were two horses, covering our manes with fur-trimmed warmth. Flaxen eyes watched me, and I couldn't tell if it was fire or tension I saw there. He was taking me outside, alone. There weren't that many reasons why he might. I burned with the possibility.

He took a couple more blankets under one arm, and we pushed out into the knife-like air. My head fell back and I watched the steam of my breath rise to the stars. My head spun and breath stopped in my throat, and I put a hand out to steady myself on Heirik. He closed his eyes, just for a moment.

"Walk in my footprints," he offered. They were big enough to easily contain mine.

Even without a moon, starlight glinted off two or more feet of snow. A blue skim-milk glow, enough to see Heirik ahead of me, a dark warm giant. It was a short distance to the stables and through the ring of sod wall that surrounded the building. As we tromped there, he told me, "My brother is not the only one who can follow the stars, já? Someone here has to know what time it is." I followed his footsteps, holding my skirts and stepping up high over the snow to land down in the next crater and the next one.

The animal stalls were open to the outside, like little caves in a snowy rock face. He led me to one of the openings. The stink overwhelmed my lungs, then mellowed into a constant and familiar smell. A faint echo of sunshine in fleece. Heirik built up a little snow bank just outside the sheep stall and lined it with blankets, so we could sit with our feet inside, but still see the stars. He sat and rested himself against the snow, his feet extended into the warm stable.

When he looked up at me in welcome, my heart skipped. I sat beside him to share the little snow bank. I leaned back like he did, into the frosty cradle, our bodies near but not yet touching. Why not touching? Up close to him, the sheep aroma was replaced by his leather and the cinnamon of fur. Or perhaps that was the natural scent of his skin. I wanted to press my lips to his throat and breathe in, to memorize what he himself smelled like, without fire or tools or clothes.

He settled in, an arm behind his head, as though this little snow bank was a mess of down pillows in a vast wintry bed. "The snow will warm us soon."

It was clear at once that his room in the house was not his real private space. This world was his place. Not a bed made of polished wood, but of snow or grass or field, with a ceiling of sky. He could stretch out here, the full length of him.

Knee-high boots wrapped tight in leather laces hugged the shape and contours of his calves. I stretched my legs out beside him, crossing my ankle-length boots. Leather touching, bodies meeting in this one small, hot place. I almost forgot to look at the stars.

When I did, they pressed in on me as they had before. The immensity made me feel tiny and pinned to the earth, snowbound underneath a million far-off fires, each bigger than all our world. To Heirik it was likely a dome, lit with sparks and flares from a god's firestriker. I liked that. It did look that way.

"Look at the brightest only. Three in a line." He drew the line in the sky, a child's lesson. I wanted to take his fingers in mine.

It was a shape in the stars, and an arc came to mind, about a hunter drawn with imaginary lines. It was barely perceptible to me, among the crush of fainter stars within and around it. If I hadn't already known it was there, I would have struggled to find it in the sprinkling of that god's sparks and flying embers.

"Frigg's distaff," he told me. "Beside it, her spindle."

I liked the hunter with his bow drawn tight, but a woman spinning *was* potent and lovely. I watched through Heirik's eyes, imagining the great goddess generating the clouds that sometimes floated on the breeze or chased each other through nasty storms. Not always, though. Did she rest her spindle on clear nights like tonight?

We watched the slow changes of the sky. Each star turned watery if I stared at it for long. After the initial bite of cold had passed, I'd begun to feel the warmth Heirik had talked about—our snow bank gathering and giving back our body heat. The warmth of sheep at our feet. Use every part of the animal, I thought, even its breath.

In the long quiet, Heirik shifted and turned toward me, resting his calf against mine. It was a gentle turning, a tentative suggestion through layers of leather, but it burned through me so thoroughly, it might as well have been a fiery tumble, the crush of hips and tongue. I shifted my own calves ever so slightly in response. The whole vastness of the sky gave way, and I could think of nothing else but the small point where we touched.

I tried to drift into the world of clouds and giant distaffs, but I felt his eyes acutely, watching me watch the sky. I glanced down at our bodies, side by side, such hunger between us. When would he kiss me?

I rubbed my leg along his, gradually increasing pressure, contact. I reached under his furs and found his hip, followed the slope to his waist, so warm and hidden. Spoke a breathless word, against his chest. "More." Knives and belt were in my way, and I slipped my fingers under.

Heirik made a sound of longing under his breath. He murmured something I couldn't understand, spoke a choked word into my hair. He was touching my shoulder. But he wasn't embracing me. He wasn't pressing his mouth to mine like he had at the coast and in the pantry. I wanted to get my hand around enough of his waist to really hold him, to bind him, but I was too small. He went rigid with restraint.

"Ginn." It was apologetic.

The cold rushed in. Something was wrong. Miserable snow was inside everywhere, between us, in our clothes.

I felt the pressure of his chin through the fur on my forehead. My hand still rested on his waist, fingers trapped under his belt, frozen. In the brittle silence, I extracted them, and curled my hand up inside my coat instead. I pulled away to see his face, and his dark lashes swept the soft skin under his eyes.

He gripped the snow between us, crunched it in his fist. "I want to take you, crush you." His words started a brush fire, his voice as violent as his hands had been the first time we touched. I held my breath and waited for the rest. The wrong part. There was something wrong. "I can't."

When he opened his eyes again, they were piercing like ice. I could hardly make out their color in the night.

"I'm marked by the gods. This blood—"

He was worried about his mark? But it was meaningless to me. He must see that.

"Heirik—" I tried to stop him, to tell him. Better than meaningless, it was part of him and his beauty.

"—Nei." With a word, he commanded me to listen. "Many close to me have died. My parents, my brother's wife. His son."

I opened my mouth, but he cut me off again.

"The day we rode to the sea, I watched you on your horse, thought I could someday hold you. You kissed me." His words were choked with disbelief. "Minutes later, you were at life's end. In Ageirr's grip." His words dripped pain and rage.

"What Ageirr does is his own fault, Heirik, not yours."

He wasn't listening. "—After … I came to you. I brushed your face." His fist loosened, eyes misted, his mind gone back to that moment, with me in the sleeping alcove. "Your lips opened and searched for my hand like a small bird." Whole parts of his speech went missing. "Desire for your mouth, any way you would give it." I pressed my forehead to his chin, and he pressed a kiss there, despite himself.

Composed again, he pulled away. "Ginn," he said with an air of formality. "I promise you." Though we were lying in the snow, he looked at me with such intent, such submission and resolution, it was as if he knelt before me with *Slitasongr* to swear on. "I will not invite danger again."

What did he mean, that he wouldn't invite it? I saw it in my mind, danger like a mist coming in under the mudroom door, or a giant black bird crashing into the house, fanning the hearth-flame with its wings. How did you ask danger to come to your home, to the woman in your arms?

Oh.

Salty, freezing sea water seemed to trickle into my gut. Oh, nei. He wasn't holding me, because he thought he was dangerous. We were dangerous.

I was alive, though. Here I was. "Look," I whispered, "I am fine." I exhaled gently on the back of his hand where it rested between us. He groaned and turned away, lay his head back, and his throat was exposed to me. The thrust of his chin, his parted lips, tortured me.

"Heirik, I am not afraid."

He shook his head. He watched the stars, but was seeing something beyond them, or deep inside.

"I am," he finally said. "I will not."

The force of his curse was powerful. Powerful enough by far to overwhelm the fragile thing growing between us.

I struggled with tears, trying not to make a sound, but he must have felt me shaking, where we still touched, his leg resting against mine, his hand on my hip despite his vow. I didn't dare move.

Moments later, he spoke again. "You have a family somewhere."

Another cold stone dropped into my gut.

"A husband," he told me with dead determination. "You are so beautiful. Someone is searching for you."

"Nei." I wanted to tell him, I have you. Always you. "Nei."

"I will help you find him."

Terror was quick in my throat and gut. I grasped onto him without thinking. And I begged.

I begged Heirik not to look for anyone. Not to make me look. If he made me go, if I had to leave Hvítmörk, oh gods, I couldn't wrap myself around him enough, make him know that he had to keep me. He was huge with furs and cloaks. My arms were insufficient. His hand came up behind me and pulled me close and shushed me. He opened up the fur around him to take me inside, and he rocked me like a child, as much as he could in the snow. He held me, and even as I struggled with hitching breath and terrible fear, I sank gratefully into his arms. I belonged right here. Couldn't he see that?

He deliberately pulled us apart. "It is hard, Litla." He disentangled our arms. "The hardest thing I will ever do. To be so close, and stay away from you."

I knew it in my bones and skin. Já, I knew exactly what that was like. One hand clutched at him, wishing him back.

"Would it be okay?" My voice was wobbly in the endlessness of snow and stars, my fingers like talons in his clothes. "If I wanted to stay?"

He looked right into my eyes. "I want you to." His voice sounded thick. And he seemed surprised at what he'd revealed, as if the truth had snuck out into the air between us.

Nothing made sense. He wouldn't touch me, but he couldn't let me go. Even as he admitted his desire, he took it away. His body against mine would bring violence into my life, disfigurement, loss and death. Blood would spill on our union, and a murder of crows would follow us when we rose from our bed. He wanted me, and would never do this to me.

As long as we wanted one another, I would stay. Though the gods themselves tried to keep us apart, I would not leave his side. I unclenched my hand and let his clothes go.

"I will not leave here."

He rested his head in the snow and stretched out, his gaze once more on the sky.

"Já," he said in the faintest voice. He looked at the stars, not at me. "Good."

I wanted to nestle into his chest and press my body against the length of his. I could lay my head near Thor's hammer and feel his pulse.

That moment wouldn't happen, though. I felt him shifting, as if we'd get up and go back soon. And all the polar air and snow I'd been denying came rushing in and my teeth started to chatter. I trembled and then began to shiver more forcefully. So cold without him, though he was inches away.

"Inside." He said it like a command, but softly, with a lover's voice. It broke my heart.

Another man would have given me his hand and helped me to stand. Heirik turned away and surveyed the grayish valley, taking in the snow-bright farm. When I stood, my limbs were heavy and stiff.

He turned to retrace his deep footsteps, and I lifted my skirts high to follow.

He'd just made a vow to protect me. And I made a vow of my own, right then, to the gods and the night and his big form ahead of me. As long as I could be near him every day, I would slowly soften his heart and ease his mind. I would coax him like a wary animal. And one day he would have me. I would be his.

The little gable over the back door shone with starlight, its dragon heads crossing forever at its peak. Heirik smacked the wood with his palm in satisfaction, and hunks of snow fell and broke up on the stones. "The house is good."

Já, it was, I thought.

We entered, and a blast of heat and steam moistened my face. I let my hood down, and I watched him let his hair free from his hat. He was beautifully flushed.

"It is good, Heirik," I told him in that same soft lover's voice, meaning everything—the house, his family, his soul, heart, blood-stained body.

Then I noticed Svana was there, in the mudroom.

An unbearable sensual tension remained between me and Heirik, despite his promise that he would never act on it. I was sure we looked sex-tumbled with our damp hair hanging down, and the intimacy of our touching lingered on us like a scent. We stood still for a second, like two foxes disturbed in the wood.

He nodded to Svana, stamped his boots and sat to take them off. I did the same. And looking up from under my lashes, I tried to send her a silent message with my eyes. I pleaded with her to get out and not say a word. She raised an adorable eyebrow and ducked back into the house.

The days and weeks were long, sometimes spent in close quarters with each other for endless hours. Sometimes Heirik would leave the house for a day or more, heading off alone on snowshoes or skið, to places no one wanted to guess, or could imagine. I missed him, then, so much. Even though being close to each other was harder, I wanted him near.

Then he would come home and things felt worse. A terrible gloom settled over the house, or maybe only I felt it. It weighed on me, like something massive pressing down on the roof, pressing in on the walls. One morning, I drew out the ice blue dress from under the sheepskins. I smoothed it over and over until it was a perfect, lovely square, then wrapped it in a soft skin and tied it. Sealed it with my tears. It wasn't mine to keep, and so I gave it to Hár, to make sure it went to its rightful place.

Then after some time, no matter how enduring our desire was, the desperate pitch of emotions just couldn't last. My wishes came and went, sometimes flaring up at the sight of him tucking hair behind his ear or tossing away a piece of wood, dissatisfied with carving. But sometimes the yearning left off for a while, leaving behind a tranquil tenderness.

He stopped leaving so much. He broke into smiles for me all the time now, brilliant and touching. He stayed in the main room of the house more than anyone could remember, and even if we didn't speak much, I knew he was here just to be with me, and I would smile to myself.

We played tafl together, until it became an every-night ritual, struggling our way into friendship. And instead of suffering because of his vow, Heirik seemed to be freed by it. He settled into wanting me with a loving and patient grace. I would be patient, too.

When Heirik and I played, every eye watched us, with the cool composure of hawks.

No one, not even Hár, was bold enough to openly stare, but the sidelong attention was palpable. The chief was different because of me, and even if we remained only friends, that alone was dangerous enough to cause bony fingers to clutch charms in the dark. Many times, I wished that we were doing something illicit and delicious enough to deserve it. I wanted forbidden things, thoughts with dark wings, bodies slick with sweat.

But the hawks wouldn't find much. While the chief and I longed for each other, there were no revolting trysts, no electric lust allowed to flow between us and fill the shadowy spaces of our house with demons. He kept his promise, and I kept mine.

During the long days, I occupied myself however I could. Magnus tried to teach me to ski, and I bumbled around outside, sinking in the snow and lurching for the house.

Inside, I played with the little girls. Ranka and Avsi would comb and braid and pile up my hair, involving circlets, crowns of straw, white kerches borrowed from Dalla and Kit. Since my hair was so long and so straight, and I was so willing, I became their primary subject. I most liked when Ranka made two thin braids around my face and left them hanging free as she gathered all the rest of my hair in a low ponytail. A leather strip set around my forehead and tied in back made me feel becomingly Viking.

Hár's daughters let the girls play with them, too, but most often let their long hair hang, a dark blond gift from their Da. Svana swirled her flaxen curls up in buns on either side of her face, with a few tendrils falling to perfectly frame her creamy cheeks.

Betta, plainest and most straightforward, still braided her hair tight every day. She watched me get my hair done sometimes, from across the room, and her big green eyes were lonesome and clear. I had a feeling I could get her to let her hair down.

Grinding winter boredom would abet me, and Ranka would be my excuse, but really I wanted to transform Betta. I wanted to reveal the flowing vision beneath her restraint. I wanted to see her glow like a painting of Freya, palms upturned, fingers combing sensually through her own long hair. I wanted to see Hár's brain fall out. It was a project that might lift the boredom, slowly working on her to get her to let go. I felt like everyone I cared about needed so much coaxing, Heirik and Betta like little animals sniffing at my feet.

Dalla's baby found its voice, and it began to practice, "Da da da da da da da." Her husband smiled as though he'd won a contest, and I didn't, couldn't, break it to him that "da" is one of the earliest sounds any voice can make. Miraculous and meaningless.

I had to get out of here. Outside. Somewhere.

I found relief by taking a lot of baths. Betta went with me, and we'd soak under the tremendous sky.

I'd told her, of course, about most of what had passed between me and Heirik. About Ageirr taking me hostage, and Heirik saving me with the swift and gut-curdling throw of a spear. And later—the night when he'd spoken to me out under the stars—I'd gone to my sleeping alcove and burrowed into a nest of blankets, and she was there, and we whispered and I cried. I told her about Heirik's awful promise to protect me by refusing to touch.

Even so, I always kept our kissing a secret. Those moments at the sea's edge were ours alone, mine and Heirik's, a private memory still alive on my lips. An intimate pressure still echoing on my wrists and arms and forehead.

I listened to Betta tell her stories, of learning to dye as a very little girl, a skill passed down from her mother. Of coming to Hvítmörk at age eight, full of grief and dreams.

We were out here now, under the press of a billion stars.

She dropped her dress onto the stones. Her underdress, too, and shift. The water was silver skittering over black, reflecting the moon and stars and Betta's torch. I sank gratefully into its warmth and she stepped in and sank down beside me. The water made unbearably soft sounds as it moved. I lay back against the stones, deeply warm. Betta rolled over like an otter, on her back, then again to fold her arms on the edge, her chin on top of them.

"It's already hard," she said, her words muffled by the pressure of chin against arm against rock. "To find times to walk away from the hearth." She was thinking of Hár. She moved a finger against the stones, tracing nothing. "I miss him."

It had been only a couple weeks, and I wondered how long this winter would grow to seem. I pictured an endless polar landscape.

"In good weather, it was easy," she said. "Everyone is out. Sometimes we even left the house together." She laughed a bit bitterly. "We are so unimaginable, we're invisible."

Images came to me, no matter that I didn't want them. They flew into my mind's eye. In the space of a sigh I saw Betta and Hár in the woods in molten sunset light, him sitting against a tree, pulling her up to straddle him, his rough hands on her skirts and her ass, pulling her close. Her long fingers in his messy hair. In this vision, Betta was smiling.

Here next to me in the wintry bath, she was sullen. She sat up as though something stirred on a horizon we couldn't even make out. She looked down at her hands, then, and ran a finger across her knuckles. "Sometimes I want people to see."

I wanted to give her something, an assurance that someday they would marry and everyone would know about them. He'd let everyone see how he loved her. I wanted to tell her that one day she'd have his babies, and he would place his hand on her belly when anyone was looking, and for a moment I wished I was the one with the sight of things to come. But these dreams were certainly ones she had pictured herself, and they were as impossible as summer snow.

In my silence, I must have been radiating stray lust from my image of her and Hár. She told me, "It is not like you think, by the way."

Exactly what I did think was still my mind's own secret. Even with her gift, she couldn't get at it exactly. But she could usually sense not only the wash of emotion in a room or in one mind and heart, but also its direction, like a tide. It was uncanny, a detection of the slightest rise in pulse or wave of hormones.

"Já? And what do I think?" I teased. My fingers rippled the water and light danced.

Betta settled like a kitten in a bed to tell me.

"We still just sit together and kiss," she said with a smile. "He asks no more. He puts his arms around me, whispers to me." It was so basic and dear. A very different image came, of them side by side in the grass watching the sun fall, his crude fingers brushing her slim ones, yellow with dye.

Over weeks of getting used to this staggering truth, that Hár and Betta did these things, I hadn't asked her how it started. I'd been absorbed in my own twisted romance, spending tender time with my non-lover, or acting as accomplice for my friend and the old man. Now with the endlessness of a winter night stretching before us, I asked.

"My love didn't grow like a flower," she stated first, to get any notion of silly romance out of the way. "I'd seen him a thousand times, of course, since I was a girl. A big man, a grown up. By the gods, he made toys for me!" She shook her head, as if just now remembering this, probably recalling his younger hands giving her a boat or small arrow.

A memory struck me like a blade, sharp and quick, of the vision I'd had. A beaming blond man handing Betta a wooden doll. An eerie cold spread through my spine and hips and stomach even though the bath was hot.

"What?" she asked, accusingly.

"Nothing," I said. "I'm just imagining you and Hár so much younger."

"He was the chief's father by the time I moved here" she went on. "I watched him become strong and gray. I saw him every day of my life." The rest was inexplicable. "Then one time I looked at him and I saw a man. And he was my man, and I was stricken with it." I remembered my own heart-struck moment, when I knew that I loved Heirik.

"I looked at him so many times then," she confessed. "Over a whole month at least. I'd see him doing the smallest thing, strapping his boots, tying his hair. Pieces of it fall out right away, you know? All around his face."

I did know. Perhaps not about Hár, but I knew the rapid beat of the heart that could come from something so small and unexpected, a man's hair escaping from its ties.

"My eyes would go soft," she said. "I was constantly looking out from under my lashes, a stupid hen."

"And so he noticed," I finished for her. I was surprised. Hár seemed particularly unsuited to detect such things, but he had.

"The first few times he smiled," she said. "Like someone's Da, like he didn't mind I was having a crush." Hár's expression typically hovered somewhere between snarling and bursting into uproarious laughter. His smiles, shared among men usually, were wicked. I tried to picture how those smiles looked just for her, gentler. A single raised eyebrow of disbelief. A nod or two. One night she was handing out bowls of food. "He was sitting back from the fire, alone. I handed him his bowl, and he hooked his finger around mine and whispered." A tough charred whisper, delivered with a wink. "'Shield your eyes, Maid. You'll have every hawk here looking down its beak.'"

Betta and I laughed.

At the time, she'd been mortified. She dropped something, knelt to pick it up and found herself at Hár's knee. He looked down, an amused god, and his face softened for a second. He told her to meet him just before sunset, down at the woods. Then he put the steel back in his eyes and turned away to eat.

"I met him right where we go," Betta told me. "Where we gathered lichens, when I first told you." It was a mile's walk from the house, and on the way to being alone with him, she had time to realize she was scared. It was the first time she would be anywhere with a man, let alone such an unfathomable and fearsome one. What would he do to her? Her heart raced the last third of the way. She wrapped her shawl tight and, thinking a hundred times that she would turn back, she stumbled through clods of dirt and long grass. And then she saw him.

Betta seemed to look inward as she told me, toward the past, toward her first sight of Hár waiting for her. His back was turned, eyes to the sky. "Freya painted it with amber streaks that night. She lit him in gold. A companion fit for her, not me." I watched Betta become infused with the goddess now, as she sat next to me in the bath, and I could imagine her flushed, beautiful and bold, when she met Hár. She didn't care what he would do with her, what he or anyone might think, she simply wanted him.

"He didn't say anything. He touched my cheek, and his fingers were rough. I knew they would be." She touched her own lips, remembering him. "I raised my hand to touch his face, too, but he caught it. He closed his fingers around my whole hand and he asked me, 'What are you about, Woman?'"

Betta sounded just like him, and we laughed more. Of course, she hadn't known what she was about. She was acting on instinct, a seventeen-year-old's yearning, inexplicable and true. She'd never even spoken more than a few words to older men, outside her Da. Much of her knowledge about sex came from Hár's own teenaged daughters. And what she was feeling seemed less about sex than some all-consuming need for body and spirit and everything that made the man himself. She wanted to possess it all and know what he was.

Hár told her to walk with him, and they talked, as much as either of them was capable, about mundane things. A broken ax, animals taking to the highlands, a luscious ochre dye sprung from lichens, the changing hours and colors of the sky. The evening sun was finest, he said, from a place overlooking the valley. He asked if she would ride with him another night. He would take her out on Byr.

"And you know about that, then," she told me, meaning her first horseback ride with Hár. "We've gone many times now, já?" I didn't know a Viking word for wistful, but her voice was the essence of it.

"He did finally let me touch his face," she gave as an after-thought. It was all scratchy beard and ridges and ruts of scars, and Betta had leaned over him where he laid in the grass and she traced and luxuriated in every one. "His lips are the only soft spot. I like to place my fingers there."

She shook herself.

"Gods, Ginn, I can't tell you anything more." She sighed away her very bones. "I'll slip into this water and never come up again." She did slip under then, and she came up laughing and spitting like a little kid, and when her face was like that she was so pretty.

"Oh no. Look at you, Woman." She floated up beside me and used her wet thumb to gently wipe under my eye. I hadn't realized I was crying.

"I'm just happy for you," I told her. I was, whenever I watched her so free and in love. I wanted her to be able to feel this way forever.

She tucked a few strands of my hair behind my ear, generally putting me together like a mother with a sad, messy little girl. "The chief doesn't let anyone touch his face, I know." She misunderstood the reason for my tears.

"Oh," I told her. "I have."

And then it was out, like a frozen puff of breath. The fact that I'd touched Heirik in such an intimate way. That we'd been something near to lovers.

"Mostly with my lips," I said, with a small smile. Betta's brows drew together. She thought I was joking, and she smacked me, splashing warm water. Then she glared, waiting for me to admit it wasn't true. I realized there was still time for me to giggle and take it back, to lie and claim I was kidding. But I wouldn't do that. What Heirik and I had shared was honorable and real, and I wouldn't deny or demean it.

The fact was, the very few times I'd ever touched him were kisses, on his eyelids, temple, throat. I'd kissed his marked and unmarked skin alike, and neither had singed my tongue. I remembered tasting salt on his cheekbone, the first time. Tears, I thought, just realizing it now.

Betta's eyes were so wide, she looked a lot like Ranka. "You kissed the chief's face?"

"Já," I sniffled. "I did." She shook her head, awed. She sat back in the water, looking at me differently, making the kind of mental adjustments I'd had to make when I found out her secret love was Hár.

"The chief is happy," she said incredulously. "But he struggles to stay away from you." There was something wistful about her tone, and her words seemed to come from a mile away, out of a deep and forgotten place. "He can't hold out forever."

Betta brightened, and she took me in her arms. I felt her small breasts press into me, her nose against my ear. She was warm and sleek. "You will hold him again," she promised. And I wished she had the sure sight of things to come, too.

Finally, Betta let me.

At night, after another sluggish and boring day, there was no reason left not to. She sat before me, facing away, on a bench before the fire. I laid out my tools, a magnificent bone comb, curved and carved, a bone needle and thin thread, strips of leather and a straw circlet Ranka had made. I had gotten my hands on some precious oil that didn't stink of whale. It was steeped with herbs and used only for special occasions. Ranka attended me like I was a surgeon, grave and ready.

Betta sat taut, probably a little afraid. She didn't think she was pretty, even had her moments of incredulous doubt about why Hár wanted her. She was gawky and not the most gorgeous, nei. But I tried to tell her what I saw from the outside, a powerful woman emerging completely and gracefully from childhood. She was capable of being free and sensual. Maybe the hair had to do with the family looking, witnesses to some bit of passion that might never be fulfilled or requited. I untied the leather thongs on her braids and separated the strands. I thought her scalp must be on fire every day, she pulled them so tight.

Her hair was long and brown and indecisive. Not exactly straight, not exactly wavy. But freedom was so rare, it tumbled forth like a stunning waterfall, coursing over the prominent bones of her cheeks and shoulders. I combed it over and over. Wasn't there some traditional or ideal number of strokes?

When it was combed I coated my palms with the slightest sheen of oil and smoothed Betta's hair down her back. I thought of Hár. How he'd done exactly this with his tough hands, looking out over the valley. Her sharp shoulder blades rose and fell with a giant sigh.

I gathered hair from around her face and made two thin braids, lighter and looser than any she ever wore. Then I shaped the hair around them into soft coils that relaxed, when I let them free of my finger, into ocean waves turning back from the shore. Using thread and needle, I sewed on the straw crown that sat low on her forehead. She turned to let me see.

She was a handmaiden of any fertility goddess. A creature of the woods and flowering underbrush. Her eyes and all the angles of her face seemed to soften in sympathy with her locks. I used my fingers and a bit more oil to shape the ends where they rested on her breasts.

There was a familiar stomping and gusting of wind in the mudroom, the particular sound of wooden snowshoes on dirt, and the sonorous voices of men. In a minute, Hár ducked low to enter the room.

I sometimes saw him as Betta did, a gorgeous man hiding a romantic soul behind his scratchy beard. Just now it was sparked with fresh snow, turning to water on his lips. I wondered if the scattering of scars on his face and hands were from fights, or simply forty years' accumulation of the common accidents of farm life.

Hár stopped when he saw us, and he changed at the sight of Betta. He gave away nothing to the men who stood behind him, but from where I sat I saw instant heat and sex and love fill up his eyes. A fearsome blue flame. Anger, too. He seemed perplexed and mad at what she could do to him without so much as moving or speaking. Arn and Magnus reacted, too, smiling at us girls playing dress-up, and surprised in a friendly way at Betta's prettiness. Magnus smiled broadly. "Betta," he said. "You steal my breath." Hár failed to completely stifle a growl.

The old man flipped his knife over in his hand, slipped it quietly inside his sleeve, and grumbled that he'd forgotten the blasted, short-witted blade back at the stable. He'd have to go out again. He disappeared back into the mudroom. A few minutes later, I made a moderately conspicuous request of Betta, that she go out and start cleaning up the back room. I'd be there to help in a bit.

Minutes stretched out, the comb hard in my hands, turning over and over in my lap. I was jealous. I imagined what was happening between them in the dark. Maybe sitting on the bench, Betta straddling him, his big hands pulling her close. Gods, what was wrong with me? More likely, they were just enjoying a moment of closeness and intimacy. He was probably touching her cheek so softly with the back of his hand, like a wisp of smoke from a sweet juniper fire.

A long time passed. I started to worry they would be caught talking closely or embracing in the lamplight.

I found them in the mudroom, oblivious to everything but one another. They didn't even hear me, didn't notice me at first.

Betta sat across his lap. His hand covered the back of her head, strands of hair caught in his fingers as though he'd dragged them through savagely, past reason and consciousness. His head was bent to her, so loving, his eyes closed, seeing the glory of the world beyond. Her hand was snagged in his hair, too, drawing it back from his face, shaggy and lit with silver in the small flickers of light.

"Are you trying to kill me," he whispered between kisses. "Elskan mín?"

Oh. My heart melted. To hear him call her *my beloved*, to speak of his feelings, and to revel in them, so freely. Betta laughed and with her free hand she traced the line where his beard met bare skin.

"Nei, Old Man," she told him. "You must live long enough to love me. Ten thousand times."

A free father would have every right to kill Hár where he sat. But Betta's Da—no more than an exalted thrall, and meek, plainer than she—would never take such payment from the past chieftain, grandfather of his known world. Hár could take whatever he wanted, and no thrall would wreck it. And while I saw the truth—that Hár loved Betta with a tortured desperation—the reality was, he held her very life in his groping hands. I wished I had a charm to touch, wishing safety for Betta's heart and her honor. I breathed deeply through my nostrils, fiercely protective of my friend, and Hár's head snapped up. Betta gasped and twisted to see who was there.

Hár considered me from under his brows, annoyed and curious.

"Old Man," I said, and my voice was not as light as I expected. "If you mean to boast your accomplishments to the whole house, keep at it."

I tried to say it with affection, but I didn't quite succeed. He growled at me, just a little, and then set Betta on her feet. He brushed off her skirt for her, such a gentle gesture. Betta reached a hand and grasped his shirts right over his heart, not gently at all. She held his linen in her tight fist, a quick taking before they would part. Before they would spend the next twenty hours, a hundred days, a million weeks, in an impossibly close room around an impossibly public fire.

The calm clarity of this winter was the talk of the house. It was almost warm, people said, and still, as if the wind slumbered. The snow that seemed so high to me, was a subject of great interest, remarked on as so minimal it was like none in known history.

And so tonight's storm was a thing of giant, swirling terror.

A horde of beasts circled and seemed to provoke the house. Wind moaned, audible even through the thick sod walls. The roof was closed up tight against the pounding, swirling snow, so we huddled around hot stones. I held a warm one in my lap, while Heirik and I played a game of tafl.

A game of strategy, the only game we had. Betta had taught me to play, the first week of winter.

The squat wooden pieces were just a little rounded on the bottom and gathered to gentle points on top. They reminded me of pictures I'd seen of acorns, small enough to fit in the cup of my hand. One of us played a chief who sat hunched in the center of the board, flanked by his men, and one played an invading army trying to capture him.

Heirik was of course a natural, having lived through—nei, orchestrated—more complex strategies in real life than anything we could build on a little soapstone board.

Tonight, I played the invaders, watching the stone chief, waiting for him to accidentally leave some opening for me.

My head and shoulders ached, perhaps with the ridiculous fact of our roles and positions on the board. Or perhaps with the weight of my hair.

Ranka had created a little girl's braided masterpiece on my head. She'd plaited three long braids down my back, then woven those three into one giant braid. She piled the whole thing up on the back of my head in a mass. By this time of night, spiky ends escaped everywhere, and bone hairpins bore into my scalp.

I envied Heirik his freedom. Two braids framed his face, but the rest of his hair fell loose. In fact, he was utterly unbound, a winter farmer, relaxed and drowsy with nothing to do. He lounged, stretched out on the bench, resting on his elbow and with one knee bent. No gauntlets for working outside, his sleeves loose at his wrists, even his boots were simply tied at his ankles with no bindings.

The contrast fascinated me—his ability to swiftly blunt his speech and close his features into an imperious mask, and yet his natural physical ease. Comfort and efficiency on any horse, with any tool, doing any kind of work. Simply standing, arms folded, he seemed to have sprung from the grass itself, and moved over it like a native animal. The deft turning away, the hiding of his physical scar, was an extension of this easy control. As natural as breathing.

He seemed designed by the gods to torment me.

Now the bench, the game, his clothes were all burnished with lamplight in the living room. I watched his hair absorb bits of firelight and then let them go in flame-like blue.

"You play like a lame fox," he said, moving another of his men, uncovering an unexpected escape route.

"Hah!" I snorted. "Now you are …"

I wanted to say *talking trash*. The sentiment was pure 21st century boxing, but it came out in Norse. "Bragging with a short blade."

He threw his head back and laughed, and it was a rare and gorgeous sound that no doubt shocked every ear in the house.

"Such a poet," he said, and with a charming smile he flicked one of my game pieces off the board and into my lap. I glared and replaced my piece, and he returned to studying the map of the board. He absently tucked a braid behind his ear, a little boy for a second. Unaware of how I watched him in such minute detail.

While I waited, I reached up and removed the bone pins from my head, and the giant braid fell with a thump on my back.

Heirik looked up at me and froze.

Oh. Something was off. It was another sinking moment, when I'd done something unexpected, wrong. I dropped my hands to my lap, and my giant braid fell over my shoulder, the ends brushing my breast. He glanced there with a stricken look, then dragged his eyes away and up to my face.

"You would sit with me to do this?"

I lifted the braid, and his eyes shifted again to watch my fingers play with the whitish strands. I could see him struggle to swallow. The moment was awkward and hot. With his irises so pale, his eyes almost disappeared.

"Why not?" I asked. I wasn't sure if we were talking about hair anymore.

We were, actually.

"Another memory you've lost," he said. "A woman taking her hair down at day's end is done before her husband."

He looked past my shoulder and out into the room. "It is not something that would disgrace you, if you did this here, with me." His voice dropped low on the last two words, holding them preciously on his tongue. He picked up a game piece with slow and deliberate form, still resting on his elbow, studiously casual. "It's not a formal gesture. Just a quiet moment to end the day."

I drank in the sound of that. A quiet moment together, an end to the day, the beginning of a shared night. "It would be okay, then?"

Head bent to the game, he looked up from under his black lashes. "I have longed for it."

The house and all its scents and murmurs seemed to drop away with those words, and we were alone. Arousal rose right to my skin, lighting up my neck and arms, and I couldn't stop it, no more than I could stop the oil from burning in the lamps.

I tipped my head back and closed my eyes, undoing my big braid, relieving my scalp. When I opened my eyes I found Heirik concentrating on the chieftain, a hunched figure at the center of the board, besieged on all sides by acorns. But I knew he watched me.

Betta watched me, too. I felt her now, like a night bird in the dim room, shifting and settling her feathers, owl eyes open. Seeing me—us, Heirik and I—doing something so intimate. I looked over at her and smiled and she ducked her head.

I undid everything, and brushed my loose hair with my fingers, letting the braids fall open. I looked at the game and made another move. Matter of factly I said, "Now let me do yours." I flicked my chin toward a dark braid that fell across his cheek.

He made what might have been a light joke, "Everyone in this house would be planning our wedding feast." But his voice was flat, and out loud it sounded bitter.

We dropped like twin stones into a strained quiet. Heirik had already made a vow to me—a kind that came without ceremony or feast. No swords or ale or catcalls following us to our marriage bed. It was a promise that came without joy.

Into the quiet, Magnus burst into the room, in a swirl of cold and snow so violent, it looked like the blizzard had lifted him and followed him right into the house. He shouted, his breath ragged, "Four sheep are missing."

Heirik was up and moving before I could take a breath. Every man in the house followed, grabbing at wool cloaks and hats and boots in an orderly madness. Women lifted children and toys out of the way. Food and drink were dropped in an instant, warm rocks tossed into the hearth.

I drifted behind them, following the men to the mudroom, and I hovered there with Betta by my side. I saw Heirik open the door to the storm, and if he hesitated for one second he didn't show a sign. He walked into pure, blistering white. And every man in the house waded in after him.

NIGHT SKIING

At first we did things like move our plates and sewing around, all of us women pretending nothing was happening. If we didn't look at each other, we didn't need to ask with our eyes, how long will it be? Will everyone come back? But after a short time, the tasks ran out and we started to pass glances like hesitant questions. Will your man return? And yours? I wondered, too, about how many sheep would return. Maybe enough. With Heirik. He would bring them home.

We tended to children who were confused by the silence, paced and bounced the littlest ones. I held Lotta and pressed her head to my shoulder. She was heavy, almost too much for me to carry, but I held onto her tight with one arm cradling her under her bum. We sat by the game board, and I showed her the little pieces and murmured silly things about the little men they represented.

Soon, we each sat around the hearth and were still, with no will left to pretend.

Haukur was the first one back, holding a two-hundred-pound sheep in his arms like a bride, Magnus right beside him holding the door. The sheep was let down on the floor by the heartstone. It looked already dead, its eyes obscured and crusted over with snow, blank white as if nothing stirred under the frost. But the animal shifted, moved some more, and let out a weak cry.

Hár soon followed with a big animal in his arms, and the other men stumbled in after him. Two sheep saved, and every man back except one.

The bluster of men and sheep died down into an awful silence. Heirik wouldn't come back.

No one would say such a thing, but it had been too long. Too stunned to speak, the family started going about business now. Dalla fussed over her husband and Thora over her brother and Da, the men trying to shrug them off. The family immersed themselves in cleaning up and herding children and sheep. Hildur secured the animals at the end of the main room, and the children were drawn to them. Lotta poked a handful of something at their faces, trying to feed them, and I watched her fondly, trying to ignore the growing panic in my gut. I counted the twists in her little braids. Started again.

People glanced at me and then down, an unexpected, half-hearted acknowledgment of what Heirik meant to me. Too little, too late, I thought.

Betta watched Hár blatantly, clenching her hands in her dress, unable to go to him and wipe the cold water and worry from his face. Instead, she took my hand and looked down at our twined fingers. I couldn't stand the kindness. I pulled away and picked up a game piece, so compact and contained. My palm closed around it completely.

"He plays with you," she said.

My panicky sickness was disturbed by her voice. "Hmm?"

"The chief. He plays with you."

"Já," I answered, as if she were dense, and I showed her the game piece. "We were just playing now."

"Nei," Betta said, "I mean he is ..." She searched for a word she didn't find. "Is like a small dog with you."

I thought of the littlest house dog, how it wagged and snapped and rolled over. She meant playful. She meant that Heirik laughed and batted game pieces at me. I thought of him splashing me in the ravine, racing on our horses.

Though my heart clenched, I tried to sound light. "Já, he is like that sometimes."

"Nei," Betta said. "Nei, he is not. I've never seen it in my life."

"I hope you will see it again," I stated, so cold now, not even warmed by her words.

It was a long time, or maybe a few seconds, before I dropped the game piece and stood up, drawn to go wait. Hár stood at the exact same time, and the two of us walked to the back mudroom in unspoken agreement. Hildur and Betta were drawn too.

Hár opened the back door and stood like an expectant dog waiting for its master. Wind and snow whipped into the room, and the biting cold stole every wisp of warmth.

"Shut it, Fool," Hildur crabbed at him, but Hár held up a hand and silenced her. He stared into the blizzard, a white and silver wasteland. And Heirik came. He lurched into the mudroom, four hundred pounds of sheep under his two arms. My heart soared for a second and then crashed in a bedraggled heap of relief. He was alive.

He dropped the animals, as if both irritated and satisfied, and stumbled past us all to his room. He was barely able to work the latch with his frozen fingers, and then he was through the door, leaving Hildur and Hár to tend to the giant, frozen sheep that filled the room. Leaving me wide-eyed and without a purpose. Betta put her hand to my back, and I felt her soft pressure of reassurance, but it hurt as if every nerve was on the surface, raw. I shrugged away and started cleaning up the room.

Dozens of wet cloaks and boots littered the floor, puddles forming all around, and I picked them up and felt the unpleasant, icy drips start to seep into my sleeves. Thoughts and questions gathered. Was he okay? How had he ever found the sheep? How did he make it back? I knew the answer. He simply had to. He made it by sheer force of responsibility, his honor like an ax over his head. And a deep desire to be good, to be needed, even by fools. He was behind his bedroom door now, safe.

The two additional sheep had been herded into the house, and the mudroom rang with that special kind of silence that comes after chaos. Then Hildur's voice stung the air.

"It is Signé's blessing," she said, efficiently wrapping up the episode.

"Nei." My voice split the air like a crow's call. "It is not."

It startled us all, the words out of my mouth without thought, my skirts flying out as I whirled to challenge her. My anger was greeted with an echoing blankness, Hildur shocked beyond reckoning. I went on, my voice even and cold. "It is Heirik's doing. He stayed out there until he found them, and he carried them home with his last strength, while you stood here griping at Hár to shut the door." It felt so good, I couldn't stop. "Beiskaldi," I spat out. An elegant and compact word for *bitter-cold-griping-bitch*.

Hildur's face closed, and so did her fist, around the charm at her waist.

She looked like an animal, cornered and aggressive, thin lips pressed together ready to hiss. My breathing rasped unbearably loud in my head, and I hoped and wished she would leave the room before I cried. I was on the edge of it. Just seconds away.

And then she did go, with an abrupt turn of her heel.

Hár had been watching me, stunned, and once she was gone he raised an eyebrow.

I asked him, my words blunt, my chin thrust toward Heirik's latched door. "Can you open that?"

Hár's giant sigh filled the room. "Já," he said with great resignation. He went to the door and unlocked it—something no one else knew how to do—and then he stepped aside. "Já, I can." He let the door handle go and walked away.

I pushed the door open a crack.

"I'm fine, Uncle," Heirik said from the shadows.

"Nei," I called softly. "It's me …"

I walked in, shut the door and put my back against it. A soft light illuminated a space so small I would scarcely have called it a bedroom, not in my other life. It was more like the size of the pantry, maybe ten or fifteen feet deep, though it stretched out indistinct and shadowed. Dim and deeply private, smelling of birch walls. Closing the door sealed it in an intimacy more complete than I'd expected. For the first time all day, I felt hot.

There was a real chair, its wooden sides curved like cupped hands. He sat in it now, hunched over with his elbows on his knees, hands hanging between his thighs. At his side, a small upturned box held a flickering lamp. At his feet, the smallest hearth sat—just four pieces of slate standing on end to form a box. Steam rose from a few hot rocks and struggled to escape through a window that was no more than a rectangle cut high up in the sod wall. It was partially closed with a leather shade, tied down against the howling wind and clogged with mounting snow.

A cold room, but even through my boots I could feel that the ground underfoot was warm. There was subterranean water.

The place was sprinkled with weapons, two axes leaning in a corner, a knife on the table and a smaller one that sat, forgotten, on the ground between his feet. The offhand presence and handling of danger, of violence. An honest to god sword hung on the wall over the bed.

Oh gods, a bed! The tiny room was dominated by it. Heaped with sheepskins and furs, it looked like a sumptuous nest. The bed had been built, I guessed, by his father's father. It was long like the men of his family and it had a mattress! Longing flared up, not for Heirik this time but for a cushion under my bones, filled with downy feathers. I imagined what the soft bed and silken fur would feel like against bare skin. His leather gauntlets were tossed there. I'd like to feel those, too, touch them again. Perhaps bite his wrist playfully as he reached for my face.

"No one comes into this room," he said, but he wasn't angry. "My brother sometimes, or Hár."

"I'll go." But I didn't move to do so.

"Nei." His answer was immediate. "Please," he added, and I wasn't sure whether it applied to me staying put, or even to me at all, or whether it was a general plea to any god or goddess that might pertain.

His hair was a wild mess, pieces plastered to his forehead and cheeks, and his eyelashes flashed with ice. Snow melted and ran down his throat. I thought maybe he couldn't move. When I stepped toward him, he looked up as if to sit straighter, as if to reach for me, but he did not.

Then he told me gently, "I am fine alone."

"Nei." I said, with my new bravery, the thrill of telling off Hildur still fresh in my blood. "You are a bad mess. Where's your comb?"

He seemed to be amused, but also impressed. Resigned to let me stay, to let me help.

"There." He raised his chin toward the dark corner.

A worn, wooden chest stood there. Just a few feet wide, it seemed mysterious and almost excessive in its privacy. I thought of my measly treasures folded and wedged under my sheepskins, and I felt a pang of jealousy. He had his own things and a place to put them. These walls of his room, this chest in the corner, were luxuries, and I wished I had a place like this to hide and curl up inside myself. I almost felt wrong being here.

Almost.

The chest was nearly full with clothes and furs. His dark blue wool, and the icy dress—his mother's—that I'd worn just weeks ago. A lifetime, it seemed. A time when we still thought we might be able to have each other. When we still thought we could kiss and touch and hold. I imagined him returning the dress to this trunk in a solitary moment, folding it gently and putting away all notions of loving me.

I moved some things around and within the nest of clothes I found a drinking glass, a small knife with a trailing vine motif engraved in its hilt, safely contained in a leather scabbard. I found his fine bone comb and a soft towel. And underneath the towel, I found a box.

It struck a match in my heart. It was so familiar.

No bigger than two of my hands across, the wooden box had two doors that closed and met with a dragon's-head clasp in front, a small lock threaded through its teeth. In my mind, I saw the electronic images slip by as if on the surface of my eyes, ghosted contact images. Scans of the decayed wood, rusted hardware just like this. I pictured the images of the book that had lived inside the little case for centuries. Her farm notes. Her words leapt to my mind, bringing back shearing and fleece and blood. *Rinsing his hands, he is sweet to my eye.* Could this actually be it?

Nei, the people here weren't right. There was no savage chieftain, just Heirik. No shape shifting wife. The box sat buried in this chest, not tucked in among the belongings of a remarkable woman. Even so, it looked exactly the same, and I struggled again to decide where I was on this island. Was I anywhere near the place where the farm diary had been found?

The wood was rough and fresh under my palm, not yet ravaged and transformed by a thousand years' time. I pressed my hand to it, to try to absorb its truth. But it was just a box. It could contain anything. More knives, probably. Heirik liked knives. Heirik, whose room I was in, who sat behind me right now waiting for me to comb his hair. I let the box go and turned back to him.

He was standing in the middle of the room, lifting his damp linen shirt off over his head.

The comb hung in my half-open palm. My lips parted and I breathed a small sound of surprise.

I'd seen his body in the bath, but it was not at all the same. It looked different to me now, in a dimly-lit chamber, so small that we were breathing each other's air. His height that seemed so reasonable to me outside—his kiss would just brush my forehead—was overwhelming in here. His body was sturdy, bred for farm work, but not fleshy. A body like none I'd seen in my time.

When he saw me, he mistook my expression. He dropped his shirts absently on the floor. His words were corrosive and yet soft. "Now you see me," he said. "Now you can forget this." He looked around at his room, as though "this"—my persistent belief in love?—might be there on the floor with his shirts. As though I could forget it.

His mark was shocking. Dark and ugly, it looked exactly like blood spilled by a divine hand. And he did scare me, after all. But I remembered holding him, too briefly. I'd felt his heart beat against my own chest, fully human. There was nothing about his fearsome mark that could scare me away. It was he who was afraid. And I would never run from his body.

"Do you want to see more?" He reached for his waistband. "Will that do it?"

Oh gods, I wanted to see more, but quickly I said, "Not like this!"

He sat, and he seemed fed up with himself. He folded his arms across his chest and looked down at them. I imagined he was shocked at what he'd done, at finding himself without several layers of wool between us.

"I heard you scold Hildur," he said, and then he smiled a wicked, charming smile and shook his head. "Beiskaldi." His chest shook with suppressed laughter. I was still shaking too, with the aftershock of adrenalin, with a creeping fear about facing her again. And with the shock of Heirik baring himself. His amusement melted my heart, and I felt good, then. And even more courageous.

I went to him and knelt at his feet, and the floor was eerily warm under my knees. I took him by the forearms, placed his elbows on his knees and made him sit with his face close to me that way. So close together, I could feel his breath on my forehead. I started to neaten his hair. I pushed the pieces back off his face, and he let me without a word. I worked on the leather tie on one of his braids. It was frozen and intricately bound. While I worked at it, I traced his jawline with my eyes, watched for any reaction, but he was withdrawn.

"Don't misunderstand me, Heirik," I told him, as I teased the knot with my fingers. "You are sweet to my eye."

I was very close to kissing him. If I just moved an inch, just tilted my head. Instead I leaned in to rest my forehead against his and he met me with an answering pressure. "I want to see all of you. I want to touch and take." I went on, now loosening his other braid. He didn't move, just breathed ragged breaths. "But only when you want me to. Not when you are trying to scare me."

"Já," he said, concisely.

I wanted so much to kiss him, but I didn't want to rush. I pictured this intimacy disappearing like a white tail in the woods, and so I hovered my hand over his knee, then very softly placed my palm there. I felt his bones and muscles under damp wool, unexpectedly hot. He sucked in air but didn't pull away. In fact, he leaned in to me, his nose to my ear. He seemed to be catching my scent. As if he were truly bewildered, he asked into my hair, "What will I do with you?"

Ravish me, I thought, take me, love me. Maybe kiss me for a start. But with a curl of a smile on my face, I said "Let me cut your hair?"

He laughed then and sat back. He folded his arms again, but he wasn't withdrawing, just considering from a distance.

"Some," he said. He would let me.

It was all I could do to drag myself away from his knees, to stand and brush off my skirt. I walked around to the back of his chair to work on the dark thicket of his hair.

It was as dense and tangled as the birches in the inner forest, and I hardly knew how to begin. I tried to comb my fingers through. At first his hair all felt stiff with ice, but when I warmed it in my palms and ran my fingers through the braids to let them loose, it was dry and silky underneath.

With my thumbs, I smoothed the nape of his neck, under his hair, slipping one thumb under the leather knot that always sat there, and he took in a sharp breath. He'd probably never felt this before. I drew my fingers through his hair like two combs, and my hands were moon-like against the night woods.

I pressed against his scalp with my thumbs, and my fingers curled loosely around his throat. He tipped his head back with a low sound of pleasure, almost a growl. I pressed my hips into the back of his chair in response. I drew my thoughts back to the job.

Truthfully, almost all of his hair needed to be cut off. I briefly pictured his hair like Magnus's, cut at his chin. He would be even more gorgeous. But he'd said "some," and I knew he didn't want to call attention to me grooming him, all eyes noticing the difference and knowing what I'd done. I had no skills to give him a good haircut anyway. Gods knew, I didn't have any idea how to do it, and the most I could manage was, hopefully, a straight line.

I held a handful of his hair to my cheek first, and smelled his cinnamon scent. It was him—that scent—not his clothes. Now I knew.

His hair made a shushing sound as I cut it, spilling from the comb and my little pair of shears to form black pools on the floor. Concentrating, I murmured, "I've never cut anyone's hair."

The muscles in his back flexed just for a second.

"It's okay," I assured him. "I'm not going to make you look like a sheep!"

He laughed, but then more seriously he said, "You just seem so sure you haven't done this."

Sure of my past. I'd let my guard down and forgotten to be vague. Not to lie, really, more like bluff, I told myself. But every time it hurt more, to love him and not let him know where I was from. He noticed the slips, the awkwardness sometimes. But right now he wasn't really waiting for any kind of answer.

He sighed.

"Já well, no woman has ever cut my hair," he said. "So you are the best."

I cut a straight line, just fine.

Once his hair was a little shorter and a bit less tangled, I pulled it all into a thick ponytail. I held it in one hand and stroked it. I placed it over his shoulder, out of the way so I could press my palms to his shoulder blades, one pale, one tinged with deep red. My thumbs followed his upper spine and found the back of his neck. He made a small sound in his chest, speechless contentment.

I was happy. Dizzy with satisfaction and craving, both. And a wicked sense of pride. I'd made the chief sit and be petted.

My touch lulled him into a kind of abandon he needed so much. I could feel it happen. His breathing became slow, regular, and his head fell to one shoulder. He was starting to fall asleep. Exhausted from the storm, from the adrenalin rush of finding the sheep and the impossible job of bringing them home. And perhaps from desires denied and buried deep in the furs of the bed that sat here beside us. Did he lie here and think of me sometimes?

Unsure what to do, I just luxuriated in watching him sleep. The light sputtering from the flame made him look burnished and brown and gold.

I removed one hand so slowly, so carefully. He was motionless, slumbering like a stone. I picked up his gauntlets from the bed, retrieved a half-carved tiny boat from the floor, and placed them both on the table. And then I gently pressed his shoulder, whispered for him to wake up, just a little. He drowsily opened his eyes.

"Stay sleepy," I coaxed. "Just move to your bed." And like a little boy, he did.

I drew a wool blanket over him, then sat in his chair beside the bed and brushed my fingers along his cheekbone. I sang to him, an ancient lullaby, though he was already asleep. *Bye bye. Hushabye. Can you see the swans fly?* I made small circles against the taut muscles of his jaw, and I sang first in Old Norse, then in English. *Half asleep in bed I lie. Awake with half an eye.*

The sound of the door opening made me freeze in place, and my eyes darted to find Ranka there. She gave a guilty gasp and shut the door tight, disappearing behind it.

I stood abruptly and looked around the room in hesitation, not sure what to do, hoping an answer would appear among the axes and knives, the shirts and dark hair that littered the floor. For the first time, I thought about the facts. I'd told off Hildur, the head of the household. Then I'd spent the last hour in the chief's room, my hands in his hair, his clothes on the floor, a sensual mess.

Inside this room, nothing mattered but the two of us. But he was in his bed now, asleep where he belonged, and I would have to return alone to stares and retribution. I pictured myself shunned by every eye. Worse, I pictured myself in the bitter blizzard, thrown out of the house. I'd be dead before he woke.

There was no way around it. I would just go. I kissed my fingers, lay them briefly against his cheek, and went out through the weaving room to the main house.

Most of the family had gone to sleep. A few were awake around the heartstone, drinking and rehashing the story of the lost sheep, and likely committing to memory the inconceivable tale of Ginn calling Hildur a bitter cold bitch. A couple of them looked up when I entered, but quickly drew their eyes away. Even Betta did not rush to me. I slipped into my alcove wishing I were a spirit, swift and unseen.

Alone, I drew a blanket up and leaned into the wood-scented corner, where the heaviness of restrained passion and fatigue found me. I should have been sorry, perhaps, but I wasn't. I should have been desperately scared for my place here. All I could think of was Heirik's forehead against mine, his beard close enough to brush my cheek. With a smile on my lips, I let sleep draw me down and hold me close.

The sound of my name woke me.

"I saw Ginn." It was Ranka, in her family's sleeping place, next to mine. I struggled up from the bench where I'd sunk. "She was with the chief, in his room."

I came alive, the hair standing up all along my body. I hoped she was speaking only to Kit, and that what I had done with Heirik would remain private. I tensed with listening.

"Child! Lower your voice." It was her mother, thank goodness. And she was admonishing. "Have you lost your mind? What were you doing looking in there?"

"I heard the singing," Ranka argued in a whisper, heeding the warning to lower her volume.

"Singing." Kit inflected the word in that special way of mothers who were skeptical of their child's wild stories.

"It was Ginn. She was brushing his hair like this." There was a short pause. "And singing him strange words."

Kit made a sound I couldn't interpret without seeing her face. A combination of já, and huh, and right, next thing swine will fly. "You were dreaming, Ranka. You were in your blankets."

"Nei!" she almost shouted, in the voice of a child who'd been disbelieved. Then she lowered her voice again. "I wasn't."

"Uh-huh," Kit challenged. "And just what was the chief doing, then?"

"Sleeping." Ranka sounded as wistful as I had felt in the moment. "Just sleeping."

There was a quiet pause, then another undefined sound from Kit, as if to declare the conversation finished. Ranka didn't say more, and I heard the rustling of blankets as she settled into her warm little den. I kept my own head down, eyes closed, and drew my cloak around me.

It was morning when I cut myself.

I sat by the hearth, girls and women all around me, a circle of us working close to the heat.

Hildur sat right beside me, and once or twice I turned to her and found her watching my sewing work. Perhaps I wasn't applying myself enough. I didn't care. I let the fabric lie in my lap and picked up my little shears. Flipping them over, I looked at them with new tenderness. I squeezed them once, twice, watching how the elegant little curve of metal sprung open and shut. Then I drew up the little whetstone that hung at my waist and rasped it against the blade.

I closed my mind to the individual words around me and let the voices melt. The overall rise and fall of murmurs tuned to the shinking sound of my whetstone, and then the wash of sound fell behind as my mind left the house. I roamed over snowless hills, green and bright as day, down a steep rockside into the pretty ravine. The sun hit the water and shattered the blue like glass, obscuring my bare feet, distorting them. The water was unusually slow, moving peacefully, not racing past my ankles with its shivering violence. It was serenely passing, and I drew arcs in the surface with my toe. I looked to Heirik, building his fort.

A barked reprimand split the air. Hildur's voice, snapping at one of the girls. Her elbow shot out with her irritated words, and she bumped me. My shears skipped against the whetstone and buried themselves in the heel of my hand. I shrieked, then swallowed the sound as fast as I could.

A soft sickness spread in my throat when I looked and saw the little blade sticking out of my body. So wrong. Something turned inside out, in my gut, when I drew the shears from my flesh.

My instinct was to curl up around the blood and hide it. I didn't want a fuss. No attention. Most everyone had seen, though, and Kit was immediately at my side, pressing a soft piece of linen to my hand. My teeth ground together, and my eyes shut against the wincing pain.

Betta came to my other side, took my forearm firmly from Kit, and held my palm up to scrutinize. She peeled the linen back.

"It is nothing," I hissed, completely unconvincing. Blood ran down my arm, dark red against my pale skin. It had been a near miss, the tender film of skin over my wrist so near, veins showing greenish blue under the surface.

"It is something," she declared, and pressed the bandage back to it, as if pressing a little gift into my palm. "I'll get water."

I held the cloth tight and looked at the shears in my lap. The ones that had cut Heirik's hair and then, the very next morning, turned to bite me. I shook my head at the bewildering coincidence. Every time I got close to him, it seemed, I ended up hurt.

It was the beginning of another long winter stretch. When the chief learned of my injury, he shied away from me again. We didn't even play games.

THE FROZEN STONES THAT RIMMED THE BATH FELT SHARP ON THE nape of my neck. I closed my eyes and felt the wash of polar air and sting of spray that came up from the bath with the wind.

Betta was humming in a wandering way, not quite a song. The water swished and curled around my shoulders as she made circles with her bare feet. She was bundled in wool and fur, but had taken her boots off to soak. A torch burned next to us, where she'd lodged it between two stones.

"I need to get my hands on some thread," she sighed. "I need a cauldron boiling outside, under the sun, so I can watch colors turn. I want to smell the lichens and flowers cooking."

A long ago memory of tea came to me, of my kitchen and sleek glass cups steaming like this bathwater. I tried to conjure up the once-familiar flavors of mint and bergamot, herbs almost as precious in the future as they were here.

"Do you ever drink the dye water?" I asked her.

She laughed brightly. "My Da says to, for certain kinds of sickness, but many think it's dimwitted. Not allowed by the gods, or at least not brosti." *Smiled upon.* "Water over the bruised root can cure a griping stomach. A concentrate can keep a babe from coming."

I raised an eyebrow. I hadn't known that.

"Broth is nothing compared to the symbols my Da makes," she added. "On the bones."

I asked her what she meant. "He scratches runes into the bones of animals. They can heal mortal wounds."

Written words were powerful here. I pictured Bjarn carefully carving them, thinking they would save a beloved person, draw someone back from death. I wished for a screen and pen so I could form some that would cure our sadness and clear this snow.

"Já, well, I crave the sun too," I said, and stretched in the water. "I'd like to run in the grass with a dog at my heels. Ride Drifa fast into the valley." I concluded with some dry irritation, "I'd like to shoot something."

She laughed some more. "Já," she agreed. "I would love to shoot something right now."

She patted at the surface of the water with the bottoms of her feet, then plunged them in.

"Do you think everyone knows about us?"

Her voice was steady and calm, not worried. But I fretted every time the subject of her and Hár came up. I saw them look at each other across the heartstone, and I knew she was losing all sense of danger about her relationship with him. All sense of what she could lose if it were found out. Her chances to ever marry, her place—and her father's place—in this family, her heart and honor and soul? And yet I knew how losing all those things, losing everything, seemed worth it.

"I don't think so, nei," I told her, and my voice was warm and thick in the night. "I think that Heirik and I draw their eyes away from anything else."

"Já, you're right." Little waves lapped at my throat when Betta stirred the water. "You two are confusing, Woman."

"We are?" I laughed. Nei doubt, I thought. I was confused myself.

"So serious, each of you alone," Betta mused, "and so light together. If I didn't see it every day I would not believe the chief could turn so."

I let my toes drift up to break the surface.

She continued, a smile, and a hint of disbelief in her voice. "I like him this way."

"Me too." I had to agree.

We sat for just a moment more, and then I teased her and myself alike. "You think I'm too serious?"

"Grave," she said immediately. "Grave as the chief." And though we both laughed, I knew it was true, that the gravity—my loneliness and wistfulness, his quiet resolution, sense of duty—those were what people knew of us. The lightness we'd begun to share in the warmth of the winter house was an inconceivable surprise.

In a second, she was back on the one topic that drove her very breath and owned her mind.

"Hár says I will want to marry someday, to a man my age. I think it's because I'm not important enough for him." She was matter of fact, as always, but her voice wavered. "Gods, why did I fall in love with the foremost among men? So dumb. I should have found a boy."

Inside, I had to agree. But it couldn't be helped, what love demanded.

Then Hár came. He emerged from the mist like a ghostly raider. Always bigger than I expected, and more tender. He carried four slim skið.

Betta smiled for him, and she splashed me as she drew her feet out of the water. While she pulled her socks and boots on, I watched the old man, his face eerily lit from below so that sinister hollows and shadows moved across his cheeks. So far above me, so dark and angular, his gray-blond hair loose and almost colorless in the night.

"Woman," he addressed me, sighing wearily and crouching to place the skið on the ground.

He raised his eyes to Betta, and something complex came alive in them. A kind of panicked wonder, and resignation. He looked like he'd accidentally caught a sleek white fox and knew it belonged to the forest. It was the face of a man who was watching her go. Hár was the most committed creature I'd ever seen. Holding on as long as he could, but ready to do what he had to. He didn't think Betta was too young for him, or too low. He thought she was too good.

They found these ways to cheat on honor. Hár and Heirik. Hiding, holding back, in the name of protecting Betta and me. I shot water through my teeth as I watched him sweep her into the night. As if any mortal man could hide his smoldering eyes from honor itself. As if a man could hide the wildness from his own heart.

It would not be alright, if Betta and Hár were found out. And the times they stole away were stretching longer and longer with the winter, tempting disaster.

There was no concept of dating or courting, just marriage or not. There might be love found in that institution, accidentally. And then there was this. They had a word for it, meaning *the great passion*. The most disorienting and ruthless love. A messy emotion trying to find its way in such a black and white landscape. Here where Hár preserved Betta, where Heirik protected me, by withholding themselves. Withholding the only thing we really wanted. Just them.

I sunk to my chin and laid my head back, my bare neck bit by cold stones. I let my feet float up gently. Honor itself seemed to rise around me like steam from the bath. I imagined it drifting away, following Hár and Betta. Honor would find him and get inside every chink in his armor.

Gods, I was bored.

There was nothing for me in the house, and I lingered in the velvet water. I splayed my toes, and it was a warm surprise between them, between my legs as I spread them. I let it in, let the water explore every sensitive surface. My fingers drifted down to join it.

One hand rested lightly on my belly, the other touched the places where I wished for someone else's imprint. I closed my eyes, and he was there.

The scent of spice and iron in his hair, his eyes soft amber. In my dream, he sat on his bed, and I straddled him, my skirts magically out of the way, his clothes conveniently gone. I tangled my hands in the blackness of his hair and pulled and tipped his head back so he would give himself to me. He let me touch his marked skin without shying away. Face to face, so close that our kiss was more of a crush. His mouth and tongue were sensations I actually knew, but the rest I imagined. He was so hard, I was so ready, all I had to do was lift my hips to capture him, lower myself onto him, so slow we both groaned into each other's shoulders. Gorgeous agony rose in me so fast. He thrust up into me and I bore down to meet him, once, twice and I lost count, lost all will and sense, and came, my eyes and voice and mind lost for that one moment. Holding him. And he clung to me, just the same.

I opened my eyes to the night sky, in the bath alone, my sex throbbing in my own hand.

Time was vague in the constant winter. Sometimes it dragged like a cloak full of stones, and at other times the force of it would lift away and let me drift. Leaning back on the rocks, I looked for Frigg's distaff among the stars, seeking the patience of billions of years spinning in place, forming something as great and fleeting as the clouds. Never finishing, always casting what was made into the sky and watching it dissipate. A thousand needles of icy wind came and stung my cheeks, and it felt good to let them do their work, scrubbing and cleansing. The water rippled, and my toes broke the surface, immediately beginning to freeze. Ten little points of blue ice. I drew them back under. I was waterlogged and chilled despite the pool's heat. I needed to get out.

My clothes sat in a pile by the tunnel entrance, and I snatched them up fast and wrapped myself tight. Inside the little doorway, I had time to fix myself. My wool dress was a rigid, ineffective towel. I pulled my shift on in a flash and wrapped myself in a big wool cloak instead. Shivering hard, I took my dresses in one hand, my torch in the other, and started out fast through the tunnel.

I tripped on something, stumbled, and in the stuttering light saw a knife on the tunnel floor. It glinted once, and then disappeared as my torch died. In the pitch black, I knelt to find it, but my scrabbling hands found only dirt. Heavy and close, the tunnel started to choke me. I stood too fast, head swimming, orientation gone. Which way? I ran, my dresses clutched in one hand, useless torch in the other. My shoulder caught on a dirt wall, and crumbles went down the back of my shift. I slewed around, confused, scared now, feeling thousands of pounds of earth pinning me. I told myself to calm down. It was only the bath tunnel. The only way out was home.

When I saw the faint light of the mudroom I lunged for it.

I dropped the cold torch on the bench and sank beside it, drawing my cloak tight around myself, muttering shushing sounds along with the beat of my heart. Wool scratched at the moist skin of my throat. I'd made it. Everything was okay.

Heirik was there, sudden and silent, just a few feet away.

My eyes swept up from his dark boots to his waist. His belt was bare, and it was strange to see him without the fire kit and clattering of knives that always hung there. His chest where his shirts were open, and his face were flushed, red everywhere, as though he'd been traipsing outside, letting the icy wind scour his face like I had. He was burnished by the snow, smooth and shining with fresh cold. But his boots were dry, his legs unbound. I looked around for his snow shoes or wet cloaks lying where they'd been shed, but everything was in order in the mudroom, put away.

His eyes were gold with anger.

"You will not go alone again." It was a rough, graceless demand.

To the bath? Me? He spoke as though reprimanding a child. "Take someone," he told me. He looked toward the tunnel door, then back to me with fresh fury. "Someone who will stay with you."

My heart dropped like a stone. He knew about Betta.

He must have seen me sink, maybe I even I shook my head. He whispered, but not to me, to the wall maybe, the cloaks and furs and snowshoes. "I know what happens in my house."

I thought of Betta, happy out there in the snowy landscape, and I wished I could send her a message to never come back. That it was over for her here.

Of course Heirik knew. He was god here, and every slight stirring of the night, a single animal's exhalation, a feuding man's darkest thoughts, were known to him. How had Betta and I—and Hár especially—thought that this insightful, observant man wouldn't know everything that happened in every corner of his farm and lands, from this mudroom down to the sea? His scrutiny of me, personally, was something I had wished for but hadn't really understood, and I felt it now. Some part of him watched me, listened for my voice, moved with my movements and breathed with my breath. I felt all of it from the past six months settling on me with an amber gaze.

I turned from it. The cloaks looked rough and primitive in the lamp light. I focused on them, trying not to shake, trying not to cry. He was behind me, angry at Betta, full of a calm rage. I didn't know what he would do to her, to both of us, but I wouldn't flinch, no matter what he said next. For both of our sakes, I would not be scared.

He grazed my spine with the backs of his fingers. So lightly, I wasn't sure it was real.

Oh.

He touched me lovingly, a whisper of his knuckles against my bone. Full of rage, yes, or something just as powerful.

I let the layers of cloaks slide off my shoulders and bared myself to him, the wide straps of my shift all that covered my skin. His finger traveled to just where skin met wool, no further. He laid his forehead on my shoulder and grasped my upper arms. I hovered between breaths, closing my eyes as if I might seal this moment, draw it into me and hold it.

"I want to kiss again," he said. Such a simple desire. The idea of kissing him rushed into me, everywhere. His words, the pressure of his head on my shoulder, his fingers on my damp skin, formed one tenuous and gorgeous moment.

Without moving, not wanting to scare him, I asked, "Do you want to kiss again?" I whispered, smiling. "Or do you want to kiss me?"

"What do you mean, Woman?" He almost snarled into my ear. He'd never called me that before, so tenderly familiar and exasperated, and I felt a wicked smile fully form on my lips. His fingers tightened. He took in my scent, and turned his head to let his deep voice flow into my ear, into the soft skin of my throat. "Kissing and you are all one."

Oh. The words went deep into my body, softening me beyond what the pool had done, what my own hands had done. My smile slackened and my lips opened with desire. I fell back into him.

This couldn't last, this impossible moment, his body pressing now against my back, a low hum of desire against the place where my raven would have been, a groan of lost resolve. His hands moved, his fingers brushing down both my arms, a million tiny fires sparking in their wakes. The cloak fell, and I stood in my shift, scant fabric between his heavy arousal and the base of my spine. I'd never felt him against me this way, so ready. I tilted my hips and pushed back against him. His fingers found my wrist, and my skin was insufficient, like he might sink into it, into my bloodstream and bones.

I turned in his arms. He bent to press his mouth to mine, a hard demand that turned to a kiss. And I whispered. "Let go, Sváss." I called him *Love*. And he let himself go, poured himself into me, and I took him, his tongue and scent and heat.

We kissed, and then he drew away, his breath coming hard and fast.

My voice was hoarse but steady. "Take me somewhere," I rasped. I glanced at the door to his room just a few feet away.

"Nei," he said. "Not there."

I didn't care where. He was impossibly willing, and though it was only a few feet to his bed, I would go where he wanted, would do it anywhere now, anywhere he wanted this to be. I only wanted to know that nothing could stop us this time, no danger, no cries of warning in our hearts. I stood, terrified this moment would crack like newborn ice.

"Put on skið," he said.

Skis.

I looked at him blankly. He wanted me to put on skið and go outside?

He was pulling away from me already, and he looked down at my shift. "And clothes, já?"

He rummaged in the corner, and I sank down hard on the bench in interrupted bliss. I watched his hips that I'd so lately felt against my body. My lips felt bright, and I placed my fingers on the fullness of the lower one, to press and keep him there. To capture his presence. But I could feel it disappearing like frost flowers in the sun.

When I came to myself, I found him quickly tying bindings around his ankles.

We got ready so fast, a steady stream of socks, woolens tucked inside, boots, bindings, hats and gloves. Signé's gorgeous coat, the melrakki fur silver and sensual against my skin. More cloaks on top, hood pulled tight at my throat.

Heirik knelt on one knee before me and strapped the ungainly skið to my boots. How could I ski with him? I'd tried only a few times, always flailing. He lifted one of my feet with such restraint and reverence, my foot felt tiny and beloved in his hands. His eyes met mine as if to show my own little foot to me, something shiny he'd discovered. Then he tied it with urgency.

He drew me up and to the door. So fast and thoroughly bound and ready. I noticed my dress, a red puddle on the bench. I bent awkwardly, balled it up and shoved it underneath. And we took off.

I followed him, curious and yet not desiring any explanation. I only felt the thrill of skiing, and I realized I was doing it without thought or awkwardness. I didn't care about slipping or falling or anything. I didn't care where he was taking me, only that he wasn't leaving me behind for two or three or ten days. We were fleeing together this time, into the sparkling, knife's-edge night.

The thought nagged at me. Something to do with a knife.

As I sped over the snow, I thought of the dark tunnel. There'd been a knife there on the ground. I pictured Heirik's cold-wrought skin, his empty belt, and clarity came sneaking into my head. Had he been there? Had he seen Betta and Hár ride off together? And then. *Oh*, nei. Had he seen me?

He stood and watched me, I knew it, as I'd once watched him in that bath. He'd heard his name from deep in my throat, seen my ecstatic face, the only thing lit for thousands and thousands of miles.

I smiled into the night wind. He'd been with me then, after all.

Freedom coursed through me, like cold and roaring water clearing my head. I flew down a ghostly, snow-bright slope, everything electric blue and violet, a wintry scene so much more savage and real than my naive skating fantasy.

Perplexed, yes, but I knew Heirik was taking me somewhere. He knew where. I thought, as the wind hit my face and froze my nose and eyelashes, that it was going to be somewhere wonderful. And there, we would be lovers.

WE SKIIED TO THE FAR EDGE OF THE WOODS. NOT SO FAR FROM home, but far enough to be utterly gone, so free in the snow, that my mind felt cleansed of everything pinched and tense. We left everything behind us in the smoky house, and Heirik and I stood alone in our beloved and immense landscape.

We took off our skið and waded in to the woods, knee deep in untouched snow. It became less deep a few feet in to the tangle of birches, but still as we pushed through, the slush and wet under-brush froze me up to my thighs. My whole legs—calves, knees, everywhere—burned with a searing pain, and then went blessedly numb.

Nei matter. I was a graceful creature, a beautiful thing, made for this wood, this night. My breath gathered and hung in the air, always a step before me.

Despite the moon, it was ink dark inside the birches, as if the trees had all burned and now stood as charcoal remains of a great fire. Heirik dissolved into it, and more than once my heart and lungs spasmed with the fear that I'd lost him. But I always found him, a steady, denser shape against the black.

Long moments of walking passed, and my eyes adjusted. The branches and leaves and shapes of underbrush became clearer. I could see him, then. I watched him inside Hvítmörk, moving through it, and though he was bundled in twenty pounds of ani-mal skins, I remembered his summer body—hot from haying, shirts open at the throat, linen sticking to the curves and hollows of his arms and back. He'd been so exhausted then. Gorgeous, but falling down tired. Tonight he was suffused with a quiet energy. In his place and time. And I in mine.

Heirik stopped and turned back toward me, drawing aside the low branches of a tree and welcoming me to come to him. I could see his smile now. And just beyond him, I could make out an even blacker place in the dark, an opening. The mouth of a small cave.

I could see he'd been here many times before. Heirik knelt to strike up a tiny fire on a flat rock at the cave entrance, using dry tinder he had stashed here. I could just make out a great roll of blankets and furs against the cave wall, and the spot where he bent to light the little fire was marked with the soot of flames past.

He blew gently on the tiny orange light, coaxing it out, and my realization grew with the same soft glow. This was where he disappeared to sometimes. When he was gone for days, he was here.

This stark and rocky place broke my heart. But I knew the relief of being away from people, especially at my most desolate moments.

The cave wasn't quite high enough for him to stand inside, but it was wide, and big enough to call a room. Deep enough that I could just barely make out its contours and limits. And toasty! I thought I was dreaming, hallucinating that the little fire was making more heat than possible, but as I stepped deeper into the cave, the glimmer of heat grew. I wasn't imagining it.

He said, "Go all the way in. Get warm."

As I moved into the dark, I heard a delicate trickling—not quite strong enough to call a rushing—of water. I squinted to find it, and I knelt beside a tiny, steaming-hot stream. It was no bigger than two hands across. I couldn't tell if it was boiling.

"Is it too hot to touch?" My voice echoed strangely in the misshapen room, coming back at me from odd angles, some of it lost in unexpected eddies.

"Nei, not enough to scald."

I touched the water lightly, and it was on the absolute edge of skin-burning temperature. I dipped my fingers in, and they sang with pain as they awoke.

The stream changed everything about this place, and the notion of loneliness flew. It wasn't severe here. It was snug, and there was life. It felt blessed and calm. I let my fingers trail in the water, let it move over my skin, unhurried, but with purpose, until I couldn't stand it anymore and had to draw away.

I turned back to Heirik and he was unrolling the big clump of sheepskins and furs.

He took off his bracers and dropped them on the floor of the cave, then stooped over the fire, drying the edges of his sleeves. I dropped my wool cloaks and hat into the pile of furs, deepening the nest. But I kept my coat on. Underneath there was only my shift, and I was still cold.

I leaned back against the pleasantly warmed cave wall. Taken by a sudden calm, a sense of unhurried freedom, Heirik and I just sat together on a bed of furs. I savored the moment, my fingers brushing through fur, my knee brushing his.

"This is where you go sometimes," I said.

"Já." He looked around and smiled as though it were a great house. When he continued, though, his smile faded. "I found this place after."

After. His sentence complete, his thought remained half hidden. I felt the weight of his mother's coat. Looking at me wearing it, in this private and wild place, he would surely think of Signé. He didn't talk about his parents' death, only what followed. "When I became … this." He looked at his hands, as if being chieftain were inked there, a physical thing he'd grown into. As if he wished he could wipe it off.

"It's so close," I said, my voice dry and cave-strange. "I always imagined you going far away."

He cocked his head, and it looked adorable to see the great chief confused. "You thought of me?"

I shook my head and drew my brows together. Would he ever understand? What could I tell him that would make him see?

"When I first came to Hvítmörk, you and I talked at the ravine." I rested my hand on my own knee, palm open, a gesture so much like his, it made me smile at myself. "Right after that, you went away for ten and a half days."

He stared openly, maybe still disbelieving, or maybe finally getting it. Realizing that I remembered the first time, maybe every time. I knew how many days. "When you go," I told him, "I miss you."

He spread his palm over mine. His fingers moved up inside my fur-lined cuff, grasping my wrist loosely this time, not too hard. He turned to face me, and with his other hand, he traced the arc of bone above my eye. I leaned in to the pressure, coat sleeves slipping off my shoulders, pooling at my elbows, warm air kissing my throat, skin slick with steam.

"I never thought I would have someone," he said, and his voice was steady, his thumb a promise on my brow. "That I would know someone."

My heart dropped into my gut.

Know someone.

The truth came and sat like a sickening weight inside me. I felt the cave too close around me, a small place, not mine. I'd led Heirik to trust me, coaxed him until he was entirely vulnerable, and here I sat in his most intimate world, a liar. He thought I was the impossible, a companion, a heart open to his. He thought he knew me. But I had never let him.

His thumb stopped moving. He'd felt me stiffen.

I let the words tumble out before I could think. "I know where I'm from."

Heirik's features were calm and even, but his hand closed tighter on my forearm. His other hand was gone from my face. And then he let my wrist go and withdrew entirely. He drew his knees up, a wall between us. Closed. His eyes gave nothing away, but his body tensed and turned inward, waiting for betrayal. Waiting for more loss, for another thing he couldn't have.

There were moments I'd practiced what I might tell him. Now, when it was time, it was so hard to get the words out.

"Saga sent me," I said. "From more than a thousand years away."

I thought this explanation would sound ridiculous. That he'd laugh at me, or treat me kindly, since I was insane. But hearing it now in this sacred place, it was true. Some goddess or spirit had come for me in my glacial, lonely future, and had drawn me back here. For a purpose I couldn't fully name, she had done this, and I had come, to take my rightful home, to be his. And here I sat by the same streamside that Saga did, somewhere deeper in these white woods.

I felt her with me. And yet, I trembled with each breath, waiting while Heirik said nothing. He'd absorbed what I just told him, his face closed in his practiced way.

Two, three, many more inhalations, and then I felt tears start to sting the corners of my eyes. I was losing him. A great hollow opened in my chest. My hands closed on fur, wanting to grasp instead at his clothes and beg him to accept me anyway. Accept the liar, the stranger, the unnatural thing I had just become. I felt ugly and wrong, a freshly born monster. My heart curled in on itself and wished.

Then he reached for me.

With one finger he traced the strap of my shift, lifting it slightly, moving it aside. He eased it down my arm.

Breath hovering, I reached for him too. I untied the binding at his ankle and began unwrapping it slowly, unwinding up and up his calf to his knee. He knew it all now, everything about me, and yet we were here in this dreamed-of moment. It sank in. He'd accepted—nei, believed—in Saga's hand in our lives so easily. And now we would make love to each other, truly, nothing unknown between us.

I took his hand, lifted his wrist to my lips. I skimmed my teeth over the skin there, and he looked at his own arm as though he'd never seen it.

"Come lie with me," I said, and we went down into the fur.

Thought abandoned, and Saga sent back to her water, it was just us. Mouths on throats and cheekbones, arms and legs entwined, his bindings loose, my dress tangling. Our hips and thighs sought one another, wanting to be closer. My shift was too much between us, and I lifted it up my legs, pushed all my clothes away so I could rest my leg on his. He hesitated, and I took his hand and brought it to my thigh. He grasped me too hard, his fingers rough, my breath coming shallow now, together with his, punctuated with a small, animal whimper, a pleading, *never stop*.

I placed my hand over the back of his, matching my fingers to his, and I guided him. Showed him how to cup me gently. "Easy," I exhaled, trembling with the need for him to move his fingers against me, in me. I rested my forehead on his shoulder and breathed. The idea of looking in his eyes was unbearable. I moved our hands together, slipped our fingers—one of his, one of mine— inside me. I moved against him, showing him, and humming now, a needy sound lost in the linen of his clothes. I pressed my head against his shoulder.

"Hverju?" Heirik's voice was rough and quiet. *Why?* Why would I want this, want him?

It broke my heart open, and a wave of love came, the pleasure and agony of a single moment, lost breath, crying. My voice filled the cave, and I imagined the sound of my pleasure reaching every creature of the forest. Heirik told me, full of wonder, "You are so alive."

My hands were inside his shirts, flat against him, sliding down, moving to untie the threads that kept him from me. My hand felt small and cool to me, when I touched him. He made a savage sound. Precious language was gone, ripped away with his clothes, lost in the fur with his linen. He strained against me, strangled a sound in my hair, and gave himself up to that wordless moment, alive and hot in my hand.

Our pulses matched in the cave-dark, and he found one word. "More." Something I had once asked of him, and this time the answer was yes.

"Lie back," I told him. As in my dream in the bath, just hours ago, I climbed on top of him. He reached for my hair, grabbed it in both fists, and pulled me down to him, hard, to kiss. I imagined the blood red of his fingers moving through the snow of my hair.

For hours, the steam held us close. It slickened our skin, kept us warm, hid us, and we were alone. A small fire, a rocky bed, in the snow-stricken wilderness. This place had been his, but we made it into ours, blessed it with the work of our bodies.

A long time later, Heirik's words startled me out of drowsiness, at the edge of sleep. "Tired One," he said. I rested on my side, Heirik behind me, and his mouth was against my ear. "You need to rest."

"Nei!" I didn't know what would happen when we left this safe and intimate burrow. I didn't want to ever know, just wanted to stay and stay and stay. "I don't want to leave here." I said it like a child, desperate with the desire to stay up past bedtime, to never give in to night.

I felt his chest move with a silent laugh. "You don't have to, Litla," he said. "Not yet. Just sleep here." Then, quieter, as though he didn't want to say it out loud. "I have longed to hold you while you sleep."

He fit himself to my back, my bottom, my bent knees. Solid, surrounding me, he matched all my curves.

He spoke in his most gentle voice, his lips against my hair. Each word was made just for me, and he held it before giving it to my sleepy ear. "Bi, bi, little bird," he shushed, and began to say the words of the lullaby. He'd heard me, the night I cut his hair.

The little bird sounds seemed even tinier coming from such a serious, grown man, and I grinned, sleepy.

He did not sing, like I had, but he spoke the poem, lulling me just as the song was meant to do for babes throughout a thousand years, and I felt it in my bones. I pressed my hips back into him, snuggling into his big body, his arm heavy around me, his hand resting on my breast.

"Hush your beating wings," he told me. "Sleepy as the birds go by, awake with half an eye."

The words were not exactly the same as the ones I'd learned in the future. At the very edge of sleep, I noted it. "It's different," I sighed.

I woke with my hip pressing painfully into the floor and the black smoke of a dying fire in my nose and eyes. The stones were chilly now, but I didn't care. I laid in Heirik's arms, and he burned.

"Are you cold?" He asked me.

"Nei, you are like a heartstone." I felt him laugh against my back.

We stayed there longer, quietly holding, thoughts slow.

"I am grateful, then," he said, continuing a conversation long past. "To Saga." He kissed my ear. "She guided me to find you at the water."

"Nei," I told him. I turned in his arms and buried my head against his shoulder. "Nei. I found you."

The trudge home was long and uphill, but I could have climbed a mountain, built a house, I was so brave and strong and full. Where I was going stretched out before me now, instead of where I'd come from. My past—the cold city, lost eyes and hearts of millions of people—was freed like a cut rope. While my body, tired and sore, struggled to get home, my heart was already there.

Heirik carried me the last part of the way, on his back, as if I weighed nothing. The snow was not quite up to his knees, the sky calm and star-struck. He walked easily, maybe suffused as I was with the great strength of possibility. I held on to him and our four skið. He felt like a horse under me, bone and muscle moving steadily, calmly, untiring.

I never would have found the house. It was no more than a gentle roll in the land, a nondescript hill, though once we came close I noticed the pale smoke climbing weakly, mixing with the gray dawn, the same color. The light time was beginning for the day, the five or six hours when the sun almost rose, reaching and not quite making it to the horizon.

I felt born to hold onto Heirik. And yet, gods, I was ready to get down! Relieved when we reached the house, I dropped the skið heavily and slid down off his back. He turned to me, and even as we both shivered, frozen through, we still could not go in.

He seemed emboldened by the night, and he pressed me up against the stiff, cold grass of the house. He planted a hand against the house and leaned over me, and I waited for his kiss. But he hesitated.

"Undra min," he said, so softly I could have missed it. *My surprise.* Then he looked away into the night, considering something unseen. He looked back at me, paused. And then all his boldness and grace dissolved.

"Ginn," he started, his voice broken, and then he stopped, closed his eyes and waited until it seemed he could speak again. "Jul is soon," he said. The holiday feast? He confused me so often, with so few words. "I want you by me." He closed his eyes. "I want—"

The door closed with a muffled thump, and we both turned.

Someone had been there.

GOD-MAKER

PEACEFUL MORNING CAME. I SAT UP IN MY BED AND DREW THE curtains open, then rested with my knees drawn up and simply looked out. The house looked pretty, wintry and cozy, with furs all around. The roof was open and a fire burned today, cheerful and strong, not just smoking embers and hot rocks. The murmur of voices grew and resolved into words. *Hemline* and *fish* and *fool*. I watched Betta counting out bound stitches to Lotta, who sat pressed to her side, nodding seriously. One of her chubby baby fingers poked at the stitches. Ranka sat right next to them binding a sock, such a bigger girl already.

Heirik had been angry when he heard that door close last night. Just a couple hours ago. It ripped us from a dream, destroyed a fragile moment between us.

He left me in an elegantly silent fury, gone into the house, but he didn't find anyone there.

Then we went to our beds, he to his and I to mine. Not angry, nei. Frustrated. Wanting more. We would figure this out tomorrow. And now the day had broken, and it could start to happen.

Thinking of his words about the Jul festival, my heart felt light and skittery like a beach bird. I want you by me. His voice was tangled with the words, nervous, urgent. Only later, dreaming of him before my eyes closed on the last hours of night, did I figure it out. He didn't mean he just wanted me near him at the party. He wanted me beside him on the high seat. His wife. He was asking.

The house breathed with me, and it was calm and lovely, flickering fire, braided girls, strong, playful men. Lamps gave more light to the work, and a soft scent of rosemary rose from a few where precious bits of herbs had been added. My house dog panted under the bench across from mine, dirty paws sticking straight out.

For a shining moment, all of it was mine.

"Child!" Hildur called to me, snapping me out of my reverie. "Butter and fish." She held her iron ring of keys out rudely, arm extended, waiting for me to get up out of my blankets and come to her. Butter and fish. Any one of six people were sitting closer and could have helped.

One more morning. It wouldn't help to argue now. With a taste of defiance in my throat, I climbed out of bed and went to the pantry.

I turned the biggest key over in my hand before I slid it into the lock. It had an iron shaft, as long as my fingers and palm, that twisted and curved into three big teeth on one end. Tiny dents pounded all over formed a twining design. It was warm. Hildur had sat by the fireside all morning, and it held the heat of her skirts, her body, but soon it would be mine. I rubbed my thumb over the curves of its decorative swirls, and I thought about Heirik so close in the next room. Wondered when he would come to me.

Bringing butter to the hearth, I felt something underfoot. A toy? In a dream, I saw the butter flung out from my hands, the dry strips of fish flying up and ever so slowly floating down, caught in a moment between joy and horror. And I fell—arms outstretched like a lost lover—into the flames.

Hands and skirts thrashing, I felt people pulling at me, up out of the fire, into cool arms. Someone drew me close, drew my head back to look in my eyes. They called for Bjarn. Pain came seconds later, the side of my face, left arm, hand exploding.

I yelled for Heirik. I screamed for him, and when he didn't come I shrieked, "Where is he?!!" Pain clawed up my throat. Breathing was too hard, and I struggled with it. I heard him, finally, and even his voice couldn't stop this. I reached for him, desperate.

"Leave the house," he said, in the voice of the chief.

Dresses rustled, children cried, doors closed. He was behind me then, his body big and snow-cold against my back, his arms came up around me, holding and rocking, talking low in my ear. "Litla," he said, "Shhhh." He pressed my unharmed shoulder tight to his body, trying to gentle and calm me.

My mind lit for a second on each of a string of simple things. Pain, hands, tears on my face. Heirik. Just him, not even the man but him as a spirit, a thing. Lullaby words, *hush, hush.* The implacable flames that still burned in front of me, orange and mean, gray closing on all sides.

I woke in misery. The hearth fire was in my blood, eating my skin. I looked at my arm, expecting to find it swarming with biting insects or angry spirits. It was flung out at my side, expertly wrapped in linen from my elbow down to my stinging fingertips. The sparking pain there was almost a comfort. I still had fingers.

I would not touch my face.

"Ginn," Betta's voice came clear and low. She petted my unhurt arm, steady and assuring. She spoke over her shoulder to someone else. "Tell the chief she is awake."

I closed my eyes again. I felt him there, suddenly, his weight shifting the bench, his scent coming near.

"Hello, Litla," he said. "You are here." His fingers were light on the arc of my brow. Now I thought of it as his sweet habit, a favorite way of touching me, hand to bone. It made me smile, and the smile turned to pain.

I tried to laugh through it. "I am not small, you know."

He laughed too, silently, and continued to brush his fingers across the unhurt part of my forehead.

"Já, well, I am not handsome."

So there we were.

Bjarn came and broke up the moment. He held something about as long as my hand and wrist, smooth, ivory-colored and hollow.

"The bone of a wreck, Herra," he said. A beached whale—a gift from the gods. Heirik took the bone shard and examined the markings on it.

"They stand uncurved," the chief agreed somberly, then took the bone and tucked it in the blankets by my side.

He just sat with me for a while, his hand now resting on my hip, pressing steadily to gentle me. He kept the pain down. His presence, and an odd sense of tingling life that came from the bone resting against my ribs. When the pain in my skin clawed and scraped, the whisper of the whalebone and Heirik's words, the soft surety of his touch, all mingled and covered me and made the pain bearable.

I would bear it, já. For weeks after that. And every day felt as long as a lifetime, knowing I had lost him.

HEIRIK WOULD STAY BY ME THROUGH ALL TIME, HE SAID, BUT WE could not be lovers. "Too many times, you have been hurt after holding me," Heirik told me. "I can't risk hurting you again."

There was no worse pain he could have inflicted than those words. They made my chest tight, made me clutch my stomach alone in the night. But they weren't surprising words. I'd known they were coming from the moment I woke in bandages, when he looked at me with such sad, caring eyes, regret rising off him as thick as smoke. He'd sat by me, and his fingers had traced the contours of my face. Now I realized he'd been memorizing me. Already saying goodbye.

He didn't leave the house and go to the cave like I thought he might. He checked on me every day. But he always stood back, looking serenely objective to anyone but me. I saw his hesitance, as if a single touch would complete the job and burn me to a pile of dust.

Other than those gloomy moments with Heirik, I had a perverse need to stay by the fireside. I sat, linen wrapped around my head, ugly as a monster. Unable to sew, just staring for long periods. Betta would come talk to me, wrap a blanket around me like an invalid, and tell me little stories about goddesses and elves and what it would be like to go to the great meeting in the west.

Each day, Bjarn changed the bandages on my hand and face. I knew when he took me outside, he would apologize and then scrape at my wounds. The pain seared away all thought, and words died in the sensation. I felt every swipe of rough cloth, felt the bones of Betta's hand ready to break in my grip. Bjarn would pour soothing honey and herbs on me, and glance nervously around, searching for someone. Did the chief watch him?

On the fifth day, Heirik did come, and he loomed over us while Bjarn peeled the bandages back and inspected my hand. The chief leaned so gracefully against the house, his everyday ax hanging lightly in his hand, looking just the way he had when I fell in love with him—dark and forbidding and decorated with blades. In the distance, I noticed Ranka peeking around the corner of the house, everyone watching.

Bjarn looked at my palm, my wrist, and he swallowed hard. "It is good," he stated, then let out a long breath.

Heirik turned away for a moment, looking up the hills. Then he leaned his ax against the house, turned to nod at Bjarn and smile at me with a brilliant, warming smile—the sweetest since my accident.

That day, my skin throbbed and stung for a long time. It burned hotter than the companionable pain I'd come to hold day by day. After sitting by the hearth for more than an hour, I stood with a surge of frustration and anguish and asked Hildur for the pantry keys.

I made it to the cool solitude of the little room and closed the door behind me. The pantry wall was the sod of the house itself, and it felt yielding and smelled brown, with the promise of growing things. Roots, seeds, a future. I leaned my head back against it and breathed. I turned and pressed my one good palm to it, listening to my heart galloping.

I went to the deep barrel. With one hand and one hip, and with grim determination, I rotated the giant lid. A rangy, milky scent flew out like a moth that had been caught, waiting under the surface. I dipped a small bowl into the sour milk. It was cold to the touch, and I soaked my hand in it.

I slowly got food out for dinner. A bowl of butter, a basket of dried meat. I set aside skyr and dried berries for a second trip, and for the hundredth time I dreamt of an orange. Radiant. Its specific scent so sweet and pungent. My palm curled around the cold bumps of its skin. My fingernails longed for the soft resistance of pith and peel. My teeth and tongue wanted that faint pop upon biting. I felt the juice on my chin and fingers.

Here in the real world, I snuck a handful of horribly wilted weeds that we'd collected in fall, to sustain our teeth. I filled a bowl with fish halves like crackers. These dried cod, and the flat grainy loaves Ranka made, were the closest we got to bread. Oh gods, I wanted bread. I wanted a crispy, chewy baguette to fill my senses, on the heels of the orange. I would bury my nose in it, if it were here. I would sink to my knees on this hard dirt floor and consume the entire thing.

The orange and baguette got caught up in each other. They swirled together with the base hunger brought on by Heirik's last kiss, and something else—a tiny, invisible fear—in my stomach. The notion, growing unseen like a root, that he might be right. He might be cursed.

I put my arms around myself and crouched in the pantry, staring at the bowl of fish at my feet. Sometimes I still couldn't believe where I'd come. I thought I'd wake to find Morgan at my bedside in a hospital, telling me I'd been sleeping for two hundred days.

I snapped out of my dreams when Ranka bounded in. She stopped short just inside the door and stared at me, obviously holding back a question.

"Já, Ranka," I said, still crouching on the floor. "Are you here to help me?"

"Lady," she started, and she spoke slower and more carefully than usual. "Why did the chief look scared?"

I asked her what she meant.

"When Bjarn changed your bandages, the chief got a funny look, like he saw a spirit."

She'd watched us, and seen Heirik hovering over me. A spirit had passed. *Oh.* Realization came suddenly and my head swam. He'd been holding that big blade for a reason. He'd meant to use it, if my hand was dying. I remembered his ax sliding out of his palm to rest against the house. I could only imagine what expression Ranka had seen on his face.

"Dear Child, sit with me." We sat on the floor, and I spoke to her eye to eye. "I don't know how I came here to Hvítmörk. That has always been the truth." It was a bent truth, but I didn't actually lie to her sweet, open face. "Even so, I can tell you that I am no spirit. I'm just not afraid of the chief."

I said it out loud, testing the words myself, and they wavered like light on water. My own voice told me the truth, I was scared after all.

"But he is fearsome to everyone," Ranka said, reflecting my thoughts. She spoke to me clearly, as though I were dumb, or I'd told her the sky outside was yellow.

"Child, know this." I tried for a fierce conviction. "To my eyes, the chief is beautiful. I see no curse." The tie on Ranka's braid was loose, but with only one hand I could not fix it. I brushed my fingers through the silky ends. "Only a lovely family with a very good farm."

She looked deep into my eyes, and I thought, or perhaps just hoped, that she would believe me. That she'd see there was room in this world for the possibility that Heirik was not a monster. But how could I convince her, when my own voice wobbled?

"Já, then," I straightened up slowly and smoothed my skirt. "Let's get this food out there where everyone can eat it."

"Já, Lady, let's do it!"

I turned to face the family, for once relieved that Heirik might be gone into the depths of his room.

Soon after we learned that my hand was saved, Heirik began talking to me again.

The news released a black and ugly spirit back into the night. It flew off, leaving only my man, the way I'd always known him. And he seemed to need my company like he needed fresh water and air.

I needed him, too. I needed his assuring presence, even if he wasn't in the room. Just knowing he was here at Hvítmörk. His voice came to me from another part of the house, sometimes, and it brought back my first days here. I'd made it through that. I would make it through this.

And so we settled into a twisted sort of lovemaking, with words instead of bodies.

At the same time, the fear I'd felt in the pantry grew, ever so slowly, a stealthy little newborn creature at the back of my consciousness.

For days and days, we played tafl and talked for hours over our game board, holding phrases between us with unfathomable tenderness, caressing with voices, weighing pieces in our palms. Too disgusted to try to capture a chieftain, I asked that we change the names of the sides. Sometimes with great humor we played circling birds against Ginn. More often we were ravens wheeling around a fine warrior, or fishermen and a great whale.

Sometimes we touched. Our hands might come together on the game board, and we gave and took sensual brushes. A palm moving up a forearm when no one observed. Hours might be easy with camaraderie, and then a single moment would flare with longing. Confused. We could not have what we wanted, and yet we couldn't stop.

My hand, no longer bandaged but still far from healing, was now red as his. As bold and scared as cornered animals, we matched ourselves to one another.

Soon my strategy got good enough for me to win a few times. Every once in a while, my defending whale got away, or on the other hand my small round pieces blocked Heirik in.

We spoke ever so quietly about the future. People steered clear of us anyway, so it was easy, when we played at night, to confide and ask and answer questions. In a handful of dirt, I drew a map for Heirik, of Iceland as seen from space.

The chief wanted to know about farming a thousand years from now, how families lived in the land in new ways. I could hardly answer. How could I tell Heirik there were no farms, no animals? That food was made from other food, not cows and goats, and Hvítmörk itself was gone so completely that no one even remembered its name. It would be as hard to accept—or even comprehend—as it would be for me to imagine a world without voices and speech. It would break his heart.

How would I describe everything, anyway? I thought of drawing a city in the most basic sense—a place where houses were strung together, with rooms that were perfectly square and bright. Whole families lived right next to each other, so close they could touch hands through a window, or even a single person could live in a space as big as this house. I imagined telling him that the expanse of this beautiful island sat packed with such boxes, until there was no room left for a single fox to house her cubs. Then layers of more stacked on top. People living up off the ground, suspended right over one another. And another layer and another, until the houses touched the clouds, and their floors trapped the mist under the ground.

I wondered if he could imagine enormous glass windows, entire buildings made of the precious material of frost cups. Lamps and candles that burned acid-bright without stopping, a light so intense it ate the sky, eclipsed the sparks of Ymir's skull and left only a handful of stars.

Smaller questions seemed more approachable. He asked what the men wore.

"Many things," I said. "Not just one like here." I tried to explain that in the future people played with clothing on a lark—a difficult concept, when here every bit of fabric was precious, made of the animals Heirik raised, painstakingly spun and sewn by the women of his family and his thralls. A length of wool cloth took weeks of a woman's life, and a shirt was a love token of the tenderest worth.

I thought of Jeff's t-shirts, torn, thrown away without a care. "The one man I knew the most," I started to tell Heirik. And then it hit me, how long I'd been away. Memory woke like a bow shot in my brain, everything about Jeff coming back. His hands, faded jeans, long lank hair the color of strawberry sun, tattoos circling his wrists like Heirik's silver bracelets. I heard Jeff's easy laugh in my mind, smiled at the memory of his shameless flirting.

"He wore much tighter pants," I said with a small smile.

Then I recalled Jeff's cold, listless eyes, never truly looking at me. His great height. I could never stretch up just so slightly on my toes to place my chin on his shoulder, like I could with Heirik. I was faced with the wall of Jeff's chest, thoughts opaque, dreams never shared. Or maybe he had none. Though Jeff had been the one man I knew the most, I didn't really know him at all.

My eye was drawn to the hollow of Heirik's throat, the silver hammer there, his linen ties hanging loose. "And he wore two shirts like you." I reached out casually, tugged at one of the strings.

Heirik didn't play. He looked from the weaving room out through the door into the depths of the main hall.

"You are lost from him," he said without looking at me. "You did have someone like me."

"Nei," I told him, the word fierce. "Look at me, Heirik. Right in my eyes."

He did.

"Never like you," I told him, and I wrapped my fingers as far as they would reach around his ankle, to draw him, to make him understand. My fingers couldn't reach all the way around. He took in a sharp breath and looked down at my grasp.

I shook my head with the impossibility of Jeff, or of anyone ever taking Heirik's place. I told him, "No one is like you." My thumb went under his linen, past his ankle bone.

His reaction surprised me. "Já, then," he said, and smug as a house cat, he blinked slowly, a very small smile forming at the corner of his mouth. "I believe that."

Gods, I wanted to smack him. It wasn't fair, I thought dumbly, that he could draw away from me, perhaps never do again what we had in the cave, and yet still smile. Still revel in the fact that for me, he was the best. No man compared to him.

I drew my hand away and swatted at his chest and he laughed hard. "Brusi," I spat out at him playfully. *He-goat.* His smile was almost, but not quite, broad across his face.

A draft came from the ceiling vent, and the passing cloud of smoke stole our mood.

"There will never be anyone like you," he said to me gravely, our touch completely wiped out, gone like the draft that had broken it. He picked up a game piece, held it loosely and let it roll out of his hand. It made a hard sound as it scrabbled across the bench.

He seemed to ask the game and floor and house itself a question. "What will I do with you?"

He'd said it before, and I didn't like the sound of it.

JUL CAME SOON.

Hildur set a small world into motion, preparing for the feast. She called up the thralls who trekked to the house to do the hardest work. She had the boys bring up food and drink from an underground store. More riches I hadn't known about. Amazed at the abundance of meat and fish and cheese and the vast quantities of ale that came into the house, my mind turned to counting, over and over. I had a deep desire to manage it all, to be sure there was enough to extend the chief's generosity.

Instead, I was set to helping Avsi and Lotta polish cups. A hoard of lovely pewter cups sat in a basket by our feet, next to the hearth. We wiped until they shone, using pieces of worn linen and handfuls of ash.

The girls were so little, chubby in their smocks, each with a tiny purse at her belt and a few beads draped across her apron dress. Lotta was all golden and round. She paid serious attention to her task, pink tongue sticking out at the corner of her mouth as she worked.

I swirled a cloth inside a cup and watched her. Since the night Heirik and I shared in the cave, I'd prayed to all the gods and goddesses that I would have our child. Or, I wasn't sure if prayer was the right word for it. More a wish in the gods' direction, a kiss to my palm, sent into the night. But that possibility was past. Absently swiping at cups, I imagined it anyway. What it would be like to have a little girl Lotta's age, but with midnight hair. A girl who looked exactly like her beautiful daddy.

The thralls tramped up the long hill on snowshoes and worked to ready our house. Men and women cleared the ground of its waist-high snow, all around the doors and walls and out to the stables. They dug fire pits and filled them with stones, and children scattered the ground with precious hay. Tents were raised, with thick red and white fabric and floors of even deeper dry grass.

In the house, I helped Ranka hang juniper boughs over the sleeping spaces, dark berries still clinging to the sticky wood. I tied the boughs and watched my left hand, healing but still angry red. I thanked the gods no infection had spread and made it dangerous to keep. If I were a thrall myself, what would happen then?

And why wasn't I a thrall, for that matter? A slave come by cheap, found on the beach like a shell that would make a good spoon. I wondered if it was only my rich clothes—an accident, the result of some play-Viking's clumsiness in a coffee shop—that led the chief to welcome me as an honored guest. Was it because of my cherry dress? Or was it because I called him Heirik instead of Herra, with a voice full of nascent longing. Was that why I hung lovely boughs and polished cups now with two adorable girls instead of hauling hay and digging pits in the frozen ground?

A day later, the first boys arrived. In the lung-searing cold, they came coughing and shivering at the door, and they had news. The fabled man named Egil—the rich one—and his children were making the trip. They were on their way, skiing three days, camping two nights, to make it to our house for Jul.

Gossip circled, swift and bright. Egil would be the guest of honor, an important man, almost as rich as the chief, whose great house sat further east along the coast of the island. The big meal, the official beginning of a long and raucous festival, would take place tonight if the gods helped his family along in time.

This meant a lot more people. Not just the man himself and his close family, but dozens who would follow in his tracks. Hildur paced the house to check on everything a hundred times, chasing chickens into corners over and over, tugging at tent fabric, testing the hay in the yard with a stick.

In a fit of anticipation, it was decided we should bathe and dress.

I sank into the pool and with a sense of blankness, I listened to women chatter around me—Svana's, Thora's, Betta's voices all swirling with the water churned up by their arms and floating toes. I turned away from the water, rested my chin on my folded arms and watched Ranka mashing something dark and powdery in a small bowl. She saw me staring.

"Cinders, Lady," she said. "For our eyes!"

She loved to teach me things, but her half-answers often made no sense. I'd given up on asking every one of my questions. I'd wait, and explanations would come some time, and so I forgot the bowl of ashes and floated with an absent mind. Something bitter just at the back of my throat, but I didn't know what.

I washed myself slowly and stood in the freezing air a moment too long before I put on my red dress. I watched the fabric unfold over my gauzy shift and underdress, and I swished my hips to let it fall. I pressed the cherry and amber wool against my thighs. I'd felt like a princess in this dress when I went into the tank. But it wasn't as beautiful as Signé's gown, hers the color of a cold fall sky, a time when blue was still possible.

Slicing my thoughts open, Betta talked in a low and secret voice. "Woman, you know it would not be right to wear his mother's clothes. Not now." The rest went unspoken. Not now that it was over between us, that my right to that dress was gone.

"Wear this," she said. "It will lighten your mood."

She dipped the tip of her pinky in the dish of cinders and told me to look at the sky. I jumped when her fingernail stung the soft skin under my eye. She smudged the black ash. The stars wobbled in my wet vision. With her finger, she swiped away my tears so they would not show in front of all the women.

We helped each other with belts and jewelry, and Ranka did my hair. She liked to create braids and loops that hid my scar, but today I asked her to pull it back tight on top and just let the rest fall. I was in no mood for prettiness.

In all of time, there'd never been anyone so capable and determined as Viking travelers in winter.

In my old life, winter was a landscape of tunnels and lighted, covered walkways. It wasn't hard, and was not at all special, to arrive somewhere. To the guests here, it would be an act of sheer will, their own and the gods'. Braving the wind-driven cold, camping some place isolated, maybe a cave in the woods, they would come on skið and snowshoes, unstoppable.

After the boys, who now sat choking down fish and warming themselves, came a group of men, ten maybe, traveling together and no doubt steered the last mile by our smoke.

I approached the front door when I heard Magnus talking to them. The mudroom was dark, and I saw him silhouetted against the snow-bright and moon, standing at his greatest height. He told them they could keep their small knives, but they had to leave their hatchets at the door.

His voice flowed without breaking, solid and deep. "No skull cleavers in the chieftain's hall." He stepped deliberately over the threshold and rested his hand on his own ax, which I noticed was allowed to hang by his side. "Drop them, or leave this house."

The mess of grumbles thrilled me. All new voices! I closed my eyes to savor the sound, and in the darkness, I felt Heirik step up beside me. Eyes closed, I knew him, his weight, the space and air he took up, his scent. We stood together in the doorway, and I opened my eyes to gaze out at the guests, a bedraggled crew, snot dripping from red noses, ice in messy beards.

Every one of them had forgotten Magnus and was on bent knee, gaping up at me and the chief.

I turned to Heirik and saw him in his midnight dark clothes, commanding and beneficent. I imagined the picture of him and me together barring the threshold, our serious eyes of ice and fire, mine rimmed with black ash. Hair pulled tight, scar shining, still red from the inferno. Heirik wore his hair the exact same way as mine, his own scar similarly on show, priceless silver at his throat, clothes the color of death.

"We make quite a pair." I whispered so the men could not hear me. "Welcome to Hvítmörk, já?"

Heirik laughed out loud. The rich sound I loved filled the air, louder than ever before.

The guests cowered. And for a moment I saw the chief's eyes and bloodied face as they did, heard his laugh rumbling like savage weather. I saw him through their eyes, and he looked demonic. I wished for once that I hadn't lightened his mood.

A dozen ax handles thumped against the wall.

Once the men had bowed to him and dropped their weapons, the chief was through with them. They were released into the party like sheared lambs. Heirik turned me away from the door and backed me up into the shadows as all the grumbling men passed into the house. He was so quiet, I almost couldn't make out his words. "It would be an ill omen for a man to die in my fire."

My laugh was like a mad bark. "An ill omen, indeed," I said.

He came even closer, and I felt the whisper of his breath, deep with ale. I backed up against the cool wall. He was a little drunk, and it surprised me. He didn't do this before toasts and blessings and the first dangerous and tedious hours of a festival were through. He didn't ever, in fact. But this was one of those nights when his emotions ran high and confused, when adulation and duty and entitlement and fear mixed into a mess.

A drinking horn hung from his hand, half full. He was loose and very, very near.

"There is something wrong tonight." He could sense my emptiness.

I breathed deep and felt the blood rush through me at his closeness. I didn't want to talk about my unrequited wish, the lost idea of a little girl of our own. My need to take care of this home, to see to it that his generosity was great. My need for him. I wanted him to hold me and tell me that these things would happen one day. I nodded my head. Já, there was something wrong.

"I am sorry," he said, swallowing more ale. He wiped his mouth with the back of his hand, and then his eyes settled on me. "This was our night."

Oh.

The memory was quick and brutal. Him pressing me up against the wall outside the back door, talking about Jul. This was the night, tonight. He'd intended to seat me next to him at the head of the table, in front of all these people. Had intended to place his sword on my lap and make me his wife, make this my home. He drank tonight perhaps to forget grief, or at least to get through this party, when his vision of it had been so different.

I reached for his cup and took a mouthful of ale myself, swallowing tears.

Like a breath across my brow, his fingers brushed the place he'd always loved to touch. I gasped with pleasure and surprise, and I took his hand and pressed it to my scar until it hurt.

"I want you," I told him, resting my face in his palm, so that he could feel the words as they formed. "I would do anything to kiss you right now."

He dropped his forehead to my shoulder, and his breath caught on his answer. "Until later, Beautiful One," he said. His tone was vague and unreadable, his hand gone from my face, head lifted from my shoulder before I knew it. I couldn't tell if he meant he would come find me later, maybe to give me the kiss I craved, or whether he meant goodbye.

Just minutes later, I heard the news.

I'd walked out onto the big cleared space of the yard, with a woolen wrap pulled close around me, a fur trimmed hat on my head. A brief whip of wind came, and my dress blustered like a spray of blood around my ankles. The fur of my hat fluttered against my forehead and eyebrows. I stepped inside an empty tent.

I was surprised at the warmth it gathered, how much it blocked out the cold. I trailed my fingertips along the taut, thick fabric. The perfume of sweet and grassy autumn rose up from the hay floor and brought memories of sunlight and blistered hands, of clearing my acre, of kneeling in snowblooms.

I dropped to my knees in the dim tent and ran my fingers through hay. I lifted a few pieces to my lips and kissed the grass we'd gathered and stored. Maybe this hay was mine, that I had cut. No matter how Heirik could or could not love me, I had a place here.

"… A new wife in this house."

The words shot out sharp and clear from among the women's spiraling voices and chirps of excitement.

"Unexpected match," someone else said, breathlessly surprised. "Beautiful," another voice added. My heart beat swift and hard. A wife, here. We would meet her tonight.

Heirik was afraid to take a wife, wasn't he? Afraid of holding a woman close to him, afraid of what evil spirited children a union might bring. The whole family feared it. He wouldn't do this, já? The little, nibbling fear in my gut suddenly grew. Disgust and fear drove me down onto my hands and tears clogged my throat, trying to come up. I asked the air and the hay, "What about me?"

Women still gossiped outside the tent, about how there was wind but not much snow. Egil's daughter would be here with the old man. "They are hearty people," another voice said. "Even she, at such a young age. And her father, he is like an ox." His house was grand, they said, the only other in Iceland as big as this one.

It would be a powerful union.

There was some logical reason Heirik would do this, and that fact made me sick. The chief would always think, and his logic was always elegantly hard and true. Yes, he would do this if he felt it was the answer to our tangled mess.

He'd said goodbye to me, just moments ago. This was why.

Something thumped on the outside of the tent. A loose flap of fabric, beating like the wing of a massive bird. I shook my head and stood, brushed hay off my dress with shaking hands. Outside the door, I looked hard into the unknowable expanse. As if conjured by the women's frosty words, four dots of light crested a hill. They floated and bobbed like fireflies, tiny in the vast valley, but as they climbed toward the house they became steadily larger.

I pressed my hand to the tent frame and thought of Saga, asked her what the hell she intended.

Egil was a friendly bull. He entered the house in a gust of frosty air, arms spread wide in greeting, and cheers erupted from the dozens of people already drinking inside. He owned the room with that sense of authority and privilege that I'd only seen in the chief.

Quiet as a shadow in comparison to Egil, the chief nonetheless drew everyone's attention when he approached. Silence hovered in the air until he formally welcomed his guest. Heirik greeted the man with a small but real smile, his eyes bright against the wool of the blue swan.

Then Egil announced, "My daughter, Brynild." He beamed, and stepped aside to present a young woman who was consumed by cloaks. Her face was rimmed with a charming gray and white fur hood, pulled tight so that all I could see were dark eyes and a button nose, red as meat. "She skied like Skadi herself," Egil said with broad pride. His voice was like the eruption of Hekla.

"I was not staying home," she stated tartly. She drew the fur hood back and golden-red hair sifted down, straight and sleek. She shook it out, down past her shoulders, and its brilliance shamed the hearth fire itself. "I am old enough to travel, Da."

She sounded like any fifteen year old, but she said it without a pout. Inquisitive, smiling, her voice and her years could not keep up with such bold and smoky eyes. Such a spirit, and powerful body to match, as though she were born from a giantess of the mountain snow.

Heirik bowed his head to Brynhild and cold fingers climbed my spine.

"I've heard so much about you, Rakknason," she said. "The God-Maker."

I'd never seen a woman look him over without revulsion or at least hesitance. Her eyes took Heirik in actively, and she pursed her lips, undecided, and then moved into the room. My face felt hot and my stomach roiled with sickness. I didn't like how she consumed him with her gaze. How her voice sounded when she called him a name I'd never heard before. God-Maker. Nei. I'd rather die than ever hear it again.

I didn't like how she looked at our house. It was beautiful tonight. The big room glittered with a hundred little fires from lamps hung everywhere. The curtains on the sleeping alcoves were all drawn aside, tied back in pretty swags, with juniper boughs over every bed. Long tables lined the room, every bench draped with furs and people. The heartstone crackled with a cozy flame. Brynhild took it all in speculatively, as if she were buying it.

Heirik led her in with a nod, and if he were willing, he would have taken her by the elbow, an honored lady. As they walked past the fire, he turned and caught my eye and a small, drunk smile touched the corner of his mouth. It was mean and humiliating, and I left the house.

It was serene and cold outside, just me and the stars and tents. And a single dog, who sniffed at the house. His head lifted for a moment, but he found me uninteresting and followed a smell away toward the stable. I went inside a tent to get warm.

Soon Haukur came out of the house and headed in the same direction. And moments later, he came back drawing a small horse by a rope, taking it right into the back door of the house. For the blót. The Jul sacrifice. Heirik would be with Freyr again tonight, and already full of drink, sitting near such a woman as Brynhild, his emotions running wild. I feared going back inside to see what he would become, and so I stayed in my tent and sat alone in the hay.

It was on a day like this, when Freyr was in him, that we almost kissed for the first time. We talked about these animals that now lived in the stable right outside. How many could live, how many we would eat. The horse selected for just this night. Heirik's hand had rested close to mine in the scratchy grass, and it was a moment of turning, a singular bit of time when he and I could still happen.

Ageirr had interrupted us. The thought of him made me shiver. I hadn't seen him tonight, and it worried me at the back of my mind.

I mumbled my thanks and wishes alone in a cold tent. "Freyr, we are mindful of your power and blessings. Please let us have a good year," I said under my breath.

He would have touched the horse's blood to his lips by now. Would have sprinkled it on his honored guests, perhaps climbed the high seat and now heard thanks and petitions from men on bent knees who came forward to speak. Our weaving room, where we sat and played together, transformed into the chieftain's hall.

"God-Maker …" I heard a drunk voice pass by. Brynhild had called him that. What did it mean?

The dog came nosing at the door of the tent, pushed the fabric away and came inside. He checked first, dug with his snout to see if he could get inside my locked arms.

"Nei," I told him. "I have no snack for you."

Instead, he sat close beside me. He leaned his weight into me, wanting warmth.

Was it a new name for Heirik, to take the place of Rakknason Longhair? A name that didn't sound at all demeaning. Much the opposite. It was a name a bold girl would say to his face.

My teeth chattered, and soon I had no choice but to head into the house. I could lurk at the door. It would be alright.

That was my plan, which was soon shattered by Hár's strong hand pulling me along.

"Woman," he said. "I won't have you hide in this house."

He lifted me from the ground and I laughed, but the sound was harsh. I thought he might throw me over his shoulder, but instead he carried me like a bride, past the heartstone and through the sparkling room I'd decorated. The boughs passed by me in a blur. He brought me across the threshold into the weaving room, where the long tables were drawn together. Dozens of people were digging into heaps of food and dipping cups and horns into cauldrons of ale. My eyes found Heirik instantly, but he was talking to Egil, his head bowed in conversation.

Hár set me down, and then took a place by my side.

I needed more ale, a lot more, and Hár supplied it to me over and over, drinking with me until my head felt pleasantly glossy and disconnected. The old man himself drank three cups for every one of mine, becoming more and more bizarre and rambunctious. His emotions and actions swooped from glumness to a kind of frantic jollity that made people duck and sent cups crashing. He snarled and ate pieces of meat with his hands. A small part of me wondered if he would keep this up for two weeks. And I wondered where Betta hid, what she thought about her love right now, ripping into animal flesh and drinking himself raw. Another minor part of my mind, far behind all immediate thought, wondered how the house would smell for a month after this. About cleaning up all these cups and bones.

What if I just walked away? The voice in my head was bitter. What if I just left it all for Brynhild to deal with?

I was about to say this to Hár, when my thoughts were interrupted by a crash and bellow. It was Egil. He got up from the table with a pound of his fist and shouted to conjure up dancing.

Somehow, at his bidding, drumming and song sprang up out of nothing and tables were drawn back just enough to make a small space.

Before I could speak or even think, Hár picked me up and literally handed me over the table, my skirts knocking over cups and dragging in meat. Egil's arms went around my waist, he set me gently on the floor beside him, and then we danced. I didn't know how and didn't care. People clapped around us, faces blurring as we turned in circles, ale sloshing in my belly, my mind free and slack. Others danced too, impossibly crowded, we bumped into each other with great force and laughed. No space for bumbling embarrassment, just incomprehensible motion, faces blurring as Egil and I spun.

Then I was flying. He lifted me by my waist, high off the ground, and whipped me in a dizzying circle. The scene of my house, my hall, sprawled out below me, Egil so alive, his hands, the music, his grinning face. I let something go from under my tight ribcage. It felt like a bird that had been struggling in there. It now flew swiftly from me, over the heads of the dancing, drinking, happy people and out over tents and stables and into the polar night.

The music ended, and Egil set me down, robbed of all breath and sense. And right in front of me, I saw Eiðr—Ageirr's brother.

He was the one Svana had called smart but ugly. Not good looking, it was true, he talked to two little girls about the ages of Lotta and Ranka. He dropped a kiss on one of their silky heads then drew them into a hug, and I was struck in my gut by the sight of his arm with no hand.

I sought out Hár, my drinking partner, and dropped down breathlessly beside him. I had the notion that Heirik's new byname had something to do with Eiðr. Hár would know.

"He is called God-Maker now," I said, my voice weak and wobbly.

"Nei matter," Hár sighed. "The hand price will be nothing."

"The hand price?"

My mind swayed drunkenly, but I found the memory, words from an arc that lay long buried in the recesses of my mind. *Oh.* The chief would pay, literally, for taking Eiðr's hand. A sum that Hár said meant very little to Heirik, considering the value of his exact and strategic revenge.

The old man gave me the story.

Heirik had cut Eiðr at his wolf's joint—his wrist—so called because the god Tyr had sacrificed his hand to bind the great wolf Fenrir. It was a physical blow, certainly. But it was also a subtle metaphor. To render the man a god, while making him impotent as a farmer. A swipe of ax that demonstrated mastery and yet mercy. He would let Eiðr live, promising to feed and protect him for the rest of his life with no promise of work in return. He'd let him live, in shame.

"Já," Hár murmured, watching Eiðr, as though he could read my thoughts. "Já …" What more was there to say about such inhuman cunning?

Hár gave a sigh so big it made the bench dip and sway. "They call him God-Maker now. As if he needed more fear."

Rakknason God-Maker. It was beautiful and terrible.

I tried the name on my lips, whispered it, and shivered at the depth and elegance of Heirik's cruelty. With impossible speed, he'd calculated this poetic horror and carried it out on a moving horse in a hand to hand clash. It was more than his mark, and his position of power, that scared people. They should be afraid. A part of him was twisted and ruthless.

The bench was hard under my tensed thighs, and I shifted and wondered how it was possible that I could love such a man. Heirik was a creature beyond anything I understood, brilliant and fierce in a way that curdled my blood. As frightening as the raven Hildur imagined him to be. I saw him that way, the blue of his hair like the heart of a flame. And knowing that I did love him anyway, I trembled. Knowing that I could rise to be like him, to stand next to him, terrified me.

I looked to my hands in my lap. Could I still tap out? I hadn't wanted to try. But what if I went to the water? I could get there on Drifa, and I could try. Somehow I knew that at the ocean Saga would find me and take me.

My fingers looked unfamiliar, separate from me, as they tapped speculatively on the red and twisted skin of my wrist. I could get away from everything here, the cold and the endless night and the dark person that was Heirik, get away before he consumed me and I became nothing. Or became like him.

Something powerful drew my eyes his way. I saw the chieftain, sitting casually back in his seat of furs, drunk, watching me and Hár with a half smile. He'd been observing me, with eyes so pale I could hardly make out their color.

Now I really knew him, his smile seemed to say. Now what did I think?

Could he actually see the moment I learned to fear him? My thighs rigid on this bench, fingers tapping anxiously at my wrist. He knew what that meant now, that it was my way back. His knife-like vision made me swallow with a dry and useless throat.

I glanced over at Brynhild, and she was unafraid. Confident and beaming like her Da, all clean and copper. She noticed me and did not draw away. On the contrary, she cocked her head and seemed to savor looking at me. I felt my own eyes acutely now, rimmed with ashes that felt juvenile under scrutiny. I wished I hadn't blackened them. Pale and small, I tried to smile back.

I took a cloak from the back mudroom and pulled on someone's big boots. I needed a place to think.

This time I did not want to be alone, but I didn't want these people, either. I wanted the wordless company of a creature who wouldn't challenge or scare me.

The clean air off the North Pole sliced my lungs, and I squinted against the moonlight on the deep snow. A dirty path was already trodden between house and stable, and I followed it to find Drifa.

In the shadows of the stalls, I heard murmurs of human voices, the tense spitting of an argument, laughter too, and in one dark room the speechless pants and sighs of lovemaking. I moved on until I came to a quiet stall, and I called softly to see who was in there.

After announcing myself, I held my torch up and looked around the corner of the wall. It was Vakr, towering in the dark. He snorted, narrowed his eyes in warning, and then stopped and seemed to reconsider. His snout reached out, nose trembling and questing, and he found something in me that calmed him. I'd been close to Heirik. He'd been touching me earlier. Maybe the horse smelled him on me and wondered where his master was.

I secured the torch into a space in the earth wall, then turned my palm up and pulled back my furry sleeve. I buried my own nose in my wrist and tried to find Heirik, and I did smell the scent of spice underneath the wool and smoke, like a voice down a long hall.

A bristly, warm face came up against mine, cheek to cheek, and I gasped. Vakr, the terrible beast, dipped his heavy head and rested it on my shoulder. He leaned into me, and I pet his side in big, soothing circles.

"Maybe there is somewhere I can go, *Awake One*," I called him the plain English words for his name. He muttered in return, in a language so far beyond me, I'd never know. I rested my face against him and felt his great eyelashes flutter. I wouldn't live here anymore, I thought with serene clarity. I would go to the ocean and tap out. It could work. At the same time as I began to hatch a clumsy plan, my heart clenched with the awful idea of leaving this world. This time and place that I fit into like I never could in the future. I could go to the assembly—the Thing—in a few months, meet people, and find another home large enough to take me in. Maybe even Egil's house.

"A trade," I told Vakr. "Me for Brynhild."

"I don't think my cousin would allow that."

I started at the sound of Magnus's voice. I had to raise my lamp to see him, he sounded so different, so deep and grown up.

"What are you doing here, Woman? You will freeze." He came all the way into the stable and then saw me with the horse. His eyes went wide and he broke into a broad smile. "Gods, the old beast is kissing you."

"He is!" I laughed, and Vakr made a whuffling sound in my hair.

"So," Magnus persisted. "What are you doing so far from the table?"

What could I say? I couldn't stand the joy I felt dancing with a stranger? Or that grief tore at me when I looked at the empty seat at Heirik's side? Or perhaps that the God-Maker scared me to death.

What I did say was, "Brynhild will make a good wife."

There it was, in the open, hanging in the frozen air between me and Magnus for a second. Just a split second before he answered. "Já!" He said with joy. "I am a lucky man."

I drew my brows together. "What do you mean?"

Taken aback, he actually stepped away from me. "She will be my wife at midsummer." He said this as though it were impossible I could not know.

My head filled first with humiliation at how stupid I'd been. Then my chest expanded, my whole body relaxed and I breathed for the first time all night. All desperate ideas and plans to run away dissolved. My love was not marrying. Magnus was! How had I misunderstood so much?

Maybe because Magnus was a child, and not someone who could possibly get married. In the torchlight, I realized that was no longer true. He looked so much like his father, his hard features carved like stone in this light, but his mouth ready to laugh or grin at any moment. His silky blond hair was like silver in the night, falling around his big shoulders. He was no longer gawky. Before my eyes stood the proof of how long I'd been here in this time and place.

"It was arranged in fall," he said. "But the chief only told me today, when Egil's messenger arrived and said that they would come. I was stunned." He was excited, and though he tried not to show it, his words became as fast and wide-ranging as Ranka's. "She's beautiful," he said. "So strong and smart. She skiied here, through days and nights. Her father is also in need of a wife, himself. They'll stay two weeks, and I will get to know her."

I couldn't stand his happiness. I wanted it for him, but I couldn't take hearing about it.

"I saw that man, Eiðr, again tonight," I said. "With his children."

Magnus stopped and slowed his exuberance. Vakr's hair was rough where I pet him, his nose heavy on my shoulder.

"His nieces," Magnus said, and then nothing more.

"Your Da told me what it meant, what Heirik did." It was quiet, only the three of us breathing, and I knew I could tell Magnus what I felt here in the dark.

"I'm scared."

He nodded. "My cousin is a fearsome person." It was a plain fact.

"You're not helping, Fool." We both laughed easily, casually, but when he spoke again the tension rose like a sudden wall.

"You sit close to his fire, Ginn. You don't know what he can bring himself to do."

Heirik's fire. An ironic and witless way to say it, given the scar that I could feel whenever my fingers checked the side of my face. And yet, it was perfect. I did think of Heirik that way—as a flame, his spirit and body both hot, something leaping up between us when we were near.

Magnus meant something else, too. He was speaking of the chief's intensity, his capacity for cruelty, the way poetic and violent plans leapt to his mind in an instant. The ability to kill curled like a dozing wolf behind his eyes.

My boots squished in the snow, and I reflected Magnus's words back at him. "What he could bring himself to do?"

"To protect you."

What Heirik might do to protect me had, I thought, included things like burying a spear in Ageirr's shoulder. I knew he would throw himself in the way of any weapon meant for me. But when he drew his hands and body away from me, for my own good, it was more painful than any wound.

Heirik looked at me with such fury sometimes, and I knew it was anger at himself for stumbling, for failing at his vow. How might he keep from failing again?

His words came to mind, those he'd said more than once. *What will I do with you?* Could he have meant literally?

Oh. Oh gods, the logical answer came to me.

He could do something to separate us. He had the power to set us so far apart that temptation would be irrelevant and desire would become a distant ache. He could send me away. What had Magnus just told me about Egil? He was in need of a wife, too. Would Heirik really do such a thing to me, to us?

"Já," Magnus said softly, as though he could see my thoughts forming. But he didn't really know what I'd been asking myself. He was just gathering up the many threads, and deep fears and questions we'd talked about, into that one lovely expression. Perhaps as an explanation for everything—the way the seasons turned, and the stars around Frigg's distaff—he added, "Well, the chief suffers the ástarœði." The *fury of love.*

Magnus tossed this to me like a hand tool, as though it were as casual and obvious as a length of rope or small blade. Heirik loved me. With a desperate heat.

Cold swirled in to the stable and around us, everywhere, and I saw the truth. In a beat of my heart, it didn't matter how cruel or dangerous he was. Heirik and I shared something I had wanted forever. He knew me, and he loved me.

I brought my hand up to the side of my face, pressing my fingers to the slick scar there.

I sat too close, já. Far too close to his fire. Every time I thought of him, the hem of my dress seemed to catch in it, and the flames leapt to life and traveled over and through me. Heirik's fire devoured everything, my clothes and hands, my braids, my eyes and spirit, with a delicious light that didn't hurt at all.

He wouldn't give me to Egil. He wouldn't. He loved me.

"Woman," Magnus said. "My feet are cold. Come into the house."

THE HOUSE SPILLED OVER WITH A GROWING REEK OF BODIES AND old ale. And the smell of two sour-milky babes I took into our bed, so they wouldn't have to join their parents and sleep next to cows. Women crammed into sleeping alcoves and men slumbered propped against walls, whole families living with our sheep, just to be here for this celebration. This joyous time, so close to the gods that Odin, Freya, Freyr seemed separated from us only by a thin veil of wool, gauzy as my shift. And yet entirely absent in my heart.

I wanted Betta, but she was always busy, mostly helping her Da. Bjarn tended a steady stream of men who'd been dislocated, cut, crushed and punched senseless in small fights that sprung up all over the yard, all through the week. He removed more than one sore tooth, too, from men and women who'd been waiting for Jul to see him. Betta, emphatically silent, bent her head to change bandages and bring ale and honey and herbs and water.

A flock of women ate meals together, and so Betta blended in. In fact, most times she dissolved into the background of the house. She avoided talking privately with me. It stung my heart, the way she was always asleep before I turned in, as if she planned it. Or she waited until I was asleep before coming into the bed herself. In the morning, I'd find her covers rumpled.

Brynhild was a distraction. She was fawned over and chatted at, with plans for a big wedding, until her bright red hair and bold laughter became a symbol of midsummer—the heat and sun seeming like a far country that we all believed we would someday reach. Magnus watched her with fascination and longing, afraid to speak, and I laughed fondly inside, thinking about his life with this spirited woman. I liked her after a while—the bold and sensible way she pushed most of the attention away. She kindly but firmly let everyone know she was not the blushing sort of bride-to-be.

But she was only of momentary interest. What I wanted was my best friend.

The party went on for over a week, becoming louder and more boisterous the drunker everyone got. It was hot and crowded, and I started to loathe even the new and fascinating voices. Moments after Betta cared for the sick and broken men, they would be drinking together again, laughing. Their gestures and sounds—such a sensual treat at first—became inescapable and overloud. Every few hours, my body and mind would spasm like a trapped animal, and I would stand abruptly and press my hands into my skirt to try not to growl. Sometimes, I'd go to the back mudroom and put on snowshoes and tramp around the house.

I counted my steps along the back of the house, a habit now, and laughed as I fell and sunk into deep swells of whiteness. I smiled as I counted, because the total was coming out so different than my summer number. My steps were fewer in the knee deep snow, clumsy with the bulk of wooden nets tied to my feet.

I rounded the curve of the pantry and ahead of me was Heirik's room. The outside shell of it. I groped along and half walked, half lunged for it, and I placed my hand hard against the place where he probably sat right now on his bed.

He was so seldom seen, after the party's first night. I missed his laugh and stolen touches over our game board. Missed the every-day moments from before this endless festival.

He came out a few times and got uncharacteristically drunk in the snow with a few of the men.

I wondered if he even bathed, and thought probably not, with so many people in our house and yard, the bath clogged with them night and day. Maybe he washed in the snow, in the woods, alone. Maybe he stole away to the cave. I imagined him drawing up scalding water in his cupped palms, pictured the slick curves of his body where it ran off him in runnels and turned to steam.

Here in reality, I leaned my cheek against the cold wall. Skeletal fingers of frosted, brown grass scraped my face, gently.

There were more little ones—raucous adults, too—who needed the songs and long stories that would fill up our dreams and let us sleep. Very late at night, after even the near-constant feasting and drinking and fighting died down, the clanks of ale cups became softer, the mood of the party more contemplative. Children would come together and sit on the floor, parents all around, and Hár would lean in and tell a story.

Tonight, he told of an explorer and raider named Hundr Blacktooth, "for he was truly that ugly." I smiled. Hundr meant dog, a singular insult to a Viking man, though I liked the actual dogs I'd met.

Hár told us that Hundr was beloved by his loyal men, and he sailed with them to the glorious places of the world. Here Hár might as well have been describing the moon, having never been, as far as I knew, anywhere but Iceland. He told of many wonders, nonetheless. They went to the end of the known world, Hundr's crew, where they traded for slippery cloth spun by insects and drink that could make a man fly. They went across the far sea, to a coast with white sand and cunning little shells of sea creatures that could fit in your hand. "And to Norway. Where there are cows as big as horses, and grass as tall as your old uncle." He hovered one hand above his own head, and the kids laughed.

Hundr was an honorable and brave man, Hár said, and his ship bore him faithfully. "Its lines were sleek, seams well sealed, and its sail great enough to fill the sky." He'd had many adventures and battles in that boat, and so Hár detoured to tell the children about them, taking as much time as possible to put every one of them to sleep. We held the little ones and rocked them in the smoky den. Hár met each of their wide open eyes with a steely gaze, commanding them to sleep and dream. I started to sway with tiredness myself, and I leaned against the wall and closed my eyes.

A pair of fearsome birds lived in the ravens' nest atop Hundr's mast. One day the birds returned from roaming the sky, and their cries were loud and wingbeats mighty. Hundr took up his sword to defend himself and his men.

Hár continued, "One of the ravens croaked at Hundr as he swiped with his sword, 'Come follow. You will see.' And a great eel rose alongside the ship. It swam to the prow and it drew the ship's dragon, who was very hungry after a dozen years at sea. And so Hundr came to an unknown land with trees as white as snow and sand as black as the chief's beard." The children didn't laugh this time, and I thought they must be rapt and a little scared. I thought of Heirik's beard, and how dark the sand was on that beach, where I arrived.

"Do you know what Hundr found there?"

There were a couple guesses, and a boy called out "a smelly troll." Áki, a little boy of about three, added "A troll!" as though it was his original idea. Hár laughed with the sudden delight that sometimes exploded from him. "Nei," he told us. "He found a beautiful woman."

There were great groans from the boys.

"This is a good story, já" Hár defended. "Because she was no ordinary woman." Kit made an indignant sound, and I opened my eyes to see Hár laughing silently.

"Her hair was spun of copper," he continued, "her skin aglow like a midnight snowfield. And her eyes were of the most fertile farm, the exact green of grass waving in the sun."

The children's mouths hung open in concentration. Áki picked his nose.

Hár went on to describe how the woman led Hundr through the trees and to a sunlit, yellow clearing where there stood a strong house. The house was for him, but he would have to stay and clear the land and farm, leaving his men to sail his ship without him. While Hundr very much liked the beautiful woman, and went so far as to kiss her—which was as glorious as entering Valhalla—he said no to the house and farm. "Because he had a stupid idea." Hár faltered, started again. "He had this idea that things would be best if he returned to the sea."

He gathered himself fully and went on. "That night, Hundr slept on the deck of his ship where it sat on the sand, and he was sore and tossed and turned. And he was visited by one of his mad ravens. The bird woke him with a beat of its great, black wing. And then it spoke to him. In dönsk tunga, já?" The *Danish tongue*.

The bird told Hundr that she was the goddess Lofn, in raven form. It made me think of *loaf* and *oven*, the English words blending into a sound that was yeasty and plush. I began to slide into familiar, sensual bread dreams.

"The goddess of unions of the heart and body," Hár explained, and his low and resonant voice drew me back. "Lofn told Hundr he should stay and farm the land. That if he did, an endless green valley would be his and his daughters' and granddaughters'. But he drew his sword and chased the bird off the boat a second time."

I opened my eyes with a start and found I'd missed some piece of the story. Some oaf among Hundr's men had accidentally set fire to his ship, and it had burned until it was a black hunk on the sand. Hundr saw the raven wheeling overhead and understood, in a moment of clarity, that the fire-setter's great stupidity was topped only by his own. I turned to look around the smoky shadows, and saw that Áki lay with soft abandon, asleep on his father's lap. Wetness glinted at the corners of his pillowy mouth.

Lofn had done what she always did, the thing that was her special skill, her superpower. She had removed all obstacles—including Hundr's ship and even his own stubbornness—so that he could have a union with the beautiful woman.

Hundr wanted the woman then, and he worried it might be too late, so he ran and crashed through the deep, dark woods to the farmhouse in the yellow clearing, where it was suddenly daytime. The woman stepped lightly from the door in a delicate dress, a single braid falling over her shoulder. Her form was finer than the curve of his ship.

Hár paused, and for a second his eyes rose to look deep into the dark of the house. It was as though he saw the ethereal woman in the flesh, her dress cool and white, a bare foot stepping from her farmhouse door. He shook it off, but his voice was a little broken.

"Hundr knelt before her and bent his head, holding not the sword of a raider but the ax of a farmer." Hár leaned forward with his elbows on his knees to almost whisper the greatest part of the story to the children who remained awake. "And the woman was revealed as Lofn herself, who had spied Hundr on his boat and wanted him for her own, no matter that he was ugly as a boar." The girls all gasped and the boys shook their heads and said nei. One of them tossed a little chunk of dirt at Hár's feet in protest, and the old man gave him a look of steel, making the boy sink back onto his bench.

"And Hundr Blacktooth became a great chieftain, a prosperous farmer and consort of a goddess," Hár finished, and I knew I wasn't imagining the hitch in his throat, a single note of wistfulness swallowed by the thunder of his voice. "And he gave Lofn many daughters."

BETTA'S BACK WAS TO ME IN THE PANTRY. SHE STOOD ON HER TOES, drawing something down from a very top shelf, and her shoulders moved with irritation as she shoved boxes around.

"Why won't you speak to me?"

She stopped moving and settled onto her heels, but didn't turn around.

I grabbed the biggest bowl I could find and just looked at it, waiting for her answer. Afraid, but needing to know. Wanting her back. It would have been the simplest thing, back in my original time, to buy a hundred bowls this size. Every one the same.

I filled it with dry fish, and I waited some more.

Something sunk in my belly. Would she say she no longer wanted me? We weren't friends after all? Tears came quick to the corners of my eyes and I felt my whole face crumple.

"What do you mean, Woman?" She finally spoke, and it was so good. I held her raspy words in my mind. Yet it was no answer.

"You know what I mean, já?" My voice was slippery, and I hugged my bowl of fish. Finally she turned to me.

Her answer surprised me. "It is Hár," she said.

Oh. Tremendous relief flowed through me.

Hearing it out loud, it seemed stupidly clear. This wasn't about me. Ever since the first night of the party, Hár had been expansive and desperate. He crashed through the week, breaking things, fighting, drinking until he fell down into the snow and slept there, freezing, while Betta doggedly wrapped bandages and set bones.

"He's out there shaking the house with his sighs," I said. "And beating up anyone who looks at him."

"Well …" Betta started, then, "já …" She squared herself up, then came toward me. She lifted herself up to sit on the high bench—the same one where Heirik had placed me when we kissed. I placed my bowl down and ungracefully made it up to sit beside her and waited until she was ready.

"I told him I am eighteen in summer," she started. "I am obviously not going to be married to anyone young, and he is a burlugalti and dishonors me."

I wanted to laugh at her description of the old man, a *clumsy wild boar.* But it worried me, that she'd challenged his honor. That was dangerous.

I felt like I was dipping my toe in icy water when I carefully asked, "And?"

Betta let it out with a short breath. "And," she said. "If he won't marry me, then we are done."

The color rose on her face. "I won't be hidden like a small fish." Her description of herself was cutting. A small catch, too embarrassing to bring home.

"You're right," I told her, and I took her hand. "He loves you, and he should not use you like that." And I took her in my arms and she turned to me and shook with quiet crying. Her hair caught in the tears on my own cheeks. I'd once promised myself that we would get the man she pined for. I'd been so naive. But at least now I could hold her through this. My shoulder was all for her. She was heavy, and I bore her up as she cried. She pulled away then, and her strong eyes filled to the limit with tears tore at my heart.

She wiped at them and straightened herself. She trailed her fingertips over the bench between us. "He will sleep here."

"Here?" I asked. Befuddled, as always. "Sleep on this bench?"

"It is his rightful room." She said. "It became so, after Heirik grew up."

I hadn't thought about the arrangements before I came here, about where Heirik slept when he was a boy, where his uncle did. This was the only other room that locked. Hár would begin to sleep in the pantry to hide from everyone and perhaps beat the walls with his stupid fists.

Winter into spring

IT WAS A LONG SNOWMELT.

Everyone talked about how the winter was mild but everlasting, the longest in memory. Outside an eerie white and electric blue permeated everything, refusing to lift into yellow and green.

Inside the muffled bulk of the house, we found the same things to do. Tension electrified everything, even the most mundane task, making it exhausting to sew a seam or repair a sock. Hár grumbled and made char cloth in the corner, and, after each meal, tramped off to the snowy stables or the pantry. Eyes followed him, people wondering without asking what drove him back to sleeping there now, after years of not caring to use that bed.

Heirik hardly ever came out. He passed his time alone, and at many points I was sure he'd left the house altogether and was gone away, probably in the cave.

The snow was no longer high, but instead a relentless slush filled every crack in the ground and made its way in under the mudroom doors. Everyone was miserable and began to talk worriedly about animals and planting the homefield. An unearthly spring, too long in coming. It was a curse, Hildur said, but to no effect. After a long winter, not even the most superstitious among us could hear her pronouncements anymore.

She looked around like a hawk and often her gaze rested on Betta with suspicion, Svana with irritation, or me with open fear and hostility.

The children, dreadfully bored, tried to make frost cups, just like the chief's rare, clear drinking glasses. It was almost too late in the season, but they desperately hoped they might still freeze. Magnus and Haukur helped the littles ones clear snow away from a spot where there was no underground stream. They dug molds deep in the hard ground and let the children fill them with water.

It might just work. There was enough cold still gripping the earth. I crouched over the little freezing cups in their hole in the ground, with my skirts hiked up out of the slush. I looked at the big, gray sky and laughed hard, a single sharp sound that went into the atmosphere and was lost. I thought I'd surely come to rock bottom—a place and time where the most interesting thing to do was stare at a pit, waiting for water to freeze. I vaguely thought that in spring, when it was dry again, I would have to do something, go somewhere else. But spring seemed like a dream from another life.

After more days of this than anyone could bear, I thought I saw daytime starting to return, the grayish play of noon light becoming stronger, the landscape's waking hours longer.

I thought I might be delirious, but then it was there again, the sun, and I realized it must have been happening gradually over a long time. Opening like a flower, so that even as I watched, I could never see the exact moment it changed. The smoke vents in the roof started to turn a paler blue, like an eggshell seen in an arc. For hours at a time it became easier to see.

And with this weak and newborn sun, our spirits started lifting, sluggishly as though we'd been sleeping off an epic ale feast. We talked about how everywhere else in the world, everywhere outside Hvítmörk, it must be spring by now. The woods and waves would be passable. Farmers in other parts of the island and as far as Norway must be planting their homefields, letting their animals free. It wouldn't be long until we did those things, until we saw grass again and smelled dry dirt.

The days became bright with promise, as if the oddest things might be possible.

Even so, it was shocking when we heard that Brosa's boat had been spotted.

The chief and Hár were on their horses in seconds, a spray of gray slush thrown up in their wake. I watched Heirik go, and I pressed my fingers to my lips and then the wind, hoping so hard. Hoping that when he got to the water he would find what he'd sought in his heart all this long and dreary winter. Not the blades and berries and honey from Norway, or cloth and silver from the east. But his brother.

Our hearts that had been tentatively lifting, suddenly soared. Everyone woke all the way up and beamed with energy. The house itself seemed to wake too, shaking winter and stretching like a giant dog. We knew somehow that Brosa still lived.

It took a long time for Betta and I to put away the honey, nuts, dried fruit, spices, casks of mead, all the while an unease gathering in my stomach.

I'd peeked at Brosa, já. He was a large bundle of furs silhouetted against the heartstone. I heard his voice calling out names and greeting family. It sounded less dark and forest-like than his brother's, more a medium, earth-colored brown. Something in me didn't want to get close enough to really see him.

A dozen men had returned with Brosa, all of them gathered here in the heady triumph of making it home, everyone drinking and boasting and laughing at once. When Betta and I emerged from our dim and cozy cave of provisions, I didn't go to join them. Instead, I went to the back door and stepped outside. I scooped up wet snow to wash my face and adjust my fluttering heart.

I'd put it off by working in the pantry, but now the little strange feeling inside me uncurled and unnerved me. I rubbed my face hard with cold, slushy crystals. I felt relief and joy for Heirik. He had his greatest love back, his little brother, and the punishing ache could end, the months believing Brosa was dead and yet holding out just enough hope to twist his heart. Those months were over. So why did I hesitate?

I looked at my wet hands, and an answer did come.

Oh.

I stopped still, snow sparkling in my palms. "So selfish," I growled out loud at myself. He was a brother. He would never change anything between me and Heirik. It was the notion, though, that struck me. The idea, however vague, that Heirik could love anyone else, anyone at all.

I recalled playing games with him, and smiled privately at his wicked humor. I luxuriated in the memory of his skin, the feeling of him against me, inside me. I remembered singing to him as he slept, and it was even more tender, somehow, than making love. Some of the rare future words that had passed my lips in months— they were for Heirik.

I shook out my hands, wiped the last wet bits on my apron, and made my way inside.

Everyone was gathered around the heartstone, and a big fire had been built in the hearth. The ceiling was open wide. After such a depressing winter, and now with Brosa's return, the frigid outdoor air, sweeping down off the North Pole, felt like a fresh spring breeze.

I lingered outside the circle of light, until Dalla made room for me to come close. My cheeks were damp, and when I lowered my eyelashes I felt every one as a miniature icicle, melting into dew around my eyes. I looked up to the flames, and there he was.

Brosa was wrapped in wool and lit by flickering orange and blue. Everything about him was broad—the bulk of his body amplified by layers of cloaks. His hair was spun gold and brown, unbraided and tangled from riding, with strands strewn across his forehead.

He looked so much like his brother. But where Heirik was dark, Brosa was sunlight. And where Heirik was colored with shades of berries and blood on his face, Brosa had a white scar, a jagged line that followed the path of his brother's birthmark. I watched this living expression of Heirik with fascination and a sense of danger in my gut. Oh, so much alike.

And yet a wholly different man. I could see that at once. Telling stories of their travels, he seemed able to talk and joke and listen to everyone at once. When he laughed it was easy and washed his face in light. An overall radiance warmed the room around him. He didn't look away from anyone, didn't calculate or consider the air over their shoulders, just looked straight at them with a frank friendliness.

He looked up and noticed me staring. Inquisitive and confident, he stared back at me for what felt like a long time. He looked at my hair, my face, lingered over my scarred cheek, took in my dress and hands. Even in the erratic, insufficient light, I could still detect the color of the sea in his eyes. They must be staggering in daylight, the blue-green of waves and far horizons.

He raised his cup and drank. When he peered over the rim, from under his golden lashes, those eyes were playful. He nodded a barely perceptible bow to me and turned to speak to someone at his side.

Someone. Right.

Sitting next to him was the chief. Heirik was right there, so close his leg was against his brother's, and I had forgotten about him. For the first time in months, for just a few seconds, I didn't even know he was there. I flushed with the heat of the fire.

His head bent in conversation, Heirik's hair was drawn back on top and damp around his face and shoulders, and I could see now how he was leaner. Brosa's face was less hollow, more accustomed to breaking into a grin. But they held their bodies just the same way, elbows resting on bent knees; they nodded similarly at a comment by Hár. The wolf pups, Hildur had said.

And já, I had forgotten Heirik, but only for one startled second. When he lifted his head and saw me, he gathered me in, and the world could have burned down around me. I'd never have noticed. I knew nothing but those gold eyes. They didn't draw away this time, but looked right at me with elegant, pure happiness. He smiled like his brother, broad across his whole mouth, every feature lit with it. I beamed back at him, so full of his joy.

Brosa caught my eye and raised one eyebrow in curious surprise.

"Come, Ginn," Heirik called to me.

Brosa had surely been told about me on their way home from the boat. There were things to tell, about Fjoðr's death, Ageirr's aggression. And news of me.

Heirik introduced me anyway. "Ginn has been a guest here for half the year." Heirik looked at me so warmly, with such pride, as though he'd carved me into existence himself, an intricate little boat upheld in his palm.

Brosa seemed torn with fascination, absorbing both me and Heirik at once. I wasn't sure which was more impossible, a strange girl who'd appeared on the sand with no memory, or his brother looking happy.

"Já, the girl was saved from the sea," Hildur broke in over my shoulder. "She has no memory of her people." Suspicion pinched her words, but Brosa answered smoothly, gliding over her rudeness.

"Well then," he said with a smile, "Things have been more exciting here than in Norway by a boat length."

Gods, these brothers charmed me.

Brosa spoke of the water as if it were a living beast that carried them, and yet sought to kill them, too. Churning waves, freezing spray, like fingers, like hands buoying them at times, and then reaching for their bones and sucking them down to their death. He talked about Moki, a man who had fallen in, and how they pulled him out with one of the long oars, landing him like a giant sopping fish.

"It was close," Brosa said, without laughter. He looked at me to explain. "A man can live only two minutes in that kind of water before he loses his sense and will. No more than ten before he dies."

The sea was the *whale road*, the choppy, frigid way home, and his words resonated in me. I felt the salt and sand in my nose and lungs, thought of the wheeling birds and sucking waves and wind. The whale road might be the way home for me, too. And for that reason, I would always avoid it.

Voices lifted and settled back down like leaves in the white wood.

We talked of nothing special—the daily life of the farm that Brosa missed, the new horse Drifa. Heirik noted with a wry smile that I'd named her before I'd had a chance to live through a winter here and learn to despise the snow.

We laughed about so many things, all of them so minor they wouldn't have caught anyone's attention for a minute in the future. Every small moment that had happened here became a story, many of them more entertaining than I'd realized.

In the midst of the story about the lost sheep, I saw Heirik change. He withdrew, became quiet, and like an unmoored boat started to drift away. Pain came to my chest, to see his easy pleasure leaving.

"Lady, Lady!" It was Lotta, tumbling toward me, so reckless and so close to the flame that I caught my breath and lunged for her. She fell into my arms and breathlessly blurted, "It worked!" One of the children's little ice cups sweated in her clutching hand.

She gave it to me, and I held it up and looked through it at Heirik, smiling to draw him out. "Look, Chief," I said. "Now she is as rich as you."

Brosa laughed, but Heirik didn't. Instead, he stood and said he was tired, that he would go. Instead of goodnight, he said "Do not follow me, Ginn."

My face flushed with rejection and embarrassment, and my shoulders folded in and curled around my heart. I watched Heirik leave without the breath to speak, let alone go after him.

Brosa was kind and generous. "You have no idea how many times I've heard those words from my brother," he said. "And still he cares for me."

Brosa's voice was a rich but lighter brown, not as thick and resonant. I wanted to look at him and see the truth of what he said, but instead I watched the frost cup in my hand. I felt it changing, dissolving, running down my fingers and wetting my wrists.

Almost immediately Svana came. She sat by us, joking awkwardly that I was keeping Brosa all to myself. I left him to her and went to bed.

I woke early, feeling like a troll frozen in sunlight.

I got up quickly to get my blood flowing, rubbing my calves and shins briskly, before climbing out of bed. A half dozen men who'd come home with Brosa were sleeping everywhere, against walls, on floors, and yet it didn't even seem as many as were here last night. A few slept in the stables, probably. Two men rolled over on the floor as I stepped over them, careful not to snag my skirts.

In the mudroom, I pulled on someone's large leather boots, brittle cold under my fingertips. I was about to step into the tunnel, when the friendly slap of a man's large hand against the wood of the door frame—as if admiring its sturdiness—alerted me to stand back. In ducked Brosa and Hár, stamping their feet and filling up the room with their fur-laden shoulders and the scents of frozen leather and icy clean hair.

They were covered in snow! It gleamed white again beyond the door, as if the winter had merely paused long enough to let Brosa come home. Their faces were vivid red. Brosa's hair was sun-kissed gold, with ice crystals dissolving in its waves. He saw me out of the corner of his eye, then turned to me and winked flirtatiously. I was dazzled by the whole of him. His presence, his smell, the disarming curve of lips that smiled so sweetly for such a bearish man.

He was trouble, and for some young lady he would be heaven.

He went inside the house, pulling the wooden door behind him. I needed to breathe, needed scalding cold in my lungs. Instead of ducking into the tunnel, I stepped out the door into the blinding white world.

I breathed deeply of air that had come straight off the North Pole. I had to clear my head and still my disorganized heart. The paving stones were snowless, and I stood with my head lowered, sorting their gray forms. I recalled Heirik's face, the feel of his hair through my fingers, the length of his body pressed into my back, curled around me. The warmth of his skin under my palms. I took a deep breath, gathered myself and went back inside to take the tunnel down to the bath.

When I returned, I shut the door to the main room behind me and was struck, as always, by the cozy prettiness of our house. It was opulent and warm beyond anything I could have imagined in the future as I pored over electronic scans of rocky remains.

My expectations had been wrong about so many things—accents, phrases, the house, birds. Everything. I'd never imagined apricot-colored curtains in a plum and russet winter living room. Never imagined the starlight twinkling of adorable lamps, the iron forged like cupped palms, filled with shimmering oil.

Heirik sat close to Brosa by the fire. He turned a long blade over in his hands, but I knew they must be talking of so much more. Their fierce love and affections passed between them in terms of sturdy walls and honed tools.

Brosa looked up and saw me, and when he smiled it was just as the women had said, just like the sun bursting through a bank of silver-blue clouds. He was shameless in his attractiveness, and I almost stumbled across the threshold.

Heirik looked blank in that calculating way that was never good. It reminded me of when Fjoðr died, when, as Betta said, the chief was thinking. Looking at me standing here, and yet looking through me as if I were made of mist, what logic path was he swiftly following in his mind? I felt his consideration like ice poured down my spine. I came close to the heartstone and said good morning, smiled at Heirik, but he did not give me anything in return.

The night was clear and brittle, bone-cracking cold. Betta and I were out beyond the bath, in the place where we peed. The tunnel made it easy to get fairly far from the house, but the rest of the distance was a slog along a slippery path in the snow, where dozens of footsteps had churned up mud before ours.

I told her I'd just start back by myself, and I lifted my skirts up high to step into the snow.

Being alone struck me. It had happened before, several times since I'd come here, but tonight somehow it was raw and new. I felt my body acutely, as an animal thing. No technology could find me through my eyes, track my voice. No one in any place or time knew my coordinates, the ambient temperature, where I stood in proximity to the closest coffee shop. I fell onto my back in the snow and accepted the pressure of it. The crush of being unfindable. The thrill of no expectations. I flung my arms and legs out to make the shape of a snowbloom.

The sky stole my breath. Unthinkably deep, and I the smallest animal underneath it, solitary and wild. I bared my teeth at no one.

"Betta," I said. "Do you feel it?"

There was no answer.

I called her, loud enough that she should be able to hear, and again I got no response.

I sat up and looked around, and I was off the slimy, muddy path. I'd paid attention to the stars and wilderness and I'd wandered. The joy of being unfindable quickly turned to worry. I grasped the snow and looked for Betta all around. I didn't see her anywhere, didn't see anything but snow. I tried to scramble to my feet, and I sank up to my knees. I struggled, too many skirts and furs, too much snow. My heart started beating fast. I needed to return to people and fire, to the sturdy house. I looked up to go to it.

It wasn't there.

A fine, gray mist obscured the world. I hadn't seen it massing around me, didn't know how long I'd lain unfocused, wondering at such freedom. Now I was inside a smothering pillow. It was getting thicker and grayer fast, and soon the stars and moon were gone.

I turned in every direction and twisted my skirts. Lurched toward nothing. I called Betta, three times, four, five, my heart pounding harder and harder. Flailing in a darkening sea, any direction could be wrong. Tears froze on my face, mixing with gray mist. I called her one more time. My voice sounded weak.

Water was seeping into the place where my boots met my wool pants, making miserable trails, circling my calves. My feet were two dumb blocks. The cold seemed lethal, all of a sudden. I was a vulnerable body that needed to be warm. I blinked desperately, a help code, and then laughed at myself like a bark in the wilderness. My eyes hadn't worked that way in months.

Trying to use my long-lost contacts brought me back to my senses, and to where I really was.

Specific questions calmed me. How long had I been gone, and how long might it reasonably be until I was missed and someone came to find me? Was I near that limit? Would they be looking yet? How could I help them find me? I stretched my toes and fingers to move blood around in them. The questions helped, but I didn't seem to know any answers, and a blank sleepiness came like a great and gorgeous weight.

Walking would keep me awake, but if I ventured from my spot, it could be the wrong way. I could move farther and farther from the house, swimming through thigh deep snow into oblivion.

I let my brain turn off, then, and tried to sense the answers instinctively. I quieted myself and tried to let my animal brain remember which way I'd been going before the swirling gray, the subtle clues that I knew in my muscles and the delicate bones of my inner ear. Where the house was the last time I saw it, the angle of my approach and how fast I'd been walking.

Completely opaque now, the mist stung my cheeks. It was moving, picking up speed. The mist changed from smothering cotton to a living thing, a biting wind. Soon snow crystals whipped my face, a swarm of needle-like beaks on a million tiny birds. I turned around again and fell hard in a heap of wet skirts and furs. And I just sat, unable to try again.

Each individual eyelash was stiff and heavy. I started to count them in my mind.

I would die here. I pulled my cloak up over my head, though I felt sorry I had to melt my icicle lashes. They were probably pretty.

I breathed out slowly, filling up the cave of my cloak with warmth, then took my own air back in, enjoying breathing deeply. I was in a state of grace. Going soon, but still alive.

Would I even know it, when I was gone? So tired. A deep, dark kind of sleepiness came like a heavy blanket. I thought of Betta being lost, too. Was she feeling the same thing?

Betta! I struggled up again. She must be in danger, too. I had to find the house and get help for her.

For Betta, I stood and considered everything again. I couldn't see. Solid white now surrounded me, and I groped at it aimlessly. It seemed so solid, when my hands went through it I was shocked. I only knew it was moving because of my hair whipping and hitting my face, and the moaning of the wind, an unearthly, divine sound. So loud, hearing human voices would be impossible.

The wind paused, and I was left deaf in the stillness. Then it gathered itself, organized itself and came at me all from one direction, strong and fierce. I pushed into it, as if pushing a boulder. And on the wind came the faintest, most familiar scent of smoke.

My chest spasmed with desire for that fire. I pushed toward it, right into the wind, and yelled over and over for help.

I shrieked when a hand grabbed me by the arm.

Someone strong lifted me off the ground and pulled me in tight. I started to shake. "I'm sorry," I apologized for no reason, and the words were eaten by the wind.

A gentle hand cradled my head. A scratchy beard brushed my cheek. "Heirik," I said roughly, eyes closed.

"It is Brosa," he said. "You are safe."

I opened my eyes and frantically called for Betta.

"Shhhh, Woman, she is safe, too. My uncle found her."

I pictured her in Hár's arms for just a moment, his breath close against her cheek before he backed away in secrecy, cursing the wind and his own stubbornness. How he must have wanted to hover by her side, speak to her in lover's tones, of comfort and the future.

The next day the snow was gone.

THE WATER'S EDGE

Spring

IT WAS JUST A FEW DAYS LATER WHEN WE HEARD ABOUT THE whale.

A messenger from the fishing camp rode up to the house to tell us there was a beached animal—a wreck—of such size he had never seen. Soon there was a flurry of readying. Horses and supplies and baskets and children, tents and bedrolls and wraps and furs. Cunning egg cartons made of sweet-smelling, dry grass, each big enough to hold dozens of eggs.

Nearly everyone would go. A beached whale on our family's sand was a sublime omen and great gift, and claiming it would be a festival.

So I sat atop Drifa, traveling again to the sea.

The land opened up before us in different shades this time. Newborn grass shoots fuzzed everything with the most delicate, sunny green. Wild, and promising to become unruly, they grew in the crevices of jumbly rocks of all sizes. The rocks were strewn everywhere to the horizon and beyond, and they stood out darker now, in the light of spring. Birches were sparked with buds, kissed with a fragile life. Snow gone, everything was newly open to the sky. It spread above us, simply blue, touched with white clouds from a storybook. The air felt clean, and breathing it was delicious.

What seemed like this wild, unruly mix of grass and crumbly rocks and hills, was actually the byway, our defined course to the sea. The route had been controlled by Heirik's family for three generations. Once I knew this, I could see it—a suggestion of a path worn into this stony ground, where for forty years men and women had chosen safe and efficient routes.

Along the ridge, the stone sisters stood guard. It was our gloriously flowered, grassy, rocky passage, and no one else's. I wondered what would befall someone who contested the rights to this land, and I remembered Eiðr's hand falling clear of his body in payment for the life a horse. What would the price be, for a stab at this beauty?

The horses were sure-footed on the steep decline, and this time I wasn't as scared. Not entirely able to sit loose and easy, still I trusted Drifa and knew what to expect. I looked out more this time, at the vista. I could see the place where the ocean would be, the idea of it introduced by an absence of hills, a somehow greener sky.

It would be my second time there, not counting the day I arrived. Already, I looked back to my previous trip and thought of myself as naive. Back when I thought I could have everything, when I thought it would be simple, and yet I feared so many easy things—birds and horses and steep rocks that we traversed to get to the water. Now I sat taller on my horse. I'd been to the edge of my heart's fear, and I hung there still, every day wondering what I would gain or lose. A steep decline felt like nothing.

When we hit the flat ground, the horses took off as they had last time. I watched the men and boys ride off in a glorious explosion of hooves and light. Drifa and I came right behind. The thrill of wind in my hair shocked me out of my reverie. Thoughts turned to hanging on, breathing, a glorious dizziness from adrenalin and love for this horse, this terrifying land. Past my tears, I could just make out the chief, and this time his brother by his side, flying together along the great curving river that would bring us to the sea.

We neared the last rise, and I heard everything first before I saw the scene. I heard the waves' rhythmic crash and suck, the reeling birds' thready calls, the shouts of men who had gotten here first and were welcoming us with something like a song. The hvalsaga. News of a whale.

When we topped the rise, I looked down on the great black-sand basin and it stole my breath.

It was familiar now, this vast and savage place, spreading for miles below. This stretch of coast was contained on one side by the cliffs to my left. Hundreds of feet high, their bases curved like a great enfolding arm around the sand. Tucked into the curve nestled dozens of tiny caves, where Heirik and I had sat together so long ago, where Ageirr had found and taken me.

Those caves looked inconsequential from up here at the top of the great rise. The sight brought ragged emotions up, bile in my throat, tears whisked from my eyes by the wind. I looked to my right instead, and I saw the fishing camp far down the beach, the hut and several boats pulled up on the sand beside it. In the water, beyond the camp, I saw the delicate curves of a Viking longship. The dragon's head just visible from here.

And straight ahead of me, the wreck.

We were separated—the whale and I—by several tiers of brush and stone and wood and sand. From where Drifa and I stood, a steep and long slope led down to brushy flats that extended to the caves and off into the distance toward the camp. Another level down would bring us to a rocky section, made of a million stones so big I could just lift one with two hands. They came in every shade of gray, steel and black, and were scattered over with skeletal driftwood from kindling-sized sticks to massive trunks, twisted, cracked, rent in terrible, reaching shapes.

Another step down, and we would wade through knee-high, electric lime colored brush. Snowblooms! They were just babies now, this year's new plants massing everywhere. Then one more step down, and the sand would level out, become moist and then wet and then meet the sea. And there it lay.

The whale, now dead, lolled on its side and offered its striped, white underbelly to our view. It was gently and softly tremendous, limp and yet proud in death. From my vantage point a hundred or more feet away, I could see right down its length.

Long parallel ridges widened over the massive hump of its middle and tapered at its tail. They called a beached whale a wreck, and I saw the reflection of a destroyed boat in its body. The proportions and graceful lines exactly like a Viking ship, its proud hull lying vanquished and upturned. Its ribs hauled up dumbly on shore.

But wreck was not a word of devastation or loss. It was a poetic and tender word in the old language. Something carried by the waves, given to the sand. A gift.

A gust of wind lifted Drifa's hair and mine and the stench came, overwhelming and rotten. Acid leapt to the back of my throat, and the smell of an astounding hunk of dead meat. I choked and doubled over from the physical blow, and Drifa had to shuffle and dance to catch us. When no bile came up, I sat tall and let Drifa make her way to the beach.

Despite the smell, I needed to get close. I needed to see this thing that had come to lie on the sand, to be found and consumed by this family.

True to her name, Drifa floated down the slope, moving with the laze of loose snow on a breeze. She didn't stop until her nose almost touched the giant animal. She sniffed at the whale, had almost no reaction but a quick shake of her mane, then began to slowly walk down its length as if to give me a personal tour.

So close, the whale obliterated all other thought or impression. Half the size of the house in all dimensions, blotting out the sky as my horse and I ambled its length. It was higher than me, even as I sat on Drifa's back. I touched a finger to it and slowly drew a line in the slime on its belly. The whale's skin felt both rough and slick at once, with short bristly hairs poking out here and there. I stood fascinated, in the shadow of its once-majestic body, feeling it begin its long slide into dust. An incredible creature. I thanked the waves for sending it.

A hand clasped my leg, not roughly, but it startled me.

"A little help?"

Sitting on Drifa, I was well above Brosa's head. I looked down at him questioningly, but he had turned his back to me and was lifting and gathering his hair. He'd pressed a leather tie into my palm. I swallowed with surprise. I had become so used to avoiding touch, this intimate request made me uneasy and a little breathless. It seemed casual enough, even offhand, but it left a fluttering in my belly.

I gathered his long hair in my hand and wrapped it with leather. It was rough and wavy and smelled pleasantly like juniper and smoke. Not the choking fumes of the heartstone, but an outdoor fire. A wild and spicy scent that could just manage to distract me from the nearby whale if I leaned in close enough to his curls. I naturally touched his shoulder to let him know I was through. It felt softer, not as lean as Heirik's.

"Takk," he turned to me and smiled.

Before this, I had always looked up to his sea green eyes. From above they were different. I could detect the gold flecks in them, the kin of his brother's.

"You might want to get away now." He planted a long stick in the ground, and a giant blade gleamed perilously close to his face. He grinned. It was a big scythe handle—made for the tallest man—fitted with a mean, long cutting edge.

I still looked at him, realizing that I'd been completely mute this whole time.

"We're about to cut the level."

I didn't know what it meant, but I didn't want to be near.

"Já, okay," I said, brilliantly. I turned Drifa and we tripped lightly away.

Down the beach, women gathered like shore birds, and I half expected them to scatter when I rode into their midst. Instead they just turned to look past me, from where I'd come. I turned around too, pulling Drifa up short. Brosa had stabbed the blade deep into the whale's skin near the tail. He and another man were putting their considerable strength into the scythe handle, very slowly and steadily cutting a line parallel to the sand. Two men followed behind and put all their weight into pulling the slippery wound together, keeping tension on the skin. They were splitting the whale horizontally.

The animal was already dead, but there was something cruel about cutting into it so deliberately and dispassionately. It would have been more humane, somehow, to attack it with spear and ax. At least it would have met a glorious end, not this cold surgery.

About a third of the way along the underside, a mass of gigantic pink intestines emerged. They billowed out gracefully at first, then sagged to the ground. The pink tubes looked to be as big around as Hár's thighs, and the whole pile was taller than Brosa, who deftly ducked out of the way. Steam filled the air around the rent in the body. The whale had died so recently, and was so well insulated with blubber, it still held pockets of heat.

The smell traveled far down the beach, even more revolting.

I dropped lightly to the ground and opened my pack. The organized and grassy nests of the egg cartons seemed a world apart. Their orderly lines and hay-like scent were a haven, daylight amidst a nightmare of dead innards. I breathed deeply of their dusty sweetness.

"I need to take a walk," I told no one in particular, and I absently handed Drifa's reins to one of the girls and walked away.

Just a short way down the beach, I came to a maze of eerie, gigantic rocks. The sight struck up a soft pounding in my chest. So familiar.

When I'd first woken on this black sand, I'd seen rocks of all sizes stretching in the distance. I knew—though I couldn't really remember—that these were some of them. I'd been right here, I thought, dipping the toe of my boot into the moist ground and making a little impression that immediately filled halfway with water. I'd lain near these very rocks, but without the strength or sense to even see their bizarre attraction.

The smallest was twice my height, and it joined to another, larger rock to make a slick, gray arch for me to duck under. I went through and explored a gallery of several more.

Rounded and massive rocks, they looked like benignly big, lumpy monsters. The shaggy seaweed that grew all over them completed the image of beasts, slumping toward the sea. Seaweed looked like hair, shimmering in coppers and slimy greens. Here and there what might have been one house-high rock had split into two who almost touched, seemed to bump noses. I had the impression that though they seemed stationary, the beasts actually moved in a slower timeframe, so slow I couldn't apprehend it.

The ocean's sound rushed and echoed around inside the rock maze. Birds like dots swooped far overhead, their cries just audible above the water's din.

Some rocks were undercut with elf-high tunnels, obviously carved by a brutal force of water, still oozing mud from the last high tide.

It was coming in again. The darkest midnight water, iced with a pure white reflection of sunlight on its surface. It crept closer, and when I turned to look back, the entrance to the rock world looked far away. The tide came faster now with each surge. I skirted the foam and tried to stay up high and away. I gripped my dress in my two fists and started immediately back.

I heard a shout and looked up to see Betta, far up on a plateau above the beach, what seemed like a hundred feet above me. She waved, speck-like against the sky. I saw a couple other women there, too, not faces, but the shapes of skirts in motion, silhouetted against white clouds. I looked around for the way up and saw a gentle climb across some boulders, that wound around to the top. I climbed until I met them up there, and breathless with the effort, I came close enough to the edge to look down on the scene below.

The thralls had set up a half dozen A-frame tents, the ones we'd used at Jul, and they looked like little play-houses. The red threads running through their fabric lit up against the beige and gray of the landscape. I could see children running around and women carrying things, moving things, indistinct from up so high. I could see the men, teeming around the whale. They seemed so small.

WHEN THE SHOUTS CAME, OUR HEADS ALL WHIPPED UP LIKE A startled flock, and we moved toward the edge of our high plateau. I crawled on hands and knees to the very edge to see what was happening.

The otherworldly rocks I'd wandered among, the ones that glistened at low tide, had enticed a child to climb. The tide was coming in fast now, and he was stuck.

My chest spasmed with fear. I remembered how those elf-high caves looked, carved into pure rock by the force of this sea. At high tide, they would be boiling with seawater, waves seeking their way in and then exploding high into the sky.

More memories came, darker ones, from many months ago. The water dragging at my boots, my skirts, the bone-crushing cold.

Brosa had said what? That a grown man could survive two minutes before losing his will, less than ten before death. But never a little boy. He would be dashed. The foaming and crashing would eat him alive, too small to swim against the surf, too thin to withstand the cold.

From where I crouched I could just see that it was Áki, no more than three or four years old. He scrabbled on his hands and knees on top of the slimy rock, and I imagined his panicked tears. Over the surf, I could barely make out words, bleak and small. People yelled, "Don't move!" I heard Heirik calling, "No time for a boat." I found him in the mess of people, and saw that he was shouting to Brosa, waving to him. He caught his brother's eye, nodded to him, and then the chief waded into the deadly ocean.

Heirik was in the water too long, trying to reach Áki.

I looked down and watched him swim to the slick rock, saw him talking to the boy, probably gentling him, trying to climb up to him, but with each attempt Heirik slid back into the sea. I stretched out on my stomach so I could see over the edge of the cliff. I saw his dark hair fanned out in the water, his heavy clothes dragging down. My lungs filled tight against the ground, my head dizzy from breathing along with Heirik, willing him to reach the boy, wishing them back to shore.

He'd stopped trying and began to just float alongside the big rock, and I wished I'd been counting the minutes. Was it two now? More? Then I saw what Heirik was thinking, I hoped. He was waiting as the waves came higher and nearer, waiting for the water itself to take him to the boy. He was so close.

Time moved too fast, seconds bleeding away, and yet the waves grew too slowly. I swore I could feel Heirik's focus shift and dissipate. He held his body differently, giving it up to the cold, slipping away though I willed him to stay. I imagined his thoughts slowing, suspended, not focused on what his loss would mean to anyone, just on that little boy. On keeping his own eyes open one more second, then one more.

Into the eerie scene, a wind came whistling hard and pressed me down into the dirt and grass. My own viewpoint seemed to draw back and away, and from my high perch, I watched Heirik begin to die.

Then a wave raised him close enough, and in a heartbeat he grabbed Áki, pulled him close, and swam for shore. I stood and watched them reach the beach. And like an arrow released from a bow, I ran.

The child was wrapped in cloaks, his mother holding him fiercely, ushering him away with a look of bewildered fear. I stumbled past her, pushing people aside so I could reach Heirik's tent. A few women were already there throwing blankets and cloaks inside. They wouldn't go in, but they helped, rounding up every warm thing they could find to save the chief, the hero, only now at the end of his life beloved.

I pushed past them and stepped inside.

I'd never seen anyone morbidly cold. I expected shivering or chattering. He stood simply in the center of the room, his arms crossed on his chest, looking confused and vaguely hostile.

"Áki?" He asked through intensely clenched teeth.

Heirik's hair was slick and freezing in ropy strands, soaked with salt water.

"He's with his mother," I said, already moving to gather the dozen or more blankets from the floor. "He's going to be fine," I added without really knowing. I needed Heirik to stop worrying about the boy and help save himself.

"I'm making you a bed, Heirik." I tried to call up a soothing, gentling voice, the kind I'd heard him use sometimes to lull people into obeying him. I reached to draw him closer.

"Woman, get off me!" He growled and pushed me away and I scudded backwards into the cot. At the most reasonable of times, he would've pulled away from me, and right now he looked insane. Pure aggression in the line of his brow and golden light of his eyes. He slurred his words, like he was drunk. "I'm sorry, Litla," he said.

I stood slowly, caught in the same sluggishness as he was, probably in shock. I watched him strip to pants and boots, his clothes making heavy sounds as they hit the dirt floor. He stumbled to the bed, laid down and dragged a single blanket over the whole sopping mass of himself, as if he were lying down for an afternoon nap. Hair dripping black with seawater, face pale as milk, he seemed smaller under the covers, and no warmer. Not at all. Though he had escaped to dry land, the sea was slowly claiming him.

I went to my knees on the floor by his feet, moving in a nightmare. I worked his freezing boots off bit by bit. Then I pulled back the blanket to untie his pants. He grasped me hard by the wrist.

"Enough," he hissed. His eyes were blazing, emotions careening.

"Don't be a fool." I told him matter-of-factly, "You will die."

He shook his head, then tried to command me with his chief voice. "Leave me." Not in a million years, I thought. He didn't know how mellifluous and tender that voice sounded to me. It could seduce me any time, but it didn't scare me into obeisance. Certainly not now.

I pushed him down and held his chest with my knee so I could get his pants untied, and he watched me with slow and listless eyes. I'd thought so many times about how it would be to touch the bones of his pelvis where they pushed up against his skin. I remembered his reaction when I finally did, a hiss on his lips, a buck of hips at the ticklish sensation. I shook my head and put those thoughts aside.

He stopped my hands with one of his own and told me gently that he would do it.

I turned away and let him. I didn't want this miserable moment to be the second time I ever took the clothes from his body.

"Too much wool," he told me. "I'm warm enough." When I turned back, he'd pushed the blankets away in a heap—every cloak that the women had thrown into the tent in terrible haste went across the floor, but for one he kept to hide himself. I picked up all the furs and blankets and piled them around him again, reasoning with him like a child.

I got him tucked into a mountain of wool. But without any body heat to speak of, there was nothing for him to trap inside the layers, no spark for the tinder. I cast my mind about, trying to recall what I could do. Then I remembered something I'd read about twelve hundred years from now.

I dropped my cloak to the floor and started to take off my boots. He watched me with curiosity.

"You will die of …" I had no word for *hypothermia*, and I was in a hurry, taking off pounds of brooches and necklaces and belts and dropping it all to the floor. "… cold. Heirik, it's serious. You need to get close to another warmer person."

When he realized what I meant to do, his black brows drew together. As my apron hit the floor, he started shaking his head. "Nei." Another useless command. "You will not."

He had to give up the argument when his body seized in a fit of convulsive shivering.

By the time his shaking ended, I was standing before him in just my shift. Freezing air whipped against the tent, and my nipples stood out hard against the paper-thin dress.

He smiled slyly, his eyes on my body, his emotions taking another swerve. At the very edge of death, he was aroused, joking. Drunk with cold, thirty seconds ago he forbade me to join him under the covers. Now he asked through gritted, trembling teeth, "Do you wish to meet the ravens, too, or are you getting in?"

I burrowed into the covers and pressed the length of my body to his. I expected to recognize his shape, his skin and the contours of his bones, but it wasn't the same at all. Not like in the cave.

It felt as if he'd been carved from one of the thirteen glaciers. He didn't feel human. I wrapped myself around him and nestled my head into the space under his arm. Raging spasms began right away, and I had to hold on with all my strength.

Slowly, over a long time, the spasms slowed and came at longer intervals, finally giving way to the smaller tremors, then everyday shivering.

My cheek—sticky with sweat from hanging on to his buck-ing body—now fit perfectly against his chest. I closed my eyes in wonder at the feel of his skin and Thor's hammer against my fore-head. I'd longed so many times to lay my head in just this spot. I had protected the memory of the moments when I'd been allowed. But I never dreamed of a moment like this. When we fell into bed together in my dreams, it was hot and slick and delicious, with entwined legs and yearning flesh. Here we lay strange and cold, no part of us twined or hungry.

We began the long climb to warmth. In the stillness, I began to take on his cold, splitting what heat I had between us, until a fragile warmth took hold inside the blankets.

At some point, I knew he would live, and then I realized just how close it had been. One more minute in that water and Heirik would be gone. We would be covering his corpse with these blan-kets. Now that the possibility seemed past, I gasped and sobbed, and he held me now, until my own tremors stopped.

After an even longer time, we felt truly warm. Small stir-rings of the muscles in his back and legs suggested he was safe. His shoulder felt alive under my fingers, and for the first time I consciously realized that I was holding him. Really holding him again, after so long. I was under a mountain of blankets with my arms around Heirik. It sent a thrill through my body, everywhere at once, washing me in arousal.

It brought to my attention many other sensations, too. My arm and hip were numb. Sand and pebbles tormented me. I shifted my weight, and without exactly meaning to I pressed my hips into his.

They met so naturally. If he were carved from a great glacier, I was the other half, made to fill the spaces in his body as he could fill mine. We slipped together. I felt him react, then, becoming hard against me, shockingly sudden and intense. I sucked in air, my lips against the cold skin of his chest, and he made a sound deep inside, underneath my kiss.

But he was stubborn among a family of stubborn men. He didn't give his hips to me, pressing with sensual slowness, didn't roll me on my back and violently shove my shift out of the way to take me. He didn't make a single move in fact.

"Thank you," he said, formally. Even as I felt the solid heat of his arousal growing against my damp shift, he whispered, "You should go."

I went dead, though my breath continued to make a moist warm spot on his skin. My voice continued to work. I murmured a question into his skin, asked him something simple. "Forever?"

The quiet was long and brittle, and I held my breath. I sank into the pleasure of his arms and waited there, knowing I would have to go soon. Savoring this single moment before he said the word I didn't want to hear.

"I cannot be with you." He said it with certainty. "I will not lead you to think I can."

It was reasoned and confident and final. In contrast to his words, though, he held me tighter. He wrapped a large hand around the back of my head and pulled me close. His lips touched my forehead. It was a press, not a kiss. It was the closest I would get.

I TIDIED THE TENT BEFORE LEAVING, AND IT FELT LIKE A RITUAL. I folded blankets and put off the pressure of a coming wave of grief. While I stayed here, we were not completely severed.

Heirik had turned to face the tent wall, and so I took my time. I took off my wet shift, and I put on my wool dress right against my skin. I combed my hair out with my fingers. Put my apron and jewelry back on, a cloak over that, a blanket too.

With each layer of clothing, I felt a little stronger, a little closer to being able to go outside into a world where Heirik and I were really gone.

Finally, I watched him breathe for just a moment, willing him to turn around and give in to me. Please, I thought, giving it one more second, and then one more. The fabric of the tent flap felt rough under my fingers, and the sky darkened outside. Please, again. One last time.

I stumbled off away from gaiety and people and whale stench. On a rise above the beach, I found a big piece of driftwood, and I spent some time laying out my shift to dry and making a little space in the sand so I could sit and lean against the big trunk. And finally there were no more tasks to do and I sank to the ground. I held my head heavy in my hands. And I faced the truth and began to say goodbye.

I conjured up each one of Heirik's features and gave the image a Viking burial. The dark silk of his hair, so beloved. It was the first part of him I'd ever noticed. I said farewell to his beard cropped close about his strong jaw and lovely chin, his dark eyelashes, his long, straight nose. A deep pang came with my whispered goodbye to his sidelong smile.

I remembered private looks, when we played tafl, when we laid in the snow under stars. His scent, the feel of his skin, in a dark cave full of steam. His body held with such fierce elegance on his horse, laid back in the saddle to turn and fight—that one was like a dagger in my gut. So beautiful. I silently said goodbye to names, shoulders, stance, every small moment. One by one I let them go like ships.

I couldn't face saying goodbye to his voice. I remembered his first words to me—he'd asked my name, he'd told me his own. I thought of him calling me small, his surprise. Calling me Ginn. The way he said it, so honeyed and loving. He'd made it my name, even before it really was.

The moon wobbled. The deadly sea, the people, all blurred. Two dozen or more men and women and children, colorful by the fire, framed against dark sand. They talked and handed around cups and smiled and joked. They didn't realize they were huddled against an endless wilderness.

Someone big approached in the dark, but it didn't even startle me, I was so dead.

"Woman, what are you doing alone? And so cold?"

Brosa sank down to sit beside me, washing me in warmth and life. I hadn't realized that I was freezing. Shaking from sobbing and a slow-growing cold that had blossomed while I wasn't paying attention, I moved closer to him. He took a very big fur off his shoulders and draped it over my back, then put his arm and cloak around me.

It was distracting, the ways in which he resembled Heirik. His body so similar, and yet a softer, rounder version, not made lean by constant farm work. The body of a strong man who'd spent nearly a year on boats and drinking by other men's fires, not out on the land with ax or scythe.

I had the impression, since the moment I saw Brosa at the fireside, that he was another version of his brother. But this close, I saw now the many ways he didn't look like Heirik, how very different his face was. How his life had carved a permanently different aspect.

Bits of black sand clung to his hairline. He must have washed with it. Surrounded by abundance and wool and safety, I closed my eyes and leaned into him. He smelled good, like rocks and sea and soap, a clean smell that had nothing to do with being elbow deep in whale. I breathed him in gratefully.

"How is he?" Brosa asked.

"He'll live," I said with some bitterness.

He answered with an eloquent "já" that combined relief and gratitude with something like regret—an allowance that things might be easier for Heirik if he were dead—and finally chagrin for thinking so. We stayed quiet for a while, then, each thinking about the chief.

"You love my brother." He stated, sure of it. He didn't need to ask me.

I couldn't explain how Heirik's spirit and voice and eyes lit something inside me the moment I saw him on this very beach. The moment I heard him speak, I was at home. "I have since we met."

Words came out of nowhere, and without thought or reason, I told Brosa about the fight here at the sea. About how Heirik saved my life, how he protected me. Brosa knew about it, of course, but he seemed surprised at my role in it. Surprised that Heirik had had to save me from Ageirr. Heirik hadn't even mentioned that part? My brief abduction was a minor event in a long war—a feud that sprang from Brosa's own tragedy. When I remembered his and Esa's part in it, I felt hot remorse for being so self-centered. Of course Brosa wouldn't have thought about that fight in terms of me. It was about his lost wife, the lovely Esa, only a child herself. It was about blood and honor and a cold baby he might have held in his hands. It was about Heirik standing in for him when that honor was challenged. I was a random detail in a thing beyond my reckoning.

Brosa moved on.

"You've seen my brother fight." He said it as though this explained everything, from my love for Heirik to the turning of the stars. "Everyone who has seen him battle is fascinated."

"Quite a change came over him." I touched my wrist where Heirik had gripped me before he kissed me. Where Ageirr held me roughly not a half hour later.

"He's the raven, já? But come before death."

I shivered at the similarity with the image I'd seen that day. Brosa shifted in the sand so he could hold me closer.

"It's alright, Ginn," he said, returning to what lay unspoken about the fight. "I am not afraid of what is past."

It hurt my chest to take a deep breath. I allowed a moment to acknowledge his reason and strength, to wonder at the sheer will of happiness that drove him.

"You love your brother, too." It was so clear how much he did.

"He's been my brother always. He taught me everything about how to be alive."

"Hmmm." I murmured into his warm chest, trying to picture them as children. Brosa, here and now, was so welcoming, so easy to melt into.

"Not just the good," he mused. "Heirik has been a fine example of how not to live, also. He won't allow himself a full life." After a moment he added a final statement. "He won't ever take you as his own."

I had just said my mental goodbye to Heirik, and this—from the person who knew him best, or at all—pounded the last spike into the hull. "I know," I said bleakly. I crushed my hope and grief into a tiny ball and wished it out into the Arctic sea. It stayed with me, though, stubborn as the man who inspired it. So I pushed it way down deep where I could forget about it. *"Goodbye,"* I whispered.

Brosa didn't ask about the English word I'd spoken. He rested his chin on my head, spoke into my hair. I felt the heat of his breath as it ruffled the loose strands there.

"A man who has you wanting him is a lucky man."

He drew back to touch my chin, to lift my face.

"My brother is a fool."

His lips were warm and easy at first, a brush like autumn leaves and the faint sweetness of angelica. His kiss was gentle and considerate. He wanted to be sure it was okay. And I pressed my mouth against his harder, and opened my lips and said without speaking that já, it was.

He took my waist in one big hand and gently pinned me against the driftwood. His fingers moved up and around my back and shoulder blades. It felt good to be embraced, and I instinctively moved to give him the same in return. One of my arms went under his cloak and around his sturdy body. My other hand found the back of his neck, and the knotted leather and hot skin there.

He was light with his tongue, unhurried, and I couldn't stand it. Brosa swept his fingers over my breast, and I reacted with a soft cry that was so unexpected, so uncontrollable, I ducked my head in embarrassment. He kissed my forehead then, and my eyelids. The soft brush of his beard moved across my nose and cheek. His hand moved up my leg, my skirt bunching around my knees, then higher. His thumb kneaded my thigh, stirring up flames.

"Stop." I gasped, urgent.

"Not now." He was breathless, drawing me onto his lap. His kisses no longer light, but demanding. Through the wool of my dress, through his clothes, I felt him hard and ready. He pressed his hips up slowly into me, and I met his body with mine. "Let go, Lovely One," he whispered, and I felt the past several months dissolve, every minute, as if they were taken by a swiftly churning stream. Gone, until I knew only his mouth, again and again, his hands, his fingers, dark words in my ear.

A laugh came from down on the beach, so great it was like thunder. It woke me, and I drew my face away, pressed my forehead to his shoulder. My heart hammered. What was I doing?

With a strong hand on my chin, Brosa made me look at him. His eyes were not the open and easy ones of a few minutes ago. They had turned to wolf's eyes. He would have me, they said, in every way that his brother would not.

My eyes burned, and I clenched them shut, willing everything—the entire night, my whole tumble into the past—to go away. I didn't have any more ideas on how to get by. I would die right here and dissipate into the sea.

Then Brosa lifted me effortlessly and placed me in the sand. His voice came low and easy, coaxing me back. "Ginn," he said. "I'm sorry. It is alright."

I opened my eyes and he was normal again. He'd put aside the possessive intention that had gone straight to my heart and gut and he was smiling lightly.

"Stay and talk with me, já?" He stood up and handed me the blanket he wore. He dug in the sand with his foot. "I'll strike up a fire."

Brosa left to walk the immediate area and search for twigs and logs. Left me alone with my slowly down-shifting body and mind. He must have been taking the time to adjust, too. We'd both been immediately, fiercely aroused. I envied him the task of gathering wood, something to do, to calm and center himself. I hung my head and shook it, but it didn't clear.

He returned and knelt by the small pit he'd made, and he crushed little twigs until they formed a delicate nest in his palm. He set it in the sand. Sparks fizzed and flew from his fire-steel and caught in a piece of touchwood. Brosa was good at making a fire. Of course. He was good at everything.

He dropped the touchwood into the nest and exhaled the slightest breath into the tangle of twigs, where a small, pink-orange spot grew and took hold. When the fire had started, he sat back to feed it and to talk.

He told me stories about his ship, of a voyage that was wonderful and disgusting and dangerous. About Norway and the amazing things that could be had from as far as the unknowable east, the honey and hazelnuts and new linen and delicate horn cups, trimmed with silver. Soapstone and leather and exotic ink, sold in miniature bottles stopped with corks. Slender bones, sharpened to write with. Bracelets and fillets of rare beauty.

He told me about his uncle. Stories of Hár caring for him like a father, teaching him about axes and stars and boats. He loved him almost as much as he loved Heirik, or more but in a different way.

I told him about summer and spinning and distaffs billowing with clouds, about the fields and walls. I told him about learning to ride Gerdi, and we laughed about her somnolent way of transporting me. I could walk faster than ride that girl, but I had some affection for her. I told him about Drifa. About how I felt so at home in the white woods. It stabbed my heart to think about Heirik there with me, but if felt good to tell Brosa about the beauty of the quiet, and the baskets of leaves and herbs and lichens for dyeing. I told him I'd yet to find Saga back among the trees, though I could feel her presence there. And somehow Brosa's way of listening made these minor adventures seem as exciting as a trading voyage.

In the quiet moonlight, something made him change direction entirely—perhaps our talk of the goods he brought home, or the cloth and bread and bandages I'd made. The things that would sustain us. It was almost a whisper. "This wreck," he said, gesturing with his chin toward the whale. "It is my mother's blessing." Wreck was fond. A way to name the whale. Something good, given by this lethal sea.

"I know," I whispered back. The animal would feed the whole extended family for some time. There was abundance, beyond enough, just like every year since Signé married Ulf. "I've heard very much about her."

He smiled, inwardly watching his mother. Then he looked at me. "I could tell you one more story, before you fall into sleep." Brosa touched my toe with his, in a friendly way. It was true, I was tired.

His grandfather, Magnus Heirikson, was among the first settlers. "They were rich," he said plainly, nowhere near describing their wealth. "They came in two great ships with people and animals and thralls. Jewelry and weapons and tools." He chuckled and shook his head in wonderment. "I think of my grandmother on a ship, with sheep at her knees. I don't know where they thought they were going with their glass cups and furs. But I am glad now that they brought them," he said, and with his foot he nudged the fur that now lay across my lap, much bigger than any Icelandic animal, a treasure beyond price. It brought to mind Signé's fox jacket. The one Heirik let me wear months ago in the snow, the night we were lovers.

How could I really let him go? He'd pushed me away finally this time. Absolutely. But I'd felt his need first tonight, not Brosa's, in my heart and against my thighs.

I drew their grandmother's fur around my legs and rested myself heavily in the hollows of my log. I had a powerful urge to go to sleep, to put aside this muddled mess. Put aside the unassuming but steady fact of Brosa's foot still resting against my leg.

"They waited until dark on the night the farm was born." He looked into the firelight and began to tell it like a children's tale, the way he must've heard it a hundred times in his blankets, curled into the body of his loving uncle. "And Magnus took his fastest horse and lit the fires all around." He poked at our small fire with his stick. "And Amma could see it from the hill where she waited, the farm lighting up like a fiery ring in the wilderness. And where she stood, they built our house." He drew a rectangle in the sand, to be the house.

His voice was deep, the cadence reverent.

"Then what?" I whispered, in a kind of trance.

"Já, well," he said at full volume. "Then, a whole lot of back-breaking work began, and everyone was very sorry they'd come to Iceland." A laugh rumbled in his chest.

Awake, I kicked his foot, a bit harder than he'd done mine.

"Alright, alright." He smirked. He got up and came to sit next to me again, putting his arm around me. "But you have to close your eyes, Litli Sládreng." Words like *small* and *slain* mixed together to mean *tired little boy*. What he was called, when this story was told to him?

He stroked my shoulder and started in again with the bedtime story, wrapping me up in a rhythmic, slow litany of all the things that were blessed with sacrifices of all kinds and sizes. The fields and house and barn and woods and bath and sea. The weapons and tools, the hearth, the horses, the walls as they were built. The beach where we sat now, the fishing camp. And the gods were very pleased, and Magnus and Amma had many children, including two sons, Ulf and Hár. "Ulf married a beautiful princess named Signé. And Ulf and the princess had two pups."

I could feel him smile at that. As a child this part of the story must have been very exciting and silly, when it got to the part about himself. I smiled, too, and nestled into the darkness of Brosa. In the second before sleep took me entirely, I heard him whisper, "And Ulf and Signé died and had no other."

I woke, curled around the silver remains of a driftwood fire. Its warmth had faded to a few embers, and I shuddered with a deep cold, blinking my stiff eyelids. Then I felt him, warm against my back, and I smiled. I pressed myself into the solid heat behind me, snuggling into him. I remembered waking once before like this, his voice a murmur against my shoulder.

I caught my breath and went still.

It was not Heirik. It was Brosa's hand heavy on my hip.

The previous night came back to me in half-forgotten voices and images, bit by wretched bit. I had thrown off my clothes and slid into bed with Heirik. I'd done it to save his life. But I knew how we were. I'd felt the call of my body, and the solid and steady response of his. With the slightest movement, his hips had fit into mine. He'd pressed his lips to my forehead. I went away marked as his, without hope of living in that love. No hope of living in a daily state of grace, expressing my burning in a hundred small ways, making food and clothes for him, tending a cut on his hand, tying the leather strips of his gauntlets and braids in the morning. These notions were really over.

I felt sick and lightheaded, and more aware of the man who laid against my back now. I'd allowed this brother to embrace and soothe me. Taken powerfully by the radiance of Brosa, I'd let loose all my fresh anger and lust.

Brosa let me go, but something carnal and possessive had been awakened. I had the sense—nei, the knowledge—that his was not just a generous kiss in my loneliest hour. I added the memory of his animal eyes to the heap of shameful moments.

They were so much like his brother's, those eyes, Heirik's sun reflected on Brosa's sea. I confused him with his brother more and more as I laid here, staring at tough grass and sand. I tried to remember the difference. I had to look and find it. I had to see Brosa right now and observe with cold objectivity that he was a separate man. Already open and easy when he was awake, I wondered how he looked in sleep.

I turned over, slowly and stealthily, barely breathing, until I could see.

The sun was making a first weak attempt at the horizon, and in the bluish pre-dawn, his white scar seemed to glow. It came so close to his eye, dipping into the crease of his eyelid like Heirik's mark did. My heart sped up with fear for him, even now, though he'd cut himself a decade ago. *He was too pretty to be like me.* Heirik's mournful voice echoed in my mind. I imagined this grieving boy with dead parents, desperate to belong with his big brother.

I dragged my objectivity back into place, like a heavy, sea-soaked dress. It was a physical struggle to put feelings behind me and just study. His nose was too short. His hair, though kissed with joyful gold, was a mess. I imagined the sea green that hid under heavy eyelids. His eyes, when he thought no one was looking, seemed tired. His eyebrows menacing. He slept with gravity. Rather than the reckless abandon of a child, this seriousness was what sleep released.

The heaviness would be forgotten when he woke and smiled. He laughed a lot, so hard that he often slumped against a wall to recover, thumped a friend's back, raised a cup. He was constantly alive with a kind of jovial kinship. I couldn't quite understand that this was him. Mirth was his strongest feature, a part of him as much as an eye or ear. It was missing as he slept, and it was almost as though Brosa was absent.

His beard was trimmed close, except for a ski slope of a point on his chin that made him into a benevolent blond devil. Svana's touch—she had trimmed his hair just days ago. I felt a pang of guilt as I secretly touched my fingertips to her handiwork.

I ghosted my finger along his bottom lip, afraid to wake him, but he slept like a stone. The skin there was unbearably smooth, so soft I could barely feel him. The memory of his tongue sent a rush of blood to sweet places. I didn't want to get up and run from him, run down the sandy hill and slip into the chaos of waking bodies to pretend I'd never been here. I wanted to stay.

A violent shake startled me, and Kit's fierce whisper. "Get up, Woman. What are you doing?"

A good and simple question. I tried to imagine how I looked, lying on the ground with Brosa, one finger lingering on his sleeping lips.

Kit glanced down the hill to assure herself that no one else was looking. "It's a good thing we came up here so early." It was then I noticed Ranka on tiptoes, trying to see what was happening while her mother pushed her behind her skirts.

I sat up quickly, my drowsiness gone with a nearly audible snap, furs and cloaks tumbling off me. Brosa stirred and opened his eyes.

He was instantly charming. "Vaenn dagan," he said to Kit, with a wink. *Beautiful morning.*

"And you stop, Man." Kit had been instantly softened by his charm, but she managed to add a "já" that sounded like a deeply indignant tisk. Reproof slipping into affection. "What are you trying to do to Ginn?"

"Not a thing," I snapped. I stood and brushed black sand from my skirts. "He built a fire and talked to me."

One of her eyebrows rose in doubt.

Brosa sat up, a broad smile on his face, his own eyebrows, and his hands, raised in a gesture of adorable innocence. Kit hissed affectionately at him, and pulled me along with her, down to the tents for morning meal.

I sat in the scraggly woods of the high ground. A number of women surrounded me, spread out in all directions, dresses sprawled out and snagging on roots and juniper. We picked through the brush to find gripe grass.

"Or you can call it toothflower," Ranka told me, and she pointed out her good teeth. "We ate it all winter."

Of course I knew that, having eaten it all winter in stews, or by stolen, uncooked handfuls in the pantry. The only vegetable. Ranka showed me anyway, how to spot the delicate cup-shaped leaves, each curled around a sparkling bit of dew.

She never tired of informing me of everything, and it was nice to let her voice blend into the sussurations of women all around me, and the waves far down on the beach. To let her chatter and announce and instruct in tones that jumped and fell.

I pulled at grass and willed my stomach to stop roiling, but the more my thoughts circled the more it grumbled. I would silence my thoughts then for moments at a time, picking at the greens. Feather-light, they drifted into my basket.

"Look, Lady!" Ranka was calling me.

I gasped when I saw her.

Her lips were stained a deathly blue. She laughed at my surprise, and the darkness dripped like raven-colored blood. It spilled from her mouth onto her white chin. My vision narrowed until I saw only her laughing face, stained teeth flashing, tongue reddish blue. Her eyes shone. The raven, come before death.

"It is just berries," she teased me.

Betta asked, "Is everything alright, Ginn?"

I shook myself and looked around, pressing my hands to the ground to steady myself. My voice wobbled more than I'd hoped. "Berries?"

"Já, they are juniper," Ranka began, and she told me they were second year berries that overwintered on the plants. I pictured them hunkered down low under dark, clutching branches. The juniper plants sprawled throughout this little wood above the sea.

Her finger brushed my lips, applying some to me, too. I felt her fingertip stop and touch the space between my teeth. She was still fascinated by it.

"You finish," she said, and turned away to do someone else's.

I sat still with my finger halfway across my lower lip, feeling the skin where Brosa's kiss had been. I'd cheapened and confused my own heart. So weak, reprehensible, to cling to someone who was so obviously a substitute. Gods, how embarrassing.

I looked around me at these women, every one a blue-stained witch, and wondered how many knew that I'd woken in Brosa's arms. Probably everyone, all over this beach. The chief included. A pang of regret came quick in my chest. I could hardly imagine the pain it would cause Heirik, to hear that news. When in fact, my heart and everything else about me were all for Heirik.

But I was angry at that coward. My emotions veered and swerved.

Ripping gripe grass felt good. I yanked away at plants and thought of the litany of what I'd given him. My heart, my body, the work of my hands. My faith in a future that he couldn't see. Or wouldn't risk enough to grasp.

He'd pushed me away a dozen times. This would be the last one, I swore.

The girls and I emerged from the brush with our baskets of moss and greens and tripped down the hill toward the sand. I looked up and noticed Brosa hacking away with a hatchet at something gross and glistening, and as naturally as though we'd called his name, he turned to see us. He stopped chopping and looked up, seemed to notice our supernatural lipstick. Then he put a hand to his heart. "One kiss, Lady," he called to me. "It's all I need."

The men all stopped hacking and looked up. The girls around me laughed, and I ducked my head shyly, a lovestruck maid. He stretched his arms broadly to appeal to me once more. " I swear I don't stink ..." he shouted. "Too bad." Everyone laughed lovingly at his charm, and I found myself smiling despite my unsettled mood.

He set himself to chopping again, but not before he gave me one of his devious winks. Gods, he was too easy.

THE WHALE WAS BROKEN DOWN EFFICIENTLY, MADE INTO PARTS—muscles, organs, blubber, bones—every one precious and packaged for home. Gone so that it left nothing but a ghostly impression in the sand and an assortment of curious birds.

Hundreds of eggs were packed in Hildur's nest-like cups, every shade of blue-green, from sun-drenched ocean to a shell so pale it seemed tinted by the exhalation of a sea spirit. Juniper berries for drink and medicine were packed in a big basket, and a leather bag full of shells would serve us as scoops, spoons, ladles.

We were ready for home, but we lingered one more night for a celebration, to thank the gods and the whale. Boys and girls gathered shellfish for our evening meal. Ale and butter were taken from the sledges the thralls had brought from home.

I sat on the rise above the beach, leaning against the big silver log that was starting to feel like my own. Still wanting to be far from happiness. It wasn't for me. Not with everything that had happened these few nights, what Heirik had done to me, what I had allowed to happen between me and Brosa. Thoughts circled like an infinity of crows.

Betta and Kit thankfully scattered them by appearing with horns of ale. It tasted sour and watery, but it gave me numbness and freedom. I thought Kit must have had another cup or two already. She was happy in the dark, free of Ranka and the baby. She smiled at me, then watched me watching Heirik.

He was bent with some kind of terrible mood. Sitting on a fur-strewn setberg—a seat-shaped rock—that acted as a high seat. Removed and above his family, he was all striking coldness. He sat uncomfortably, drinking and watching. Bunched in irritation, without his typical poise, he was almost beastly.

"Já, he is fearsome tonight," Kit said, deftly reading my mind.

He softened just once, when Áki's father approached and thanked him formally for his son's life.

"There is nothing to thank," Heirik said gently and genuinely, as though taking the man by the shoulder with his words. "Only remember, when the boy is old enough, he trains with me with ax and spear."

The man ducked his head, probably terrified, and yet thankful, blessed.

So smoothly, Heirik had turned a father's humility into great honor. And Heirik himself was transformed by the task. These times when he took adulation from this family still thrilled and saddened me, and I imagined they did the same to him. He would feed them with the work of his own hands, save them at the cost of his own life, and he would and had killed for them. At once a father and a savage. No wonder they were so devoted to him.

People murmured to Áki's father as he returned to his family by the fire.

And in the man's wake, Brosa came forward. Heirik instantly returned to his foul mood. He sat up straighter at his brother's approach, an uncharacteristic rigidity to his spine.

Brosa dropped to one knee. He planted his ax before him like a sword, as though pledging his fealty. Everyone hushed.

He was stunning. Brosa's clothes were new and opulent, brought from his trading voyage. So crisp they shone. He wore leather as blond as his own beard, lighter than any I'd seen in this land, knee-high boots strapped tight around his great calves. Cool white linen showed at his wrists, unbound by any gauntlets, his sleeves hung loose over silver bracelets. His shirt was open at his throat, just enough to allow the glint of Thor's hammer to show.

The pale leather and linen contrasted with a tunic dyed the deepest auburn with an underlying touch of crimson—a difficult and rare color to achieve. Embroidered with the palest yellows that reflected and lit up his beard and the streaks in his hair. And oh, his hair. Parted in the middle, he'd plaited it tight against his head the way that Betta wore hers, but just to behind his ears. The rest tumbled wild, halfway down his back. Even with my fingers caught up in it, I hadn't realized how very long and heavy his hair was.

He bent his radiant head before Heirik, then looked up at his brother. Silence and tension hovered. This was something special, a declaration, or a request so great as to warrant splendid clothes and a stance of submission. Something drew me to my feet, to stand and listen. Betta and Kit stood beside me.

"Heirik, Broðr, Herra," Brosa began in a strong voice. *My brother, my chief.* There was not another sound, not a breath, in the whole crowd.

"I ask with deep respect, and with our family as witness, that I may have a contract to marry Ginn."

A puddle of skirts and blankets whuffled about me where I sank into the sand. Betta and Kit knelt quickly beside me, and Betta grasped my hand.

If possible, the entire family—probably two dozen adults and assorted children gathered around the high seat—became even quieter. Not even a toddler wriggled or cried. For a second, a silent current passed between Heirik and his brother—a complex and intimate conversation, wordless and quick.

"Brother," Heirik said. "It is a good night for making such a request." He gave Brosa a half smile, but it turned sour. "A union born of this wreck will be a good one."

A fist tightened in my chest. What?

He paused, and then leaned in, elbows on his knees, as if to speak only to Brosa. "You are a good man, Brother," he spoke intimately, as if none of us were there. "We go to the althing. If no family of hers is found, then be well with your bride. The marriage can take place in summer."

I listened to Heirik's dark and beloved voice give me away.

My next breath didn't come, then another failed to come. I couldn't get air.

Betta turned me toward her and shook me. And I woke up suddenly like breaking the surface of the sea and gasped. I collapsed into Betta's arms, air finally moving through my throat.

I cried into her. Thoughts tumbling, lurching, coming back. I thought of shining Brosa, his great will to live despite tragedy, his sensual touch and hearty flirtation. I cried for him, for his asking, for his wanting me. Then I remembered Heirik's luscious, complex, private smiles. His body, hot arms around me, his breath in my hair, taking him inside me. A love not allowed, the anguish of a thousand moments, so close, so very close. I wept harder again.

With one arm Betta held and rocked me. With her other hand she soothed my hair over and over, rhythmic and calming. Finally, I laid limp in her lap, my face turned toward the sea watching my betrothed with dead eyes.

Brosa didn't seem to mind—or even notice—that I was not present at the fire. I suppose I was secured, as far as he was concerned. After he'd bowed to Heirik again, he stood, half a head above almost everyone, and a dozen men tried to clap him on the back at once. He talked and toasted with them, and smiled like a teenage boy. The boy he should have been, after all, but was not. A nineteen year old man who'd lost one wife already, lost a baby son, fought for his life and earned wounds and scars. A man who made honorable promises and strong friendships, who gave himself fully to everything he set his mind to. And now that would include me. I felt ungrateful for this magnificent gift.

I shuddered in Betta's lap, my breaths hitching and jumping as they sought a normal rhythm. And then it hit me. I struggled up in a sudden panic. "I have to go to Heirik."

I scrabbled to get out of Betta's grasp, and she let go of me, but Kit grabbed my arm and held me back. "You will not, Woman."

I felt wild when I turned to her, like I could strike her. "Let me go!"

She held me tight. "You will not do that now." She took my face in her cold hands. "Calm yourself. You've cried."

I looked for any sympathy, even a hint of understanding in her face, and found none.

"Now," she said matter-of-factly. "Wipe your eyes and go greet your beautiful husband."

Betta hadn't said a word. With the silent confirmation of my best friend, I knew it was real. This was happening. I was to marry Brosa.

The brush was thick around my knees, and wet. I slogged across the slope above the beach, trying to go unnoticed in the dark.

At Heirik's tent, I stopped and breathed and calmed myself. I looked up at the stars and silently asked them why they didn't come forward, witnesses. They had seen us together, in love, in the snow and wind. They'd shone above me as I walked in his footsteps, hearing my solemn promise to stay by his side. Now they stood, unmoved.

I called softly to him and then peeked inside the tent.

He sat on the big piece of driftwood in the center of the tent, his forearms resting on his thighs and his eyes to the ground, he hung pondering or in dull misery. He looked up at me, and fear shone as clear as daylight in his eyes. Fear of facing me. It broke my heart to see him look that way because of me.

"Take it back, Heirik." I told him, in a voice much like his, the way he'd told me what to do so many times.

His brows drew together, fear turning to the first glimmers of anger.

"Don't challenge me."

He spoke coldly, and so did I. "Don't give me away, like a sack of grain."

And then everything good and strong in me started to falter, and my voice wavered with one more word, all I could get out. "Why?" I sucked in a deep breath to steady myself.

He hung his head again, and it was quiet for a long while, so long that I was afraid I'd been dismissed. And then he broke the silence.

"Just hours ago," he told me, without looking at me. "You came down that hill with Betta. Your lips were stained." We'd been painting ourselves with the berries. "I could see the space in your smile."

He looked up then, eyes focused on my mouth, the gap between my front teeth. My lips opened to his gaze.

Then he continued. "You need someone who will kiss that mouth."

Brosa had comforted me two nights ago, and had kissed my mouth, yes. Kissed it so thoroughly my lips might still glow like the pink ember he'd nursed before sparks and fire took hold. His kiss was good, so easy and lush. But what was that kind of kiss worth, if Heirik was here, so close to me, for the rest of my life? Did he intend to stand by while Brosa shared every tender thing that came from my heart? Taking my hair down, placing a berry between his lips, cutting a shirt for him and tying back his hair. Making love. Lying entwined with his brother, so close that I might feel I could reach out and touch Heirik instead.

"It should be you," I told him.

"Ginn." He shook his head. "You are so good."

"The mark on your skin," I started to say, and my hand unclenched as if he'd let me trace it. But his eyes glowed with instant fury, a terrible force, and I backed up against the tent wall.

I spoke anyway. "I don't think it's a curse. I think it's just …"

I had no idea what caused such an extensive mark, and the sudden realization was strange, as though the gods were just as good an explanation as any. As though it could have been an ancestral spirit in diaphanous clothing who swept over Signé as she slept, Heirik growing fierce and strong in her womb. What force made a child grow into this man?

"A coloring in your skin," I settled on. "Nothing more."

His voice was carefully neutral. "I've promised to protect you any way I can. Do not push me to break a vow."

His eyes weren't sad. His gaze wasn't lust-sick or yearning. It was caring. And that devastated me.

"Leave me my honor," he said, ducking his head and speaking so quietly I could barely hear it. It was a request as tender as any marriage proposal. His honor was that important to him, and that delicate. The most important thing in a man's life, more vital than any one element of love or family, a bound up whole that could not be reckoned or parsed, that defined everything he was in this life and the one to come. I couldn't bear to take it from him, to break him like that.

And so I closed myself. Like a shutter, like a fan, all at once and quiet. Just as he so often closed his features and emotions, now I closed my heart, and he became no more than the chief to me.

"Já, Herra," I told him. I ducked my head and backed out of the tent.

I left him, honorable, and headed out toward the sea.

I waded down the beach from everyone, near the rocks. A dark and misty place made to be haunted by the ghosts of traders and warriors, the unchosen. I stood with my feet in the freezing water, and it seeped into my boots.

Reki. The word rose in my mind, and I spoke it out loud. A thing drifted ashore. In my tear-muffled voice it sounded like another word, rekingr. *Outcast.* The tenth century was a wilderness, and I was alone in it, sent out among animals with teeth like Svana's and sneers like Hildur's. Without Heirik's constant presence, his unstated devotion beside me. He thought he was protecting me, but tonight he'd pushed me outside his circle of light, into the bewildering dark.

My mind stumbled back to the sleeping alcove during my first day here. And it came, fear like acid in my throat, as vividly as though I'd been plunged again into the water of time. Immersed in the same confusion and terror, the cold closed on me, around my ankles. I shivered and reached my hands out in front of me and fell ungracefully to my knees. I knelt in the freezing sea, and my shift and skirts soaked up black water. Salt stung inside my nose, behind my eyes.

Tiny, cold pebbles lodged under my fingernails, and my hands began to numb. Heirik had taken honor too far, and he'd become a frozen thing. I could do that, too. Crawl into the water I came from, until a numb freeze took my breath.

Or I could go home.

The thought struck me like a blow to the head.

I'd always thought that water would be the way back. That was why I'd feared and skirted it. I hadn't wanted to go into the dark sea and hope not for frigid death, but for the cool refuge of the lab.

I looked at my hands in the water, lit in the moonlight like little fish swimming in place, never moving forward. I lifted one hand to my other wrist. I tapped out.

A ripping opened in my brain.

A howling of metal, it felt like a blade through soft, pink flesh. I saw my own hands flicker in the water, disappear and reappear like a glitch on a screen. I would go, right now. Splitting my brain, savage sounds, yes, I was going. And suddenly I didn't want to. A mistake! I threw all my weight against the pull. I struggled to my feet, ripping my hands up out of the sea, stumbling backward over heavy, wet skirts. Oh gods, I was going. It wouldn't stop.

"Ginn!" His shout came from the darkness.

He ran to me, called to me, and I stood in a blurred panic, found him. I went to him. I burrowed into Brosa's chest.

"Woman, shhh, what is wrong?"

He shushed me until I could answer. The truth, I thought. "I was so scared, alone here."

One truth, anyway.

"Oh nei, elskan mín, nei." His arms crushed me, sorry he'd failed to protect me already, and not even betrothed an hour. *My darling.* He held me tight. He was suffocatingly large and ardent and it felt good. "I won't leave your side now." He kissed the top of my head, kissed my hair, a promise.

I turned my head to rest on his chest, and looked up the beach. I saw Heirik there, and my heart sank. I felt the pressure of twelve hundred years of rightness and desire. I had traversed time to find him and no other. These strong arms, Brosa's, wouldn't work. I would always mourn Heirik.

He stood outside his tent, arms folded across his chest, looking to the sea. He appeared much as I felt. Miserable. Contemplating a numb death. Then into his solitude walked Svana.

As scared as she was of Heirik, she came to appeal to him anyway. She wanted his brother for herself. She would ask the chief to overturn this crazy decision, just as I had. I couldn't imagine she'd sway Heirik in some way that I could not. But it was worth a hope, that she'd wheedle and try.

Instead, something odd happened. I couldn't make out the words, just the song of her voice, and it was not beseeching or fearful. Her voice was lilting, happy, a little bird chirping. In his typical manner, Heirik looked away while he listened to her. He looked down the beach, and I wondered if he could see me. Me, in his brother's arms.

Then Svana brushed Heirik's wrist, as anyone might when sharing laughter, casual conversation. I could just make it out from here. Svana touched him.

Heirik didn't pull away or even stiffen with shock. He simply turned and walked beside her to the big fire.

Brosa felt me shiver and murmured "shhhh" and stroked my back. I was so lost.

"Sit with me, Litla."

I recoiled at the familiar name. Gods, it was strange how he chose that. "Please," I asked into his chest. "Please don't call me that."

He pulled back to look at my face, and then I saw comprehension and surprise grow in his eyes. I thought maybe he hadn't really understood it until just now, or believed it. That Heirik and I didn't just feel attracted to each other. We had a relationship. We were in love. Heirik had a sweet, intimate name for me.

"I will not again," he promised, and he picked me up like a child and carried me back to where it was dry. He settled me beside him. His hand was warm and confident on my chin. Sea colored eyes found mine, and he smiled his big-hearted smile. And I melted. Exhausted, distressed, needy. Soaked. I sat under the weight of his arm on my shoulders.

"Brosa" I struggled feebly. His comforting, darling nature surrounded me. I had to hurt him now, not wait until it was worse. "I love your brother, not you," I told him. "He is my heart and blood."

"I know." He was calm and unsurprised. "I have seen it."

He surprised me with his honesty in answer to mine, and with an easy pragmatism. "I don't love you, either. But my brother will not have you. And I will." He touched a finger right between my eyebrows and slowly traced the slope of my nose. Somehow it wasn't patronizing, it was slow and charming and seductive. "You and I will grow."

Gods, how far I had come. Lost in a wide universe that this man didn't even comprehend. Somewhere so different that love didn't matter to a good marriage. True love was something to give up if one had to, and new love could grow as casually and inexorably as a wildflower on a roof.

The fact that I was attracted to him was a bonus, já? That I had found and secured such a beauty as Brosa, such a profoundly happy and honorable man, was the dumbest, incredible luck.

"We will figure this out later," he said. It was a statement, not a question.

"I will hurt you," I told him.

"Já, well, let's enjoy ourselves tonight before you get started on that."

I actually smiled. In the heart of this miserable night, he made me laugh.

The morning came brisk and clear, with a fine, friendly spray off the ocean, as if it had never been a roiling beast trying to steal the chief and Áki. Trying to steal me. I walked along its edge, skirting the foam and feeling sorrier than ever in all my life. Pressure and dull pain tried to fight their way out of my skull, and I held my wrap tight around my shoulders. I'd pulled my hair together tight, but bits of it splayed and stuck to my face.

Betta bounded up behind me, loud and fast, and she threw her arm around my shoulder. "Too many horns at night, and a woman is thirsty all morning." She laughed at my expense, and surely to mask my dark mood in front of Hár's daughters.

"Too true," Thora added, looking peaked herself.

In fact, Dalla, Kit and Betta all looked drained and wan, wrung out by drink from last night's party. Svana was conspicuously absent.

They wanted to talk about me and Brosa. They wanted to say how very lucky I was, how gorgeous a husband, young and rich and strong as a boat. He would have his own ship made, they said, a rumor that floated on the morning breeze.

Everyone knew I had a strange relationship with the chief, a kind of intimacy and passion that no one wanted to imagine or examine. My betrothal to Brosa took care of that once and for all. No more swiping at charms or whispering in corners. Their sails filled with relief, they bore down on me with excited plans and questions.

My mind skimmed over the tops of their words, dipping down once in a while, listening just enough to say "hmmm" or "já, I know." I tried not to hear phrases, just looked at the sand and pictured my lover sitting on his horse by this water, his shoulders strong. I raised my eyes to the row of little caves worn into the rockface and remembered the first time we came here together, how his hand looked when I touched it for the first time, we sat right in that spot, right over there.

"My Da will marry, too."

Thora's words made me snap to attention. Hár would marry?

"I heard him myself, talking to the chief last night. He said he would not comment on Brosa, but he had the matter of his own need of a wife." Heirik and Hár had then moved too far away for her to hear more.

"To think of my old Da," Thora laughed. "And thirteen babes already. Is it not enough for his balls' pride?" She and Dalla laughed hard.

I waited a moment to be safe before glancing at Betta. Her face was a mask. She turned away and stooped to pick up a shell, while the girls chattered about who the impending wife could possibly be, from what house, and would she come to live with us, and when, until they soon ran the subject out and turned to my betrothal again.

When Betta and I had a chance, we stole off high up the slope above the beach. The moment we were far enough away, she fell to the ground in a heap of skirts. She looked up at me, and her heart was laid open.

I sat down beside her and put my arms around her, and she shook without a sound, for long moments. She drew a few deeper breaths, one more harsh inhalation, and then she spoke against my shoulder. "I knew, já?" She said. "That he was important, that he would be needed someday, for the family."

She drew back and looked down into her own lap, seeming to be fascinated with her own white fingers, how they gripped one another. "But now that it is happening, it hurts so much." Tears broke on the last few words.

I knew that stunned feeling. I knew how it felt to sit where Betta was, staring into a future without someone.

She looked around herself, behind her, as though she'd lost something, and then she lay back in the brush, her wide green eyes seeking the sky. I laid down beside her, and the heavens sat there, indifferent, a blue-steel gray above us.

How would Betta live with Hár's wife in our house? How could she go on while he held someone else right before her? How could he even do it, for that matter? Betta would need unnatural, impossible courage to watch while he walked out with his wife at night, bedded her there in the pantry, had babies upon babies. My mind raced with the horror of it. The litany of questions that applied the same to me. How would I live with my own husband?

I could never really agree to marry Brosa. When the shock passed, I would really talk with him. I would hurt him, soon. His natural smile would fade because of me.

Men—the whole idea of them—sat like a bundled ache in my stomach. I glanced at Betta and considered whether we could fall in love without them. But no, I loved her, but I didn't feel that way. I felt something so utterly different. I felt lust for, I had to admit, two brothers. Love for one.

"I knew this would come," she said to the sky. "I already stopped seeing the fool." She sat up tall, wiped her mouth with the back of her hand and blinked hard, as if to cleanse herself of sadness. But her voice was a hoarse whisper. "I just … wanted him."

The way she caressed the words, it was like she was touching Hár's face right now. I could see right into her, feel what it was like when she watched him move and smile. Someday she might have marveled at his features while he slept, perhaps seen them echoed in the face of her child.

Her heart had crashed ahead without knowing how difficult this would be. She couldn't have imagined it. I snuggled against her side, as if we rocked in the same leaky boat.

It was afternoon when Hár cut his finger off.

Betta and I came out of the woods and brush, full baskets in our hands and determination in her eyes. She'd made peace with needing to face him, and once she'd made up her mind, her courage couldn't wait. She was that little girl sometimes, the one who wanted a simple, happy life. She needed to see Hár's face to know it was true, that her hopes were over. It broke my heart to watch her tripping down the big slope toward the beach, baskets and braids swaying, me right behind.

About a third of the way down, we heard a furious bellow followed by a series of poetic Viking curses about goats' balls and troll piss, loud enough to carry a half mile. Betta dropped her baskets and ran like a scared little kid. I dropped mine too, and matched her.

If I focused on the driftwood, I didn't need to watch Hár's hand bleed, didn't have to see his finger lying in the sand. The wood looked pretty, snowy gray dripping with ruby and cherry and amber. Blood soaked his clothes, and his ax lay slick and red at his feet. We arrived just in time to see him kick it viciously out of his way, calling it something I could only translate as *incompetent cock sucker*. He stomped to the nearby fire, where men had been hammering and sharpening their blades for the past four days.

He sat on a log, as if to warm himself and contemplate the stupidity of his accident. He opened his palm and considered his left hand, now missing half its first finger. Magnus came breathlessly with a soaked cloth. Hár wrapped it—not around his wound, but around his remaining fingers, wincing only slightly though it was streaming with salt water. He curved his fingers into a fist, and without hesitation he thrust his hand into the fire.

Betta turned white as snow and sank to her knees. She rocked back onto her heels, then up again on her knees, her hands like claws in the folds of her skirt, wanting to run to him. But she stayed away. She had such an iron will.

A dozen people had gathered. Thora fussed at her father's side, and Magnus knelt to ask if Hár needed anything. Hár answered with a roar at both of them. "Get off me!" He grumbled more curses, looked around and barked "Let Betta come."

The beach became quiet. Even the relentless rhythm of the waves seemed to pause to be sure he'd said "Betta." Betta stood with great poise and without looking at anyone else, she approached him. Thora stared open-mouthed at her Da, as he melted from angry old man to tender lover at the sight. Betta knelt beside him, and took his forearm to look at his wound, but he pulled his hand away.

"My hand is no matter, Woman. I need to talk."

If it was possible, even more of the blood left her face, and she was a ghost, ready to dissipate. But she placed her hands steadily on her own knees and waited.

"You've heard I will marry."

She nodded, holding back all emotion, more controlled than I could ever be. I thought of myself just yesterday, accusing and pleading. The things I'd said to Heirik. *Don't give me away like a sack of grain.*

"I meant to talk to you before there was word," Hár told her, and his voice was gentle. Betta dropped her head, then, no longer able to bear what he was saying—giving her this speech, and in front of half the family. Her will failed, and her features crumpled with pain.

Hár was still talking, "And before this happened." He gestured at the inconvenience of his severed finger.

Then he saw her face and quickly took her by the chin with his good hand. "Nei, nei, mo chuisle, shhh." She had taught him the Gaelic words, and his voice was like I'd never imagined it could be, caressing the words, caressing Betta with them. "What are you about?" He shook his head, as if bewildered by the emotions of women. "I only wanted to know, first. If you would say yes."

Her angled brows drew together, and I watched as his words very slowly made sense to her, and then her eyes widened and she just said, "Oh."

They smiled just for each other, as if none of us were there. He cupped more of her face, covering her cheek, his fingers tracing her hairline where her tight braids began, and she tilted her head and leaned into his touch. Her hand came up to cover his, and her eyes slid shut in bliss and relief. Tears traveled down her pink cheeks.

"Well, hjarta mitt?" He added ruefully, "Are you through with me now that I have but one good hand?"

She burst out laughing, and so did all of us. And she told him she wanted to marry him.

He nodded then, that taken care of, and told her he'd need some new clothes and asked if she'd go find them.

They didn't kiss, didn't hold one another. Betta gazed up at him a bit longer, though, and it was stunning how they transformed each other. She was a gorgeous woman. And for a moment, Hár wasn't a gruff and dangerous Viking. He was a lover, a husband of the heart.

On my muddled trip home, everyone else ranged intensely high, full of joy and whale and weddings. I heard music, but it came from far behind my back and belonged to another world, a small and colorful one. Here where I rode out in front, everything was washed out, colors indistinct, clouds unmoving in a plain sky. The luminous and ever-rushing river we followed through the valley, now slogged along through new grasses and shifting mud. We walked its banks, against its course.

I pushed on up front with my betrothed, still stunned at the word. Floored by the whole experience of meeting Brosa, let alone marrying him. Whenever he shifted to walk close to me, I tensed—Drifa snorting in response and tossing her head. Didn't he see what his brother meant to me? Why did he persist with this?

Brosa tried to cheer me. He talked to me in bright and easy tones, but his voice was just a bit too smooth and light, the differences always coming to mind.

Mostly, I heard Svana's teeny yips up ahead. "Herra!" She called after Heirik and spurred her horse up behind Vakr. What could that vapid girl have to say to him?

I would not tag along after them to find out.

I'd passed hands between brothers like an ax or horse.

Back at the house, I stood at the center of a storm of horses and whale meat and fat and bones. Provisions and shouts carried past in all directions. Home now, things that happened at the sea would become real, become everyday.

In the midst of the flurry, Svana stood beside Heirik. "Let me help you," she said, and she tied the laces on his bracers. A simple gesture, at the end of a long day. Time seemed to slow down for me, every second a lifetime. I watched her hands shake as she touched him. Heard him say "Já," distracted, staring into the homefield, maybe thinking of seeds and light. Not desiring her touch, but a *yes* nonetheless.

Beyond them, the house seemed to change before my eyes, from a protective and playful creature to a closed, frigid lump. The grass shriveled and turned to gray fingers and then to solid ice. A trick of the light.

When Svana was through, Heirik looked down at his hand, flexed his fingers and shook out his wrist. What did he see when he looked down at the top of her blond head? Or into her upturned spring-sky eyes?

I watched his future start, without me.

WE DIDN'T SEE THE CHIEF AGAIN FOR FIFTEEN DAYS.

Brosa seemed to know this would happen, he fell so easily into his brother's absence. It gave us time to know each other, he told me, as if it had been arranged. And over many days, I did settle into this quiet time, too, and into Brosa. I learned to like him very much.

Brosa didn't seem to believe me when I told him we couldn't marry, could never happen. He charmingly wooed me, shooting arrows with me in the yard and walking to the stable to talk privately with the horses. He sat with me by the fire, moving closer until our bodies rested against one another and I felt heady with his presence.

As the mornings and evenings passed, I felt Heirik's absence less, felt almost disconnected from the thread of him. A sensation of freedom and sickness in my heart. When I recalled Svana touching Heirik casually, speaking gently to him, it felt like those things happened in another lifetime. Here, now, Svana's gaze would rest on me and Brosa, and her little teeth had never looked whiter.

Brosa came to me again and again like a puppy, until finally, sometimes, I played. Tonight, I agreed to walk out with him, and he'd led me halfway around the field where barley was beginning to grow. He pushed me gently back into the homefield wall, deep in this unfathomably soft spring evening.

The loam smelled damp and clean, and he cradled my face in his palm. My cheek fit into the cup of his big hand. He bent to kiss me. Undeniably delicious, his lips carried traces of after-dinner honey. His beard scratched my chin. He pressed into me now, pinned me to the wall. The pressure and weight of his body, the heaviness between his legs, carried me off. I closed my eyes.

My hands went to his hips and I found his curves so familiar. I swept his broad back with my fingers, the nape of his neck. His hair felt just like Heirik's. With one hand, I gathered it roughly in a ponytail and held it that way, and when he uttered a soft sound of desire the image was complete. For a glorious moment, it was Heirik who had me against that wall, ready to love me well, until I forgot my name.

He bent farther to kiss my collarbone, the sensitive skin above the neckline of my dress. I whimpered without thought, and it made him harder. Instinctively, I rolled my hips. They weren't a perfect god-made match, but in fairness we were standing, slipping then, melting into a grassy wall. Sliding down to the ground, my cheek against the grass, hands caught up in his hair. I was on my back, then, Brosa a gorgeous weight on top of me.

Nei, I would not.

"Stop," I told him, and this time I meant it. I pushed him away, and he drew back to search my face.

He must have seen my conviction, because he nodded and rolled off of me. He laid on his back, staring at the sky and panting like a house dog. I struggled with my skirts and sat up, my back against the homefield wall, and we both breathed and calmed ourselves. We stayed there together, slowly returning to the world—to the grass and earth and moonlight surrounding us with silver. The complaint of a goat.

It was hard to imagine a less sensual sound, and we both laughed, broken free from the trance of sex.

I sat against the wall, Brosa's head in my lap, and I stroked the hair off his forehead. It looked like gold, unstoppably sun-drenched even in the dark. His weight was simple and intimate, and holding him this way was more familiar than I expected. It was effortless, his eyes watching the sky. I traced his cheekbone with my thumb.

We didn't talk. Mainly he looked at the stars, and I looked at the field around us, the immediate grass, the darkness beyond. I indirectly looked at him, and he was breathtaking, his eyes upturned to the sky. He seemed not to notice me, not even notice my fingers in his loose hair. I didn't know what he might be seeing.

"Esa had already died when I named my son."

He said it as though he'd picked this statement casually, like a wildflower. But his voice was smaller than I'd ever heard it. Smaller than seemed possible for such a bear of a man.

He reached up to his forehead as if to stop my hand, then just held onto me there, both of our hands against his cheek. He looked into the sky, not at me, and he was so young, so lost and scared. He was back in the moment, stunned by quick grief and confusion. He told me how he'd gone to his knees beside Esa, holding her hand. Hildur had been there, had dragged him up off his knees and told him to sit on the bench.

"She told me to hurry and take him in my lap, that he would not last." Brosa absently made the sign of Thor's hammer on my hand, the same way he had blessed his child. "I wanted him to die as part of the family."

A sighing of grass in a small breeze drew my attention to the fields, the valley I knew was out there in the dark. A quiet moment passed.

"I named him Arulf," Brosa continued. I had heard this whole story from the little birds while spinning, but I knew Brosa now. Now I could imagine him in his moments of loss. He'd held the child, and named him for his own father, Ulf. "Arulf Brosuson."

Hearing the child's full name was a sharp stab. I opened my palm against Brosa's head, pressed and held him there.

"A good name," I told him through my tears.

The wall at my back sheltered us. Brosa smiled then, and turned his head to burrow into me, into the warmth of my lap. He crossed his arms on his chest and closed his eyes, lashes against my red wool dress. We could sleep here, I thought, just stay still and he could breathe deeper and slower until the waking world passed, and I could follow him and sleep, too.

"I can never replace them," I whispered into the air, my fingers finding his curls, soft like those of a little boy.

"Já, I know." He spoke into my dress. Resigned, but hopeful too, in the admitting of it.

I told Brosa, "You can't replace him, either." And it was good to hear it out loud between us. "It's okay. You're beautiful for trying."

He smiled, comfortable against me, his eyes still closed.

"What has my brother done, then?" He asked me, with a wicked smile. "Enchanted you?"

I laughed out loud, a scattering of sound. The thought of Heirik bewitching me was somehow funny.

Then I thought of the ravine and what had happened there the first time Heirik and I were ever alone together. He'd walked toward me with such intensity, and I'd backed away in fear, yet by the time we climbed the hill back home, I was lost in love. Even without my knowing it. I thought of how he'd taken me to the woods and I'd been thoroughly seduced. Not far from here, he had first called me Litla. I suddenly felt my love for Heirik as if it were a live thing. An animal, not far away, watching me and what I'd just done with Brosa.

I breathed deeply of the green and brown smells of night, and I had no answer. I leaned back into the stout wall, and Brosa snuggled into my lap, and we did fall asleep, for a while.

Little bits of sticks and grass stuck everywhere in our clothes and hair. We stood outside the door of the house and I dusted off Brosa's shoulders. I ran my fingers through his beard and the hair that fell around his face. He inhaled deeply and held his breath for a moment.

"Careful, Woman." He stopped my hand and held it to his cheek. "You'll find yourself up against a wall again." He grinned and picked a twig from my hair.

He confused my heart, messed it all up. Admitting he didn't love me, knowing I would never replace his wife, but still insisting on marrying me. And playfully offering to take me like animals against this grassy house.

"You and I are over," I told him with a smile, a kind but insistent hand against his chest, pushing him away.

"Turn around," he told me. "Put your hands on the house."

The sod was cool and yielding under my hands. He brushed me down, starting at the nape of my neck. He stopped along the way to pick out debris. The scratchy wool dress attracted every kind of grass, twig or bit of dirt. When he reached the curve of my buttocks, he brushed a little slower, easier, cupping me in one hand, and I swore I wouldn't let anything start again.

Then he smacked me good and declared me fit to go inside. I turned, put my hands against his chest to laughingly push him away, and he grabbed the back of my head. He kissed my forehead. Sweet and familiar, like an old married couple, I thought, and then shivered.

"It's a little cold, já?" A word for *triflingly chilly*, nothing at all to speak of. I felt it come from deep in his chest, where my palm rested. "We can go in."

"Just a second." I wanted to count every star, say goodnight to every one, before going back inside to smoke and body odor and my sad little bed where I dreamt of other, different futures.

The air moved, clear and delicious around us. I looked back at the sweep of the spring night sky, and there came three girls out of the dark, as though they'd sprung like land spirits from the cool valley. Dalla, Thora, Svana having a walk before bedtime. I wasn't sure how much they'd seen of our affectionate grooming, but they surely found Brosa and me in an embrace. I felt caught, guilty for enjoying him. It wasn't right to enjoy him.

He let me go so he could hold the door with exaggerated gallantry, winking at Dalla. Hár's daughters smiled sweetly as they went by. When Svana passed into the house, though, her eyes burned inside a cold and lovely face.

LOTTA TURNED FOUR YEARS OLD.

On her day, she sat cross-legged in the grass, and we did her hair in spirals and a flower crown. She bent over obediently, staring into the heart of a plucked flower the color of an egg yoke. Lotta offered her ash blond hair to Betta to comb, and it fell all around, slippery straight, so silky, it kept escaping from Betta's fingers. And Betta, whose bony hands were always competent and sure, kept dropping and losing the strands. She swore under her breath. A bitter, perfect compound phrase somewhat like *shaggy-headed skirt chaser*. She sounded a lot like Hár, and I smiled but hid it from her.

Her hands started to tremble as she picked up Lotta's hair again and spoke to me, her words focused at the house, beyond the little girl's head.

"He is sorry now that he asked for me. He made a mistake."

Betta dropped Lotta's hair, defeated, and thrust her chin into the breeze, looking far down the valley, a tear on one cheek. Lotta lifted her head, but didn't get up and run away. She waited and listened in that way of little children, invisible, absorbing everything. She twirled the wildflower.

"He takes me with his eyes, fiercer than ever," Betta pulled on a clump of grass. "But he has not walked with me, ridden out with me. He wants me," she ripped the chunk of grass out savagely. "But not as wife."

Hár had been staying as far from Betta as the house would allow. I'd seen it clearly myself and wondered about the endless tours of the walls with Magnus that kept them away for whole days, until hunger drew them home.

"Do you think he'll take the offer back?" She looked directly at me, wanting a straight answer, but also desperately craving assurance. "Pay it off?"

My brows drew together in confusion.

Oh. She thought Hár would pay her father, to dissolve the contract that had just been struck. She really thought so. Tears waited, ready in the half moons of her lower lids.

"Have you lost your mind, Woman?" I asked.

She pursed her lips, and it seemed she really wasn't sure. Couldn't even understand what I meant. I'd noticed it before—her second sight didn't work at all when it came to her own heart. To Hár.

"Betta." I shook my head. "I don't know what he does all day. But the way he looks at you. I have never seen a man's heart so exposed."

Lotta turned her little blond head over her shoulder and asked, "Is he Grandda?" She flipped the flower over and back, loosening the petals.

"Já, Child," I answered her. "Your Grandda is going to marry Betta soon," I admonished Betta with my eyes, "and be her husband forever."

Lotta nodded gravely. "Will there be a party?"

I told her já, and I took over braiding her hair. I wove a story about a big party with songs, and honey in her milk. Grandda would have a shiny sword, and there would be a pretty crown for Betta and snowblooms and she would ride in on a horse. She would look like a handmaiden of a beautiful goddess.

I heard Betta sniffling. Out of the corner of my eye, I saw her pick her own flower and slowly, carefully pluck the petals off. She gathered them in her lap, like drops of sun against her linen skirt. I could feel her relief like a great cloud clearing and letting the warmth in, bathing our skin. I stole a glance at her face, and she was smiling just a little. She might not believe me entirely, but she was okay.

The bandage was just unwieldy enough to drive Har insane, as he tried to change it himself, one-handed. He sat, grumbling, on a big upturned log, one of the few in the yard that would accommodate him. A bowl of soapy water and a pewter cup cowered at his feet.

I watched from the shadows of the door as he tried to untie the bandage, then tried again and growled louder. He stood, picked up his ax from where it gleamed in the grass. He turned to face the big log, and with a controlled rage he hacked it neatly in two.

I stepped from the doorway and shielded my eyes from the sun, walked up to him and with my full five feet and three inches I ordered him. "Sit." I gestured with my chin at the next biggest log in the yard, and he went to it. I took the sudsy bowl on my hip, the cup, which held clear water, in my hand. There was a small cup of honey, too, and new cloth.

I knelt in front of him and worked slowly on his hand, wondering how I could start to ask. Why was he ignoring Betta? I didn't know how to begin, and so the silence grew. He dropped a statement into it. An answer to a different unasked question.

"I could not watch the sons of my brother," he said. "Watch their stupidity, and not act."

He stopped then and lifted his eyes to me, and they were apologetic. But he didn't back down from what he needed to say. "I couldn't watch her go to another man." He looked far down the hill at Betta, where she played with his granddaughter, tossing a flower at her. He seemed to forget about me. "I love her too much."

This love was a word I'd never heard before I came here. It didn't appear in any of the sagas or poems and certainly not the legal documents—the words that were used and kept in public. It was private, unwritten, and I could tell in a heartbeat what it meant. A gorgeous mix of sounds and words, *cherish, want, take* all turned into a single verb. It melted my insides with the thrill of an unknown word and the depth and resonance of his voice as he gave it to her from afar. I love her, he'd said. Too much.

Suddenly I felt very, very angry at Heirik, and it came out like a black wave at Hár. I yanked on the bandage too hard, and spat my words at him. "Then where are you all day?"

He stared at me, completely blank.

"Why don't you show her? Ever since the coast—"

I stopped myself. After all my help with their clandestine meetings through the long winter, I felt comfortable with Hár. But I was snapping at the one man who had admitted his true feelings and expressed them in a proposal based only on love.

I tried for gentle curiosity. "Why do you ignore her?" I took a palmful of soapy water and bathed his hand.

"Her father." Hár winced at the burning soap. "He sits like a hawk on a branch."

I laughed out loud. He glared at me, but I laughed some more. It was too good and too easy. Relief passed through me like a tremendous, delicious wind.

I dropped my eyes so I could hide my giggles, and I watched as the bloody runoff from his wound turned the bowl pink. Staring at the swirling colors, I tried to hide my continuing laughter, but my shoulders shook quietly. I couldn't stop thinking about this prepossessing man thwarted by Betta's weak, simpy Da. This patriarch, father of thirteen, reduced to a love-stricken, horny teenager.

"But …" How could I say it kindly? Bjarn wasn't even a man, fully. He was a thrall, and Hár had a right to marry his daughter without even asking. Yet, Hár feared him? It was impossible. "… Bjarn?" His name was nearly swallowed as I tried to contain a little more mirth.

I dipped my fingers in golden honey, and it was silky, with a promise of tenacious stickiness to come. It smelled like late summer as I applied it to Hár's wound. He sucked in air and gave me an evil glance.

"Já, well, since I asked for marriage, he has grown a backbone."

I smiled and tried to be gentler. Tried to imagine how Betta would handle these beloved, damaged hands, with their promise of protection and pleasure. Hár saw Bjarn as a father, who had dreams for his daughter, no matter how far-fetched they had once seemed.

"I'm sure you could persuade Bjarn to let you take a walk with your betrothed." I tied a final knot in clean linen.

"Nei," he sighed, contemplating his fresh bandage as if his hand were new to him, and inconsequential. "He is protecting his daughter. For a man such as Bjarn, it is the greatest moment in his life."

Hár looked across the vast yard to Betta. Far down the hill with the children, she twirled, and her green skirt floated open like a trumpet flower. He looked with kind, thoughtful eyes. Then he shook his hand out once and grasped his knees, ready to get up and go back to work. With a deep breath he added, "I will not take his honor."

I looked up sharply at the echo of Heirik's words. *Leave me my honor.*

"Child," he said to me, so gently. "You must know that Heirik grieves."

It was the first time I'd heard Hár use his name. The old man smiled. "He is trying to save you and all of us." He looked around the yard and down into the valley, as if to measure what was saved, and it was impossible for me to tell whether he believed it himself. Then he added, "And he is a stubborn, stupid ass."

GATHERING

AFTER TWO WEEKS, THE AIR ALL AROUND THE HOUSE CAME ALIVE with an almost audible buzz. The exact kind of tension felt just before a bow-shot.

Brosa now went to the walls with Hár in the daytime, leaving me many hours without his warm protection. I tried to help with cooking, sewing, anything, and every time I touched a tool or bowl or spoon, Hildur would look up as though she could feel my intention, and she would hiss, "Rest, Girl. You've done enough."

Instead, I walked outside for hours, wandering in the twisty birches or sitting at the top of the sheer drop to the ravine. I squatted down to look at flowers and mosses more closely than I ever thought possible. I collected bits of pumice, pretty white florets of lichen, feathers.

In the dying sun one night, Svana and Betta walked with me. Every time Svana's pale hair and pink complexion came into view, I tensed and thought of her fingers, her hands, on Heirik. It drove me mad.

Now, we stood at our ravine, the one that I felt belonged to me and the chief. We gazed out over the twin waterfalls, Betta, Svana and I quietly standing together and listening to the rush, the two courses of water always meeting just before they hit the roiling surface.

We watched for a long while, each of us with our arms folded across our chests, as the light turned from pale sun to steel to navy blue. A velvet sky, spread out like a wing over our heads. Svana turned to me out of nowhere, her teeth flaring up tiny and white in the dusk, her words a sharp crack. "You cannot have every man in this family." She walked away in a huff and sweep of skirts, one blond braid swinging out behind.

I turned to Betta, who had a hand clasped hard over her mouth, eyes wide. I ducked my head and laughed silently, too. But ice melted down my spine. She'd gotten past Heirik's boundaries. I wondered what she was capable of, the little creature. And what she meant to do.

When the stubborn chief returned, he had ten more beastly men with him. More and more were coming along, gathering to go to the assembly, the Thing. He left them camping in the yard and spent his hours in his room, or gone off alone to the woods. He hardly met anyone's eyes, least of all mine.

Men, women and children had arrived at our house by the dozens. Among them, Eiðr came with his older niece, but not Ageirr. He hadn't shown himself since the fight on the sand.

By the day we left for the gathering, at least fifty of us set out together under a puff-clouded sky the blue of eggshells. Betta's dream come true. We would camp three nights out under the stars, and ride four days to the Thing.

Down by the river that ran just below the house, I turned Drifa back to look up once more at its snug greenness, the strong slope of its roof and sturdy doors.

"I will be back," I told the house, as if telling the dog to stay.

THE DAY STRETCHED OUT LONG AND LAZY, AND WE RODE WITH our cloaks thrown off in the sun.

The chief's family rode ahead of the crowd, and so I was surrounded by Brosa, Betta, Hár, Magnus, Svana. The sweep of sky seemed to lift and pull us along, leading a great train of people and animals. I could smell and hear the moving feast that slowly ate up the ground behind us. Voices joined and writhed, sparked with shouts and jolts of laughter. Children's cries and infants' squalls. The mellow stink of ale carried on the breeze whenever it whipped my hair forward, and the reek of sweat and horses pressed against our backs.

Ahead of us, a vast wilderness opened wide and green. The rocky ground was lush with moss and complexly layered with white and copper lichens and tufts of spring grass, stretching farther than I could see until at last it disappeared in a cloud of ever-present mist. Framed against it all, Heirik rode out far ahead, facing the landscape alone and first. Every so often he would fall back to talk with his uncle or brother. Or Svana.

The few times he came near, she spurred her horse to meet him, a little fox cub at his heels. They would talk until he turned away.

Heading across the island to the meeting place, the route was different than our familiar byway to the sea. The rocks felt wrong under Drifa's feet, and there were no stone sisters, only smaller cairns with different aspects.

"Bit-meyla." I spat the words out loud, then looked around to be sure no one had heard me. *Biting little girl.* I felt so stupid, then, I pressed my forehead into my hand.

I couldn't hear what she and Heirik talked about. Couldn't hear anything but a sound like a savage ocean in my head.

On the second afternoon, we came to a tremendous valley, miles wide. It sprawled under the sun, fuzzed with spring grass and framed on either side by woods of short, ragged trees. I walked off far ahead with Brosa, and at his side Drifa and I dropped down into that endless lawn.

His boots rustled the ankle-deep grass, and the woods' edge crackled with movement. Underbrush snapped and shivered. A pair of foxes lifted their heads as one and watched us pass. With a sudden harsh breeze, grass laid flat from our feet all the way to the horizon. Birds wheeled, threads of voices far up in the air. Snorts and hoofsteps, hundreds of them, moved behind us, always catching up yet never coming close.

Brosa walked beside Drifa and talked about boats. How long they should be, of what wood, how the planking should be layered. A good snekke had a keel ten men long. He drew the swoops and curves of hulls in the air and told me why each shape worked to slice the water, ride the whale road. The dragon's eyes and mouth should be wide open, he told me, to eat up the waves and clear the way of spirits.

He told me about the beauty of light glancing off the water, and I thought the color of his own eyes captured the idea perfectly.

"I can see it, when you tell me," I said, and he ducked his head, somehow shy after all.

Drifa matched his footsteps, keeping a slow and easy time. He told me more. About the nausea of a terrible storm, he and his crew near to death. The seething black water and freezing rain seemed impossible from where we stood now, in this warm, yellow light. He remembered the desolation of too many days afterward, not knowing if they were still on course. He spoke of the burning of frozen cheeks and cracked lips, the anguish of hunger, of not enough water. "The stink of the other fools in the boat, as you might imagine," he said, glancing back at the army that followed us.

"Then there was a day when the raven flew farther ahead," he said. "And there was home."

He looked at me with plain happiness.

"And when I got home," he said, in his way of turning everything into a bedtime story, "there was you."

"I was a surprise, já?" I smiled.

"Not by the time I got to the house." He laughed. "My brother took one minute to be sure I still lived, and then he told me about you. Many things about you. All the way from the sea to our back door."

My laughter sounded like chimes in the crisp air, so light and happy I hardly recognized it.

"He talked of me?"

"Well, já," he said, "for quite some time. I knew all about how you came to be found on the sand, how you cut an acre of grass, how bad you are at spinning thread. I knew about your voice, and your lovely blue lips."

I closed my eyes and smiled, breathed in the whisper of a breeze laced with juniper smoke and ale. I felt Drifa move underneath me, her hips dipping to one side and the next, over and over, a confident and forceful little girl. Heirik's gift to me, even before either of us understood how we felt.

"We'll camp here," Brosa said, and I opened my eyes to find I was at the center of an eddy, horses and people drawing up on every side, nosing around, milling, trying to stop for the night.

We camped in the lee of a rock at least six times my height. It loomed above our heads, encrusted with moss and copper lichens, and topped by a handful of scrawny birches. They looked black now, without a hint of green in the twilight.

Cozy inside my blankets, I lay hip to hip with Betta. No one slept near us, two weird women betrothed to important men. Clouds passed in front of the moon, obscuring its bright arc with swirls of gray and deep lilac. The light filtered through the birches' stark fingers, and my eyes drifted shut watching it, closing once, then again.

"The chief thinks you will find your family," Betta stated, waking me. "A husband you are lost from."

"Nei," I muttered. "He doesn't."

I spoke without thinking, the truth slipping out through sleepy lips. At first, she didn't say anything in return, and I almost thought she might let it go, let the words dissipate, unquestioned. But not Betta.

"What do you hide from me?"

Her voice sounded flat, dampened by our hard bed. It seemed like a simple question, but I knew her and I felt the complexity in it. She didn't mean just now. Her question was patient and old, and I wondered how long she'd seen a lie in me.

She was up on one elbow now, surveying me, and under her scrutiny, I hid. Out of habit, a trick developed at her own urging. I shielded my real self even as I turned under the covers to face her, and I dug in my heart and found one true thing I could tell her. Something that had been waiting behind my breastbone, ready to burst out one day. Now it did.

"I have lain with the chief."

Betta's face went blank.

She tilted her head like a housedog with a sore ear. She looked harder at me to try to find the joke, but I nodded. She continued to stare at me, with no wit, no chiding, no expression at all. Betta was always so easy-spoken, so funny and cutting. I felt a silly satisfaction at stunning her speechless.

"In his room?"

I laughed out loud like a joyful shout, amused that this was her question.

"Nei," I said. "Are you crazy, Woman?" I hastily added, "And don't ask, because I won't tell you where."

She laid her head back on the ground and stared up through the birch fingers, letting a long breath out through pursed lips. In the silence, I considered what she must be imagining, his body heavy over mine, what she thought he looked like without clothes. How she believed sex was accomplished at all, for that matter. She'd seen rams to ewes, and other animals, but she needed to know so much more. I was waiting for her wedding day to tell her about loving a man. Now I wondered if in her mind she saw any small bit of what had passed between me and Heirik that night.

"Things are changing," she said, moonlight sparkling in her eyes.

I could almost feel her thoughts turn, away from Heirik's body and mouth and hands all over mine. She was drawn back to the Thing, to her raging excitement about this trip, and she began talking again about how Hár told Magnus the meeting might soon split into many smaller Things across the island. "This might be the last time, Ginn!"

Through the murk of a variety of hopeless dreams, she'd struggled to get here. Past her mother's death, her move to Hvít-mörk, the mean girls, her low status, the whole ordeal of her and Hár. I pictured her slogging through muck, her mud-clogged skirts bunched in her fists, to get to this bed beneath the giant sky. On her way to the assembly! Elated to have made it, her teeth lit up brilliant in the moonlight.

Snoring rose on all sides of us, and the sussurations of dozens of whispers, punctuated with snickers and laughter. Farther off, the thread of a song. The kind of anonymous talk that gathered and dissolved and became, somehow, quieter than silence.

Betta reached for me under the covers and laid her hand low on my belly. The heat of her touch stole into my clothes.

"He has been here?" It was both a question and a statement. She still struggled to believe me.

"Já," I said. "He has been everywhere." I laughed and elbowed her, and at first her eyes went wide with shock, but then she laughed too.

I sat up and crossed my legs, not really sleepy.

"I still can't believe you," she said. "Your hands have touched … him." She picked one up and looked at my fingers. Then she dropped it, giggling, and she twisted and settled against the hard ground as if to fall asleep.

"Ageirr is not with us," I observed, drawing her awake, and letting slip one more thing that had been on my mind. I'd wondered about him this week, but I didn't have the heart to bring it up with Brosa.

"Horses would need to drag him here," Betta said, her voice muffled by wool and fur.

A cold stone bit into my thigh and I shifted. "Why?"

"Because at the law rock, they would settle their feud," she explained, patient after months of learning that there were many simple things I didn't understand. "He's not yet goaded the chief enough to raise the stakes."

She summed it up plainly. "If they settle, he can't kill Heirik."

Hearing his name in her dusky voice was a shock. I thought maybe it was the first time I'd ever heard her say it. It came easily to her, as though she'd said it herself before, but this was the first time I heard it out loud. She thought of him as human, and the warmth that stirred in me was almost enough to blot out the chill of her statement.

Ageirr could never kill Heirik, anway. Not the way Heirik fought with such calm determination, skill, controlled passion, *Slitasongr* loose in his grasp. I smiled, the moon no doubt lighting up my teeth too, leaving a dark absence between the front two.

"Oh, Ginn," Betta said, and she struggled to sit up facing me. "Please don't find anyone."

I caught her eyes, and her hands. I looked deeply and directly into her soul. I didn't know when I would tell her who I really was. Always scared of losing her, always telling myself that she was more accepting than that, I put it off until someday. And when these moments came, where it seemed right, I thought of Morgan's empty eyes, thought of the pain during the Jul festival when Betta turned away from me. And I just couldn't do it.

"Betta, hear this," I told her slowly. "I will know no one at the Thing. And not one of those people will know me."

I squeezed her hands, and I loved her more than ever for her immediate nod. She took our clasped hands to her mouth, and kissed our fists like she was turning a key.

As we got closer to the assembly, the chief and immediate family started to hang back instead of riding ahead. Brosa pulled Drifa up close to him, and we slowed our pace. We would get there last, and everything would be prepared for us. And so after days of traveling, we sauntered the last hour, my body rocking, eyes drifting closed.

We climbed a hill of dark brown boulders, the horses never wavering. We crested the top, and my eyes opened wide to see Thingvellir—this sacred place in the land.

The gods had ripped a great gash in the earth, and it dominated everything. A place where tectonic plates clashed and carved a canyon perfect for speaking. Throughout time, those plates would always diverge, break off and move away from one another until more massive cracks would open all around. Now, the small canyon's floor lay green with moss and grass. The law rock—where men would come together to make appeals and hear cases of theft and mortal insult—jutted up like the tail of a great, dry beast.

I wondered who had first discovered the acoustics here. The way sound was amplified at the law rock had changed by the time I studied voices. The land displaced, ground together and torn apart every few hundred years. The crack had deepened, and on both sides towers of shops, restaurants and apartments climbed into the sky, teetering close to the edges. A glass elevator plunged to the bottom of the rift, where, eyes twitching with information, people walked its shadowy length. *In 1789, Thingvellir was struck by a wave of earthquakes lasting ten days.*

Today, the rent was just deep enough to echo songs and laws, shallow enough to walk down into and lay among sun-touched grasses. Around it, the land spanned the horizon, a crash of black earth and deep emerald, with yellow greens flaring up throughout. The vast landscape was threaded with sparkling blue streams and rivers of all sizes, separating and joining in a twining mess, and the big lake, standing open and free under the sun. I smiled into its warmth, thrilled with the possibility of hearing people speak here.

Brosa left me to walk with Betta, and our horses waded into a stream of people. Hundreds of them, a thousand maybe. Their faces were sun and wind burnt, tough, scarred. Full of life, unlike the blank faces of the future. But the volume of them, the crush, reminded me of the city. Of sleek trains stuffed with people in the clothes of dozens of places and times. The clean usherings of subterranean transit, taking thousands of us across all of the City of Iceland. Impossible, now that I knew this place from the inside. I'd taken four days to cross a thumb's width on a map, the country around me bigger than the gods.

The only distances that mattered now were the immediate ones. To the booth where we would sleep. Here to home, in another two weeks. The distance between my hand and Betta's. She rode exactly beside me, and I closed my fingers around hers. Even with her at my side, the press of bodies made me nervous. People pushed too hard, too many of them, with their frank smells and ugly teeth. Far too many of them, like in the future.

"Heirik." I called his name softly, listening for his reassurance.

"It's okay, Ginn," Betta soothed me. She sat tall on her horse, smiling, in the midst of more people than she'd seen in her lifetime.

We reached our booth.

It sat apart at the head of a long line of living spaces. Like spacious cow byres, they sat in a neat row, built with minimal materials, a few crossed logs, dirt floors. The chief's booth spanned the space of three of them. It sprawled in luxury, as big as the house, with canvas curtains drawn back to reveal wooden cots heaped with sheepskins. A red and white cloth tarp was pulled tight to form a roof and logs were set up as benches around a cheerful fire. We set foot into our little home, our best horses following right in beside us.

Heirik nodded to the men who'd come before us and set this all up, and they bowed their heads. He handed Vakr over to one of them and then the chief disappeared into a curtained-off room in the darker depths of the booth.

The smell of meat cooking made me swoon with hunger, and the sight of the beds made my bones yearn and ache. I found my place, where a few of us women would sleep, and let the curtain drop around me. I smiled, thinking of Drifa in her place in this same house.

Brosa, Hár and Magnus talked outside the curtains, about making their beds near the entry, in case of revelers or other fools sneaking in with sticks and knives. They laughed, recalling one especially hapless drunk last year, who stumbled into Hár's cot and almost lost an arm. Instead, the man had been given more ale and propped in a corner. When he woke the next day, Hár and Heirik were sitting right before him, sharpening knives. "The dumb goat pissed himself." Hár's laugh rumbled through the booth, mixing with horses' whinnies and people calling and singing outside.

Secure at the heart of this bustling, voice-laden world, I closed my eyes.

The market sat inside the mouth of the rift. Rock faces enclosed us all around, and we pushed and scurried within. Betta and I, in our dark green and red dresses, got carried on the current of people.

She was unafraid. And not just because Magnus walked ten feet behind us. Betta lived with thirty people around, saw maybe twice that many at haying and Jul. She closed her eyes at night thinking of just one. Here there were more than a thousand, and instead of overwhelming her, they fed her energy and joy.

Naturally fearless and curious, Betta had been growing even stronger now that the one vision that terrified her—the day she would have to give up Hár—had vanished. He would be there when we returned to the booth, as solid and alive as a wall, and so she was free.

I tried to emulate her. To open my eyes and see everything. A chaos.

People, a hundred or more at a glance, sprawled outside of tents. They sold everything I could imagine wanting, and their voices rolled and pitched like the sea. They spoke of bowls and ale horns, of furs piled higher than my head. They talked about fabric in a thousand shades of ochre and brown and gray. They laughed and shouted, voices lifting up above all our heads, swirling in a great gyre.

Within them all, a single voice caught my attention. "Rakknason," someone said. "God-Maker now." My head snapped around, but I couldn't see who it was. Who was talking about him? No one had the right to speak about Heirik like that, to utter that terrible name.

I ducked under a curtain of dead birds and fish that swung on strings, past a family's cooking fire, an iron pot hanging above it. My skirts swept the ground and snagged peoples' feet. They were laughing all around me, talking about griddles, spoons, etchings in leather, discussing belts and bracers. Ale slopped everywhere, in buckets, in peoples' drinking horns, down their chins and chests. The tang of drink filled my nostrils and sat at the back of my throat. I would never find the person who'd dared to speak of him.

I raised my eyes above the throng, and saw the climb to the law rock, so patient above this seething mass.

Heirik would not go there to pay for Eiðr's hand. He would leave that be for now. Justice took time.

Betta and I had silver, more than we needed or knew what to do with. We searched for food and drink to bring back to the booth, but the market overflowed with so many things, we wandered and explored. Magnus walked protectively behind us, letting us roam and talk to every merchant.

At first, I'd resisted the idea of spending Heirik's money, any of it. I hadn't imagined there would be so many things I wanted here. Sharp spices for cooking, dried herbs for perfume and sweet bedding, and honey enough to last for years. Bins of nuts and dried fruit. Rows of tiny leather boots. One man sold knives with carved handles in the shapes of boats and animals with shining eyes.

I thought of all of Heirik's knives, gleaming at his waist, balanced in his hand and slipping through his fingers. I wanted one that fit my own palm.

"Deer antler," the man pointed at one. "And this one is hvalrif." *Rib of a whale.*

I ran my finger over the delicate twining designs carved into the bone. The blade was slim, the whole thing not much longer than my hand.

Even though Heirik hadn't handed the silver to me personally, I knew he wanted me to have it. I bought myself that knife, and a leather sheath for it, and I made room on my belt.

Minutes later, Betta and I came to a jeweler's tent. His workbench was surrounded with a dozen women cooing and pecking at beads and needle cases.

I didn't really intend to spend any money, no significant amount anyway, but the smith liked Betta and me especially. He seemed to have an inkling that we were worth more—perhaps a sense like Betta's, an ability to read the most subtle gestures or clues. And so he showed us sparkling beauty.

Hundreds of glass beads blown with the care of a skilled firebreather, spun with color and capped with silver. Men's bracelets, thick silver curves and coils that slipped and turned around and around on our small wrists.

The smith winked a bloodshot eye at us and slipped something unimaginably beautiful from under his bench. A man's torc, a twisted bronze neck ring. It was lit with the glory of a farm sunset, all amber inlays and orange sky. Translucent lavender stones were fixed as eyes within the hissing faces of two stylized cats that met at the throat. Freya's cats, I thought, and then I heard Betta's voice in my memory. Like he was watching Freya paint amber streaks in the sky.

Betta made a small sound of awe when she heard the price, and then moved on to look at more delicate things, but I saw her tracking the torc out of the corner of her eye. She seemed resigned, melancholy about it at first, and looked back only to moon. But I watched a realization creep over her like light up the wall of the house—that she was someone different now, someone whose betrothed could wear such a thing. She was someone who could buy it for him. I watched her watch the necklace.

When we had looked at everything, I drew the man aside. "I need to buy safely," I told him. "I will return with my escort for the cats' eyes." I nodded toward the bench, where he'd slipped the torc away.

His brows rose eloquently, and I imagined he wondered many things, whether I was serious, and also sane, whether I had the money, how much was on me, how far away my escort might be. His knob nose flushed red, and he actually bowed to me. Then he hissed an instruction to his wife, waved a hand anxiously for his brawny son to step forward and watch over the inventory, and brought me into his tent.

While my eyes struggled to adjust, my skin drank in the coolness and dampness of the tent. The interior air was like water, quick and soothing, and the place smelled of metal and canvas. When I could see, I noticed a dark and intensely bored boy—another son, probably—half slumped in the corner, examining a knife's edge. He looked up with faint interest.

I thought the jeweler might stutter, he was so nervous as he asked me for assurance. He needed to know I wasn't teasing. The fact that he'd even gotten his hands on the material to make that necklace was a miracle, and the piece probably represented a year's gamble to him and these big boys, to their mother.

Physical money felt strange in my hands. I dug through the clunky pieces of silver, and I gave the man a sizable down payment. He nodded and swallowed, looking like he might cry.

"Might I show you one more item, Lady?" He inclined his head and waited for my name.

"Ginn," I said. It would have to be enough. In this world, I had no more name than my own small one. My money sparkled and clinked more than anyone else's, and he was satisfied.

Clearly, I was shopping for a man, an important one, and the smith wanted to sound the depths of my love and purse. And so in the privacy of the tent, he brought out a ring.

It flared like white fire against the rough brown cloth he laid it on. I gasped and reached a finger to touch it, but couldn't, it was that stunning. I got down close to it and exhaled, my breath misting its silver surface.

I had no other name for it, but ring didn't suffice. It was more like armor. A marauder's shield of a ring. A very thick band, it wrapped once around the finger. The ends curved back to almost meet, two dragon's heads biting at each other with open mouths and searching tongues. It would span from the base of a man's finger up to his knuckle. And yet it was somehow graceful, without bulk. The band was filigreed with lines like frost flowers. A delicate, simple, deadly weapon of a ring. I pictured it on Heirik.

More than that, I wanted it for him. I wanted to cover him with this solid, gorgeous thing. I had a fugitive vision of giving it to him, pressing it onto his finger, wedding him.

But he was not mine to cover, not with my own body, not even with a fur or blanket on a cold night, and certainly not with such an intimate and possessive gift. A woman would give this ring as a symbol of raw and proud ownership over a man. I wished I had the right.

It would be bought with his own money anyway, I thought, and laughed, a bitter sound inside the hush of the tent. The dark boy rose, sudden and wary. I told him it was only a passing thought, my outburst. His ring was in no danger from me, and it was not comical at all. It was grave and precious.

The chaos of people had thinned into a steady, sluggish stream. Children ran around our legs, chickens too, and an occasional horse pushed past us, disturbing the flow.

Betta and I strolled, with no need to return to our camp for the night. I asked her to come with me to the law rock, just to listen to the voices echoing as people sang and talked inside the rift.

The angle of the sun's light was becoming sharp. Everyone's features looked tired and carved, as if from golden stone. A horse's yellow tail, hit with a ray of falling sun, became like starkly detailed straw, dry and coarse.

Into this sleepy, ambling crowd came the man. He called me.

"Gods, Ginn!" My head shot up. But he must be calling some other woman? He breathlessly pushed through shoulders and arms, leaving irritated and curious faces all turning after him, toward me. A small space opened up around me and Betta. The man stopped just inside the circle and went still, sheer amazement in his eyes.

"It is true." His voice broke, as if with relief and joy. In a sort of trance, he said, "You live." Then he shook himself and came running to me. He took me by my waist and lifted me high in the air, spinning me so hard my hair and skirts whirled. When he set me down, he looked at me with the darkest blue eyes in the world, shining with tears of happiness.

"Oh, Ginnlaug." His straight dark hair fell across his eyes, and he pushed it away. "I thought you were gone forever." He ghosted his fingers over my cheek, eyes all wide concern when he noticed my scar. "Sváss min. I heard of a lost woman here, with hair like snow, but I could not believe it was you."

I took his hand, and with great sympathy removed it from my face.

"It is not me." The words were so stupid, meaningless. Whoever this man had lost, he thought he'd found her. It was heart wrenching, awful, this widower's delusion. "I don't know you," I told him.

A rapt crowd watched us now. The man's heavy brows drew down hard as though he might cry, and then his wonder and happiness began to fall away. "But Ginn," he said. His voice was still light, but I heard something subtly wrong underneath it, some dark and slippery form gliding under the surface of a lovely stream.

"It is me, Asmund. Your husband."

My heart dropped. His eyes were full of a lifetime of love, and he was so sure, that in a disoriented moment I felt maybe I was wrong. Maybe I really did know him. He was my husband, and the 22nd century had been my amnesiac dream. I was Asmund's sváss, his shipwrecked love. But I shook my head and backed into Betta, who was warm and reassuring. Her long fingers closing around my waist reminded me of who I really was.

Asmund was still sure I belonged to him. His hand closed hard on my elbow. "Or would you rather stay with Rakknason?" The words were bitter and cold as dried fish. "Deny me for a rich house?"

The nervousness that fluttered in my chest became full blown fear. He wasn't sad, all of a sudden. He'd turned from a hopelessly grieving lover to a threat. Suspended between his grasp and Betta's, I sent her a silent plea. *Know me*, I thought. *Don't let me go.*

Asmund jerked me free of her. Betta gasped and I could feel her falter behind me, could feel her skirts twitch, physically turning between the only choices, to go or stay. I wanted her to go get help, but the idea of her leaving me here terrified me.

"Ginnlaug!" Another breathless man made it through the growing congregation. "Brother!" He addressed Asmund, astonished. "It's true, you have found her."

I pulled harder, but I couldn't shake Asmund off. The dark navy sky of his eyes turned smug. You are my wife now, his gaze seemed to say. This crowd my witness.

His brother turned and spoke to the crowd, bursting with the story. "We learned of a woman searching for one of her family." He looked at me, then, as if he were my long lost brother-in-law. "We heard you traveled with Rakknason God-Maker. Is it true, the great chieftain saved you, good sister?"

My voice shook when I answered, but I made my eyes brave and clear. I looked right at Asmund, and I used Heirik's awful name.

"Let me go now," I glanced at the man's wrist, where he held me. "Or Rakknason will make a god of you, too."

He hesitated, drew back inside himself for a second, and he seemed to be considering meeting the chief. My words hadn't been a threat, but more a warning. If he didn't let go of me soon, he would be as good as Eiðr with one precise swipe of Heirik's blade.

But instead of stepping away, Asmund made a decision. I could see him set his resolve. He grimaced and tightened his grip. His brother grasped my other elbow. Panic began to pulse in my veins. Both of them bored into me with their eyes, telling me I'd go with them, no matter how much I exclaimed or struggled.

I appealed to the crowd. "I don't know these men!" I yanked and pleaded, "Leave me alone."

I threw my weight into pulling free, fell back against Betta who caught me in her capable arms and hugged me tight. Asmund reached for my face again, and then he froze.

From behind and above him, a shining blade slid up against his cheek, the sharp edge just an inch from his throat.

"She does not know you."

Heirik's voice was calm. I looked up, and he was dark and terrifying atop Vakr's back. His short sword rested simply against Asmund's face, the steel pricking up the hair of the man's dark beard. Every bristle was defined by the sunset, and gold and purple lit up the blade that nestled there. Asmund swallowed, wanted to speak but his voice failed. He sputtered as though his throat were already cut. He slowly removed his hands from me, and without looking at his brother croaked out an order. "Let go, Mord." Mord let go of me, too, and I lurched free.

Heirik removed his blade, and Asmund turned to look up at him. Framed in bloody sunset light, Heirik looked like a wronged god. His black hair was lit with the orange flame of late sun, his wolfish eyes committed and cold. He didn't speak. His eyes let go of Asmund, done with him for the moment, and found me. I saw terror under his vicious exterior. His fear for me, that no one else could see.

He gestured with a silent, curt nod for me to get up in front of him on Vakr. Impossible. I'd never be able to climb up on Vakr in front of a crowd. All black hair and steaming breath, he seemed a hundred hands tall, Heirik a giant on his back, and I could already feel myself falling, tumbling from Heirik's grasp. Then Ginn from Hvítmörk would die. I'd be lost here, Ginnlaug, Asmund's wife.

Heirik reached for me. He put his hand out.

For a moment, his big palm, his fingers and bracers seemed unreal, and I stared dumbly. But I took his hand, and it was solid. I stepped into the stirrup and pushed off, and with ease and grace he settled me on the saddle before him. He turned Vakr to leave.

I looked back to see mayhem erupting behind us, but to me it was a roaring silence. Men running, escaping, chasing, horses upset, a chicken fluttering at their knees. Magnus had arrived on his shining horse, Faxi. Hár had come. He held Betta against his chest. I couldn't hear any of it. I put it all behind me and looked forward to wherever we might go.

We walked at a deliberate, solemn pace, and our silence cast a cold pall over the crowd. They deferred to me and Heirik, cleared a path, and then closed again, wordless, behind us.

We were away soon, out of the market, and Vakr continued to walk out past the booths and tents of the camp city, past dozens of glimmering fires and upturned faces, past a thousand big rocks, to the water. A small river ran through the plain, branching and joining other currents and waterways that cut into the dusty land in the distance. The water gleamed a deep turquoise.

We stood at its bank and watched it go by.

A cloud rolled in, white like a fox and filling half the sky. It made the sun's last light slant and shift, throwing up mysterious sparkles from underwater rocks. The bank curved, rich with moss. Big stones reached into the water, every inch covered with the green of lichens, moss, grass. Where the grass was submerged, it had died and turned gold. The river combed it like a water spirit's long hair.

Heirik and I were beyond anyone, alone. In the presence of the river, his arm slipped around my waist, and I was still. It became hard to take any more than the shallowest sips of air. Everything was heightened. Every color, the sound of the current. Heirik's chin and nose touched my hair. The sky turned dark blue. His heart beat against my back.

After a long time, we returned to the booth, me atop Vakr and Heirik walking alongside, his hand resting on his horse's mane. The sky was gray now, but the moon made it easy enough to see our path.

I did what I'd wanted to do when we walked this way long ago. I reached down and brushed Heirik's hair with my fingers, drawing it off his cheek and back behind his ear.

"This was a mistake, bringing you here," he said, but it wasn't cold. He didn't mean to shrug me off, he was just speaking his thoughts. "Magnus will take you. In the morning, you will ride." He turned his eyes to me. "Go home."

When we reached the booth, Brosa sat at the entrance tapping on his thigh with a knife. I'd never seen him anxious before. When he saw us, he surged up and came to my side, took me by the waist as I got down from Vakr. His eyes shone with relief, but also something sharp and bottomless that took me a moment to recognize. So foreign to him. Anger. He crushed me to his chest, but I hardly felt it.

I sat in my bed, blankets drawn up around me, the curtain open just enough so I could see people around the fire and hear their happy voices.

I saw Betta far across the booth, sitting on Hár's bed. Her father hadn't come on this trip, and so the old man stretched out beside her, his head propped on his elbow so he could watch her with such adoration. She took down her braids before him.

I felt everything unraveling. Everything I accidentally found here, everything I'd built and hoped for and wanted.

Hár touched a brown strand and smiled.

The strange men—Asmund and Mord—sat tied up in the back of the booth, grumbling and every once in a while shouting curses. At times Magnus would go back there and kick them and tell them to shut up. At the fire, not far from where I sat, Heirik talked with Brosa. They discussed what to do with them. I let their words wash over me, Heirik's dark voice flowing and mixing with Brosa's softer tenor.

I turned my little whalebone knife in my fingers, let it balance in my hand, flipped it the way I'd seen men do a hundred or more times. I thought I should name it, even though it was tiny and meant for cutting fish or thread.

"Brother, you know I will do anything for you," Brosa said. My knife stopped turning. His words jumped out against the soft background of nighttime murmurs. "I will give up anything you ask. But as I do this for you …"

There was a pause, a gesture I couldn't see, then Brosa continued. "She becomes mine now."

There was more. They talked about other things. But I heard nothing else over the roaring ocean in my mind.

Heirik had planned this. He'd made Brosa ask to marry me. It was his idea.

This was a mistake, he'd said. *Go home.*

Heirik meant for me to ride in the morning with Magnus, back to the house. But I started to think of another home, where no bright Faxi could carry me, where Magnus could never go.

I huddled in my blanket and made a plan, simple and dumb. I would wait until the darkest point of the short night, then say I needed to go to the stream to relieve myself, so that anyone might hear me.

I would only need to ask a stranger to confirm the direction, but I already knew the way to the sea. Even though the ground had moved and shifted over time, I could see the outlines of the place I'd visited in the far-off future. I knew the direction I'd have to look, past this lake to the ocean, and I would ride that way and keep going through rocks and rivers and trees until I reached the sand, then continue farther, all the way to the dashing waves.

In the back of the booth, where Betta and I had our bed, I sat against the wall and shook, even though I drew the wool close around me. I trembled with adrenalin, for what was to come, and with fear and sadness, teeth chattering. I sat in darkness and could see through a space in the curtain, everyone glowing rosily, seated on benches and around the little tables and upturned logs, drinking so much ale.

Egil and another man arrived, and there were shouts of welcome and an outpouring of drink. Heirik and Brosa returned from wherever they'd gone, and they sat and visited. Heirik was in a foul mood, but I watched him hide it, until finally he became lost in business and conversation. They spoke of ships, and the new man's arrival from far-off parts of Europe. They talked about trading something, a word I didn't recognize, and of loyalty and other men who were fools. I half-listened, absorbing the sounds of grave and important talk. Words that held other men's lives in the balance.

Svana went to them with a skin of ale and quietly filled their cups. She brushed Heirik's arm with her pale white hand, and he was startled, but he didn't pull away. She smiled at Heirik, and it broke my heart, so sweet and wide-eyed, so pretty. The men were taken with her.

"You haven't introduced your wife," the stranger said, following her curves with his eyes.

Svana was coy, enjoying the man's mistake. Her eyes flashed my way, and I thought she might be trying to find me in the dark, to make sure I was listening.

"You will remember Svana," the chief said to Egil. "She is a daughter of my house." And to the new man, he said. "I have no wife."

As Svana walked away, the men watched her figure, and the rich trader cocked his head to one side. "Maybe it is time you take one," he suggested to the chief. "She is old enough, já?" He rubbed his chin, where ale had leaked into his thick red beard.

Heirik looked past the man into the dark.

"Já," he said absently. "She is."

It didn't touch me. In my mind, I was already heading to the sea.

When I went, it was with Heirik's whetstone in one hand.

I crept into his bedroom, ducked past the sheet and saw the place where he would sleep later in the night. The rough wood of the booth was not our home, and this was not his real place, but the bed was a mess of sheepskins and furs that still held his impression from earlier in the day.

He'd sat right here. Had lain his head here.

I gathered the covers up in my arms, and I drew a deep breath of him, to take with me into the future. Then I stole his sharpening stone. I didn't know what I would do with it. I just wanted it.

I held it in my left hand, and with my right I took out my new knife. It needed a name before I left. It was little, and it needed a name that felt small but strong. *Swimmer* came to me, suddenly and in English.

Before I left, I swept my eyes over the sleeping women, and it was still and peaceful. I didn't even need to tell anyone I was going to the stream. The only one who saw me go was Svana, and she nodded. She would wonder when I didn't come back, but more likely she'd be relieved. Rid of me.

Drifa was inside the tent, and so I took a nameless horse that chewed on the grass outside.

I asked a woman on my way out of camp whether I was heading to the ocean, and she nodded, looking like I was impossibly stupid. I thought maybe I was just that, a wandering and stupid thing. The horse stepped carefully through a maze of tents and sleeping bodies.

I thought of Brosa, so brave. He adored and feared his big brother, did all that he asked. He would change his whole life for Heirik, give up everything he desired. And yet he'd stood up to him today and said stop. Brosa would be alright without my kiss goodbye. He could take care of himself, and without me he could build his ship and sail away.

Betta sat on the bed with Hár, safe and joyful. I couldn't face saying goodbye to her, so I just imagined her a few months from now, crowned in flowers, holding his sword in her lap on their wedding day. She would be fine, too.

My mind was already separating from them, going ahead of my body into the future.

The flat stone fit perfectly in my palm. A dark lava rock, Heirik used it for sharpening knives. It usually hung at his waist. I held it tucked inside my closed hand, just one finger holding the horse's mane.

We rode for an endless, featureless stretch of time. The sky had turned completely dark at last, and I could feel the cold coming off the ground and up the horse's legs, under my skirts. We passed right through a birch forest, on a road that was no more than a wide, cleared space in the trees. I shivered and swayed along with the horse's cadence.

A crack sounded in the woods, and my senses woke. A tail flared in the brush, a blink of white highlighted by the moon. It happened again, a long while later or maybe just a few minutes, the sound of movement. There was nothing to see. Nothing lingered.

It must have been hours later when I snapped out of my trance again. Salt slowly registered in my brain, the smell of the sea. And then I got so close, I could imagine the crashing, and then I could really hear it. The waves.

I salivated, desparately wanting what I had come for. The oblivion I would have soon.

I slipped from the horse and let it go. Eyes soft and unfocused, I struggled on foot the rest of the way. I stumbled when my skirts snagged on big pieces of driftwood. My dress collected the smaller ones, and I brought them with me back into the water, where we'd all come from, me and the sticks.

I went to my knees in the foam, and the cold struck me like a searing burn, for just a second, before my body gave up. I swayed with the water's pull, in and out. It was time.

I placed my hands in the water, then raised my fingers to my opposite wrist to tap out.

I had loved here. I'd thought I found my soul's match, my rightful place, all those serenely satisfying moments that make up a good life. The moments in the farm notes, come to life. But I'd come to a place I could study, just like I studied that book on a screen. I could hear the real language, the way I'd dreamed. Could study the gestures and emotions. But it was their place. A place of harsh logic I could intellectually understand, but that my heart couldn't weather.

Could it?

I wondered at the simple question, and I drew my submerged hand out of the water and spread it flat so I could skim the surface, foam bubbling up between my bony fingers. I rested them gently on my other wrist, just for a second so I could think.

The diary, my romantic heart, they were what I was good at.

My sweetness had the strength of ten Viking boats. Was it really broken?

I heard a splash of something big in the water. I thought the horse had followed me, but then there was a groan, a man's harsh voice cursing. Fear spasmed in my chest. I whipped my head up and saw Asmund and Mord wading through the water toward me.

They'd hunted me, and like a pursued animal, my heart raced hard and I shrieked. My hand spasmed, fingers tapped my wrist, once, twice, and I felt the familiar endless falling, the blinding pain. A serrated knife dragged through my brain.

I convulsed on the floor of an empty lab, alarms blaring on all sides.

FREEZING

The future

THE COMPANY HID ME. THEY WOULDN'T LET ME GO.

I told everything to Jeff and Morgan. I told them about my family, about the smells and sounds of the house and farm, about haying and the ocean and feasts and axes. Morgan's interest perked up around weapons and jewelry, and she listened more closely. Words tumbled out about everything, the ravine and the enormous sky.

About Heirik. I could hardly describe him. I was loved by a powerful chieftain, had been close to becoming his wife. None of those words worked.

A long stream of people wanted to talk with me, more than ever before. Programmers, physicists, historians, therapists. A reconstructive surgeon. Even the elusive, never-before-seen owners of the company sent their people. Neurologists grilled me about the sensations I'd experienced and the physical aftereffects. Costume historians asked about the exact design of my shift, which now sat in an air-tight baggie somewhere deep in this glacier. My cherry dress—the one I'd loved and lived in for so long—laid there with it, maybe hanging, freeze-dried like a fish.

Now I wore clothes like an inmate, drawstring pants, soft t-shirts. They wanted to study me, study what happened, avoid trouble, delve into possibility. I huddled the whole time everyone came and went and talked, my knees drawn up, a big pale sweater wrapped tight, my arms lost inside.

They said I would be given the best of everything, anything I wanted, as long as I stayed put. As long as I told no one else about where I'd been. As if these were choices.

They had never made it public that one of their people was missing. The secret of my disappearance became the secret of my return—and of what they now knew the tank could do.

They gave me two impeccable, frigid rooms to live in, inside the prettiest blue cave of the glacier. I didn't struggle against it. I could have lived anywhere. I burrowed into the downy blankets of those rooms and stared. Mist crawled out of air conditioning vents, high on the walls. It formed a cloud cover, as if there could ever be a sky in here.

When I asked the room, a fire sprang up in my fireplace, without scent. Without wood or smoke at all. I looked into its blue falseness and thought of Brosa, breathing life into an apricot-orange ember.

Morgan visited sometimes, and I gave her coffee and listened to her questions, over and over, about the jewelry and knives we'd seen at the market, the bracelets Heirik wore, and for which occasions. I told her about his hands.

I let my heart pour out, bloody on the white rug, telling her how powerful my love was, how I belonged at his side, at the head of my household and farm. I told her about the fight on the beach, and she asked about spears. I talked of Ageirr's hatred and grief, how I had to tell Heirik about Fjoðr. I tried to capture in words what the chief was like at feasts, that indescribable mix of angry and entitled and proud and shy. Heirik was gorgeous, I told her, even though everyone said he was so ugly. I told her about his voice, his bloody mark, his pitch-dark hair and incandescent eyes. Told her how people didn't truly see him.

She wanted to know about his ax. The manner in which its head was attached to its handle.

"Jen," she said. "He's been dead a thousand years."

I made a small plan. It wasn't an escape plan, or even a good or honorable plan at all, just a set of instructions to get my heart to stop aching.

I would read the diary, but only after a hundred days. I'd save it, with the sure knowledge that it waited in my electronic files, just as patiently as *Swimmer* waited under the mattress of my cushy bed. And then on Day 100, I would read it all, every poetic and lovely line, and I'd destroy it. I would dissolve the files in the river of time, and they would rush away in pieces so small they could never be found.

I'd destroy anything I had left. Even *Swimmer*. I'd sneak into Morgan's studio and melt my little knife. That was my plan.

I set the apartment to count down the days, telling me how far I'd come. It was the only way I knew that time passed.

On Day 29, the psychologists and surgeons agreed I was ready to heal.

A shiny light pierced my eye, followed over and over by what felt like a tiny ice pick. A bright needle. It sunk over and over into the soft skin around my eye. In the bony places, the pain was sharpest, and I gripped the edges of the clean table. Pain hovered just on the edge of bearable. The doctors removed the scars from my orbital bone, my temple.

During surgery, I thought of things past. Moments like dry leaves on a breeze, lifted and were whisked away one by one. My traveling, my bumbling efforts to learn things, to love people. Images of Betta's capable hands, Magnus's patient eyes, Hár's lean and grisly face. Images of the green and living house, the vast, sun-warmed fields stretching out from our high hill. An image of honor itself, like a cramped and huddling cloud. Hah. It thought it was so grand.

When the anesthesiologist pricked my eyelid and asked, "Can you feel this?" I said no. I lied. I didn't trust this room, without any scent. It had no colors, and none of the people looked at me. They saw me as project laid out on a sterile table, numbers in their eyes, crosshairs guiding their work.

I breathed deep and thought of the woods—their endless whiteness kissed with a million shades of apricot, rust, orange, plum, everything revealed underneath the silver and brown bark. Here I floated at the center of a featureless, odorless white world, and nothing glowed beneath.

They talked about my heart rate, respiration, and an irritated voice said "It hurts, doesn't it?"

"Nei," I told them, my words feeling blurry, a tear on my cheek. I felt a prick in my arm, a last moment of clarity before I realized they were putting me under anyway.

My eyes slid closed.

My thoughts turned like a great water creature, slowly from the past to the future. The future as I felt it, progressing from the night I left the Thing. I saw possibilities, near ones and those farther away, every one as clear and solid as though I'd gone into the tank and visited in the flesh.

Around the heartstone, Hár was whispering a scary story to the children. Svana smiled at them, as the little bodies struggled with glee and the suspense of his tale. Svana was young as a child herself, but she fed a dark-haired babe at her breast. No more than two months old, his hair black as night against her pale skin. I thought if I touched him I would feel the hard fact of his skull covered with weightless feathers of hair. They would wave with static electricity as I drew my fingers away.

Heirik came to stand behind Svana, looking down at the child with a kind of restrained delight and awe. His eyes spoke of gratitude, commitment. He slid his hand over Svana's shoulder and his thumb stroked her throat. Mine, his whole being said. He bent and dropped a kiss on her spun-sugar hair. He looked up, then, right at me, and his mouth curved in a small smile.

I saw other ways, too.

I came up out of the sea and onto the black sand again, and it was almost twilight, the sun resting on the horizon and lighting up a tremendous cloud bank with pale purples, hottest pink and gold. Against that sky, Heirik was a dark shape atop Vakr, the horse himself no more than a shadow. Drifa stood beside them, and Heirik's hand rested on her saddle where I'd ridden her so many times, as if he were touching my thigh.

I called him, and when he saw me he slipped from Vakr slowly, warily, as if I were the vision, not him. Then he came running, picking up speed. He crashed into the shallow water, dropped to his knees and pulled me urgently in. My face pressed against his chest, so tight. He murmured unintelligible, old words. He held me so hard, his shirt was in my mouth, blocking my breath. He pulled back to see me and captured my face in both his hands.

And then I really saw him. He was a broken thing, his features hard, eyes weary.

"I wait for you here," he told me in a hollow voice. His thumb was rough against my lips. "Sometimes." The word was full of terrible longing. Hours spent walking along this shoreline, knowing just where I had gone, and hoping—with absolutely no reason to hope—that I would return. His other thumb moved along the arc of my eyebrow, pressing against bone, feeling me solid and real. His eyes searched, as if he wondered, still, whether he was dreaming.

"I bring Drifa for you." He dropped his hands and his eyes, shy. His loneliness and stupid hope were wide open for me to see. Evenings spent walking this icy water's edge, an empty horse at his side.

With a great gasp, a sucking in of a thousand gallons of air, I broke the surface of my vision. I looked around wildly at the white hospital, scentless steel surrounding me. The dead eye of a machine watching my breath.

IT WOULD TAKE TIME FOR ME TO RECOVER, THEY SAID. MY LEFT eye twitched and ached under bandages, temporarily useless. I wouldn't see out of it for maybe a week, maybe more.

Long stretches of time drifted in and out of my two rooms, along with wall-sized images of the farm that I chose and discarded. I watched the arcs Jeff used in his designs. I saw the pictures of animals he would never know, animals I could now smell and taste in memory. I watched them without depth of field, indifferent goats and placid cows, eyes lost too, theirs to grazing and tricks of information and light.

I searched beyond them for different arcs. I swiped through file after file, until my soul felt blind, too. I saw a flat Scotland laced with mist, a New England town square, a cobblestone street clattering with hooves. I came upon dance halls lined with ladies in their puff-sleeved dresses and red and ochre shawls. Skip, skip, skip. Then one caught my eye. A dark-skinned man in glowing yellow shorts. The file read *Vida v. Cruz*.

I started the arc, and pre-fight excitement bloomed on the screen. Murmurs and shouts came from a packed crowd, and two fighters shifted and bounced on their toes, touched gloves, and the fight began. I remembered it suddenly, viscerally, from a year ago. I saw it on a flat screen now, on my wall, but it was the same fight I'd seen a year ago in the tank.

It was short and brutal, and when the Locust kicked Yusef Cruz, fear seized me too late. I hadn't thought about whether I might accidentally travel, the same way I had in the tank, wrenched into the Atlantic Ocean of another time. But I didn't. I remained here in the rarefied air of my room, and I watched Mateus Vida lay the championship belt at his opponent's feet.

When that fight ended, another began, without a break. And then another. I must have sat back on my bed and pulled my feet up under me, because I found myself there later, legs numb, the artificial night of the company building gathering around me. Unfolding my stiff legs, I asked the apartment, and it told me I'd watched for seven hours.

I did the same on Day 37, and then 38 and 39.

The fights overflowed my mind and senses. The purity of purpose, the raw violence, the mixture of formality and savage freedom, all soothed me. I came back time and again to that one historic fight between Vida and Cruz. I watched Vida's elegantly powerful kick until I felt like I was falling into the screen. I wanted to kick someone that way.

I tried it.

I stood in the silver void of my room and felt self-conscious, then even more stupid when I thought about it. There was no chance that anyone would see. No people came to visit me anymore, not now that I'd told Morgan everything I knew about buckles and weapons. There was no one who might watch me try to learn, who might laugh gently at me and tell me, Woman, you kick like a lame fox.

Awkward at first, wobbling with uncertainty, I kicked anyway. I tried a few times, rewinding the scene to follow the path of Vida's leg as best I could. I set the fight on repeat, and I watched the wall and kicked, again and again. I kept at it, each kick blurring into the next until my breath came in gasps and a spike of pain throbbed in my side.

I saw flashes of images in my mind, and they mixed with the pictures on the screen. Ageirr's sneer, the men chasing me at the beach. I let each picture go, as if it could be deleted from my brain, as thoroughly gone as a twice-trashed file. Delete forever. Yes.

Food tasted metallic, and people didn't come or go, so I lived on coffee and became absorbed in the old fights. I watched Mateus Vida, and dozens of other fighters. Yusef Cruz and "Cobalt" Cabral.

I pushed the furniture to the edges of the room, and after watching hours of bouts, I'd sit on the floor and watch bios about the fighters' lives, and vids of how they trained. I did a hundred or more push-ups every day, with both arms at first, sloppy, my guts swaying, and then soon I became stronger and could do them straight as a board, then with one arm. I forced myself through hundreds of sit-ups, while I watched other kinds of matches go by—Karate, Judo, any kind of fight.

The days passed by, and only the apartment's announcements made me notice the change. My arms felt wiry, and the company-issue sweats hung on my hips.

One of my favorite fighters was Shan Rush. Called the Swift, he was balletic, a true wrestler. I called up all his bouts, everything I could find.

I liked the pair of wings he had etched on his back—dark blue, drawing the eye like blood coursing over his shoulder blades. The wings of a stylized raven, outstretched, wingtips indelibly inked on his upper arms. I remembered the tattoo I had longed for a year ago. Now, the blue swan reminded me not of poetic, romantic death, but of real, everyday meanness.

Rush had a small habit of tucking his wavy black hair behind his ear. He'd punch someone savagely into submission, then stand and push a lock of hair back, such a gentle gesture. Watching one of his fights, it finally struck me why I was so drawn by him. I halted the video and read his stats along the side, *175.26 cm (5′9″)*. It had always been my guess at Heirik's height.

I swiped the video off the screen and forced myself to eat dinner.

I drew *Swimmer* out from under my mattress, just to look at it. It sparkled as always, the bone handle seemingly made for my grip.

I couldn't help it. I sought out the fight again, sought out the raven-haired wrestler, unable to keep from watching him. I looked, now, for every similarity. Rush got his opponent on the ground and punched him hard, swinging away on the edge of control, his muscles and bones moving until it almost looked like the wings worked and he was flying.

The hvalrif handle looked pale in the flickering light of the screen. *Swimmer* felt light and steady in my palm. I touched the point to the skin of my arm, to let loose a drop of blood, and as I watched it bead, I knew what I wanted to do.

I had the doctors go back over the places where my scars had been, and decorate them with my own blue-black ink. But not with the image of a raven.

Down the nape of my neck and onto my back, the powerful lines of a whale's big body dove. I imagined it moving with a giant gentleness and confidence into unknown water. The split curve of another whale's tail curled around my eye, above my brow, below my lower lid. Exaggerated, lush blue, it cupped my eye like a loving hand. A single white tendril of scar remained from my burn, a resilient mark, that became part of a blooming swirl of sea.

My wrist was encircled with more dark blue, twining sea shapes. Things that were near-runes, meaningless marks that almost, but didn't, speak of the whale road.

Later, I wished the wrist marks didn't remind me so much of Heirik's silver bracelets. They made me think of the edge of a white sleeve falling away to let my gaze and my fingers inside. I went back and had more added, until by Day 99, the stylized images of whales and nonsense climbed my arm past the points of reminder—of bracelets, of bracers, of hunting gauntlets and arm rings. Beyond all those things.

"Day 100," the room told me, when I woke.

A sharp blue ray came through the ceiling mist and pierced my eyes. This was the day that I would do it—read the farm notes and throw them away. I'd let all my love well up and flow over and then I'd stop caring about the past. I would stop dragging my fingers slowly up my wrist, my inner arm, imagining Heirik's fingers there, remembering the small moments until they blended with the tingling on my skin. Stop pressing my small knife to my arms here and there like little tests, reminders. I would be courageous. I'd face real pain.

I did it right then, like a sharp and short rip, not a long rending. I pulled the diary up and let the reading tint close over my eyes.

I lingered on the transactions first, the trades and cows and days, with a fluttering in my belly, a hesitance to read the rest. With a twitch, I turned each page of the notebook. Twelve of them. I worked my way through methodically, reading every word, saying goodbye to each one. Goodbye to juniper on the soft skin of a throat. Goodbye to hands closing on black sand, to the scent of her husband's sweat after haying. To sheep and horsies and violet skies.

My dry eyes itched. No tears came to hinder my contacts.

Sooner than I was ready, the love poem came—the last few lines of the book, written in a different hand. I kissed my fingers and tried to press them to the words, to seal them away. To put away the unknown writer's yellow birch leaves and lattice of bones, but there was no real book to touch with my moist fingers.

At the end of the diary's pages, trailed a string of random images from the ruins of the Viking house. Sewing needles, spindle whorls, a whetstone, a beaded charm, an iron ring of keys. My breath caught on those last two. Hildur came to mind. Her fingers clutching at beads or resting possessively on her keys.

I'd forced her out of my mind, hadn't thought about her in weeks, but seeing that charm, her nastiness came back like a putrid wave. Her meanness. The big ring of keys that floated on my contacts looked so much like hers. I swiped them away, but they tugged at my thoughts, and I brought them back again with a flick.

Four small iron keys hung together, made for small locks on boxes or underground stores. Two of them had flattened heads a couple inches across, lacy with filigreed designs. The other two had been formed like cylinders, to fit into barrel style locks. Another key acted more like a pick. That one was for the dairy barrels. The longest key was as long as my hand, and it curved like a twisted hair comb, folding back in on itself. It had three teeth that fit into the pantry door.

So many times she had handed it to me.

I blinked hard and then opened my eyes wide, making the image larger. During haying. That was the first time that I'd held all her keys. When we got ready for parties and feasts, I often was given one or two to handle. The day I fell into the fire. That precious morning, when I thought for just an hour that everything around me would be mine, she'd barked at me to get fish and butter. She'd held the keys out at arm's length, and they'd jangled, looking just like these.

I saw Hildur's hard marble eyes twitching. Svana had once warned me it would happen. *Careful, Woman*, she'd said. *Where the wolf's eyes are, the wolf's teeth are near.* I thought she was talking about Heirik. Now I knew that Hildur was the one I should have feared.

My heart did not race with anger. It slowed down instead.

I sat calmly in the center of my bed, almost meditative, and small moments came back to me gently, like ashes on a light breeze. Hildur saying there would be no true wife until Brosa came home. Hildur talking alone to Ageirr the day of roundup, handing him something before he rode away to chase the other men. Her startling command that made me jump and cut myself.

I remembered a door slammed on that most intimate moment, when Heirik was asking me to marry him. The very next morning, Hildur had sent me to the pantry. I recalled her wicked hand on my shoulder, and something solid underfoot. I'd thought it was a toy, but maybe not. Was it her boot that tipped me into the fire?

On my final night at the Thing, her daughter was the last to see me. Svana had nodded when I left the booth. Soon after, Asmund and Mord—who had been securely tied—followed me.

For every terrible thing that had happened to me, Hildur was there. If not in person, then in some devious and hidden way.

Like ashes, these memories accumulated, up above my chest now. The pile rose with every moment recalled. My lungs felt dry and too full.

I pictured Heirik, the brave and terrible chieftain, dead. A young man alone, carried to his bower in the earth, *Slitasongr* by his side. And this room inside a glacier was my grave. Here on this colorless, pillowy bed, I would gratefully sink. I laid back, let my fingers spread open. I let the images go from my eyes, so that all I saw was the featureless ceiling.

"Jen."

I sat up with a jolt.

Jeff's voice called from everywhere in the air around me, the whole room amplifying him. "You need to come down to the lab. I have something to show you … off your contacts."

Jeff hadn't stopped trying to find something, anything, he could pull from my wrecked and shriveled contacts. They'd kept recording for some time, at the beach, before running out of power. He could see the record, but not the content, and so he kept working with them, on and off for these hundred days. A nerd's dream, unlocking the evidence of time travel by digging into a midden of broken code.

I walked, stunned, down the hallways, my anger at Hildur a stone in my throat that I had yet to swallow. I wondered what Jeff had found. I had no idea how big this accomplishment was. Maybe it would be a single grainy image. Tenth century seaweed. A rock. Mist from the air conditioning hovered above my head, and I pulled my sweater tight around me, locking my arms across my chest.

The wall-sized screen waited, black and full of possibility, while Jeff mumbled commands. Morgan stood beside him silently, and I thought about what she might hope to see. A knife or arrowhead. She didn't look at me, just the wall. Some code went skittering across it, a bright light flared, and then it was our beach.

The black sand. Somewhere near the fishing camp. The scene was life-sized, just as it had looked to me when I woke there.

Captivated, my eyes felt round, my mind slack.

The image cut out and came back a few times, with some slightly different angles on the ebony ground and silver driftwood. My hands clawed the beach, blue and clumsy. I was watching my own fingertips struggle. Waves pounded constantly, water churning and foaming, wind moaning, a dumbfounding rage of sound.

Then sharp voices made it through, and Hár and Arn were leaning over me.

Oh, Hár! I miss you. I went to my knees on the floor of the lab and watched as if I were there again, on the ground before the old man.

"She's alive," he called. He and Arn backed away, and Heirik came and knelt before me.

I choked with longing, one hand to my chest, the other reaching for him. There he was, Undra Min. As frightening as the first time I saw him. A man the colors of wings and straw. Of blood. A touch of a smile came, brief on his lips, and I saw it—what I hadn't seen then. From that very moment, he'd wanted me.

"My God, Jen, is he—"

"—Don't!" I interrupted Morgan. My voice was vicious, my eyes intent on Heirik. "Don't talk about him."

I moved toward him on my knees until I could press my forehead to the screen, right where he would kiss me. The picture laid flat under my hand. There was none of his scent, no fox fur or iron. My breath did not stir his hair.

The sounds of the lab gave way to those from home. I heard the complexity within breezes, the whuffles and snorts of animals, soft susurrations of the house. The grass would be long on it by now, and emerald green. It would move with the air currents in silky waves. I closed my eyes and imagined the crackling of fire and water. I heard the sound of Betta breathing, lying in the brush next to me in the hours before she faced Hár on the beach. The rhythm was slow and steady, the confident life force of a young woman who, from where I knelt now, had been dead for over a thousand years.

Life was quick. But single moments could open and flower, and bits of time that fit between breaths could expand or deepen endlessly. Twenty years with Hár, a part of each day, maybe 20,000 hours in his arms, weighed against that single terrifying moment when Betta knelt before him and silently asked Please, don't hurt me. Love me.

Gods, I was a coward. Raven starver. And so was my man. The chief and I could do better than this.

"I'm coming for you." I let the words go softly, but they didn't find Heirik. My breath came back to me. His image disappeared from under my palm.

Morgan's studio was warm and redolent with scents of burning wood and metal. She'd called me here, on the last morning of my life in this time. I didn't know why. Maybe to grill me one more time about the tools and all the silver I'd seen. I'd already told her about everything I could remember. About the many knives and hatchets and scythes, the keys, the torcs and bracelets, even the ring I wanted so much for Heirik.

But she didn't ask me anything. She messed with something on her back work table, polishing something small in her hand.

Maybe I was here to say goodbye, then? She didn't want to take the time to come down to the lab and see me off.

I waded into her haphazard place. Gods, what would Heirik think of it? What would he make of the great contrasts, the offhand wealth and filth in one stroke? Strata of junk and clothing and abundant food came with this life. A pair of flip flops moldered on the workbench next to the finest tools, shining and unimaginably precise. A lifetime of silver—even for someone as rich as Heirik—scattered on every surface, even the floor. A fine film of mold sloshed gently when I touched a coffee cup. He was thoughtful, his things minimal, ordered. He worked with plain tools, sharpened by his own hands. When he toiled in summer's night, it was only by the light of the midnight sun, not a diode.

I ran my fingers over a finely honed hatchet. I thought he might like this place, actually. He was so curious, he would be open. Confused by the people of this time, já, but not entirely. He knew about hiding emotion so deep it ceased to exist.

"Come, see this," Morgan said. She cleared the worktable with the back of her hand and set down a ring.

Plainer and simpler than the original, but still finely detailed. She'd changed the scrolling filigree to just a few strokes embossed in the silver—the firework forms of snowblooms. So subtly wrought, pure emotion came from just a few contours and lines. The dragon heads had become stylized, suggestions of wolves. The mouths searched in savage anger, and yet somehow I felt they teetered on the edge of a snarling, open-mouthed kiss.

The ring was gloriously big and strong. I'd explored Heirik's hand with mine, and I thought about the size of his ring finger. My heart was laid open, and I was back there on the beach, my fingers on his laces, under his sleeve, his fingers in my mouth.

Morgan had made this for me to give to Heirik. I stood silently and deeply stunned. She would craft something so beautiful for me? I thought of Jeff, too. Jeff would break into the sealed lab to try to send me. I'd spent most of my life in this cold and inhospitable future. Here at the last minute, I was loved?

It wouldn't make me stay. Nei, I was made for a different world. This time I wouldn't fall into it. I would dive.

The ring was easy in my palm, with an inner hum.

"You look … pretty," Jeff said over the sound system, from behind the glass partition that separated us, his voice volleying and landing in the corners of the lab.

His skin flickered with blue and white lines reflected from the screens he watched. He was reading double, data in his palm and in his eyes, and it made his focus strange, his mien like a lost and starving ghost.

He looked up and smiled a lopsided, cute smile.

I lifted my right hand to him, palm out, and waved my fingers.

It was sweet of him to lie, but I knew I didn't. I'd looked in the mirror one last time. I was the angel of death, in a dress that swept the ground like night. A black fur rose bearlike and formidable around my shoulders and the back of my neck. A tendril of white scar marred my cheek, my pale face and neck wreathed with images of wrecks. The split tail that swept my orbital bone, a great body, hidden, diving down the nape of my neck. Grim determination focused my eyes, which really did look like ice. My mouth looked like Heirik's, resolute. I would be terrifying to anyone but him.

I would have another, plainer dress when I had settled things. A happy dress. But this was the one I needed to travel. I'd sewn Heirik's ring inside my sleeve, the stitches tight and protective, made with my needle from home. The leather purse at my waist held three small satsuma oranges, and my needle case rattled with kale seeds. The only things from this time that I wanted to share.

On a chain around my left wrist, I carried a little metal cage, small enough to fit in two hands. It swung, hidden inside my draping, midnight sleeve. A real, tiny rabbit bumped around inside.

I'd gotten it from a fanatic realist, the last thing I needed before I could go. I felt its little nose poke through the bars and sniff at my fingertips.

Jeff's smile was gone, his eyes back on his sets of numbers, or whatever he looked at. I didn't know what variables such a man considered. Not wind and weather and walls.

While he readied these unknowable factors, I knelt in the lab, ready to welcome the sensation of a pummeling wash, a river, the way the tank always felt. I waited for it, and I said goodbye to many things. To glass windows, to the brilliant splash of blue-green filtered sunlight in my apartment, the humming that passed for silence. I said goodbye forever to coffee and strawberries, to afternoon naps on a cushioned couch, to the brays and croaks of city crows. All the things I felt I had to say goodbye to, even though I would not miss them. They were already absurd. Receding as though some part of me was already a hundred years away, a thousand, almost there.

I reached into my sleeve and set the tiny cage on the floor.

The rabbit fit into my hand, vibrating and silky, and when it sniffed at my palm it tickled. I exhaled on its fur and the little hairs splayed out and caught the lab light. I held the cold of Swimmer in my hand, and I appealed to several gods and goddesses, one by one. To Freyr—the first god I had seen come alive in Heirik's flesh. And to Saga, who drank from the water of time, who could see the past and the future in its currents. She could send me upstream, I was sure, and so I beseeched her. Let me get there. I would do the rest, whatever needed to be done. Just deliver me. And I appealed to Lofn, who removed all obstacles for lovers. Please, I begged her as I watched the rabbit's blood seep across the white lab floor.

I immersed my hands.

A house sprang up around me. Mean and plain compared to mine, the heartstone cold at my knees. I brought two soaked fingers to my lips. Let him have waited for me.

SWIMMER

Early Summer

I OPENED MY EYES TO THE TENTH CENTURY SEA. I WAS HERE. THE tank had taken me back.

I knelt at the water's edge, swaying, entranced by the ruffly white edges of waves. The sky was eggshell gray, just becoming light. I struggled to stay upright but my head reeled and echoed with the metal screeching and the calls of real birds, swarming overhead.

My stomach clenched. Was it the right time? The right place?

Splashing came from close by. Someone was here with me, coming toward me through the water. Heirik! It was just like my anesthesia-laced dream. He was here. He had been longing for me, waiting by the water. With great resolve, I lifted the weight of my head to turn to him.

Asmund and Mord waded toward me.

They stopped dead, their mouths falling open. Mine did, too.

Last time through, I'd been barely, intermittently conscious. Right now, even with all my preparation and grim resolve, I was slipping from all thought and sense. My head wanted to thud down on the sand.

In all the plans I'd made, the ones where I braved the disorientation, the frigid sea, the mile to the fishing camp, I was alone. In my mind, I gathered myself up and I walked, graceful and resolved, a hundred pounds of midnight dress dragging a snail's path in the wet sand. My wake filled up slowly behind me with dark seawater. I would get a horse at the camp, a white one, fast and strong, and I would ride and ride.

Of all those plans and dreams, not one included this. I never thought about returning in the very same moment I left.

We looked at each other from a safe distance. Asmund and Mord had been chasing me for a hundred and one days. Or—I stopped at the sudden disorientation—just one. One full and dangerous day at the Thing.

They'd escaped our booth, no doubt untied by Svana, and followed me all night, putting their lives at risk to capture me. Now, just a house-length away from their goal, they stood stunned. They didn't come any closer. The last fingers of waves came and wrapped around their ankles.

Oh.

In a flash, I saw myself as they did. I had been gone for months. I'd painted my body, healed my hand, learned to fight in my cold room. I'd spent lonely hours walking the halls of the glacier. To Mord and Asmund, I had just changed in a single breath. My cheerful dress had turned to death in the ocean's foam. My ghastly scars had transformed into ink. The tail of a beautiful wreck erupted on my face, dark blue fins blooming suddenly on my cheek, encircling my angry eye.

Asmund seemed to make the decision first, that he would carry out his job no matter.

He started toward me. Mord followed a moment later, taking on Asmund's bravery. They were afraid of me, but they couldn't stop. They wouldn't.

I staggered to my feet to fight.

I could still feel the raw ripping in my brain, hear the echoes of the metal shearing with the force of two ships grinding together. Wet from the knees down, my dress was a morbid tangle. My legs caught up in it, and I stumbled and went down. I fell on my cheek and salt water stung my sinuses. I watched wet boots come toward me. They made sucking depressions in the sand. One of the men gripped my shoulder like iron. I felt a rope around my wrists, and I blacked out.

I woke on a moving horse. Unlike my first evening ride in this land, no tender Viking held me up, no flying Byr took me home. This animal was slow and tired, and it flung its head frequently, trying to nip at my legs. Ropes cut into my wrists, and Swimmer was gone. I saw Asmund drop it into the pocket of a leather bag.

He walked several feet away, leading my horse by a rope, careful not to touch me. He had tied my hands in front so I could grip the horse's dirty mane. Mord rode on another swaybacked animal. We didn't talk all day.

My thighs, out of practice, became miserably sore. As the hours went by, I secretly worked the rope around my wrists, though it sawed the skin right off. When I got tired, I had to concentrate on staying upright, tangling my fingers in thick horse hair. Finally, I laid down over the animal's back, my cheek laid against her scratchy hair that smelled of neglect, of carelessness. I whispered to her that she was a good girl.

At this unnatural angle, I watched the ground go by, lichen by lichen. Small shots of adrenalin pulsed through me every time I thought of Hildur's wrinkled face, Svana's sharp teeth. For half the day I was stone bored. The other half my heart dripped with rage.

I couldn't help review it all again and again. I had watched Svana. She trembled when she touched the chief. She had become fascinated, but she didn't really want him.

Her mother did.

Hildur had worked for Heirik a long time, always in charge and yet never truly. Never powerful, like a real lady of the house. I imagined her building a bitter dream of scraping her way up to own everything. Svana, so pretty, was her ticket. Brosa would return from trading, Svana would capture his heart. Ageirr would help get Heirik out of the way, goading him until he escalated their fight. Finally, the chief would give Ageirr the license to kill him.

Except that I washed up out of the ocean and changed everything. The chief did the unthinkable and fell in love.

When Hildur succeeded in getting him to push me away, I was immediately handed to Brosa. Hildur watched everything crumble. In desperation and against her deepest beliefs, she sent her little girl in to beguile the disgusting and dreadful chief. The most powerful one.

I had come so far, and for what? To be tied up like this? Taken far from home and family?

Nei, not a chance. I had come back to live in my true home, and I would get there. I had come for this time and place. To see this sky. To challenge Heirik to give all his courage and honor to me.

With all my strength, I sat up to look, and the air seemed to lift an epic sweep of pink and flame-blue clouds until they spanned above us all. They looked solid as the land, their surfaces rough, etched with orange and gold. A spring sunset over lava rocks that stretched forever, covered with moss and cradling the light in a million tiny crannies. I breathed and watched the giant sky, until my eyes turned glassy and my head became light with beauty.

We came to a small stream and Asmund untied me, so I could take a break.

Squatting beside the stream, my enormous wet dress snagged on the underbrush. It would trip me and tangle me up if I tried to run. I looked around, scanning for anywhere to go, any way to hide. There was nothing. Twisted trees stood everywhere, all in leaf, but the forest was sparse and I could see far in toward its heart.

I had no idea where on the island I might be. To get away, I would definitely need a horse.

When I returned, Asmund gruffly told me to give him my wrists. He tied me with the rope, and I did not wince when it bit my open skin.

"Think of your own wrists." I spoke calmly. "When you meet Rakknason."

"Shut up, Witch," he told me, his voice shivering, though it was not cold.

We spoke less and less.

I frightened them, and they didn't touch me any more than they had to. I did nothing extra to scare them, only existed with my terrible clothes and skin and eyes, just like Heirik.

We stopped to camp. Asmund watched over me, sitting bleary-eyed, trembling. In charge for the night. He watched me, until I pretended to drop off into dreams. I slowed my breathing and became as patient as a stone. I heard him shifting around in the dirt, pushing at the fire with his boot, dropping in more wood. And after a long time, I heard him stop.

I opened one eye the smallest amount and saw that he was asleep. Mord snored on the other side of the fire, curled like a raggy bundle.

Asmund's leather bag was nearby, not too far. I crawled to it, two hands at once, then each knee, stopping so many breathless times to watch and listen as the men stirred. I seemed to creep forward for hours, each inch toward the bag stretching out like a mile. But they didn't wake. They were exhausted and slept like the dead.

With both hands, I tipped the bag over and Swimmer fell out. Merely a sliver compared to a man's seax, still the knife felt alive and strong to my touch. Morgan had sharpened it, and her edge gleamed with 22nd century precision. A few rusty traces of rabbit blood remained, reminding me of my capabilities. My intent.

I flipped it in my fingertips like Heirik would, and I tried to channel his grace and intention. Rather than watch, I closed my eyes and felt what I was doing. Felt the tip of the knife slide under the rope. At an odd and clumsy angle, I could get only the slightest pressure against the bindings, so I sawed gently, focused, forever. My tongue stuck into the corner of my mouth, the slumbering men almost forgotten in the task of doing this complex and real and heart-stopping task. It became contemplative, and the pain of rubbing wrist-skin burned, like mowing my acre.

When it was done, I didn't waste a second. I took the bag, took both horses, and left.

By the time I heard the shouting behind me, it was far-off, like unimportant birds.

In my daydreams, I always approached home in daylight. Dress and hair flying under an orange midsummer sky, I would reach the house. I would see it, beckoning green and yellow in the fall sun.

But it was spring, unexpected and dusky. I rode in the chill of bluish gray, still wet, freezing. I knew I was pointed away from the ocean, and with only that knowledge, I rode as fast as I dared. Every few minutes, I felt like I wanted to surge ahead, and yet felt acutely how alone I was, how I could be, right now, drifting so far off course I might never be found. Swimming down deeper instead of up, toward the air.

My eyes ached watching the darkening horizon, willing one of the cairns to appear—the ones I'd seen on the way to the Thing, on the way to the coast, anywhere, any combination of rocks that pointed the way to Hvítmörk.

The horse's ribs expanded and fell in a hard rhythm under me. She was tired. The second horse kept pace, watching me with one wary eye.

After more hours than the horses and I could stand, we topped what seemed like the hundredth small rise. I dragged my gaze up to look ahead, knowing I would see more of nothing ahead of us, and yet hoping for something. I held my breath and appealed to Saga. I've come, I told her.

And I saw them, like giants moving against the night. The stone sisters.

My heart soared like a hawk, and then my chest contracted and I sobbed, a rasping, empty sound. Fear and anger and uncertainty had blasted through me, leaving me hollow, and now the promise of home filled every space. Now I knew. I would get there. Not tonight, but I would.

I dropped down off the nameless horse, and the three of us stumbled the last mile, near to collapse with exhaustion. We made it to the base of one of the giant women. A pool of warm water barely touched the earth's surface, just enough for us to drink mouthfuls that tasted of sulfur and wet wool. The animals chewed weeds. I rummaged in Asmund's bag and found dried fish. I would be able to eat, too.

Leaning against the terrifying maiden, her head looming high above me, I crunched on fish and named the horses. Rifs, Plunder, would be the bony one, because I'd stolen such a fine girl. Lisi was the one who watched me all day. It meant something like Small Fish. They chewed and nosed close to me, and I wrapped their reigns around my wrists. I laid down next to the little pool and watched the sun drop from the sky. We would rest, and then I'd switch horses. That simple plan was all that remained in the world. I laughed at how easy it sounded, as my eyes drifted closed.

The next day, I put the stone women on my left and followed their path home.

The house sat curled into the hills, the grass on its roof blending with the land around it. It waited for me, a patient animal. In my delirious hunger and desire for this place, I could feel it perk its ears up like a giant beast and know my presence.

The horses and I crossed our river at its narrowest point. They walked right through it without a second thought, and my skirt hems skimmed the water. We rode up the path, past homefield and cows and sheep. As we got closer, the chickens came to regard us with their cocked heads.

I felt satisfaction. No skyward reaching of my heart, like when I'd spotted the great stone sisters. Not the outpouring of wonder and elation I'd felt at seeing the vast and velvet sky, the safety and glory of Hvítmörk. None of those things I'd imagined I would feel. Just a sense of numb completion. I was here.

Hildur stepped up to the threshold.

Vaguely aware of a handful of people in the yard, I saw only her pinched and vile face. I dropped down from the horse without taking my eyes from her, and I began to cross the yard, my dark skirts ragged from sleeping on rocks, a hundred and three days of hunger and pain in my chest. Every ragged edge of my heart was her work. Every brittle icicle that was left in my soul had been shaped by her. It was too much, her daring to stand there in my place.

She backed away as I approached, backed into the mudroom, her face gone white as a spirit. I followed her calmly, as she fled into the house. She was afraid of me. Good.

In the hearth room, with nowhere else to go, she stopped and faced me, and from a sheath at her belt she drew a knife. Like Swimmer, it was a cooking knife, no longer than a hand. Made to cut the heads off fish. But she raised it to me as though it were a battleax.

I'd always been docile. Even as Hildur's eyes widened in fear as they roamed my face and dress, I could tell she still thought of me as little Ginn, the one who mooned over the chief and let myself be hurt at every turn. I had always been the weak and yearning one, full of hope and love. My strength was in my capacity for those sad and romantic notions.

Not for this.

I breathed in, and even as my foot traveled, I saw the whole movement as though complete. I felt my leg unfold, my skirt a massive blue-black wing that traced the shape of my kick, defined it in the air. It was the most graceful thing I'd ever done. I felt the connection, and could hear it, too—the moist, solid crack of bone.

I kicked Hildur, and I watched her face crumple, watched her fall. Her head bounced hard off a bench and she was down.

I drew Swimmer and calmly gripped it, not even breathing heavy. The little knife glinted with confident intent, an invitation to fuck with me. But no one else here would.

I looked around, finally, and they were my family, the ones who hadn't gone to the assembly. Ageirr wasn't here. Heirik wasn't either. He would still be at the Thing.

There was no sound from anyone, especially Hildur. I glanced down and took in the sight of her flat on the floor, almost lifeless but for a stuttering, shallow rise and fall of her chest. With my free hand, I drew up my hems and gently prodded her with my foot. She was out like a stone. I used my toe to roll her onto her back. My kick had distorted her face, her jaw was shaped wrong and blood leaked from her nose.

She would be out for a while, maybe forever, but I placed my boot on her chest, in case she woke.

THIRST

HORSES APPROACHED SO FAST AND LOUD I HEARD THEM THROUGH the thick house and felt them rattle my bones. I heard Hár and Magnus calling from the yard. The boy's beloved, newly dark voice, his father's rasping call.

And then I heard Heirik. Just outside, angry and rumbling. "Ginn!" He commanded me, even now, to answer.

My pulse quickened. I'd made it, finally, all the way. I made it past months of pain, past the lab and back through 1200 years, past Asmund and Mord, past Hildur, through woods and streams, through time and fear itself, to be here where I stood right now. Separated from him by only our front door.

My pulse quickened, but nothing more. No great outpouring of love. No great emotion at all. It was like a fear response in my animal chest, cold and ready. He stepped into the house, breathless, searching for me, and I saw him for the first time in so long.

Everything slowed like in a fighting sim. He turned toward me, as if he were in a virtual cage match, suspended. He gripped Slitasongr lightly, his hand bigger than I remembered, skin blood red, fingernails black with dirt. He stood ungraceful and exhausted, his hair a horrible mess, stuck in strands across his forehead. I noted his dark brows and desperate, scared eyes searching the room for me.

He thought he'd lost me.

He had no idea.

Somewhere deep I had been bracing myself. I'd come home for honor's sake, for vindication, to release my pain and the chief's. But I also came to be with him, to try one more time to be lovers, and to have him by my side. I came to challenge him.

It wasn't tenderness, not romance, or even simple lust. He was just mine, and I was here for all that was mine.

I stood before him, dressed in death, ink soaked into my skin, cold clarity in my eyes, and I waited. I waited, and time resumed, slowly, languidly enough that I saw everything register. The shock as he took me in, his eyes traveling over my face, dress, hands. Knowledge growing, the spark of realization, that I must have gone to my other place and time. Gone long enough to change. Then his face transformed with a lightening wonder that would have charmed me four months ago. A look in his eyes that would have melted me.

"You returned," he said.

"This is my place," I told him, and it wasn't unkind, but I could hear no warmth in my own voice. "She tried to take it from me."

Heirik followed my gaze to the floor, where I held Hildur under my foot, and his eyes widened. He grinned, and it seemed the sun filled the house. Já, he thought this was wonderful.

For him, anxious hours had passed. A few days of heart-stopping fear that I might be hurt or dead, two days of anguished remorse, maybe. For me, it had been months. I'd felt bone-crushing regret. I'd grieved for so long. I'd felt my own eyes slide closed and give up to the false, flat world. And I had let them.

My relief at seeing him was tempered by all these things that had passed.

In all the time I'd prepared for this moment, I'd thought of a hundred ways to start. I'd thought maybe love would rush fast and free inside me and the past hundred days would fall away in a tangle of bodies and mouths and pledges and endearments. I thought of simply touching him and saying nothing at all, just reaching for his cheek, brushing his beard with my fingers. I thought of telling him that a glimpse of his face on a cold screen was able to wake me, when nothing else could. I imagined starting off by telling him I loved him.

"You think you are a god maker," is what I said. "You're not. You are a man."

He took a step back and cocked his head as if he hadn't heard me correctly. Brosa came up beside him, breathless, concern across his features, changing to confused wonder when he laid eyes on me.

"Woman, what—" Brosa started, but I didn't let him speak. I'd risked my life, with a desperate hope that Saga might bring me here again, and now I would say everything I needed to say. I spoke to Heirik.

"—Ageirr and Hildur are responsible for every bad thing that has happened to me. For stealing me away, for my burns and injuries. Ageirr," I said, looking around the house, though I knew he was not there. "Hildur." I spat her name, pushing at her with my boot. "Not your curse, Heirik. You are not special like that. You are real."

Heirik just shook his head and found nothing he could say. Unreadable, even to my eyes. So I went on.

"They have taken so much from us." My voice was clear like a polar morning. "If we remove them from this life, it will release us."

The air went unnaturally still, everyone waiting.

I watched Heirik closely, watched all the small motions of his features and moods that I knew like no one else. He was fascinated, and he was considering. Like a season shifting in the course of a minute, his eyes turned from golden wonder to ice-cold rage, not at me, but at Hildur and Ageirr. I watched him come to agree with me, and it was like pure fire in my veins.

"Já," he said, and that one word was vindication, promise, love song. It contained all of his belief in me, his agreement, his wish for justice. "I will find Ageirr."

It was quiet for the briefest moment. Unstated words hung heavy, as if he'd really spoken them and they'd taken solid form. I will kill him, the very air seemed to say. And more. I will do whatever it takes. Even die. There was always that chance, even though he flew like a demon in a fight. The chance that Heirik might not come back.

His features changed before my eyes, from anger to fear.

He was afraid? I'd seen him swing his gorgeous ax and cut down men all around, seen him throw a spear with cold precision. But he looked, right now, as though this was the most terrifying moment of his life. Was he hesitating to fight Ageirr? After all the man had done?

After a silence, and a painful breath, two breaths, Heirik spoke. "Be my wife."

Oh. Heirik didn't tremble in the face of death. Only before me.

He stepped close to me, finally, and it was him, my love, touching my face, tracing the tail that curved around my eye. "If only for a moment, Woman. Let us know what it's like."

I wished for joy. I wished that the softest and sweetest love would rush in, filling me with warmth and relief and the impossible glory of yearning fulfilled. But what I felt was a cold kind of rightness. It was done. I thought I should be angry. This—Heirik being brave and mine—was all I had wanted, all the time I had known him, and he could never give it to me. Now here he stood, making it seem so simple. Now, after I'd put away hope and happiness with my farm notes and cherry dress. My whole body thrilled with anger.

A thousand times over I would marry him.

"Já, then," I told him. "Be my husband."

Only after I'd said yes, did I think to look toward Brosa. His words rang in my mind. She becomes mine now. I owed him an honorable breaking of our contract. He stood, back against the wall, arms crossed over his chest, and at first I thought he was shaking with anger. Then I realized it was with amusement, barely restrained laughter. When I caught his gaze, he raised an eyebrow, and then nodded to me. His blessing.

"Uncle," Heirik called in a massive bellow as we left the house. "Marry us now."

Hár looked up from where he stood talking to Byr, and his bushy brows drew together, his mouth opened to speak. But he didn't. He just looked at me dumbstruck. Finally, he turned to Heirik and nodded.

Hár called on our gods to make this marriage strong, all the while watching me, scanning my face with frank bewilderment. He joined us with the shortest possible ceremony that would suffice for the few witnesses. When the time came, I sat on an upturned log and Heirik placed Slitasongr in my lap like a babe. "For our sons," he said with teeth gritted. At the threshold of death, he would give me such a thing.

Heirik turned to formally tell the few who stood around us. "Ginn is wife of our house now. Make sure this is respected."

"Nei—!" An ugly screech came from the threshold. Hildur staggered, bloodied, out into the yard.

Magnus grabbed her by the arm and pledged, "I will make sure, Herra." It sounded like a final vow.

Heirik bent to kiss me, and I met him with a kiss as empty as a shell. He asked for more. "Give me your sweetness, Litla."

"It's been too hard for me," I told him with clear, dry eyes. "I've given up sweetness."

He looked for a long moment, searched my face and I could tell he found nothing. What was there to find? Perhaps hard determination, sheer will, blue-black ink. No honey for him, no more melting inside and wishing for his heart, no pining desire.

His hand was heavy on my cheek.

He leaned in close and put his forehead to my shoulder, like he always did, and his beard brushed my skin. I drew in a deep breath of steel and leather, and his scent was a sharp memory. It stirred something the way a breeze might, lifting some delicate emotion in my gut and then letting it fall again.

He spoke softly in my ear, his breath waking up the skin of my throat. "Never, Woman. I will find you."

Heirik stood straight, and said out loud so everyone would hear, "Do not worry for me, then, Wife."

With cold hands, I gave him Slitasongr, loaning it back to him just moments after he'd placed it in my keeping. And he went to Vakr. I watched Heirik's back move, his head hanging just the smallest amount, just enough to cut my heart out. The way his hair fell, I could see the leather knot at the back of his neck, and a memory came to me, of the first time I walked close behind him. We paced the house, and he'd turned to me at the end and said he was all grown up.

He wouldn't turn around this time. He'd faced his greatest fear already, asking me to be his wife, and he'd gotten my stone heart in return. He would ride off in a cloud now, gone to the dust of the valley and the mist of the highlands, to find Ageirr. And he might not come back.

He looked small and alone in all the universe. It was as though I looked at my own back, bent over the ocean's edge, against the overwhelming darkness and backdrop of a million reflected stars. I was too small, too alone, and I had felt that way for too long. Ástkkván, wife of the heart, just for this minute and maybe never more.

I couldn't let that be.

"Wait!" I called, and then was running. I ran after him in a desperate mess of skirts, tears streaking my cheeks. He turned to me, and his face lit. He picked me up in his arms and twirled me in the air and we both laughed, too loud. He lowered me, and I slid down into his arms, where I fit. His hand came to the back of my head, holding me against him, pressing me into a hard kiss. When he let me go, I just stared in awe at him, and he at me.

I remembered the ring I had in my sleeve, and I reached for my knife. I ripped the stitches fast, along my cuff. I had the right now, to cover him with this ring, and perhaps only this chance to give it.

It glinted—silver that had never been touched by sun and sky. I slid it onto his finger, both of us watching our hands move together.

"Now," I said. I folded his fingers in to his own palm, closed my hands around his. When I spoke, it was as a wife to her husband. "Please, Love. Kill him."

He drew away to see me, and he so slightly raised an eyebrow. Heirik brought his other hand to cover ours, and I felt an eagerness grow in him, a voice in his hands, eyes slowly lighting. I'd woken his courage and commanded him to do the one thing he needed to do, to go out and get justice. But more than justice, he wanted revenge. He yearned to kill Ageirr. Wanted it with a great thirst. I could see it. Sultr. Fyst. Hunger. Desire.

I smiled.

He pressed one more kiss to my forehead, and he was off to climb onto Vakr, leaving dust. His uncle and his brother rode at his side. Nothing would ever stop him now, and I was comforted knowing that.

As for Hildur … "She's mine," I called to Magnus, who had her tightly bound. On his honor, he would never harm a woman. But by all the gods, I could.

"There will be a ship in the North, leaving for a new Western land." Greenland, inhospitable and mean.

I told Hildur it was her choice. "Be on that boat, or die by my hand."

No more than an hour later, Betta came home, along with everyone else from the Thing.

I saw her sitting tall on her horse, and a calm happiness stole over me. It had been months since I'd talked with her in the dark, on the way to the gathering, and now here she was, just the same. My lovely friend, I thought. I am home. I watched her get down off the animal and leave it at the stable, and when she turned to make her way to the house, I called her.

"Betta." My voice was level and sure. She turned to me, those water-green eyes open wide, and I could only say her name again and reach for her and she came tripping and stumbling into me and wrapped her thin, strong arms around me. Her kiss was warm near my ear, her voice dusky and familiar. "Ginn," she said. "What has happened to you?"

"Take these," I said without answering her question. I held out my iron ring of keys, taken from Hildur. "Make sure this house is locked down tight. Feed everyone and put the children in the pantry. And send someone for your Da."

Her huge eyes searched my inky face for anything at all, anything that could explain one tenth of what was happening. Then she took the keys, took my hand in hers, and held me and the iron together. A key bit into my palm, making my eyes water.

"Good," she said. I loved her for her faith in me.

No man to carry me over the threshold, I lifted the hems of my death-colored dress and stepped over the line.

Married now, with vows of sweet revenge, I sat on the edge of Heirik's bed. I brushed my fingers over white fur and felt my eyes water and go soft. Our bed. I'd made it.

I trembled, and then shook hard, with the shock of adrenalin. Courage and anger and resolve had coursed through me, leaving this empty and quaking body. My plan went no further than this. I laid back and stared into the wood rafters.

Vivid images came, of the fight that raged somewhere, right now, at my bidding. I'd done all I could, readied us, children safe, Bjarn at hand. Exhausted, I let Betta take care of things. And I waited.

Dreamless, I dropped like a stone. For hours, or perhaps only minutes, I slept without any visions or sounds, and when I woke it was with a brutal start. Up in an instant, I woke to shouts outside.

I flung my door open, and saw Heirik.

He was in the mudroom. Somehow he had made it home from the highlands, down off of Vakr and over the threshold. He'd made it here, inside our beloved house.

Sweat and dirt and blood were smeared into his face and clothes. Other men's blood? I could see that his own flowed, a lot of it, where he held his arm close to his chest, everything slick. Blood saturated his left side from shoulder to foot. Currents of it, too much, down his thighs and onto the floor, ax slipping, landing at his feet.

It wasn't possible, that he'd lost so much and was still here.

He saw me, and he sank to his knees in a red pool. He stared with open love and completion, satisfaction. One hand reached for me so slightly, then dropped. He smiled, the way he always did for me. "Litla," he said.

And then he closed his eyes and let go of this world.

I watched his face turn peaceful with closure, a life accomplished, a love fulfilled if just for one moment. Radiant like when he called on his gods. He looked blindly upward, where the sky would be.

I couldn't breathe, and I was glad I couldn't. I wanted to go with him.

"Stay," I asked instead. He went down.

On my knees in seconds, I used my whole body to block his fall. He hung so heavy, but I wouldn't let him go, wouldn't let him fall in this dirt. I would uphold him in death, carry him until the Valkyries came. A fierce bitterness came up in my throat, that if he wasn't chosen for Valhalla, I would rage and burn the universe to dust.

He was warm, and I felt his pulse under my hand, under the skin of his neck.

"Come," I barked, my voice thick and commanding. "Help him. He's not dead."

Hár came forward and picked him up like a sleepy little boy, and put him to bed.

I opened the door to the outside and shouted commands. For Bjarn to come. For Ranka to take the whole family away. "To the bath or farther," I told her, and her little braids swung out behind her as she focused on her task. I held Betta and Svana behind.

I took the few strides to Heirik's room—our room. He would still be alive when I got there. He would be. He was.

I quickly shoved furs behind Heirik, where Bjarn had propped him up in bed, against the wall. Chilled with sweat, his skin picked up the traces of blue in his hair. I climbed over him to sit on the bed on his uninjured side, and I touched his face, put my hand again to his throat, his pulse. There was so much blood. How could there be so much?

Bjarn was suddenly by the bedside, businesslike. "We need to get his shirts off. And we need someone to help."

"Svana," I commanded, loud enough for her to hear. With her name, a blast of bitterness came from my lips. If that bit-meyla could try to take him from me, she could sure as hell tend his ugly body, too. Let her get close. Intimate as blood.

I steeled myself to remove his shirts. Heirik would be wearing two, of course, and it would be twice as delicate an operation to undress him. I gently lifted the hems. Everything was soaked through, and it was hard to tell where he was hurt. His arm, surely. It hung limp at his side.

I watched his face, assessing. He looked blissful, as though he'd come home drunk rather than wounded. His mind was somewhere, listening to something, not in his body, and he didn't even wince as we pushed and pulled and got both long shirts over his head.

Bjarn peeled the sleeves from Heirik's left arm, inside out, as though he were removing a layer of skin. As he pulled the cloth away, Heirik stirred, and liquid began to seep and bubble from a huge gash along his arm.

Bjarn had slid a thick wool blanket under him, to catch the fresh blood. He handed the shirts to Svana, who knelt on the floor watching in mute terror. She took them without noticing what she held. She was staring at my ink, my healed hand, and quiet tears paused delicately on the swells of her cheeks before coursing down to her throat. I knew they weren't tears for Heirik, just for herself.

Bjarn tossed a pair of shears at her knees. He told her to cut the few clean parts into squares and strips.

I'd never looked into a fresh wound before. In fact, I'd turned my eyes and ears away from the wounds on the beach the day Ageirr had captured me. I'd turned from the glistening blood of Hár's finger, only willing to look later when I changed his bandages, at a safe distance of several days' healing. I had to look now. This wound was mine to bear and to live through with Heirik.

I expected it to open before me in splendorous gore. But it was not glorious, just wrong and deep. They'd cut across his upper arm, at an angle. But it wasn't a ragged knife cut. It had the clean edges of a great talon slash, from something very heavy and sharp. It went deep enough to see the white of bone. Inside his arm, it was red like the meat of any other animal.

That was my objective assessment. But darkness closed around my field of vision. It wasn't just any arm split and bleeding. It was my husband's, who hovered between this bed and the glory of the afterlife. Tears ran freely down my face. They flowed onto Heirik and me, and spots spread like ink, dark against my night-sky sleeves.

I grabbed a linen strip from Svana and wrapped it around Heirik's arm above the wound. I tied it as tight as I could. Very tight, enough to save his life. I put all my fear into tying that tourniquet, and he did wince, then, and it reassured me. I could see now that the blood had mostly clotted and dried during his long ride. The linen strip might help. It might, possibly, be enough to save him for the moment. I pressed my fingers to the knot in the cloth, wishing it to be powerful.

Then I simply touched his face, trailed my fingers along the black of his beard where it covered his jawline. He turned toward the touch and opened his eyes. Gods, he opened them, and they were as intense as the first time I'd seen them. I got lost in them now, again, as every time.

"Lofn came to me, Ginn."

"Shhh, Heirik. We can talk later."

Bjarn cut in forcefully. "This was an ax, Chief?"

"Já," he whispered. "Cut my arm." Já, I thought, it did. "The down stroke bit me." He sucked in sharply as Bjarn inspected the gash.

Betta's Da spoke quietly to me, as if Heirik weren't there. "A very lucky miss, Lady. An ax will remove an arm, a leg even, with a single blow." I had a vivid memory of Heirik swinging his own ax through the sunshine and bringing it down to cut the hand clean off Eiðr.

"I know," I whispered, my fingers hesitant on Heirik's pale face. He couldn't look at me for very long. His eyelids kept closing, lashes fluttering erratically. It wasn't like sometimes when he broke my gaze out of emotion or shyness. This was uncontrolled. He was morbidly unfocused.

"Chief," Bjarn tried to rouse him. "I'm going to clean and seal your wounds."

I turned to him in shock. "There is more than one?"

"Já," he said as though I were dim. "He is not dying from a cut to his arm." He showed me a ragged hole in Heirik's side that was darker red, ugly and slick. A gaping hole in his body as big as my hand. I turned from it with a hiss, forcefully denied it. It looked mortal.

Bjarn didn't seem to necessarily think so. He probed the edges with his fingers, and Heirik became even paler. He rose up from out of his stupor.

"This one was a spear, Chief?"

"Já," he admitted. "I suppose so."

"A bad fight," said Bjarn, conversationally. I wondered if he'd ever seen Heirik in the heat of battle. It would have taken a truly soul-crushing fight to leave my husband like this. Every man who had faced him must be dead.

And Brosa? Had he made it home?

"They stuck him and then wrenched," Bjarn said, instructively. "That is why it's so big a rip, see?" I fought not to vomit. I didn't flinch. I looked and learned.

"Hold him well," Bjarn said, and he picked up big iron tweezers, a palm's-length long. "While I look."

I pressed against Heirik's shoulders, pinning him to the wall. His scent was lovely spice, and I buried my nose in his hair and whispered, "Undra min." I called him what he had called me, my most unexpected love. I could smell just him, through the soggy heaviness and iron of blood.

I turned my head toward Bjarn and Svana. Even as I rested the weight of my forehead on Heirik's shoulder, I watched both of them. Bjarn bent his head to work, and dug into Heirik's wound.

Heirik trembled but made no sound, no struggle. He took even breaths, breathing into my hair, my ear. "Wife," he murmured, and I was pleased he knew I was here, knew exactly who I was. What I was to him.

Bjarn drew the tool out and dropped a small shard of something that thunked on the floor. I pulled away to assess Heirik's face again, and it was white like a snowbank, with a sheen of sweat. Bjarn dug again, just to be sure, to be thorough.

"I won't need to look for pieces in the arm," he told me. "An ax bite won't leave shards."

He was ready to clean Heirik's wounds. He turned a plain and sorry gaze on me, like a warning. This would be bad.

I took Heirik's hand. "Don't let go of me," I told him, and I felt a slight pressure returned by his fingers, saw a small thread of a smile on his lips. That was good.

Bjarn looked at me sidelong. "Have you never sealed a wound, Lady?"

I shook my head no. "I can't ..." I almost said can't remember, but then caught myself. I was done with those lies. "Nei," I said. This was the sort of thing done in shiny hospitals, by better trained people than me.

He sized me up. "You're too small," he said. "I can get Hár."

"Nei," Heirik said with cold clarity. He was the chief for a single lucid second, brooking no complaints. It would be me. "Ginn will do."

Bjarn took Heirik's hand from mine and placed it on my thigh. "Hold her here, Chief." He looked at me with grave doubt. "You will want your wrist for weaving."

Heirik idly stroked the soft inside of my thigh, though he didn't know what he did. Even through my thick dress, the heat of his thumb sent a rush of useless, misplaced arousal.

"Remember the cave?" I murmured into Heirik's ear, taking his attention off what Bjarn was going to do. "I did this." I moved his hand an inch up my leg. He smiled a bit, ready then, and held his other hand out to Bjarn. Bjarn placed a stick in it, an inch or more thick, and I wondered what it was for. Heirik put it between his teeth.

Oh. Já, he had done this before. I'd forgotten about the big scar on his leg, and the many smaller ones scattered on his arms and hands, just like his uncle. I'd never asked him, in all this time, where they'd come from. He turned to the wall.

Bjarn was quick and ruthless. He cleaned the wound on Heirik's side first, with steaming water, and let it run out into a big bowl. Heirik made no sound, and he didn't fight against the pressure I put on his shoulders. He clamped his teeth tight and squeezed my thigh just a little, a gentler grip than I'd expected, almost loving.

Then Bjarn bathed him with soap and everything changed. The lye burned like hellfire and Heirik groaned from behind the stick in his mouth, sudden and raw, arching his back. His hand closed hard on my thigh. I froze and stared.

"Still him, Woman," Bjarn chastised me, and I applied myself again, trying to calm two-hundred-fifty pounds of bloody Viking.

Heirik spit the stick out with a growl and batted Bjarn away.

My husband wanted to say something to me. He looked up and mouthed the words without sound. "I am sorry." Dread stole into me, quick and foul. He thought he was dying now. Right now.

"Nei." I was forceful. "You look here Heirik. In my eyes."

He seemed to swim through thick liquid in order to see me, but he obeyed my order. And then he smiled. A most rueful smile lit the corner of his mouth.

"Lofn came." With his uninjured arm, he grabbed me. I looked at his hand and hardly knew what it was. I remembered Hár's story about Lofn, the goddess in the glowing house that charmed Hundr Blacktooth. "A song in my mind," he muttered. He was having trouble stringing thoughts together.

He closed his eyes. "I regretted I would not live to tell you."

He'd meant to stay conscious just long enough to get home and tell me this, this thing I didn't understand, and he was slipping away and hadn't explained. But the little he said seemed to lift a terrible weight from him, as though his job was done. It scared me. He looked like having told me this much, he'd fulfilled his last task and was free to go. To seek that welcoming door in the dark, the incandescent, seductive hall where warriors drank, raucously calling him.

Instead, he swam up again to consciousness. He sucked in air and placed the stick back between his teeth so Bjarn could rinse his wound once with more hot water. The cleansing made him bleed again, and the bowl filled with a festive pink froth.

He shook his head, and I removed the stick for him. "That made me mad, já?" He continued, as though he hadn't stopped talking about Lofn and regret. "Though my blood poured, I fought them all to come home to you."

"Let's finish, Chief." Bjarn cut in, dryly.

He reached for a small iron knife that Svana had heated over a rush flame. I hadn't noticed her doing this, hadn't noticed him instructing her. The knife wasn't glowing red, but it was hot enough that they used a cloth to handle it. Bjarn told the chief it would be now, and he pressed the iron to Heirik's open flesh. Heirik's eyes opened wide, and he jerked up off the bed twice, three times. A big wound, Bjarn said. There was nothing I could do in those moments, just press myself to Heirik's body and let him feel my presence, if he could. Then it was done.

Heirik breathed raggedly against my throat, and my hair stuck to his face as I pulled back and let him go. Svana, when I glanced at her, was a wan blue, a complexion of skim milk and terror. But she'd done a helpful job, had cut a number of strips and small squares from his ruined shirt, and when she handed them over, I caught her eye. She was watching Heirik and me, and she was solemn, looked humbled by us. I imagined her little girl mind, watching how a man and woman love one another. I raised an eyebrow, unamused. She would soon find out what I'd done with her mother.

Bjarn covered one of the linen squares with honey and placed it face down on the fresh burn. He layered linen and dried peat moss over that. I wrapped Heirik's waist with strips to hold the whole thing tight. I sat back and watched the muscles of his abdomen working as he breathed. Too fast, too hard, but he was breathing. It was wonderful.

We had to repeat everything, of course, with the gash in his arm—including the soap and hot iron. His eyes looked determined one second, and the next the eyes of a trapped dog, wild and unseeing, fingers crushing my leg so that I knew I would stumble when I stood.

It would be okay. Hár had gone through something like this with his finger, and he'd even done it himself, sticking his own hand into the fire. Hár had done it, and probably Brosa, too.

Brosa.

Even as I held Heirik and pressed him down with all my weight, part of me thought of his little brother and willed him to be alive. I wanted him to be alive for Heirik. I wanted him here for me, too. I could tell him how sorry I was, even though he had no idea how very far, and how long, I'd left him.

As if conjured by my thoughts, Brosa burst into the room.

Brosa pushed Bjarn away, gently but in a rush. He went down on his knees at Heirik's bedside, much as he had knelt before him at the coast, in loyalty and love. He touched his forehead to Heirik's hand.

"I thought you were dead." He drew heavy breaths between words. "I brought your blood to my lips, on the field," he said, and then his voice twisted with tears. "It tasted of a mortal wound."

"It was Ageirr's blood," Heirik said.

Brosa turned and spit on the floor, and Svana flinched and pulled her skirts aside as though Ageirr's life force was splattered there.

"I thought your body had been taken entire by the disir," Brosa continued. "I wandered, grieving you. I didn't want to come home."

"Shhh, nei," Heirik said, and he reached across with his healthy arm, at painful cost. He touched his little brother. He brushed his fingers through Brosa's golden hair and laid his palm on his head. "You see I'm still here, já?"

Brosa nodded and bent his head in quiet relief and gratitude. Heirik brushed his brother's forehead with his thumb.

"Chief," Bjarn said, from where he stood behind Brosa, and his voice held a steely command all his own, in this moment when he, the healer, was in charge. Heirik nodded and told his brother and Svana to go.

The binding of his arm was a minor irritation. He looked several times like he wanted to swat Bjarn away like a fly. His eyebrows drew tight together, almost ready to complain, but in a sudden shift of features and will, he became the chief again. He composed himself and resumed dignity. Mouth resolute, face calm and closed. He watched patiently until Bjarn got the last strip wound around his arm and a final knot tied. He said thank you, nodding to Bjarn.

Not to me. Everyone else had been excused, but I would stay, would always stay now. Until his last breath, be it today or in fifty years, I would be here.

I helped carry things to the door, and Bjarn stopped me there. Salty tears dried on my face and throat, and my clothes were wrinkled from clutching and wringing, red from blood and wet with my saliva and Heirik's. Betta's Da looked with curiosity at my face, my blue ink. He took my hand and pushed my sleeve up to my elbow, revealing rings upon rings of knotted and winding tattoos.

"Your scars are healed," he said. Out of everything insane and different about me, that was what he chose to see—my healing.

He glanced back at Heirik and told me, "It is hard when it's your own."

Heirik was my own now. Já.

I STAYED WITH HIM ALL DAY AND INTO NIGHT.

At first, I straightened things. I drew the table and chair back in place, picked up shredded linen and made a pile by the door. Slitasongr lay in the dirt, thrown aside, crusted with dried blood. I lifted it, heavy in my arms like a child, and I felt its voice humming in the bones of my forearms and fingers. This was blood I'd called for, that I'd sent Heirik to get, and I wet one finger and very carefully drew it along the cheek of the blade, turning the rust to liquid red. I placed the ax carefully in the corner. Scrubbed the rest of the blood—Heirik's own—into the dirt of the floor with my boot.

I sank to my knees on that spot, and I took Heirik's face in both my hands. With my thumbs, I smoothed his brows, and he breathed peacefully but did not wake. I followed his jawline with my finger, touched the bones and hollows of his cheeks, rested my hand on his scarred temple. His beard was too long, grown over the days that he had searched for me. I looked for him in there, and I spoke to him about summer and strong walls and how we would live together in this room if he would just stir, just wake up now. He didn't. My tears fell onto his face, but he didn't open his eyes.

Standing on my toes, I opened the cover on the small window, and over many hours, I watched the rectangle of sun fade into a blue-gray absence, until just the wavering light from oil lamps remained. I watched the wooden walls. I breathed with the house, the strong scent of birch stealing oxygen and making my head light.

I sat in Heirik's chair, watching his chest rise effortlessly. He wasn't laboring to live, wasn't feverish even, just asleep. I dropped my head back and felt the air move through my own constricted throat.

Our chair. Everything here was mine, too.

Eventually, I slept.

I rode in a fast boat, skimming over dark green and turquoise waves. Glacial ice had broken off and floated in big chunks all around, but the channel I raced along was free. Fine spray needled my face, and I closed my eyes and breathed in salt. Felt a broad hand placed against my low back, a warm and reassuring pressure. I didn't turn to see him. I watched the water. A whale breaking the surface with its tail, the water falling like diamonds from its flukes.

Abruptly it was gone. The sparkling ocean turned to a dark and blood-sour room. Betta knelt at my feet, her head in my lap. Her features were cut sharp in the last light of a nearly empty lamp. She looked broken, just staring at Heirik, and yet also looking into the distance at something that was recently and irretrievably gone. Something big had died, stealing her spirit.

My eyes shot all the way open, my heart pounding. I looked to Heirik first, then he breathed, and then I did. What, then?

"Woman," I shook her out of her glassy-eyed trance. "What is it? Is it Hár?"

She sat up on her heels, but her blank look remained. Her brows drew together over washed out eyes.

"Is he," I stumbled over the worst question. How could I ever ask if Hár had been lost in the same fight that had put Heirik in this bed? But I had seen him carry Heirik. He'd been fine, já? "Is Hár well?"

She smiled and her eyes came back to life. "Oh," she perked up, and she took my hands. "Hár? Strong as a boat. He says the gash in his face is nothing."

"His face?" Absorbed into this tiny room, watching this one man breathe, I had no idea what was going on outside.

"Oh, Ginn," she broke down, then, like I'd never seen. My strong friend, finally pushed past what her love could bear. "Oh gods, I stitched his wound myself. The first I've been close to him in weeks ..." She dropped her head back into my lap and continued. "I thought he would break the bench in two where he held it. I thought I was doing it wrong, but Da told me nei, the needle hurts the toughest boar of a man."

Betta giggled, "I suppose with such a husband, I will have to learn to fix him."

"You are so good, Betta," I told her, and touched her forehead like a blessing.

"It's not as if he was so pretty before," Betta said. "But I would prefer if he stopped losing fingers and blood. And us not yet married." We both laughed then, and it was a great relief, to feel some life in this dark space. A smell of sheep's coat greased the air, and the tang of blood lurked. The room needed airing.

I asked, "Is everything well in the house?"

"Já, everyone is fed, getting ready for bed, not so worried as they were on the way home from the Thing." Her mouth twisted in a wicked smile. "Hildur is sleeping in the barn." She held a hand up to her mouth, trying not to laugh.

"The barn is too good for her," I said.

"You have taken her keys," Betta stated, looking at where they hung now at her own waist.

"Já, well, I have married the chief."

She dropped her head in my lap again, and I could feel it in both of us—as surely as if I had her gift—the many shocks of the day colliding and paling in comparison to one another.

Like it was the most normal thing, I asked, "See his ring?"

Betta turned to look at Heirik's ring, where it gleamed on his bloody hand. Then, slowly, as in a dream or sim, she went to Heirik on her knees. She dragged her skirts over the dirt floor, drawn by a powerful and unseen thread. She touched him.

I held my breath and felt the pounding of life in my eardrums. Saw her reach out and touch Heirik's ring finger, spread her hand out over his. I watched the signs of Heirik's life, the rise and fall of his chest. Betta moved slowly, as if she swam through ghostly water. Her fingers hovered over his cheek bone, touched his jaw. Brave and curious Betta. No one else had ever touched him this way, like I did, with compassion and awe.

Her voice came from another world. "The chief is not gone." She turned her head to me. "He will wake and be with you."

"He had better."

He hadn't reacted—even when I cleaned him and bandaged his wounds. Hadn't moved for what seemed like a hundred hours. He was becoming part of the bed, part of the house itself, a living but inanimate thing.

"I have something for you." Betta drew me back from solemn contemplation.

She placed a whorled, weightless ball of carded wool in my lap. In the lantern light, it looked like one of Frigg's own clouds, ready to float into space, but it had an earthy smell that tethered it here and now.

My nose wrinkled. I was suspicious of a gift of wool, and she smiled.

"The chief's fleece from last fall's shearing," she said. "He ordered Hildur to save it, in case you changed your mind."

I breathed it in, and I fell back into that sunny, sex-drunk afternoon. Heirik had been so alive that day, his eyes not only open, but on fire. I heard his gorgeous voice in my mind, freed by the presence of Freyr. Spin that fleece, he'd ordered me and smacked the wall with happiness. I had almost kissed him that day. So close. Despite his vows, his honor, his ugly curse, despite all those things, he had hoped that someday we'd be together. He was so vulnerable, not just now in his long sleep, but always.

He'd kept this fleece, sentimental in the extreme, and suddenly I couldn't wait to draw it through my fingers. As if reading my thoughts, Betta handed me a spindle.

I looked at it, wanting to spin his thread, not remembering how. I turned the wooden dowel in my fingers. Ran my thumb along the bone whirl.

"What were you staring at?" I asked her. "When I woke?"

"A wreck," she said. She tossed the word off, as though every day she saw a vision of a whale in the chief's bedroom. She sat down on the floor and drew her knees up. "In my mind, it swam in sunlit water."

My heart raced and I sat all the way up, my hands and feet tingling. "You see the whale?" I whispered, as though a louder voice might shatter the precarious truth.

"You do, too, then?" Gratitude and surprise rose in her voice. Finally, she wasn't the oddest one here, the only one with strange sight. "I've seen her for months in my dreams," she said. "I don't know what she means."

"I may," I said.

Betta's eyes shifted to my tattoo, and I watched her study it for the first time. We hadn't had time to talk.

"Já," she said. "I suppose you would."

"Not that I can explain it," I told her. "It's not something I understand. Only Saga does. But whenever it happens, I'm at the sea."

"When what happens?" Her voice was a dry whisper, here eyes huge. A child at the hearth, listening to one of Hár's stories, and I was a fairytale come to life. Or a ghost story.

Half a year ago, I would have backpedaled, hid myself, said I couldn't remember. Not now.

"I come through time," I said matter-of-factly.

She looked at me for a long moment. "I knew you were something."

The rest was unsaid. Something special? Or monstrous? Otherworldly, a creature, not a woman, maybe cursed like Heirik was? I waited and steeled myself for her rejection and scorn, for all the lies and omissions, for all the disbelief that was sure to come.

She smiled.

"From when?" she asked, and her teeth stood out big and white in the lamplight. Before I could answer, she also asked, "And can you stay this time?"

"Já," I said, sure of it. "I'm home now." I told her about the day during haying, when I first knew I didn't want to go. And then I started to tell her everything. I began with the day I arrived. "I woke on black sand," I said, and she settled in to listen.

Betta took care of things, and I stayed with Heirik all night. I sat beside him and tried to spin. I talked with him in low tones, telling him stories of my glacier, and of the island, the way I knew it before Hvítmörk. All the good parts. Coffee and pillows and fighting you could enjoy without anyone having to die. The oranges he could try when he woke up. I knelt at his bedside and pleaded with him to wake up, my forehead pressed hard into his shoulder, my body shuddering. I crawled in with him and slept, and when I woke I felt him breathing under my cheek, and I had the sensation that we were normal, husband and wife waking to start the day. But I was the only one who got up.

I cared for him, cleaned him. I washed his wounds with linen soaked in honey water, careful not to break the raw, seared skin.

I thought about going with him into death. When it finally came, would I be brave enough to go? He was a chieftain, but not the epic kind who ruled like a king in Norway or Sweden. Just here in the small world of our island. Would they push him away on an elegantly curved, flaming boat nonetheless?

I pictured his belongings surrounding him, his ax and bracelets and glass cups. I looked to the chest in the corner, where he kept precious things, and a thought came to me slowly, just a wisp of smoke at first. I let my mind wander to the worst scenario, his possessions laid out in the boat that I'd seen tied up past the fishing camp. Beloved items, his father's knives, mother's furs. And a small wooden box.

It looked exactly like the one in the archives, on the screen, only new. Just made a few dozen years ago, rather than twelve hundred. About two hands across, its doors closed with a dragon's-head clasp, it waited among the furs in the chest.

The box felt warm inside its nest, and I lifted it out like a perfect egg.

I knew what was inside. In the frigid future, I'd clung to the image of this box and its diary, the proof that at least a few settlers had written about their own lives, far before the sagas. I assumed it was just something lost to the years, obscure but possible.

Now I knew better, having lived here. No woman on a Viking farm could have kept that diary. No woman here could write. Except me.

I looked to Heirik where he slept, raven hair against cool linen. The formidable chieftain with precious metal eyes, sleeping, reckless as a child. His wife wrote the diary. And in it, she told of so many things that hadn't happened to us yet. Moments still to come. That woman, the writer, had a future with her dark-haired man. He was alive.

My fingers touched lightly over the lock. With sure hands, I dug deeper in the trunk and found the key.

The book looked so clean and new, the birch bark soft the way I always knew it would feel under my fingertips. The first three pages were scratched with dates and trades, the hash marks and awkward notes I knew so well. And then came blank pages. Nine of them.

In the box lay a few slender bones, hollow and finely sharpened, just like Brosa said. I picked up the priceless vial of ink that lay next to them, and it fit into my palm. I laid these things out on the small table.

"Everyone settled," I started to write.

I thought of how the diary looked in my contacts, and I made the shapes by hand. My words as powerful as the runes on a healing bone. Someday, I would teach him all the letters, and he could write me a love poem.

A knock came at the door, and Brosa filled the doorway.

He looked like a beaming bear, dressed in a work shirt, sleeves pushed back and crusted with mud. He'd wiped his hands on his pants, but they were still brown with dirt. He brought a gust of fresh air in with him, a waft of grass and sun, and I squinted as if he himself were radiant. How long had I been sitting here, with the edge of the bed biting into my thigh, my hand on Heirik's chest? How long since I'd seen the sky? A night and a day and into the next evening, I thought. I couldn't remember.

"How is he?" Brosa asked.

"Sleeping," I reported. "No change."

Brosa took just one step into the small room and looked from there, seeming to assess his brother and then settling his gaze on me.

"It's shining outside," he said. "You should come."

"I …" I tried to imagine sunshine, tried to picture myself walking in it ever again.

I hardly knew how to speak, how to encompass everything I felt for Brosa. Here he stood, this brave and tender man who had been willing to put behind what he loved, put the sea and wind and the lure of other lands behind him, to stay here at Hvítmörk and marry me, give me a good life.

"I am sorry," I said, my voice cracking, my hand reaching for him.

With alarm, he came to kneel at my feet and take my hands. "Nei, Woman! Why?" His nails were filled with dirt.

"You would give up everything for me," I said, barely rasping the words out, but I lifted my head finally. "And I turned from you in a heartbeat."

He looked up at me with those sparkling, sea-green eyes. "You told me that you would hurt me." Then he winked and his broad smile came. "You are close to my heart," he said. "You've given me the greatest gift any woman could. You love my brother."

I ducked my head. He was always so generous and good.

"I heard you," I told him, brushing tears from my face. "When you spoke with Heirik at the Thing. You told him I would become yours now."

"Ahhh," he said, something beginning to make sense. "Já, well, you must have missed the rest of that conversation," he said ruefully.

"The rest?"

"My brother said nei," he sighed, "and tried to take my arm off." Brosa looked down at his wrist and shook his hand out. "I reminded him it was not my idea."

He laughed, but I was quiet, my breath suspended.

"He was sick with love-grief," Brosa told me, as though it might excuse anything. Then with a big breath he said, "Anyhow, Egil and Rafnson came, and we had to make a good show of it."

I thought of Svana serving those men, of Heirik's cramped mood, deftly hidden to all but me.

Brosa continued. "We talked about you later, for a long time. About what he had done to you. What he had to do to make things right."

"Já?" My laugh was laced with bitterness, and I cast a dark glance at Heirik, sleeping. "He is devious. I can hardly imagine what else he thought he could do."

"Uh, marry you?" Brosa suggested.

"Oh."

My heart lurched. In the gray pall of that miserable night, even as I stumbled to the water and washed my hands in the tide, even as I tapped out in bleak emptiness, Heirik had been changing his mind, resolving to ask me if I would live by his side. Like a bird looking down on it all, I saw him stand with resolution inside the tent at the Thing, orange lamps lighting the canvas. I saw me drop to my knees at the ocean, the water like black oil covering my hands.

"It did take him a long time to come to that decision." Brosa's words brought me back. "And a great deal of ale to get him to admit he had been gravely wrong. Even more drink before he realized the world did not revolve around him, and that he might be too late."

"He was," I said. He was far too late. Only because I fought to come back, did we have one more chance.

Brosa lifted my chin and turned my head so he could examine the whale's tail around my eye. He cocked his head to see it from another angle. "Where did you go?"

"Where I came from," I said reasonably, explaining nothing.

"I see." His thumb traced the ink, and he seemed to decide this answer would be enough for now. He stood, and his hand on my shoulder was strong and sweet. "You will be his wife yet," he said. "He owes you that much."

I smiled and wiped my cheeks and chin where tears gathered.

"And he is a stubborn boar," his brother added.

I laughed the tears away. "Já, that he is."

I thought Brosa would leave then, but a pause hung in the air until it became awkward.

"Ginn," he started, and I looked up to him and felt my own eyes wide and lost. Brosa went on, "You need to come outside now. You are in charge of this house, and Hár and Betta marry tomorrow."

It felt like a kick to my chest. "So soon?"

"Já, it has been planned this way, you know."

He looked tenderly at Heirik, at the place where my hand now rested defensively on my husband's chest. "It's already begun," he said with a strong hint of apology in his voice. "People are arriving. We're digging. Laying the stones and starting the fires." He held up his hands, palm out, to show me dirt and char.

I sniffled. "Já," I said, slowly waking from a trance. This was what I'd wanted, had been born to do, to be the wife of this house, and yet I sat with clean hands in a small, dark room. "Já, I see."

I stood and looked around me, picked a shirt off the floor as though I could prepare for a wedding as quickly as straightening our room. I pressed my skirt flat against my legs. Then I rose to my full height. "I will need the thralls to bring up ale and food, get the tables down. The boys can finish helping you, and Ranka can bring out the cups and bowls and be in charge of shining."

Sleep or no sleep, glorious life went on growing like flowers on a house. And I would tend it.

Brosa looked at me with profound relief. "You have seen this done before, then."

I nodded and laughed. "Já," I said. "Hildur had me practice many times."

I glanced back at Heirik and bent to tuck a blanket around him. I kissed my fingers and touched them to his mouth, promising silently that I would be back, and then I walked out to join the wide, sunny world of the living. I willed him to follow.

Hár walked down the length of the house, away from me. The sun shone on his back, and he held a gleaming short sword in his hand, swinging it unconsciously, like a song. It was the one from above Heirik's bed. When Heirik and I were married in the open grass, outside this house, he'd given me Slitasongr for our sons. This sword, Heirik's great-grandfather's, would be for Betta.

At the end of the house, Hár turned back to nervously pace this way now, toward me. He wore the torc Betta had given him—the one from the assembly market, cats snarling at his throat. The bronze played against the sky of his eyes and the gray at his temples and in his beard. He wore his hair all down around his face, more supple than seemed possible. It whipped around his strong jawline in a quick burst of wind.

He smiled to me as he came closer, his hand brushing the house the way Heirik and I both did sometimes. He was all the colors of a deepening sky, the amber flash before becoming night, the way Betta saw him when they met at the woods for the first time.

"We should wait for my nephew," he said. He glowed with anticipation and love, and I knew he was saying this because it was right. But he wanted Betta. And I wanted to see them together. Something good and promising on this windy day.

"Nei, Old Man," I said. "Brosa will do fine. Heirik would want you married."

If Hár was the sunset, Betta was the tall grass, exploding with life. She rose from her spot on the ground among the flowers, out near the forge where she'd sat to do her hair. She looked green and luscious, like a gift, loaned to Hár by the land spirits.

The fabric he'd given her was rare, dyed a deep emerald that echoed her eyes. Cotton from the east, I thought—bómull, tree-wool, so gauzy it clung and fell like clouds. The dress she'd made was long and simple and flowed like mist over the subtle curves and hollows of her breasts, waist, hips. Snow white linen and pale bare feet peeked from underneath. She wore no jewelry on her arms or throat, the only adornment an intricate green-on-green embroidery that she'd worked into the bodice. It was a large square, criss-crossed and surrounded by radiating patterns that entwined just where Hár's hands would hold her. Her skirt flew out with a sudden gust, and wrapped around her legs. She crossed the few feet of grass to me and threw her arms around me.

Her bony shoulder blades stuck out under my hands, and I thought about how I would no longer feel them poking into me while I tried to sleep. I kissed her cheek, warm and dry.

We stood on the highest point, by the forge, and looked out over Hvítmörk. We gazed at the tossing mess of trees, stretching for miles, and the wind came like a god's hand skimming over the treetops and flattening the leaves. It hit us hard, too, against our backs, pressing us forward. Everything streaming forward, our skirts billowing in demented swirls. Chickens moved around our feet, and my dog came to sit at my side, pressing my skirts in place with his heavy, hot body.

This bittersweet wind had whipped all through the day. The best, most incredible day of Betta's life, a glorious day she'd waited for since she was born. But without the chief to marry her to Hár. Without Heirik, who despite ugly curses and imprecations, had always been important to her. She'd knelt in our room and touched his face. It was tender, clearly something she'd wondered about but never done.

"He was not for me, Ginn."

My heartbeat scattered, and two chickens pecked, as though they'd heard it fall in the grass. Gods, she always went straight into my thoughts, with ice-pick precision. And dumb and selfish I stood beside her, on her greatest day, thinking about myself.

"He resisted wanting me just fine," she added. Something far gone, that had passed between her and Heirik, was released. She smiled playfully and tugged on the keys at my waist. "Never you."

I laughed with her. "Nei, he couldn't resist me." It was true. "And his uncle failed completely at resisting you." I reached for her hair. Long and indiscriminately brown, shaped with loose finger curls, it gleamed with the barest sheen of oil steeped in juniper and roseroot. It whipped and tangled in my fingers.

Oska-byrr. A fair wind to one's heart's content.

"You will not believe how gorgeous your man looks." I told her.

"Nei, I won't be surprised," she said. "He is beautiful to me every day."

"I challenge you, then," I told her. "To stand unmoved when you see him."

"Fine," she said, and she pushed at my chest with her palm and then took off running. I stood baffled for a second, and then realized she wanted to me to race. I ran after her, in the crazy wind, her wedding dress flying out behind her.

They married by the ravine, under a billowing sky, with dozens of people who'd come for the party. Maybe a hundred, I calculated, wondering if my ale stores would hold.

Betta rode the few minutes to home on a horse—Hár's own Byr—carrying a bursting bunch of white flowers. Amma's crown sat low on her forehead and sparked with golden light in the late sun. Her husband walked beside, leading his horse. When they reached the house, Hár swept her off the saddle and held her in his arms. It was a terrible omen if a bride stumbled in the door, and so he carried her across the threshold. Her hair trailed over his arm, and fallen snowblooms marked their wake.

At the party, Brosa made the sacrifice and blessing, and I couldn't watch. All I saw was Heirik, like a spirit, doing these things that should be done by him. The blood of sacrifice running from his ghostly fingers, not Brosa's. A glass raised in blessing by his spirit self.

Brosa sat on the high seat, then, and as the highest ranking woman in the family, I served him ale. Over the cup, our eyes met. His always looked ocean-tossed, and tonight they were full of bold joy.

He touched my face and then bent to speak low and sweet in my ear. "My brother is strong. He will be well, Ginn," he told me. I squeezed his hand and he kissed me, soft against my temple.

By the time I'd served Hár, Betta, and a couple other people, Brosa was through with formality and shouted "Drink, Fools!" to everyone in the hall. Happy shouts came and everything dissolved into wonderful, joyous chaos.

My work was done, and I wanted to be close to Heirik. I set all thoughts of cups and drinks aside, and I backed away from the party. I would go to him now. Now that my best friend was secure and happy, I would leave, and I would lay down beside him and tell him about the wedding.

I stood for a moment, in the door to the back mudroom, and watched and listened. The voices were happy and filled the house like a packed barn. Among them, I could hear Hár's thunderous laughter.

The old man beamed at the center of a mass of people, and he lifted Betta onto his lap like she was a tiny thing. Brosa crashed his cup against his uncle's and the two drank. Then Hár dipped his fingers in the ale. "Thor, give me strength," he said, and made the T sign on Betta's forehead. "There are too many hours before I can bed this woman."

Betta choked just a little on her drink, her cheeks pink. I could see she was not truly embarrassed. She sparkled and smiled so that her teeth showed big and white. She leaned over and showed Lotta her ring, and the little girl reached out a single chubby finger to touch it.

Heirik stepped up behind me. Alive.

A tingling spread quick and low from my spine and filled every tiny space in my body, inside my heart, between my fingers and toes. His hair brushed against my cheek, and I stood still for a moment, as if moving might break this illusion, might make me wake. But he was really there. He smelled of stale sweat on linen, the most luscious scent in the world.

My lungs felt light and entirely full for the first time in so long. I sighed and breathed out a thousand cramped and tiny spirits of fear and darkness.

His shoulder was a promise when I lay my head back against it. He wasn't gone. He was here and would not go again. He would be the husband of the diary, with the fourteen good fleeces, sweet to my eye. My whole body melted back into his and he sheltered and held me up. I gave up the days of managing and ordering, the hours of cleaning him as he slept, the night fears that gripped me with the thought that he was gone. I gave them all up, and I let tears flow. His heart beat into my back and right through me as if it were my own.

"You spun," he said.

I laughed, but it was breathless. I couldn't speak to answer.

I felt Slitasongr's handle against my calf, its iron cheek against my ankle. He was using it like a cane. With his wounds, he would have lurched here with desperate purpose, just feet from our door though it might as well have been as far as the sea. To be with me. His breath came hard against my ear, nearly destroyed from the effort. His mouth, his voice a pressure and flow of air against my neck. Panting, he pressed his lips there. And we stayed, swaying gently together, his chin on my shoulder, hand on my belly, sliding farther around my waist, until his breathing slowed. Exhale with me, Love. Onda. Inhale.

He looked past me, over my shoulder at Betta and Hár.

With one finger, the old man traced the neckline of Betta's dress, and she laughed and sparkled.

Heirik's voice was like gravel, coarse and unused. His arm around me tight now, words against my throat, he said, "Let that be us."

Winter again

THICK SKATES CARRIED ME, MADE OF THE BONES OF FAST FJOÐR.
Leather thongs held them onto my boots, woven with expert twists
and knots. We propelled ourselves with wooden poles tipped with
iron spikes.

The water underfoot was solid white and thick as a little glacier. We moved on its surface, free. Air speared my lungs, brilliant
like metallic light. Heirik's hand held mine too tight, a rough grasp
of love.

Lark-like voices echoed in the ravine behind us, Betta with the
little girls. Then Hár's gruff thunder. None of Svana's lilting tones.
She lived far across the fields with her husband, Eiðr.

Heirik and I surged ahead alone. Fjoðr's bones carried us as
quick and glorious as the horse himself, slicing through a sudden
wind.

We glided over Heirik's ice-buried fort, over the frozen current that had swept away our first awkward fear. We glided over
everything that had come before. I watched him out of the corner
of my eye. He moved like a gorgeous nightmare, dark and bloody
and grinning, and I was the rest of that terrible dream. I imagined
my ink that matched his mark, thought of our eyes flashing gold
and ice. A cloud of laughter burst from my lungs and was taken by
the speed, a little puff of mist gone behind.

Heirik suddenly grabbed me and swung me in a stunning arc.
We flew off our feet and landed in a snow bank, a mess of bodies
and skirts and bone-strapped feet. The cold bit my cheeks, and his
lips burned against mine.

Above us stretched an exploding sky, streaming with white
and silver light. A storm was coming. Nei matter. We both smiled
into our kiss.

MANY THANKS

To my husband Martin John Brown who parallel wrote novels with me, and my 8-year-old son Sebastian who wrote several books in the time it took me to write this one. To Shannon Okey, a publisher who loves my book with all her heart. SCORE! To my editor, Beverly Army Williams, and to my friend and adviser Sarah Gilbert, who got me poisonous angelica root when I wanted to make Viking mouthwash. Thanks to my very first readers whose excitement made me realize I had really written a book: Stacy Crockett, Laura Stanfill, M.K. Carroll, and Rachael Herron. To Arabella Proffer, Tamas Jakab, and Elizabeth Green Musselman for their help with the making of the book itself. To my mom Eileen Golden for the quiet time and love.

To Kristin Bjorg Ísfeld for her personal tour of the Viking house ruins at Stöng and the land around Thingvellir in Iceland, and to traveling companions Zeke Healy and Brenden Jones. To my friend Dale Favier, who burst out in Old Norse when he heard about my book, and who graciously provided an excerpt of his poem, *Infanta*, for use in the farm diary.

To the librarians and reference staff of Multnomah County Library, for helping me with questions like how to cut up a whale, and for use of the cool and quiet Sterling Writers Room. To Tamlin who helped name Slitasongr, and the many other good people of the SCA Barony of Adiantum. To Tami Bridges Hawes, too, and to everyone who tried to teach me naalbinding, bless you. I'm sorry, I never did get it.

To two people I've never met, yet who helped me tremendously with my research. William R. Short, author of *Icelanders in the Viking Age: The People of the Sagas*, is a Viking fighting technique expert and all-around incredible source of knowledge (see hurstwic.org.) Also the online Viking Answer Lady. To my online writers' groups at Ravelry.com and "WA." To my friends Minka Wallace and Beate & Ron Weiss-Krull for their friendship through this project.

And to all those who supported my Kickstarter campaign to visit Erik the Red's House in Iceland. Foremost my PRESENTING SPONSOR and longtime friend Craig Cobalt. To all of you, I enjoyed sending you postcards!

Anne Garrison
Antje Hegemann
Barry Goldstein
Beverly Army Williams
Brett Hendricks
Candace Decker
Christian P.P. Donker & Coert Donker
Christopher Kaiser
Craig Matthews
Dale Favier
Elizabeth Beekley
Erica Pittman
Eric Hobberstad
Funnytool
Glenn Copeland
Harry Steinman
Jeanmarie Higgins
Jeff Sypeck
K. Jespersen

Kellan Elliott-McCrea
Laura Fitzpatrick
Laura Stanfill
Lynette Golden Fitzpatrick
Marcee & Tim Rogers
Marylee Klinkhammer
Michelle Kroll
Michelle Toich Anderson
Minka/The Olivia Darlings
Paul Cortellesi
Rachael Herron
Rich Laux
Rosalind Simpson
Rowan Rose
Sarah Gilbert
Shannon Okey
Shira Lipkin
Stephen Grout
Thor Ernstsson

Turn the page for a special preview of **So Wild a Dream.**

COMING SUMMER 2016

So Wild A Dream

The next book set in the Hvítmörk world

Sign up for news at www.LarissaBrown.net

CHAPTER 1

Svana shoved a stick into a crack in the ground. A good stick, thick and bent, like an elbow crook without its flesh. She'd been saving it for a time when she could slip away to this far field. The grass would be tall soon, up to her shoulders. Eiðr would not see it here.

She knelt and traced its line with her fingers. It angled off to one side and toward the sky, which lay blue and still over her head.

Ginn once said that a thousand years from now, people traveled by sky. Svana watched it always, these past two years, yearning to go up free into its heights.

She dropped a leather bundle on the ground with a wet thud. Tucking her dress out of the way, she untied her small knots. Why had she tied them so tight? A piece of her fingernail broke off, brittle as dead grass, and she cursed. Her fingers used to be soft and fine.

The cords pulled free and the leather fell open, baring the bloody head of a fox. A little one that had sniffed at her cooking fire that morning while Eiðr was away. She had thanked the gods over and over as she whacked at its neck with her husband's old ax.

Its blood smelled just like that blade. The iron stink hit the back of her throat, and water came up into her mouth. She wiped her face on the shoulder of her dirty dress, and bits of hair like straw stuck in her mouth. Her hair used to be soft and yellow. Everyone said it was like melted butter.

She lifted the small head, and held it out in front of her. Would it be enough?

The gods preferred horses, but gods were practical beings. They would hear her.

She pushed the severed neck onto the stick.

Slowly, she twisted and pressed. She dared not break the stick - it was a good one - so she worked the head gently, a little at a time. She swallowed down sickness from the disgusting sounds, the slick wetness. No one else would do this for her. Her breath came soft and shallow as she worked.

Finally, the head hung on the bone-pole, eyes blank, seeing into the next life. The stick bowed under its weight, but it held. She turned it slowly, carefully, toward Hvítmörk.

Svana wiped her hands on her skirt.

There.

The fox's dead gaze reached across the acres of grass and out toward Ginn's grand new house.

Svana bent low to speak into the stick where it met the ground.

"I raise this nithing pole and turn it on Ginn of no other name."

Her voice was too small for the gods to hear. She felt foolish, but she pushed her words out stronger.

"For my mother." She closed her eyes tight and pressed her palms to the ground. "For taking our places, forcing us from our home."

The words came faster. "For forcing me into a life of servitude, and the bed of a man I loathe. For leaving me alone. Crushing my life in your hateful hands like I am nothing but an egg."

Her words grew and blew a fire to life, as if flame climbed up the stick and lashed out of the fox's mouth.

"I turn this head also on Heirik Rakknason, chief and husband to Ginn. Already a boy is killing my own husband for me. He will be found with your family's ax in his back, Rakknason."

The fox's voice shook with rage and tears.

"I raise Hel against you."

A hard breeze came, and Svana's heart stopped in her chest. The head swung on its post. It looked away from Ginn's home and off into the highlands.

What did it mean? This sudden shift in an unmoving sky?

She sat back on her heels and took shuddering breaths. Her clouds, her companions, did not travel anywhere. There was no wind.

She turned the fox head back toward Ginn and uttered a small appeal for the curse to find its target.

Brosa rested his shovel and looked out over the swells and valleys of his brother's land. Their grandfather had ringed this farm with fire, among the first men to claim the wilds of Iceland. His brother, chieftain now, owned it all.

On the brink of night, the land turned gray. The far-off hills changed first, the grass turning to ash. Then the valley was devoured by a creeping, shriveling deadness. It moved fast through the land, from the horizon right down to the dirt under his feet, so that he picked up one foot and checked the sole of his boot.

The dog beside him whined and sniffed.

Brosa bent again to dig. He leaned into the shovel, breaking up hunks of grass, over and over, stopping only briefly to wipe his forehead with the back of his hand.

The sky dimmed, and the familiar sensation came, the one that had plagued him these two years since Ginn came to Hvítmörk.

The sensation of his wife. The whisper of linen on his wrists. A dress whipping in the wind, hanging from a line. The feel of Esa's clothing, and through it, the shape and bones of her thigh. Slender and strong. Her laughter as he tried to slip his hands inside. All those moments, swallowed by crows.

"I welcome it, já?"

Words given to a stiff wind.

The shovel crunched, iron against colorless earth, faster and deeper until his muscles sang with the digging, and for one wild moment, he knew his thick body had been made only for this. Sculpted by the gods so he could one day dig into her grave mound.

There she was.

Esa.

And next to her, the small bones of his son.

He climbed in beside them and lay down in their grave.

It would be his last act of usefulness, to complete his family. He would trade his family for a living one, for his brother. So that Ginn and Heirik could have a babe. Surely, some spirit would take his life in return for a new one to come. The spirit would find him here. He felt it nearing him, moving in the gray land, and its approach soothed him like a child's bedtime song.

He woke to a bird's call.

Brosa didn't open his eyes. Was he alive? Or had the spirit come for him, in the body of a raven?

He caught the breeze on his face, smelled the damp earth. He flexed his cold fingers and felt a jaw bone under his thumb. Teeth. The long bones of Esa's dead leg pressed into his. He shifted, and they cracked.

He was alive, then, já.

The call came again, and he jerked upright, eyes open. It wasn't the voice of a bird. It was the voice of a woman.

Eðna Jonsdottir dragged herself up from the sea. Slogging on her hands and knees, her dark wool skirt swirled in a wash of white foam and sucked her down into the black sand. Salt water blasted up her nose, scraping out her sinuses, and she pressed her head between her palms, choking, coughing.

"Sodium chloride," she muttered, and the words burned.

The 22nd century lab she'd left behind was completely gone, its orderly vented air replaced by the madness of sea spray and fish stink.

Good.

It wasn't a glorious arrival in the past, but it was right. The ocean, and a black sand beach was to be expected. "Confirmed, I'm in the right place," she recorded.

But what was the time?

She lifted her heavy head, hoping desperately for the wilds of the 10th century, dreading that if it hadn't worked, she might find the spindly, sky-high glass buildings of the 22nd.

She saw nothing.

Where had the waves gone? The foam, her dress? Everything black. She felt for the ground, and her hands sank. Yes. The sand was still under her knees. The waves still bumped at her back, but she couldn't see any of it. She'd gone blind.

She closed her fingers in the sand, steadied herself and shut her eyes. She let a stream of images pass by in her mind, the ones she'd collected since she was ten. For just a second, she indulged in her birds. Vibrant, ancient ones. Peacocks, plovers, snowy owls.

Calm. She would try again.

She blinked to activate thermal imaging, and the landscape sprang to life.

Yes.

Eðna knelt in the center of an enormous curve of sand—a meniscus of beach. Thrown through time, she had settled precisely where the foam met the land. Black cliffs rose before her, filling the sky to what she presumed was the east, based on her memorized map and the assumption that she had come through on the same beach as Jen.

At her back, the ocean would stretch all the way to barren Greenland. It pulled, as if to suck her back, and she lurched forward on her knees.

"Alone," she said and wiped her mouth. "I've arrived, alone, on the beach. As expected."

The sand was dark black, like winter night on her childhood farm. The silt transitioned to pebbles, and then bigger rocks, as her eyes moved up the sloping beach. Finally, the beach gave way to boulders, surrounded by thickets of pale silver plants. Their stems searched, reaching toward a dim white sun.

Eðna zoomed in on their round heads, like satellites dotted with tiny buds. Not yet flowered. Spring, then.

"Thermal imaging is functioning."

To her right, more of the same landscape continued into the distance, every grade of black and gray. No big spikes of white that signified heat and life lit the horizon or glowed from beyond the hills. No city.

She blinked to seek/accept, and glowing words confirmed: No coordinates found.

In the corner of her field of vision, a timer counted the hours and minutes since she'd left the lab. She knocked water from her ear, and the numbers zinged through days and weeks, then settled back to zero.

"But the chronometer is haywire."

Would her lenses be stuck like this, in thermal imaging mode, counting time endlessly up and down?

In a heartbeat, her contacts glitched, and the skeletal, gray thermal image exploded into eye-searing color. A bright world of green and puce and a dozen shades of blue opened up before her—the naked colors of ancient Iceland's sand and ocean and sky.

Eðna raised a hand to shield her eyes from the glare, and she scanned the beach in both directions. There, in the distance, a bit of brilliant red. Yes. Her physical confirmation sat a mere half mile away.

A wooden hut, bleached by wind and salt spray, hunched at the water's edge. Two big A-frame tents stood back from it, natural canvas with wide red stripes, textbook Viking style. An animal-prowed, elegant boat sat on the water beyond the froth. She was within a generation of her target, if not spot on.

Her achievement, already, was like nothing ever done before. To deliberately and accurately travel through time. A spark of exhilaration lifted her heart.

Here!

She rose to her feet, trembling, and stood tall. Icy water streamed from her hands and dress, and her hair stuck to her eyelashes. She lifted her chin to the clear, arctic sky. "Yes," she said, and a cloud of breath lifted and took off into the wind.

Eðna Jonsdottir had traveled through time. Here she stood, on the black sand beach of Jen's ravings. Her mission was underway.

For news about So Wild a Dream,
sign up at www.LarissaBrown.net

ABOUT LARISSA BROWN

LARISSA IS AN AUTHOR WHOSE WORK RANGES FROM SPECULATIVE, historical fiction to knitting books and essays.

Beautiful Wreck, her first novel, debuted in 2014, and her second work of fiction—the novella *Tress*—was published in 2015. The companion novel to *Beautiful Wreck* will be published in 2016.

From the open fires at an Oregon Renaissance Fair to the ruins of a Viking longhouse in Southern Iceland, Larissa's research took her across the world. She's invented Old Norse words, made Viking mouthwash out of angelica root and attempted to learn the ancient needle art of naalbinding.

Larissa posts photos of her #writingspot on Instagram to share the ongoing adventure of writing, and she's the proud owner of the addictive online generator at herosmellslike.com. She lives in Portland with her family and can often be found writing at Powell's Books or at the beautiful, historic Central Library.

Please visit!

WEBSITE & E-NEWS www.larissabrown.net
INSTAGRAM larissabrown5855
PINTEREST Larissa Brown
FACEBOOK Beautiful Wreck

And please consider writing a review at goodreads and any other retail or book sharing site.

ABOUT COOPERATIVE PRESS

COOPERATIVE PRESS (FORMERLY ANEZKA media) was founded in 2007 by Shannon Okey, a voracious reader as well as writer and editor, who had been doing freelance acquisitions work, introducing authors with projects she believed in to editors at various publishers.

Although working with traditional publishers can be very rewarding, there are some books that fly under their radar. They're too avant-garde, or the marketing department doesn't know how to sell them, or they don't think they'll sell 50,000 copies in a year.

5,000 or 50,000. Does the book matter to that 5,000? Then it should be published.

In 2009, Cooperative Press changed its named to reflect the relationships we have developed with authors working on books. We work together to put out the best quality books we can and share in the proceeds accordingly.

Thank you for supporting independent publishers and authors.

WWW.COOPERATIVEPRESS.COM

CPSIA information can be obtained
at www.ICGtesting.com
Printed in the USA
BVOW10s2356101217
502439BV00001B/36/P